HIGH TIDES

COVED

BOOK ONE

C.K. CEED

High Tides

Coved: Book One

Coved

To my dear mother, who planted the seeds of my love for reading and storytelling. From your nurturing care grew a tree whose branches now bear the fruit of my imagination.

Content Advisory

This book includes the death of loved ones, sexual acts, and severe violence, including execution. Certain scenes involve harm to a character in a physically vulnerable state. Please proceed with care.

ONE

The forest, thick with ancient trees and tangled undergrowth, seems to pulse with a life of its own, each rustle of leaves and crack of twigs amplifying the sense of isolation. Right, left, right, left, jump, duck, left, right. The instructions pound in my head, a rhythmic mantra guiding my every step through the dense, shadowed woods. I think I see something furry flash by, causing me to pause my run. I take my earbuds out, listening for the ruffle of leaves that might signal a larger animal may be patrolling. But I'm only met with the sounds of the forest. The trail ahead, barely visible under the canopy, twists like a serpent, leading me closer to the place I know so well: the Cove. A place of beauty and peril. It's that edge that draws me here. The trail veers off from the main path, one not many people know about.

The Cove has always been my refuge, a secret sanctuary far from my parents' fears and phobias about water. But the danger is part of the allure. The memory of those rebellious, reckless kids who never made it back to shore lingers in the air of the town like a ghostly warning. The water, a dark and mysterious entity, breathes in and out, as if it were living, as if it were aware of my presence. I match my breath to its rhythm, feeling the tension of the run melt away.

The music in my ears falls silent as I pull out my earbuds, letting the raw, untamed symphony of the sea wash over me.

Moments later, the trees thin, and I break through to the shore. The mist from the waves clings to my skin, a cool caress against the heat of my exertion. I inhale deeply, tasting the sharp tang of salt on my tongue. The ocean's scent, my favorite, a blend of brine and something deeper, more primal, fills my lungs. I pause, the sound of crashing waves replacing the pounding of my heart. Standing at the forest's edge, I gaze down at the water. In the summer, The Cove undergoes a natural phenomenon: high tides. Night after night, the sea rises, swallowing the beach until the waves nearly kiss the forest line. When the tide recedes, it drags the sand with it, carving a deep curve into the shore. I walk down closer to the water's edge.

Standing here on this narrow strip of sand, I feel worlds apart from the mundane rhythm of university life, as if I've stepped into another realm entirely. Lately, I've been haunted by a strange feeling, a kind of sixth sense whispering that something is coming, some impending doom lingering beyond the horizon.

I can't, for the life of me, figure it out. I'm at the top of my class at Rysen University, fresh off a strong sophomore year. I'm in a great relationship, I live with my best friend, and I have parents who genuinely care. By all accounts, life should feel perfect.

So why does it seem like a storm unlike any I've ever known is about to break over me? The thought lingers as I watch the tide roll in and out, each wave echoing the unease that's taken root within me.

"Beautiful, isn't it, Kali?"

A voice in my right ear, smooth and low, sends a jolt through me. I spin around, heart racing, to find myself staring into a pair of deep, dark-brown eyes. They hold a warmth that belies the sudden chill creeping up my spine. He's close, way too close, and I instinctively take a step back. My sneakers sink into the wet sand, a reminder of how precarious my position is. What makes the Cove dangerous isn't its waters, but the sudden rip tides that stir without warning by day and the slow, creeping tide that swallows the shore by night.

The high tides that rise on the shores of Rysen are a wonder all their own. My father once told me it was what first called him to this little town, a strange lure for an oceanographer so far from the sea. Lakes aren't meant to breathe like the ocean, yet Rysen's, resting on its narrow strip of land, does. The locals call it *the tide*, though my father insists it is a *seiche*, a hidden pulse that stirs the lake as if something vast and sleeping turns beneath the surface. The weathermen call it wind and pressure, the usual things. But my father says it's older than the wind, older than the world's first storm, a memory the lake still carries in its depths.

The man before me is tall, his broad frame silhouetted against the afternoon sunlight. I take him in, noting how his outfit doesn't scream hiking. He's wearing a long-sleeved, plain black T-shirt, jeans, and severely scuffed, brown hiking boots. The unease I feel isn't only because of his sudden appearance, it's the way he seems so at ease, as if he belongs here. I've lived in Rysen my entire life and have never seen him. He looks about my age, but I've never seen him on campus at Rysen University either.

He holds up his hands, palms facing me in a gesture of peace.

"I'm sorry, I didn't mean to startle you." His voice is calm, almost apologetic. As he extends his hand toward me, something glints in it, catching my eye. My gaze drops to the object he's holding—my student ID—the plastic card gleaming faintly in the dim light. "You dropped this." That explains how he knows my name. Something still isn't adding up.

I snatch it from his hand, my heart still hammering in my chest. "Ever heard of personal space?" I snap, sidestepping and walking around him to move farther up the beach and put some distance between us. My senses are now on high alert, every instinct screaming at me to be wary, but curiosity keeps me continuing the conversation.

"I was going to tap your shoulder," he continues, his tone unruffled by my hostility, "but I figured that might make you more anxious, so I decided to speak up instead."

I study his face, searching for any sign of deceit or danger, but I find only an enigmatic half-smile playing on his lips. "Yeah, well, try vocalizing from a foot away next time," I retort, not letting my guard down.

"Noted." He nods, the small smile lingering, as if amused by my wariness.

As the tension eases slightly, he makes an attempt at conversation. "Do you come here often?"

"No," I lie, trying to maintain the upper hand. The last thing I want is for this stranger to know my whereabouts. I'm not even sure why he cares. I also don't want others frequenting my favorite running trail.

"I hear it's pretty dangerous," he says, a hint of challenge in his voice.

"What are you doing out here then?" I counter, deflecting his attempt to probe deeper.

"Hiking," he replies simply, as if that explains everything. "And you?"

"I wanted some peace and quiet," I answer, my gaze drifting back to the water. I'm not entirely sure why I admit that to this stranger. The waves seem darker now, reflecting the thickening clouds overhead, signaling an impending storm. That's weird. There was nothing in the forecast about a storm rolling in.

I look back over the guy. He's not giving much away, which frustrates me. "The hiking trail's a bit far from here," I say, narrowing my eyes and staring directly into his. "How'd you know about The Cove? It's usually a local thing."

"Educated guess," he replies with a shrug, his eyes seem like they're getting lighter. They look like milk chocolate now. "I grew up in a small town like this. Where there's a forest, there's usually water close by."

I can't shake the feeling that there's more than what he's letting on. My instincts scream he's hiding something, but I can't pin down what. The air between us crackles with unspoken questions, and I find myself wanting answers.

A single raindrop lands on my nose, cold and heavy, jolting me out of my thoughts. "Looks like it's time to go," he says, glancing at the sky. Without another word, he turns and starts walking back up the beach toward the underbrush, leaving me no choice but to follow.

Once under the cover of the forest canopy, the trees, once comforting, now seem to close in around us, their branches reaching out like twisted fingers. My nerves are on edge, every rustle of leaves making me jump. I steal a glance at him, wondering what's going on in that head of his, but his expression is unreadable.

"Enjoy the rest of your run." His voice breaks the silence once we reach the original trail. "Be careful out here. You wouldn't want to lose that again." He nods toward the ID in my hand before turning on his heel and jogging away, disappearing into the trees like a shadow.

The rain starts to fall in earnest now, and I break into a run, heading back to the safety of my Jeep.

The encounter plays over and over in my mind, looping like a film reel I can't shut off. Every glance, every word, every flicker in his eyes feels sharper now, like the world itself is trying to tell me I missed something. Who is he? And why do I feel like that was more than a chance meeting?

I drop into the driver's seat of my Jeep, the door slamming harder than I meant it to. My pulse is still uneven, my hands slick against the steering wheel. I glance into the backseat, my bookbag right where I left it. Untouched. Except for the ID that's no longer in the front pocket but in my hand.

A shiver runs through me despite the muggy air. I drag a hand across my forehead, wiping away a mix of rain and sweat. Then it hits me.

He wasn't sweating.

No one makes it down to The Cove without feeling the burn of the trail and the steep incline, the heavy humidity pressing against your skin. But he looked…untouched. Calm. Like he could have been walking through a mall instead of trekking through the forest.

Rysen is a small town perched at the northern tip of Michigan, clinging to the edge of the map like it's not quite sure whether it belongs to land or lake. From above, it almost looks like an island, the way it juts out from the continental United States into the cold stretch of the Great Lake, water curling around it on nearly every side except for a single, thin road that ties it to the mainland.

It's beautiful in a quiet, unassuming way. The forests here are dense and alive, their canopies so thick they swallow the light by afternoon. Pine trees crowd the edges of every back road, and in summer, the air smells faintly of moss and rain-soaked bark. But beauty in Rysen has always come at a cost. When night falls, and the high tide rolls in, the shoreline disappears beneath the water, turning paths into currents and fields into shallow, shimmering lakes. People have learned to respect the tide here, or they'll be claimed by it.

Now, as the rain drums against the windshield, the forest outside blurs into a dark, unbroken mass. The wipers thump a steady rhythm, but it does little to cut through the murk. The uneasy feeling from the stranger still lingers, so I decide to see something familiar. Someone familiar.

Ten minutes later, I pull up outside the graveyard where my boyfriend works. The sight of him chopping wood with easy strength is a welcome distraction from my lingering unease. Elijah Palmer stands at six feet, three inches, after a recent growth spurt, his built body honed by years of physical labor at his dad's graveyard. I watch him for a moment, appreciating the way his muscles ripple under the gray T-shirt with every swing of the ax. The dark, cropped hair on his head is a stark contrast to his pale skin, a sight that never fails to captivate me. I continue to look his way but don't see anything as I lose myself, deep in thought, remembering when I met him in kindergarten, and he wouldn't speak to anyone but me.

"Like what you see?" Eli's voice, teasing and familiar, pulls me from my thoughts as he approaches the Jeep. He opens the door and slides into the passenger seat, his presence instantly grounding me.

"Maybe," I reply, a small smile tugging at my lips.

"Just maybe?" he echoes, leaning in close, his breath warm against my cheek. His navy eyes, filled with mischief and something deeper, lock onto mine. The tension from earlier melts away as he closes the distance between us, his lips brushing mine in a kiss that is anything but tentative.

I lose myself in the moment, the world narrowing in on the two of us. Eli has always had this effect on me, making everything else fade into the background. But as his hands roam and the kiss deepens, a small voice in the back of my mind reminds me of the stranger at The Cove, and the unease and thunder cracking that came with him.

"How was your jog?" Eli asks, his voice pulling me back to the present. I start the car and begin to drive as he takes a couple of deep breaths.

"Fine," I answer, keeping my eyes on the road as I pull away from the graveyard. His hand finds my free one, his thumb brushing lightly over my knuckles, a simple gesture that usually soothes me. "Are you ok?" I ask after his fifth deep breath.

Today, my thoughts are elsewhere, and Eli, perceptive as ever, picks up on it. "Yeah. Did you go running with anyone else?"

"No, just me," I reply. But the words feel heavier than they should. I hesitate, then add, "I ran into someone at The Cove."

Eli shifts in his seat, his grip on my hand tightening slightly. "Someone?"

"Yeah," I say, trying to keep my tone casual. "Some guy was just returning my ID. I must have dropped it on the trail."

"That's strange, you always keep it in the front of your bag," Eli murmurs, his voice thoughtful. See, perceptive. I can see the gears turning in his head, the same protective instincts that have always been a part of him kicking in. "Did you know him?"

"Never seen him," I say, frowning as I replay the encounter.

"Was everything okay?" he asks, concern lacing his voice.

"Yeah, he was just…calm. A little too calm if that makes sense. But he didn't seem threatening, just…odd. Said he was hiking."

Eli makes an expression I can't place. "Maybe we can get you some pepper spray. You never know who might be hanging around."

"Are you saying I should carry a weapon?" I joke, but the unease in my chest won't go away.

"Maybe," he says, half-serious, half-teasing. "Just promise me you'll bring it with you."

"Okay, Dad," I reply with a smirk, squeezing his hand in reassurance. But as we drive on, the sense of foreboding lingers, a shadow at the edge of my thoughts. I look over to Eli, who has his brows drawn together in concentration.

"I haven't developed mind-reading yet, you're gonna have to

tell me what has you so preoccupied," I tease, trying to draw Eli out of his own deep thoughts.

He flashes a grin, a mischievous glint in his eye. "Well, I'm currently thinking about how long we have until Paris comes back to the dorms from work. And wondering exactly how many surfaces in your apartment I can bend you over before she sticks her key in the lock." He winks, sending a thrill through me that leaves my mouth unexpectedly dry.

In that moment, I'm reminded of the power I wield just by being myself. Most people fall hard for the package they see at first glance: wide hips and an athletically trained body. The contrast of my deep skin against pearly white teeth, my hair usually in some braided style, and soft, hazel-green eyes often elicits a primal response from those I encounter. As I matured, I recognized the sway I held, not just over men but women too. Eli is different, though. His love is unlike any other, and it isn't about possession or appearance. It echoes a purity I've only seen in my father's eyes. It's a love born not of desire to claim but to genuinely cherish. While his affection is boundless, a part of me always fears it won't be enough to keep me tethered.

"Babe...Babe...Kals," Eli's voice breaks through my musings, pulling me back to the present. I realize we are pulling into the parking lot in front of the dorms. Time always seems to slip away when I get lost in thought.

"You coming?" he prompts, already jumping out of the car and moving toward the entrance.

We navigate through the pristine lobby of my apartment complex and take the elevator in silence. As we reach my fifth-floor apartment, the door swings open unexpectedly, revealing all six-foot-seven inches of Caleb Carwell, Paris's ex, or at least, that's who he's supposed to be.

"Hey, Caleb," I manage as I crane my head up to look into his black eyes, the crescent moon birthmark around his left one pale in comparison to his tanned skin. I try to mask the awkwardness that surges through me. Eli slides his hands around my waist, a silent assertion of his presence.If I have to note one thing about Caleb that has always stood out to me, it's his eyes. They're black through and through, but sometimes, if I look deep enough, it's like he's always tired, to the point that he has a semi-permanent red rim around the pupils. Other times, I look, and they're perfectly normal.

"How's it going?" I ask, aiming for casual but hitting somewhere near strained.

Caleb and Eli have a complex history. They used to be close —we all used to be—double dates, shared secrets, the works, until a rift grew last year, sparked by Caleb's messy break-up with Paris. Despite the tension, they maintain a façade of camaraderie, driven by a deep-seated loyalty that began once Elijah started playing wide receiver on the football team that Caleb happens to be the captain of. Still, every conversation feels like walking a tightrope.

"You know, it's going," Caleb replies with a strained smile, running a tan hand through his curly brown hair, acknowledging Eli with a nod.

"Hey, you're back from your run," Paris chimes in as she emerges from her room, her hair up in a towel, her timing impeccable.

"Yeah, and you're home early," I shoot back with a flicker of annoyance. Narrowing my eyes at her hair and the obvious shower she just had, I recall Eli's earlier words involving surfaces of my apartment. Honestly, there is no way we could have done anything extensive, but I was at least hoping for a quickie.

"Finished up early at the café," she replies, refusing to meet my eyes, her voice light.

The conversation falters, the air heavy with unspoken words and unresolved tension.

"I'm gonna head out, Paris," Caleb says, nodding toward me. "Eli, see you at practice," he adds before slipping out the door.

Once he leaves, Eli exhales sharply, the tension in his shoulders easing perceptibly. We make our way to the kitchen, fetching glasses of water in an attempt to wash down the discomfort.

"Awkward!" Paris declares, trailing us into the kitchen and breaking the silence that settled over us.

"You think?" I retort, forcing a smile. I'm painfully aware that Paris is my best friend and an adult capable of making her own decisions. I just wish she would make better choices.

"I thought he would leave before you got here," she admits with a sheepish grin.

"So, what are you guys like, back together?" I ask.

"I'm not exactly sure," she murmurs, her smile faltering.

"Paris!"

"I know," she sighs, her expression conflicted.

"He broke up with you with no explanation a couple of months ago, and now he just waltzes back into your life? And you're letting him?" I press, my frustration mounting.

"Well, he said he had a lot going on at the time, and he didn't know how to handle it," she defends weakly.

Eli scoffs quietly, a sound barely audible but full of meaning.

"And what do you think about this?" I turn to him.

"I think nothing. If Paris thinks it's fine, then I guess it's fine," he responds diplomatically, though his tone suggests otherwise.

"Am I in an alternate universe? Am I the only one who sees something wrong here?" My voice rises more than I'd like it to.

"Is the screaming really necessary?" Paris counters, her voice rising slightly. I look between the two as they pretend I'm overreacting.

"I need to shower. I have to be at work in an hour," I say abruptly, cutting through the rising tension and ending the conversation. I don't really have to be at work. In fact, I still have about three hours before my shift at The Kill Spot starts. I don't want to keep arguing with Paris about Caleb, though. We're young, and people fall in and out of love all the time, but I hated how easily he discarded her, like she didn't matter. I don't care what he was going through. Maybe the real underlying concern is whether Eli would do, could do, the same to me.

In the sanctuary of the bathroom, the sound of water rushing from the showerhead is a welcome relief. Water has always been my refuge, the one element that seems to understand the ebbs and flows of my life. Despite my father's inexplicable fear of open water, I find solace in its embrace, whether I'm engulfed in the sounds of the ocean or the spray from the shower. Tonight, as water cascades over me, I feel the weight of the day start to dissolve, the steam clouding the mirror and my thoughts.

Emerging from the shower, I wipe away the fog from the mirror, catching sight of my reflection. My wild hazel eyes are framed by my long box braids, thin curls cascading from each one. It's a look that could captivate or intimidate, a reminder of the potent mix of attributes that often draw people to me, sometimes for reasons they can't articulate. Tonight, I decide to let my hair down, literally and figuratively. Something in the air hints at change, subtle shifts in the currents of my life. Perhaps it's intuition or the charged atmosphere post-rain, but I sense that tonight isn't going to be just another night at the bar.

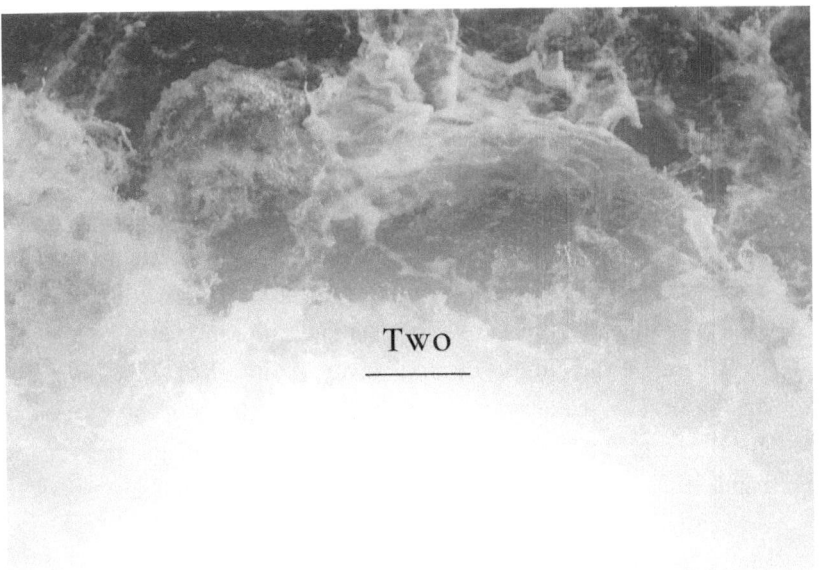

TWO

The air inside The Kill Spot hums with energy tonight. The latest hits from Little Mix blend seamlessly with the laughter and chatter of RU students and some of the town's locals. The bar, perched on a small piece of land at the pier's edge, offers a stunning view of the tranquil Cove. My older brother, Killian, opened it a few years ago with his girlfriend, Gina, after they graduated from Rysen University. Killian hovers over the bar, keeping an eye on things, while Gina expertly mixes drinks, handing them off to the other servers, including me.

The bar is divided into several sections. On the far right, plush booths line the wall with round tables in front of them, creating a cozy, intimate space. To the left, an upgraded jukebox sits next to the dance floor, where neon lights flash, giving the place a more city-like vibe than expected in a small town. The pool table and dart boards occupy the rear section. A good portion of the football team is gathered there. As always, Caleb and his inner circle stand out. They're all wearing their long-sleeved team T-shirts that match their jersey numbers.

Lucas, Caleb's best friend, barely reaching Caleb's shoulder in height, is leaning between his girlfriend Allie's legs while she perches on the pool table they've claimed. She and I have always been friendly with each other whenever the team and their respective partners hang out, but we've never developed a relationship. It's always hi and bye. Elijah stands next to his older brother Liam, who, coincidentally, is also my older sister's boyfriend. I roll my eyes as a slender girl with a sharp bob drapes herself over Caleb, laughing too loudly at something he says. A wolf tattoo curls over her shoulder, the ink catching the light before I force myself to look away. A flicker of something, maybe heat or jealousy, I'm not sure which, flares in my chest, and I clamp down on it, forcing my focus back to the task at hand. It has to be anger. Anger for my best friend who still ends up tangled with her ex every other night. That's all it is. It definitely isn't jealousy. Not from me. Not over Caleb.

Friday night always draws a large crowd, and the vibrant atmosphere is punctuated by an unusual group that settles into one of the last open booths. Their presence casts a subtle shift in the air. Among them, familiar, soft-brown eyes unsettle me with their intensity as they catch my attention.

"Kali, two Long Islands and a tequila straight for the ladies in the back!" Killian shouts over the noise. I nod, quickly getting back to work, and hand the ladies their drinks as a new group of patrons sits at a table in my section.

As I approach the mysterious group to take their order, an older man greets me first. His beard is full and silver-gray, striking against his almost youthful face. The combination doesn't make sense. His features are too smooth, his eyes too bright, like time forgot to touch him properly.

"Hello, love," he says, his voice carrying a warmth that feels wrong, practiced.

Everyone at the table shares that same unnatural gray hair and those eyes, deep-brown, too dark, almost liquid. They glint under the low bar lights like something is alive behind them. The sight prickles at the back of my neck. Alongside the older man sits a girl about my age and a boy who looks far too young to be anywhere near a bar, yet something about him feels...oddly ancient.

"What can I get for you?" I ask, forcing my voice steady as a chill works its way down my spine.

"I'll have a scotch, neat," the bearded man says. "They'll have whatever's on tap." His gaze lingers a moment too long, and my stomach tightens. I glance toward the boy, his eyes meeting mine for only a second, and in that brief look, I swear his pupils stretch and lighten slightly.

"Okay, IDs," I manage, extending my hand.

"It's been so long since I've been carded," the man says with a chuckle. The smile that follows is all teeth, too white and perfect. "We're celebrating my nephew's twenty-first birthday."

The ID the boy slides across the table seems real enough. Everything checks out. Except the face behind it. No twenty-one-year-old looks like that. Not unless he stopped aging years ago.

"I'm really thirsty," the girl murmurs. Her voice is soft, melodic, and somehow it sounds like more than words. Her eyes twitch, moving from side to side, like she's keeping watch for everyone in the room.

"Coming right up," I say, pasting on a smile that doesn't reach my eyes. I turn toward the bar, each step feeling heavier than it should. At the counter, Gina's chatting with another customer, and out of the corner of my eye, I spot Eli by the pool table, watching the group closely. I don't see when he moves, but when I reach my destination, he's already there, his expression shadowed with concern.

"Everything okay?" he asks, eyes narrowing slightly as he glances toward the table I just left.

"Yeah, just another group of patrons," I reply, though my voice lacks conviction.

Eli seems to contemplate this for a moment before offering, "I can take that table if you want?"

"No, you don't work here. I've got it," I insist, brushing off his concern. Sensing my resolve, he backs off but not without a wary glance back at the group.

When I return with their drinks, the vibe at their table has shifted subtly. The air around them feels charged, almost expectant.

"You are unnaturally stunning," the bearded man suddenly declares with a southern drawl, his companions nodding, as if privy to some secret about me.

"The most beautiful human I've ever seen," adds the woman in the group, her voice earnest.

"It's like supernatural beauty, a mesmerizing type," the bearded man continues, his companions echoing his sentiment.

I laugh off their comments, though they leave me feeling exposed under their intense scrutiny. "I'll have to let my parents know their genetics are getting rave reviews," I joke, trying to keep the atmosphere light, despite the growing knot of anxiety in my stomach.

As I turn to leave, I can feel their eyes on me, weighing and measuring. Shaking off my unease, I return to the bar where Killian and Eli watch with thinly veiled concern. The night rolls on, and the strange group departs with odd formality, each making it a point to bid me a personal goodbye, a gesture that leaves me more puzzled than flattered, but mostly uneasy.

As the bar begins to empty, the lingering tension from the encounter with the mysterious patrons hangs heavily in the air. Eli, along with a few of Caleb's friends, remains by the pool table, their conversation low and intense. I approach to clear the remaining glasses, my energy nearly spent from the night's ordeals.

"Hey, Kals," Liam greets, offering a sympathetic smile. "Rough night, huh?" he observes.

"Who knew energy could be both invigorating and drain-ing?" I say, trying to muster a smile that doesn't quite reach my eyes.

"If anyone would know, it would be you, right?" Liam replies, and something in the way he says it makes my brows knit together. There's weight behind his words, like he's talking about more than simple fatigue.

I open my mouth to ask what he means, but Eli cuts in, his tone light though his eyes are anything but. "She doesn't need any more of your philosophical musings tonight, man."

I laugh, but it comes out softer than I intend, touched with disappointment at the interruption. "Actually, I could use all the empowering words I can get," I say, glancing at Liam, trying to draw him out again. There's something in his expression, some-thing knowing that makes my stomach twist.

Liam starts to speak, then stops. His jaw tightens as if he remembers he shouldn't say whatever was about to escape. The silence stretches, heavy and strange.

To ease it, I turn to Eli, his nearness steadying me. "What is it I need then," I ask, my voice teasing, "if not philosophical musings?" I lean closer, catching the faint glint in his eyes beneath the bar lights.

"I don't know," he murmurs, his voice dropping to a whisper meant only for me. "But I remember making a promise about the surfaces of your apartment."

His words send a shiver down my spine, part anticipation, part something I can't quite name. There's a faint hum beneath his tone, almost as if the air itself responds to him, or maybe to us.

The rest of the night passes in a blur of laughter, closing duties, and the lingering echo of Liam's unfinished thoughts. When the lights dim and the last chairs are stacked, only Killian, Gina, and I remain.

"Let me know when you get in," Killian says as I grab my

coat. His voice is steady but carries that quiet, protective edge he gets whenever the night feels too heavy.

"Will do," I reply, stepping out into the warm summer air. The faint tang of salt water seeps into my every breath, clinging to my skin and filling my senses.

A crescent moon hangs low on the horizon, its pale light washing the parking lot in ghostly silver, stretching all the way to where The Cove meets the sand. The tide creeps in, inch by inch, as steady and relentless as breath. I glance at my watch. Just past one in the morning. By two-thirty, the entire beach will be gone, swallowed by the lake.

Signs line the pier and the shoreline, warning people to stay off the beach after ten when the water begins its inevitable rise. Most people listen. Most.

Killian had been lucky to snag the sale of the old seafood restaurant located on the quay. The pier itself is tall and solid, its wood blackened from years of storms and salt. It rises about five feet above the normal waterline, high enough to stay dry even when the tide climbs to its full three feet. From there, a set of narrow stairs winds down toward the beach, though some of the lower steps will be under water within the hour.

They call it the Tidal Hour. The moment when the lake turns unpredictable. The water rushes in so quickly it feels alive, as if something deep beneath the surface opens and exhales, flooding the shallows before sealing itself again. The old stories say it's the heartbeat of the lake, a pulse that wakes and sleeps with the moon.

I turn my gaze across The Cove toward the emergency pier about forty feet away. It's smaller, less impressive, meant only for rescue teams or for anyone foolish enough to be caught on the beach too late at night. The air hums faintly as the tide pulls stronger.

Looking closer at its shoreline, I freeze. A lone figure lies stretched out on the sand, motionless. At first, I think it's driftwood or a pile of clothes, but then the moonlight slides across it, revealing the curve of a shoulder, the shape of a body, a human one.

The figure doesn't move. Not even when the tide touches its feet.

The sight of his shirt freezes my breath. It's a white long-sleeve emblazoned with the number one beneath the word "Captain." Its fabric catches the moonlight in ghostly flashes. Recognition hits like a gut punch, a wave of dread crashing over me, colder and fiercer than the tide creeping up the shore. Something is wrong. Why isn't Caleb moving? I swing back to the parking lot, noticing his Trailblazer is still here.

My gaze shifts to the pier where the steps descending toward the original shoreline are now barely visible. The tide, unrelenting, has swallowed the lower steps, each wave climbing higher and drawing the line between sand and water ever closer to where he is sprawled near the edge. I take the steps two at a time, my pulse hammering with urgency, while the briny air clings thickly to my lungs. The beach below is shrinking fast, the waves claiming more ground with every breath of wind. Caleb lies beyond the advancing surf, his body too still, his arms limp and splayed at unnatural angles. Though the water hasn't yet reached him, the tide's slow, relentless crawl inches closer with each pulse. Every wave stretches forward, brushing his boots before sliding back again, as if testing how far it can reach before taking him completely.

I have to move faster. If I hesitate, Caleb will be lost to the water.

My shoes slap against wet wood. Cold spray mists my face. *I don't even like the guy, not really.* I can't explain what's driving me to risk my life for him. It feels like something else entirely, something older, deeper, pulling me forward.

The last few steps are already swallowed by the tide. I splash down into the icy water that claws at my calves, my breath catching at the shock. Even in the thick of summer, the water here remains a cool forty degrees. Each step is a struggle, the current dragging at my legs like invisible hands. The sand shifts beneath me, treacherous and soft, threatening to pull me down with every stride.

Foam gathers around my knees as I push forward. The sound of the surf fills my ears, roaring and alive. My heart pounds, a steady drum against the rhythm of the waves. Caleb is only a few yards away now. The distance between him and safety is shrinking with every passing second.

The roar of the waves grows louder, their rhythm pounding in my ears, steady and merciless. My muscles burn as I fight through the water, the cold biting into my skin, urgency hammering in my chest. Every second feels like a race against the lake's unyielding pull.

Caleb and I have always been a part of each other's lives. We grew up together, same schools, same summer camps. He was even my dance partner at Paris's sweet sixteen while Elijah danced with her. Back then, Caleb and I took dance classes together, stumbling through steps and laughing until we couldn't breathe. I spent so much time with him that an innocent crush had started to grow without me even realizing it.

By the time high school came around, I thought maybe he would ask me out. He didn't, but Elijah did. I had no idea Elijah saw me that way, so I said yes, thinking it would make sense somehow. Maybe it did, at first.

When Caleb started dating Paris, I thought it would be perfect, the four of us together, best friends, something light and easy and maybe even a little magical. For a while, it was, until he broke up with her. Until everything cracked open, and we were left standing on opposite sides of a fault line.

Now, with the water churning around my knees and the tide closing in, I can't tell what I feel. Anger? Guilt? Something worse? The lines are blurred. I don't know if I'm angry at him for breaking her heart, or at myself for still feeling something for him at all.

I push forward, the waves tugging harder, as if the lake itself wants to drag us both under. Caleb lies motionless ahead, his body slightly angled down, thanks to the way the water drags the sand back into its depths, the water curling around his boots. I grit my teeth and keep moving. Whatever I do or don't feel can wait. Right now, I have to reach him.

"Hey!" I call out, my voice slicing through the stillness of the night. No response. I quicken my pace, the soft sand giving way beneath my urgent steps. Reaching him, I drop to my knees, the cold water soaking through my jeans, chilling my skin. It's already halfway up his horizontal body, soaking his back.

"Caleb!" I shake his shoulder. Still, he doesn't stir. Panic sets in, my mind racing as I scan the deserted beach. We're alone, just me and Caleb, the tide our only company. I should've shouted for Killian.

I fumble for my phone with trembling hands, its screen a stark light in the dimness. Dialing 911, I force my voice to remain calm as I explain our location and the situation, all the while feeling the tide creep higher around us, threatening to claim Caleb before help can arrive.

I hang up and position myself to start CPR, my hands shaking as I place them on his chest. The first compression is met with the resistance of his lifeless body against my desperate force. Water begins to lap around us, the sounds of the lake merging eerily with the thudding of my heart and the shallow gasps escaping my lips. I press down, counting under my breath, each number a plea for life. The surreal feeling that the water responds to my touch overwhelms me, each push against his chest drawing the waves closer as their rhythm intensifies with my own frantic pace.

Then, as the water almost covers his sides, Caleb gasps a

sharp, sudden intake of breath that cuts through the silence like a shot.

His eyes fly open, his irises glowing an unnatural shade of purple that pierces the darkness, causing me to stop my next compression mid-motion. His eyes fixate on me with intensity as my mind races, scrambling through memories of Evolution 101 lectures, but no scientific explanation can account for the clear bioluminescence in Caleb's eyes.

For a moment, everything is still, the only sounds are our frantic breathing and the gentle lap of water around us. Caleb's gaze holds mine, a myriad of emotions flickering across his face as he seems to come back from somewhere far away.

The tension of the moment hangs heavily between us, the air charged with a mixture of relief, fear, and the unspoken questions that now lay at our feet. His hand reaches up, gripping mine with a strength that belies his earlier stillness, anchoring me to the spot, as if to say the danger isn't over yet. Panic courses through me as I struggle against Caleb's hold, the fear evident in my wide-eyed stare as I try to pull my hand from his grip.

"Kali," he whispers, his voice rough yet steady. His grip loosens abruptly, and I tumble backward into the cold embrace of the rising tide. The shock forces a sharp gasp from my lungs as I flail, desperate to find my footing in the disappearing shoreline. Caleb stands from the frigid shallows, silent and imposing, before effortlessly lifting me. I cough and sputter, struggling to catch my breath as he carries me with determined strides toward the tree line. The first level of stairs leading back to the bar is already submerged, and the water is now rising quickly. Caleb ascends the steep beach with unnerving calm, carrying me. My head sags over his arm as I look back toward where the shoreline should be and find a wall of something black, silky smooth like satin, barely visible. The moonlight casts a haunting glow across its rippling surface, and I realize it's water.

As soon as his foot touches the treeline, whatever force was holding the tide back breaks, and the beach floods in a sudden whoosh. I know what I saw, yet I still can't believe my eyes. I search Caleb's determined face, but he doesn't react at all, and doubt creeps in. Maybe my mind is playing tricks on me, the way it does when I'm starving and everything starts to look like a cheeseburger. He gently places me on the trunk of a felled tree. The cool wind of the early morning bites through my drenched clothes, and I shiver uncontrollably, the threat of hypothermia all too real under the night sky.

"Stay still," he instructs, his voice a low rumble against the howling wind. "We'll get through this."

I nod, my teeth chattering, my breaths coming in short, uneven bursts. His confidence is strangely comforting, even as the surreal nature of our situation presses at the edges of my mind. Caleb pulls me onto his lap, wrapping his arms around me. I cling to him, grateful for the warmth of his body.

It hits me that I've never been to this part of the forest before. When I run, I always stick to the same trail. Now, I don't even know where we are. I'm certain if we follow the trees back, we will find our way to the bar, but I'm so cold I can't think straight. Summer in most places means warm nights. Not in Rysen. Even during the summer, the nights here can be brutally cold, and the wind off the water makes it worse. Deadly, even.

As my shivering subsides to occasional trembles, I dare to pull back slightly, peering up at him. His eyes met mine, the purple glow now a soft light in the darkness of the trees.

"Y-y-y-y-your...e-e-e-e-eyes," I manage to stutter out, the shock still fresh.

"What about them?" he challenges, his eyebrow arching, almost daring me to acknowledge the impossibility of what I'm seeing.

"T-t-t-they're..." I struggle for words, finally managing to steady my voice. "They're purple."

"So are yours," he replies coolly, a slight smirk playing at the corners of his mouth. The wail of sirens cut through the wind in less than ten minutes since I called, but my teeth are chattering like it's been an hour.

I don't notice his hand moving to the back of my neck until he gently but firmly pulls me into a kiss.

This kiss is controlled and deliberate, anchoring me in the moment, his lips claiming mine with a certainty that leaves no room for doubt. His hands are firm on my back, pressing me closer, as if trying to meld us into one. The intensity of the kiss sweeps away my reservations, drowning them in the rising tide of need that his touch sparks. Eventually, he eases back, allowing me to catch my breath, his chin resting atop my head. A siren grows louder in the distance, signaling the arrival of first responders in what I assume is The Kill Spots parking lot. Another ten minutes pass, and I hear boots crunching over dead branches and leaves.

"What happened?" a patrol member asks as he approaches, speaking into his walkie-talkie to relay our location to his team. They meet us with emergency blankets and body warmers.

I repeat a sanitized version of the night's events to the first responders back at the bar, carefully omitting the inexplicable sections. "When I came out of the bar, he was lying by the water. I found him passed out and not breathing. I performed CPR, and his breathing came back," I explain, a rehearsed clarity in my voice despite the swirling confusion inside.

The police chief, who is also Lucas's dad, takes me aside for a deeper inquiry, his stern gaze prompting me to stick to the essential facts. After giving my statement, I ride with the now-stable Caleb to the hospital. Based on how quickly he recovered earlier, I'm questioning whether he was unstable in the first place. His mother, Elizabeth Carwell, a nurse there, meets us with tears of relief and gratitude. She hugs me, her thick curly hair tickling my nose as she thanks me for saving her son.

As I navigate the hospital corridors, a familiar voice stops me in my tracks. "I hear we have a special patient today," my mother announces as she enters Caleb's room. I turn to face her, managing a sheepish smile.

"Mom," I greet, my voice tinged with embarrassment. Kara Marrinos, Attending at Rysen Medical for Emergency Medicine.

"Kali," she replies, her tone unreadable as she quickly turns her attention to Liz, Caleb's mother. "No worries, Liz. Looks like he's stable, just needs rest," she concludes professionally, reviewing his chart.

She motions for me to step outside with her. "I was leaving work when I found him like that," I say quickly, hoping to preempt any further probing.

"You're soaking wet," she observes, her gaze sharp. "You could have died," she continues.

"Mom, he was halfway out of the water. I couldn't just drag him out. I had to kneel right there and give him CPR," I plead, hoping she'll understand the necessity of my actions.

She considers my words for a moment, then finally nods. "Okay. Okay. Let's get you something dry to wear," she concedes, leading me to her office, which is as intimidating as ever with her numerous medical degrees and certifications on display.

She hands me a pair of dry scrubs as someone knocks on the door. "Come in," she calls.

Eli enters, looking both concerned and slightly awkward. "Hello, Elijah," my mom greets him with his full name, which he dislikes. I've always had a feeling she was never too fond of him.

"I heard about the accident. Just came to see if Kals is okay," he said, his eyes searching mine for answers.

"We were just about to…" my mother starts.

"Nothing," I interrupt, desperate to escape the stifling atmosphere of the hospital. "I'm going to get something to drink," I announce, brushing past him. Eli follows silently.

The relationship between my mom and I has always been a bit strange, loving as she is, there always seems to be a barrier between us. She's a top surgeon and practically never home. I even chose pre-med to make her proud, volunteering and shadowing at the hospital. But nothing ever feels like enough. It always feels like she's watching, waiting for something to happen, for me to mess up somehow.

As Eli and I walk toward the small cafe near the hospital entrance, the weight of his gaze bores into me. He leans against the vending machine while I select a soda, his attempt to appear nonchalant failing miserably.

"Just ask," I finally blurt, unable to bear the tension any longer.

"Why were you with him?" he asks, his voice laden with unspoken accusations.

"What? I...I wasn't with him," I stammer, taken aback by his implication.

"Lucas said you called the cops," he presses, his brow furrowing in confusion.

"Yeah," I reply, my patience thinning.

"So?"

"So, I wasn't with him. I found him," I emphasize, frustrated with his line of questioning.

"You found him," he repeats skeptically, making air quotes with his fingers.

"Yes," I confirm, mimicking his gesture.

"And?" he continues, unsatisfied.

"And what, Elijah?" I retort, using his full name to signal my growing irritation.

"What happened, Kali?" he persists, his eyes narrowing as he uses my full name in return.

"Oh, wow, Lucas didn't tell you?" I reply sarcastically, feeling the tension between us thicken. He sighs deeply, his shoulders relaxing as he braces himself for my explanation.

"Babe, I just want to know what happened," he says, his tone softening.

"I was walking to my car and decided to stay at the pier a bit. I saw someone by the lake shore and noticed Caleb's Jeep in the parking lot. I thought he was just lying there…but then I realized he wasn't. He was unconscious. I called the cops. I gave him CPR until they arrived," I explain, leaving out other aspects of the incident.

"What?" Eli's confusion is evident. "Like with your mouth?"

"Seriously, Eli, it was CPR. He was dying." My voice rises slightly in defense.

"He wasn't dying," he counters stubbornly.

"Yes, he was. His lungs were probably full of water." I'm exasperated by his denial.

"How could you possibly know that?" His skepticism is palpable.

"Why are you mad? I saved his life." Frustration colors my words.

"You didn't save his life. He can't die like that." Eli's words are cryptic and confusing.

"Like what?"

"Drowning." He looks away

"What are you even talking about?" I demand, my confusion growing.

"That was all that happened? You just did CPR until the ambulance came. Nothing else happened, right?" His eyes search mine for the truth.

"Is there something else you expected to happen?" I feel a mix of defiance and curiosity. He seems to know something he isn't telling me.

"No, just asking," he lies, planting a quick peck on my mouth. "We should get back to your mom." He's already walking back towards her office.

"I actually want to see how Caleb's doing," I say, following him reluctantly.

"Oh, yeah, we can." Eli stops abruptly, tension returning to his shoulders.

Back in Caleb's room, his mom is joined by his dad and friends, a few of whom I recognize. "How's he doing?" I inquire, noticing Elizabeth's red, teary eyes.

"They said he's stable," she responds quietly.

"I'm fine," Caleb chimes in, his voice stronger than expected.

"Why don't we go get some coffee?" his dad suggests to his mom, offering a brief escape from the crowded room.

They had divorced a year ago, and the tension between them still lingers in every conversation, every glance. I remember the night Caleb told me about it, the first time I had ever seen his carefully built composure crack. We were sitting on the couch, half-watching a documentary while waiting for Paris to get back from class. His voice had been barely above a whisper when he said it, *"They're splitting up."*

Then his head dropped into my lap, the weight of it startling and strangely fragile. He stayed there for a long time, silent except for the uneven rhythm of his breathing. I ran my fingers through his hair without thinking, not knowing what else to do. When his tears finally dried, he sat up suddenly, pulling himself back together, his face slipping into that calm, familiar mask as Paris walked through the door of our apartment.

The door to Caleb's hospital room clicks shut behind his parents, the sound pulling me back into the present. The others linger near the end of his bed, voices low, their words blending into a dull hum. The slender girl with the brown bob and the wolf tattoo from earlier is there too, her presence as unnerving as ever. Their conversations about the night's events drift around me like static, meaningless and distant.

I stand beside Caleb's bed, the sterile chill of the hospital pressing through my clothes and into my bones. He lies so still, the calm on his face at odds with the chaos still raging inside me. He looks at peace, as if he didn't almost die. As if he didn't kiss his ex-girlfriend's best friend.

My best friend. But something rose in me when our eyes met, a pull that wasn't mine to command. The kiss didn't feel chosen. It felt inevitable.

The thought twists like a knife. What does that make me now, standing here and keeping that truth from Eli? The one thing I can't stand is a liar. Yet, here I am, wrapped in silence, pretending I'm still the person I was before tonight.

Eli joins me, his presence a comfort in the sanitized environment. "It's been a long night," he murmurs, bending down to whisper in my ear. "Ready to go?"

The weight of exhaustion settles over me, answering for me before I can speak. I nod, my earlier frustration with him submerged under the tide of fatigue.

Walking out the room, I glance back once to see Caleb's face against the white sheets, his eyes following me. We exit the hospital quietly, leaving behind the speculative murmurs and clinical lights.

Outside, the cool night air is a relief after the oppressive atmosphere of the hospital. "Let's get you home," Eli says softly, guiding me towards the car with a gentle hand on my back.

As we drive away, I lean against the window, the events of the night replaying in my mind. Tomorrow will undoubtedly bring more questions and confrontations, but for now, I welcome the escape into the quiet.

It's now nearing eight in the morning, and back at the apartment, I find Paris on the couch surrounded by a moat of used tissues. Her pale cheeks are stained red from a night of crying, and her eyes are swollen and bloodshot. Her dirty-blonde curls are piled into a messy bun atop her head, stray strands framing her slender face. I don't have the energy for a deep conversation right now.

"Is he…?" Paris's voice is tentative.

"He's fine," I reply quickly, hoping to cut the conversation short. "They were just double-checking when I left. You know my mom."

"How…how'd you…find him?" Her words are cautious, laced with something more than concern. Was that a hint of anger or accusation?

"Can we get into the details later? It's been an endless night," I insist, my patience wearing thin.

"I…I…I'm just trying to understand."

"What exactly are you trying to understand that can't wait until later?" Annoyance sharpens my tone, my eyes narrowing as I tilt my head in frustration.

"Er…nothing." She retreats, turning to face the TV, her shoulders ramrod straight.

I retreat to my room and let the hot shower cascade over me, washing away the grime and surreal events of the night. *That wasn't very nice*, a small voice in my head chides. If it were Elijah, I would have had the same reaction, probably even worse. She's just scared. But discussing what happened tonight feels impossible. No one will ever believe the truth. How could I explain that what should have been a simple resuscitation turned into me being the one rescued, then into a kiss so intense it felt like wildfire igniting every nerve in my body? Or that the tides, impossibly, seemed to respond to me, holding back when we should have been engulfed by water. They'll think I'm delusional. I almost believe I am.

The sane, acceptable version of events? I performed CPR. I saved his life. Nothing more.

Refreshed from the shower, I can still hear the TV playing in the living room. Paris, like me, hasn't gone to bed yet. I hate fighting with her. I need to clear this up now, so I walk out and sit next to her on the couch. Her head is hung low, tissues clutched in her hand.

"He's fine...and I know he can't wait to see you," I say, giving her a hug and a kiss on the forehead. She looks up at me with those big blue eyes full of fear. Sighing, I resign myself to explaining. "The short version is, I saw his car at The Kill Spot after work and found him unconscious by the lake. I called 911 and gave him CPR until the EMTs arrived. I don't know why he was by The Cove or how he ended up there. That's all that happened."

"You're two for two in the life-saving department: first at camp, now here," she replies. "Another save on Caleb's part, and he's going to have to give his life to you at this point." She manages a smile.

"I guess I am two for two." I laugh, rising to head to bed. I had completely forgotten when I saved him from drowning at camp. Which ended in an earful from my dad for me, something about being reckless and the dangers of water. "He breaks up with you again, I'm gonna let his ass drown."

"It wasn't him, though."

"Huh?" My sleep-deprived brain struggles to process her words as I pause in the doorway of the living room.

"I broke up with him," she clarifies, letting the words hang between us. "I broke up with him because of you."

"Me?" Confusion clouds my response.

"Not you specifically," she stumbles over her words. "It's just...I've never really felt like Caleb wanted to date me or be with me. He's sweet, the perfect boyfriend on paper, but it's always felt insincere. Sometimes I'd catch him staring at you. There was this longing in his eyes. I knew then that no amount of dates, sex, or gifts could compete with that. I had to choose, and I chose you. I'd choose you over anyone."

Overwhelmed, I return to her, cupping her face gently between my hands. Her skin is warm beneath my fingertips, but her eyes, those betrayed, wounded eyes, cut through me. "Paris, I would never intentionally hurt you. That includes anything or anyone." My voice is steady, but the weight of my words presses against my chest. I lean forward, kissing her forehead, a silent plea for understanding, before retreating toward the sanctuary of my bed.

Her revelation is like a dagger plunged into my heart, twisting with every beat. I know I'll have to tell her about the kiss eventually, about the fire that surged through me in that impossible moment. I try to convince myself it was shock, a fluke. But the truth gnaws at me, undeniable and raw: I've never felt anything like that with Elijah.

I collapse into bed, my body weary, but my mind refuses to rest. Thoughts swirl like storm clouds, relentless and chaotic, racing through my head, determined to outrun me. Sleep takes me, but there's no peace, only the weight of a thousand questions haunting me in the darkness, waiting for answers I'm not ready to give.

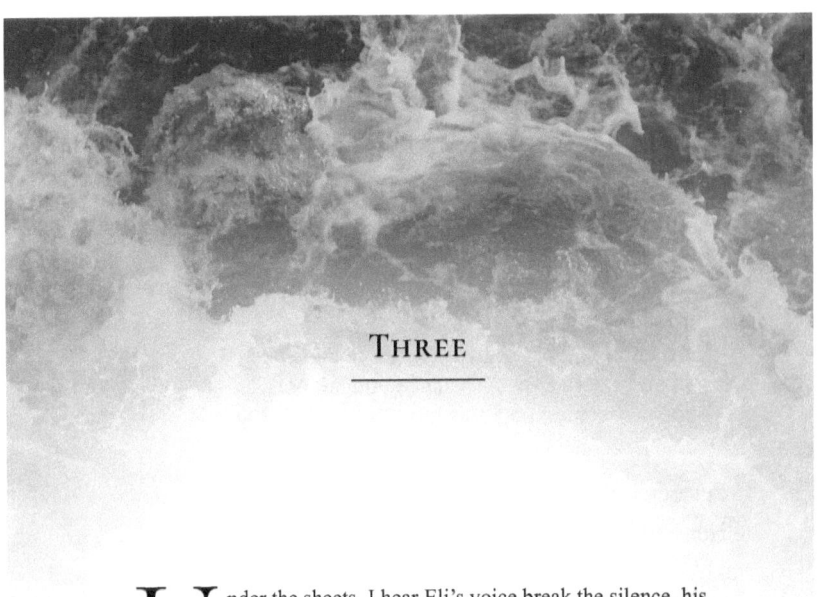

THREE

U nder the sheets, I hear Eli's voice break the silence, his breath warm against my skin as he plants kisses up my thigh. "One kiss, two kiss, three kiss, four," he murmurs, his voice a tender contrast to the chaos of the night. "Five kisses, six kisses, seven kisses, eight," he continues, his game making my heart race.

"Nine kisses…" he whispers.

"Eli, please," I breathe out, my voice desperate with need.

"I need you to look at me," he insists gently.

Lifting my sleep mask, I meet his gaze, but it's not his usual navy blue eyes staring at me. His eyes are violet.

Beep. Beep. Beep. Beep.

The shrill alarm tears through the fragile quiet of morning, dragging me out of a restless half-dream and into the disappointing reality of eleven in the morning. Through bleary eyes, I squint at the clock. The red digits blur and refocus, as if echoing my own reluctance to face the day. I can't believe I forgot to turn the damn thing off. Who signs up for a Saturday class at noon? Oh, right. I did. Last semester. Idiot.

I flop back onto the pillow for one last defiant moment

before surrendering to consciousness. The shadows of my dreams still cling to me, vivid and unsettling. Eyes glowing like coals in the dark, watching from places light can't reach. I shake the memory off, but it lingers like smoke in the corners of my mind.

A soft chime breaks the silence. My phone. I reach for it, blinking away the haze.

> MOM
>
> Dad's home. We'd both really like to see you this afternoon. Especially since you left before I could check you out this morning.

Perfect. That's code for *you're in trouble.*

Her shift ended at seven this morning. Why is she even awake? That's the Marrinos overachiever spirit, relentless and unstoppable, powered by caffeine and pure will. Mom hates water, always has, but Dad loves it. Or at least he used to, before fear took its place. He says people don't understand the dangers that hide beneath the surface. With his government clearance and all that cryptic research he works on, I suppose he probably knows more about water than most people. Maybe too much. Maybe that's the problem.

For a long moment, I lie there, the weight of inevitability pressing down like a heavy tide. Eventually, I swing my legs over the edge of the bed, the floor cool beneath my feet. One reluctant step after another, I shuffle to the bathroom, brush my teeth, and pull on a pair of leggings and one of Elijah's hoodies, the one that still smells faintly of his cologne, woodsy and warm.

Breakfast, if it even counts, is a bagel and a bottle of apple juice scavenged from the fridge. I eat standing up, the hum of the refrigerator filling the silence. With a resigned sigh, I grab my keys and head for the door, bracing myself for whatever waits at my parents' house, and for the strange, dream-born dread that still whispers at the edges of my thoughts.

The drive home is a welcome distraction. The Marrinos' estate is especially beautiful in the summer. The crisp morning air carries the scent of newly budding trees, and as I drive up the winding driveway, the they flaunt their vibrant hues, green leaves blowing in the summer breeze. With the windows down, I let the cool air and the earthy fragrance fill the Jeep, momentarily easing my apprehensions.

As I approach the imposing structure of my home, the building looms like a gothic cathedral among the dense forestry, its grandeur both comforting and overwhelming. The familiar sight stirs nostalgia in me. My parents have done quite well in Rysen. My mother is an Attending in the emergency department here, while my dad is one of the world's top Oceanographers. He's definitely paid top dollar at Rysen University. Students from all over come to the university to study under him. Parking behind a sleek foreign sports car I recognize as Killian's, I brace myself for the inevitable confrontation that awaits.

Stepping into the bright foyer, I'm greeted by the familiar opulence of white marble streaked with gray veins that ripple across the floors, walls, and even the ceiling. Sunlight pours through the towering windows, scattering across the polished surfaces and flooding the space with a blinding brilliance that feels less like warmth and more like scrutiny. Every beam of light seems to search, to expose.

My mother has always loved this clean, minimalist aesthetic, the kind that belongs in magazines rather than in a house full of actual people. With three girls and two boys, though, it never stays pristine for long. No matter how hard she tries, life always manages to leave fingerprints.

I move through the familiar corridors, my footsteps echoing softly in the vastness. The scent of pine cleaner and worn leather greets me like a quiet memory as I pass through the grand foyer and step into the den. The air shifts as I near the back of the house, carrying with it the mingling sounds of mid-morning activity, of pots clinking, low voices, and the faint hiss of something sizzling on the grill outside. Killian sits in the kitchen, framed by sunlight and shadow, a mug of coffee cupped in both hands. He glances up as I enter, his expression unreadable.

"Good morning," he offers, his smile a small knowing curve. "How was the drive?"

"Peaceful," I respond, settling into the chair across from him. "The estate looks beautiful, as always."

"It always does," he replies, his eyes holding mine a beat too long. "Are you okay?"

I hesitate, the memory of the previous night still raw and vivid. "I'm fine. Just tired," I manage, my voice steadier than I feel.

Killian nods, understanding in his gaze but wisely choosing not to probe further. "Well, if you need anything, you know where to find me."

What I love about Killian, and about our family in general, is that we aren't overly sentimental. We aren't the kind of people who say *I love you* every time we hang up the phone or make a habit of hugging just because we can. We simply know we are family, and that understanding is enough. There is a steady kind of loyalty between us, quiet but certain, like a heartbeat that never really stops beating.

I've always found it interesting how emotionally aware we all seem to be. It's as if we all had an extra sense for reading a room, for knowing what someone feels even when they don't say it aloud. It makes our house peaceful most of the time, calm in a way that feels almost deliberate.

All of us, except Kristina. My oldest sister and I have never really gotten along, which is strange because her twin, Krystal, and I get along effortlessly. Kristina and I clash over the smallest things, as if we were born on opposite sides of a line neither of us can cross. Krystal, though, feels like the balance to both of us, patient and kind, the calm after every storm. Sometimes I wonder how two people can look so alike, and yet be made of completely different things.

Grateful for Killian's restraint, I make my way outside to where my parents are sitting. The late May air carries that almost-summer warmth, soft and faintly sweet with the scent of lilac and cut grass. A light breeze stirs across the patio, cool enough to raise a shiver when it slips through the shade. It should feel pleasant, but it does little to ease the tension tightening around my chest as I approach the table where my mother and father sit at brunch.

My mother's posture is perfectly composed, her smile practiced and careful. My father sits opposite her, his coffee cooling beside a plate he hasn't touched, his gaze fixed on something beyond the treeline. The clink of silverware and the low hum of conversation fill the air, gentle but measured, as if the house itself is holding its breath.

"Hi, Dad," I greet, trying to gauge his mood from a brief glance.

"Kali," he responds tersely. His one-word reply is enough to confirm my fears. Starting with him being upset, although his next question takes me by surprise.

"Are you okay?" he asks, his voice softening slightly.

"Yeah."

"Alright then." He nods, his response succinct, leaving me momentarily confused.

"Wait, that's it? No 'the water is dangerous and you could have drowned,' nothing?" I push, unable to hide my disbelief.

"Well, your mother and I have spent more than enough time educating you on the dangers of The Cove, well water in general. But," he pauses, choosing his words carefully, "from what I gather, you did save Caleb's life. You're incredibly brilliant. I raised you to be. Meaning you must have weighed your options and had no other choice but to do what you did. I don't need to reprimand you for that." He takes a long drink from his glass, his favorite gin, no doubt, before continuing, "I nag because I know how bad it can get in open water. I just want to make sure you're okay. You, your siblings. I don't know what I would do if something happened that could have been prevented. I just want you to be safe. That's all."

"I mean…Yeah, I…"

"I also know how much Caleb means to you. You two have always been close," he says, a knowing look in his eyes.

The words catch me completely off guard. For a moment, I stare at him, trying to decide if I heard correctly. Caleb means *that* much to me? I mean, we're friends, sure, but I never thought it looked like anything more than that. What is everyone else seeing that I'm not?

A cold realization settles in my stomach. Is that why Elijah was so upset?

"Liz!" my mother suddenly exclaims, drawing our attention to Caleb and his mother as they approach from inside the kitchen. The interruption is timely, sparing me from having to respond further.

"Hello, Kara. Thank you for the invite," Elizabeth says with formal politeness, her gratitude palpable.

"No need for thanks. You're my best nurse," my mother dismisses with a wave of her hand, her attention quickly shifting to Caleb. "How are you feeling, Caleb?"

"Better, thank you, Mrs. M."

Brunch proceeds under a veil of strained civility on my part. I keep my head down, avoiding Caleb's probing gaze as much as possible. My parents and Killian do their best to keep the conversation light, discussing research and mundane topics, but the undercurrents of concern are impossible to ignore.

Feeling overwhelmed by the charged atmosphere, I excuse myself from the table. "I'm gonna go for a walk. I haven't been to the treehouse in a while. Wanna see how she's holding up," I announce, not waiting for a response as I head for my childhood sanctuary, hidden among the trees.

"Mind if I join you?" Caleb's voice calls out from behind me, his footsteps quickening to catch up.

"No, not at all," I reply, a mixture of relief and apprehension swirling within me as we walk together towards the path that leads to my old treehouse.

As we venture deeper into the forest, the sound of the hidden waterfall grows louder, its steady rush threading through the uneasy silence between us. The ground softens beneath our boots, damp with moss and scattered pine needles. Caleb walks a few paces ahead, shoulders tense, hands shoved in his pockets. His presence is both comforting and disconcerting, keeping my senses on edge.

"I want to apologize about last night," he finally says, his voice low and careful. He slows his stride until we're walking side by side.

I glance at him, then back at the narrow trail ahead. "What were you doing out there?" My tone is sharper than I intend, but I need answers more than apologies.

"I...I—"

"Look, it's just us here." I stop walking, forcing him to stop too. The air between us feels heavy, the waterfall's distant roar filling the silence. "You don't need to lie. Were you trying to kill yourself?" The question leaves my mouth before I can soften it.

"What? No, I—"

"Then what were you doing?" I take a step closer, unwilling to let the matter drop.

"I got into a fight," he says finally. He doesn't look at me when he says it, and the way his shoulders shift makes it sound more like a deflection than an answer.

"A fight that left you unconscious without a mark on you?" I ask, crossing my arms. My voice comes out half disbelieving, half fearful.

"It's complicated," he murmurs, his gaze darting toward the trees. His body stiffens, every movement taut with unease.

I frown. "Complicated how?"

He doesn't answer. Instead, he glances around again, his eyes narrowing as if he's listening for something I can't hear. Then he straightens abruptly. "We should head back," he says, already turning toward the trail behind us. His pace quickens, crunching twigs underfoot.

"If you don't want to answer me, you can go back," I call after him, following but refusing to match his speed. "I haven't even gotten to the treehouse yet." I gesture toward the faint path leading deeper into the woods.

Then I hear it, the soft rustle of leaves, the faint shuffle of something moving through the undergrowth. The sound circles us, too fluid to be the wind. I turn, scanning the trees for the source, my heart hammering.

When I face forward again, I almost collide with Caleb. He's frozen mid-step, his entire body rigid, eyes fixed on something ahead.

Before us stands a massive gray wolf, so large it looks almost unreal, its piercing eyes locked on ours. The sight freezes me in place. Caleb reacts first, stepping forward and pushing me gently behind him, his arm instinctively outstretched, as if I were something small that needed protecting.

Another rustle to the left snaps my attention around. A second wolf slips out from between the trees, moving with deliberate grace, its gaze as sharp and assessing as the first.

The air thickens with the sound of movement. Leaves tremble, branches shift, and one by one, more wolves emerge from the forest's shadows. Their coats range from pale silver to deep charcoal, their bodies forming a slowly tightening circle around us. They move in eerie synchronization, cutting off every possible path of escape.

"Caleb," I whisper, pressing my back against his. I can feel the tension in him, every muscle coiled and ready. "Caleb…"

Two wolves prowl to our right, teeth bared and hackles raised. Two more mirror them on the left. The others linger just beyond, their low growls vibrating through the air like a warning.

My eyes catch on the largest wolf again. Something about those eyes feels achingly familiar. I can't place it, but a flicker of recognition stirs in me, faint yet undeniable, like remembering a dream right before it slips away.

"Kali, I need you to stay calm," Caleb says quietly. His voice is low, almost a growl itself, steady but edged with strain. I try breathing deeply, resting my forehead in the shallow of his upper back.

"Caleb, we're surrounded by wolves," I whisper into his back, trying to keep my voice from shaking. "I didn't even know there were wolves on this property. Me being calm is not a realistic expectation right now."

My pulse hammers in my ears.

"Do you have to argue over everything?" His frustration is palpable.

"Do you hear what you're asking?" I counter, my anxiety spiking.

"Things are about to get really weird for you right now, and I need you to stay calm." Caleb's tone is urgent, his body tensely coiled for action.

"Weirder than being surrounded by a pack of oversized wolves?" My voice rises in disbelief.

"Yes, weirder than that," he replies, annoyance threading through his tense whisper.

As if on cue, a new voice cuts through the tension. "Are we interrupting your lovers' spat?" The mocking tone comes from directly in front of Caleb. I peer around him, and my breath catches in my throat. The gray-bearded man from the bar, the same man who had been a wolf moments ago, now stands naked where the animal had just been. What the fuck!

I spin, putting Caleb and me back-to-back, just in time to see another wolf transform into the stranger from my run at The Cove yesterday. My mind reels. "What the fuck!" Panic surges, and a scream begins to build in my throat, when suddenly, Caleb spins, his hand clamping over my mouth, silencing me as the circle of now-human figures closes in.

"This is where you being calm takes effect, Little Bird," Caleb's voice is a strained whisper against my ear.

"Little Bird?" I manage to muffle through his hand.

"I'm gonna move my hand, and you aren't gonna scream, okay? Kals, I need you to say yes."

I nod, fear and confusion tangling in my chest. Caleb's grip shifts, and in one smooth motion, he spins me around to face him. His hands settle on my shoulders, firm but careful, grounding me, even as my heart races.

My back is now to the gray-bearded man while Caleb's body shields me from the others. The tension in his stance tells me this is more than fear, it's calculation.

"We don't want to draw anyone else out here," he says quietly, his tone measured but urgent.

I swallow hard, the meaning behind his words sinking in. He's not only talking about the wolves, he's talking about our families.

"You good?"

"Am I dreaming?" I ask, my voice a whisper of disbelief.

"No."

"Am I dead?"

"No."

"Am I being punished for that dream I had about you last night? Because I had no control over that.'

"What? No...wait, you had a dream about me?" Caleb's tone shifts, a hint of something else beneath the urgency.

"I just watched a dog-like carnivore turn into a human. I think I'm losing my mind, and that is what caught your attention?"

"Was it a good dream?" he asks, a smirk playing on his lips despite the surreal danger enveloping us.

"Enough!" Graybeard's voice booms from behind me.

"Looks like our little Alpha here didn't learn his lesson from last night. I told you they would be together, the Alpha and his fish bitch," a girl from the bar sneers maliciously.

"We're here for the Siren. Step aside, wolf. Or this time we won't leave anything of you to save," Graybeard threatens with a chilling calm.

"You've got the wrong girl," Caleb says, his tone hard with defiance.

Siren? The word snags in my mind. Are they talking about me?

"Heath, report," Graybeard commands, his voice cutting through the clearing. He turns toward the man from The Cove, the one now identified as Heath.

"I saw her last night," Heath replies. His voice is calm but certain. "The water moved with her. By the time she found the Alpha, they had maybe fifteen minutes before high tide should have swallowed them whole. I've never seen water hold itself back before. Therefore, I can only assume it's her. She's the Siren." His gaze locks on me, sharp enough to make my breath hitch.

I swallow hard, the memory flashing behind my eyes. I had told myself the tide was just slower than usual. That's all. Just slower.

"You're trespassing on private property," I say, forcing my voice to stay steady. "You need to leave before I call the authorities."

Their laughter breaks out all at once, low, cold, and perfectly synchronized. The sound makes the hairs on my neck rise. Heat stirs deep in my chest, spreading outward until it feels like fire bubbling just beneath my skin.

"Step aside, Alpha. I won't ask again," Graybeard snarls. His voice carries the weight of command, a threat wrapped in authority.

"No." Caleb's answer is sharp and immediate. He shifts, stepping in front of me once more, his body a shield between me and Graybeard's burning stare.

The scene explodes into chaos.

Graybeard lunges at Caleb, moving with shocking speed. Caleb reacts in kind, and I freeze when I see his fingernails lengthen into curved, razor-sharp claws. He shoves me aside, hard enough to knock the breath from my lungs, but I know it's to get me out of the way. He takes the full force of the attack.

They crash together with a bone-jarring impact, a blur of fists, claws, and gritted snarls. The sounds of the fight echo through the trees, a raw rhythm of violence and desperation. My pulse pounds so loudly I can barely hear anything else.

A sharp prickle of fear races down my spine as the other three begin to circle me. The air thickens, charged with their intent. My body trembles, but something else rises beneath the fear, a strange electric awareness.

I've always been good at reading people's emotions, but this feels different. It's like their feelings are bleeding into me, each pulse of their energy syncing with my heartbeat. The girl's emotions hit first, bright and vicious. She's enjoying this, her excitement laced with hunger. The boy, younger and taut with nerves, radiates frustration, the need to prove himself. Heath's energy feels heavier, reluctant, a dull ache of guilt that barely masks his conflict.

They close in, slow and deliberate. I can smell the earth, the sweat, the sharp tang of adrenaline in the air. Caleb and Graybeard are still fighting behind me, their growls and shouts crashing together like thunder. The sound of them bleeds into the rhythm of my racing pulse.

"You don't want to do this," I warn, my voice trembling but louder than I expect. "Especially naked."

The girl smirks while the others hesitate. I take advantage of the pause, scanning the ground until my fingers close around a fallen branch. It's solid and rough, heavier than I thought. I test its weight, my hands shaking. It won't kill anyone, but it'll hurt.

My body hums with adrenaline, every nerve alive. There's a heat building inside me again, the same dangerous current I felt before. It gathers at the base of my spine, rising, pushing, demanding release.

"Actually, I do." The girl lunges at me, her movements swift and deadly. My body reacts before I can think. I twist aside, bringing the stick down, and it cracks against her temple with a sharp thud. A jolt runs through my arm from the force of it, the shock almost as strong as my disbelief.

"You bitch!" she spits, spinning to face me, rage twisting her features.

"Reflexes," I say, breathless. "You *are* trying to kidnap me, though."

She lunges again. I strike low, the stick connecting with her stomach, then spin and bring it across the other side of her head. The wood snaps clean in two, and I stare at the broken end, stunned.

The young boy from the bar moves next, silent and fast. He grabs for me, but I duck under his arm, sidestep, and jab the jagged stick into his ribs. He folds forward with a gasp. I knee him hard in the face once, twice, each hit followed by the sickening crunch of bone. My stomach twists, but I can't stop.

"I'm going to fucking kill you!" the girl screams, her fury a raw, feral sound.

"Anna, she needs to be alive," Heath says, stepping closer.

His calm makes my skin prickle. In his hand glints a long needle filled with a cloudy liquid. My pulse spikes.

"Why?" I demand, backing away, my breath coming fast and shallow.

"Just stab her already!" Anna screeches.

Before I can move, strong arms seize me from behind. They lock around my chest and pin my arms tight. The pressure steals my breath. I thrash, twist, and slam the back of my head into the face of whoever's holding me. There's a dull crack, a curse, and the grip falters. I wrench against it with everything I have, lungs burning, the world narrowing to the sound of my own heartbeat.

"C-C-Caleb," I gasp, my lungs burning as the edges of my vision start to blur. Panic claws up my throat, sharp and choking. Somewhere behind me, a deep growl cuts through the chaos, raw and animal.

Something in me snaps. The fear twists, hardening into defiance. I'm not about to be drugged by a pack of wolf people in the middle of the woods.

My thoughts scatter, frantic, but one word keeps pulsing through the noise.

Water.

I need water.

The thought barely forms before I feel it cold and slick against my skin. The arms holding me are wet. I glance down in confusion, and the sight freezes me.

Blood seeps through the pores of the boy's hands. It's not dripping from a wound, it's *pouring out of him.*

He releases me with a strangled cry, stumbling back and I twist free. I turn in time to see his skin begin to pale and shrivel, drying before my eyes. The blood that should be in his body streams out like sweat, soaking the earth at his feet.

I stumble backward, heart hammering, unable to look away. The air is thick with the metallic scent of blood and decay. The boy collapses, motionless, and his skin tightens, splitting, sinking against bone.

The others stand there, watching, faces caught between horror and disbelief.

A violent wave of nausea hits me. I double over, gagging as the stench of salt, iron, and rot rise, mingling into something unbearable. My stomach twists, my throat burns, and for one dizzy, unreal moment, the forest spins around me.

Another deep growl reverberates through the clearing, and everyone turns to look behind me. I spin, heart skittering, and we all stare at the same impossible sight.

Graybeard is on his knees, face cut and pale, and Caleb holds him like a vice. One of Caleb's hands is tangled in Graybeard's hair, forcing his head back to expose his throat. Caleb's other hand, claws bared, clamps down around the exposed neck. Tiny droplets of blood bead where the skin splits under the pressure.

"Arnold," Heath says, voice flat and bored, like he's naming a chore rather than a man in danger. Graybeard strains against Caleb's grip, every muscle trembling as he fights to breathe. He keeps looking at the decomposing boy at his feet, as if the sight is part punishment and part proof.

"Leave now or he dies. You all will die here," Caleb says, every word a quiet promise.

My brain scrambles. He can't mean it. He wouldn't kill him, not here on my parents' property. Would he? Has he ever done that before? The questions tumble through me, useless and frantic, while the taste of iron fills my mouth, and my hands go cold.

Heath nods slowly, backing away as the others reluctantly follow. As they retreat, the tension in the air slowly dissipates, leaving me trembling with the aftershocks of adrenaline. "I underestimated you. That won't happen again," Graybeard gargles out as Caleb dislodges what I can only call talons from Arnold's neck before allowing him to limp away.

Caleb stumbles over to me, his face pale but determined. "Are you okay?" he asks, his voice rough with concern.

I shake my head, unable to speak as the reality of what happened begins to sink in. We are alone now, the threat momentarily abated, but the danger is far from over. Where did they go? Is my family in danger? We need to get out of here, to a place of safety where we can regroup and plan our next move.

"Let's go to the treehouse," I suggest, the idea of a familiar and secure place appealing in the chaos. "It's right up here through those trees."

Caleb agrees, and we begin the trek to my childhood sanctuary. I walk beside him like a zombie as a myriad of unanswered questions run through my head.

The treehouse is nestled high among the sturdy branches of the oldest oak on the property. My dad designed it to be like a cozy studio, more of a guest house than a tree house. The exterior is crafted from natural wood to blend seamlessly with the forest's surroundings, and large windows wrap around the structure, allowing sunlight to flood inside. The main entrance is reached via a wooden staircase that spirals up the trunk, opening into an open-plan living space, featuring polished hardwood floors and high ceilings with exposed beams. It used to be the perfect spot to relax and take in the serene beauty of the forest, making the treehouse feel like a secluded nature retreat.

As I return from the kitchenette with a washcloth and a bowl of lukewarm water, my hands tremble slightly, betraying the calm I try to project. The dim light from the overhead lamp casts long shadows across the floor as I approach Caleb, who seems too still for comfort.

"What the hell," I murmur, not expecting what I find. I

gingerly raise his shirt to reveal his torso, bracing myself for a gruesome sight. Instead, there's nothing but dried blood over his skin, unmarred and smooth across his obliques.

"I told you I was fine." Caleb's voice is weak, yet somehow steady, cutting through my confusion.

"How?" I demand, frustration edging into my voice.

"Little Bird—"

"Stop calling me that, and tell me how you aren't bleeding out! I saw the blood…and your eyes, they were red, as in the color red. But also violet. And don't try to bullshit me with genetics. I don't remember learning about a red eye color recessive gene. What were those things? What are you?" The questions tumble out, my voice rising in pitch as I step back to gather my thoughts. Deep breaths do little to steady my nerves.

"Kali," he says, using my name as a tether in our spiraling conversation.

"Did I kill that kid? Are you going to kill me?" The question that haunts my thoughts now hangs between us, absurd yet terrifyingly pertinent.

"Why the fuck would I—" He's cut off by a sudden bout of coughing, dark blood speckling his lips.

Panic surges through me. My training as a junior EMT is supposed to prepare me for this, but standing here, with Caleb looking more like a myth than a man, I feel utterly unprepared. "It's internal. It has to be," I whisper, more to myself than to him as I kneel beside him, my hand hovering over his side where I expect to find a wound.

"I just need to rest and so do you," he insists, his voice a hollow echo of his usual tone as he leans back against the couch, his eyes fluttering shut.

"You can't fall asleep. What if you have a concussion?" My words are rapid, the scenarios playing out in my mind, speeding up my heart rate.

"I don't have a concussion," he murmurs, a thread of irritation in his response.

"Oh, I'm sorry. I must have missed the part where you graduated from medical school. Was that before or after you explained what the hell you are?" My voice is sharp, the sarcasm a thin veil over my fear.

"I almost forgot how sassy you are. That's going to be…fun, for the rest of my life," he manages a weak chuckle, his hand reaching up to smooth the frown between my brows. His touch is cold, his fingers stained with his own blood, and I flinch involuntarily.

Great, he's delirious. I pat him down, trying to find his phone, but I find nothing. Idiotically, I left mine back at the brunch table. I'm hoping sooner or later, one of our parents will come looking for us if we don't make it back in a decent amount of time. This isn't good. We're inside and relatively safe for now. Time for a real plan. Moving him isn't an option and neither is going back outside alone, too many variables. I look over at Caleb, gently placing his head on my lap, holding the damp washcloth to his forehead, trying to remember anything from my years shadowing at Rysen medical. I've been doing it since I was sixteen for Christ's sake, yet I come up with nothing. He looks way too pale for my comfort.

"I said I'm fine," he reiterates, a stubborn set to his jaw.

"I didn't say anything," I counter quietly.

"You're thinking it."

"And you know what I'm thinking?" I raise an eyebrow, half-expecting him to nod.

"It's not hard to tell," he says, his now black eyes locking onto mine.

"I don't know what to do, and I'm scared," I confess, the words coming out small and raw. My voice trembles, and I can hear the betrayal in it, the way it mirrors the fear in my chest.

I'm still reeling from the image of the boy, from the wet heat of his blood on my skin, from the way his body went slack and then began to fall apart. I know, with a clarity that makes my skin crawl, that I did that.

My hands keep twitching, as if trying to scrub something off my palms. The world is too loud, every sound magnified. Gray-beard's gurgles are still in my ear, and the metallic smell of blood presses at the back of my throat. I taste copper and panic.

"Tell me what to do," I plead, forcing the sentence out through my dry mouth. "Tell me how to fix this, because I don't know how." My mind keeps flicking back to the dead boy, to the way his skin puckers and darkens. The horror of what I made happen sits heavily in my ribs like a stone.

Caleb looks at me, and for a second I search his face for something like mercy or direction, anything that will steady me. My knees tremble. I'm terrified, but under the terror there's a cold, strange steadiness, as if some part of me already understands that nothing will ever be the same.

"Continue to sit with me," he suggests gently, and I comply. He lifts his legs onto the couch.

"Let's play a game," I propose. "Two truths and a lie?"

"I'm tired," he protests weakly.

"It'll be quick," I say not overly confident that he doesn't have a concussion.

"Okay," he sighs. "One, you're going to be my wife and bear my children. Two, I'm not a monster, contrary to what you saw today. Three, I've been in love with you ever since I first laid eyes on you," he says softly, each statement more surreal than the last.

"What's the lie?" My voice is barely audible, my mind reeling from his declarations.

"I thought the game was three truths. Oops," he smirks slightly, clearly delirious.

"You're delirious," I state, ignoring the pang in my chest.

"Maybe. You could tell me about your dream," he suggests, his eyes closing again.

"Not a chance," I whisper to myself, though a small part of me wants to share to see his reaction.

Eventually, he drifts into a light snore, leaving me alone with my swirling thoughts. Wounds don't just vanish. Humans don't grow claws or change eye colors on a whim. What the actual fuck is going on? Why would he say those things? Who are those people, and why are they after me? What is a Siren? Sitting in the dimly lit room, I watch over him, the weight of the night's revelations pressing down on me. I'm not sure what I'm expecting to happen next, maybe my sheer willpower will force him to reveal more. I look out of one of the large windows as the afternoon light gives way to darkness, raindrops pelting against it.

As I stare at him, my mind drifts to all the moments where life has seamlessly woven our paths together. We are constantly around each other, yet I've only ever seen him as a background fixture in my life. A shadow, almost. My focus has always been on Eli, on us. Caleb has been part of the scenery rather than the story. Most of the schools we attended seemed to pair us together, the most popular boy and the girl who, despite her preference for solitude, somehow managed to be just as liked. And then there was dancing. Our strange, short-lived stint in dance classes when we were twelve years old. Our parents had decided that we needed more "culture." The teacher always paired us up. Always. Of course, it came in handy for Paris's sweet sixteen when we were naturally paired together as well.

I realize we are actually good together as the memories come flooding back. In those moments, Caleb would take the lead effortlessly, his movements graceful and confident in a way that belied his age. Even back then, there was something captivating about the way he danced. He had a natural rhythm, a fluidity that made every step seem effortless, while I was rigid, constantly counting steps in my head, trying to keep up with the choreography. But with Caleb, it felt different. He made it feel natural, as if I could finally let go and trust that the steps would follow.

One particular memory stands out, etched into the fabric of my past. It was the night of our first big recital. I was a bundle of nerves, my hands trembling as I fidgeted with my costume. Caleb noticed, his eyes catching mine with an unspoken understanding. Without a word, he took my hand, his touch grounding me in that moment.

"Just breathe," he had said, his voice a calm anchor in the storm of my anxiety. "We've got this."

And we did. On stage, everything clicked. Our movements were perfectly synchronized, the music flowing through us like a current, connecting us in a way that transcended mere steps. It was the first time I felt truly in sync with him, like we were in perfect harmony, something beyond what words could capture.

Now, as Caleb stirs awake, I watch the color slowly return to his skin. The ashen pallor fades, replaced by the familiar warmth of life. His breathing, once shallow and uneven, steadies until it's calm again. It's as if his entire body has just reset before my eyes.

Reality crashes in, heavy and disorienting. My life has been a lie, and more people probably know about it than I'd ever imagined. But why didn't he want me to call our parents? Do they not know? Wouldn't keeping this from them put them in danger, too?

Once he is fully awake, we start back toward the main house. Twilight settles over the estate, the fading light casting long shadows that stretch like dark fingers across the lawn. I can't let him leave without answers. If we go back to the dorms, it's too risky. Paris will sense something is wrong. With her suspicions already circling and that intuition of hers sharper than most, it's only a matter of time before she pieces things together. Talking at his dorm is impossible with all the players sharing that house, and dragging Eli into this is unthinkable. No, it has to be now.

Unfortunately, my own body feels drained, like every muscle is heavy and unfamiliar. I lean into Caleb for support as we walk. His warmth is steady beside me, but my thoughts keep spiraling. Why didn't anyone come looking for us?

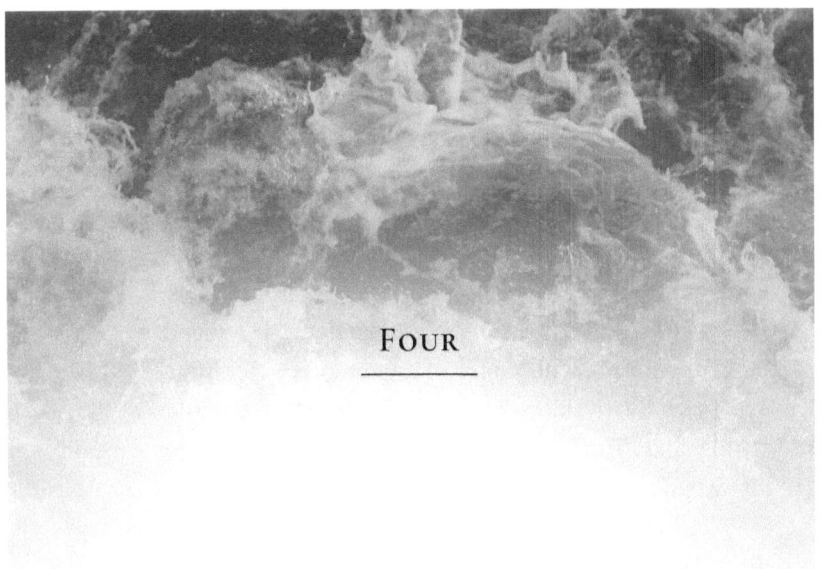

FOUR

When we reach the main house, the patio is empty. The table from brunch is cleared, the chairs tucked neatly in place. Caleb glances around once, then says quietly, "My Mom must have left."

I stop beside him, scanning the silent house. The doors are shut, the windows dark. "How do you know that?" I ask.

He doesn't look at me. "I just do."

I blink at him, confused. He doesn't have his phone. There's no way he could know that, yet he says it with absolute certainty. The confidence in his tone unsettles me, stirring the unease that has been building since the woods. What else does he know that I don't?

Something about the way he says it chills me. There's no hesitation, no guesswork, only quiet conviction, like he can feel her absence in the air.

I lead him upstairs to my room, which happens to be the farthest from where anyone else will be. It feels symbolic somehow, like even the house knows we need distance from everything familiar to face whatever this is.

He excuses himself to clean up while I sink into the chair at my old vanity. The room feels unchanged, frozen in time, but the comfort it once held does nothing to quiet the storm in my mind. My reflection stares back at me from the mirror, the same hazel eyes, same face, yet I hardly recognize the person looking back.

When Caleb finally steps out of the bathroom, the air between us feels heavier. The silence stretches, thick and expectant, pressing down until I can almost hear my pulse echoing in it.

"Am I allowed to not be calm now?" I demand, my eyes locking onto his with a mix of anger and desperation. His black eyes, usually so unreadable, are filled with a complex blend of shame and frustration. The silence between us grows heavy, almost unbearable.

"I...You weren't...That shouldn't have happened with you there," he finally stammers, struggling to find the right words.

"They wanted me?" I ask, my voice barely above a whisper, the realization sending a chill down my spine.

"Yeah."

"Why?"

"I'm not sure."

"You're not sure? Or you don't want to tell me?" I echo, my tone incredulous. "Okay, in case you haven't noticed, the cat's out of the bag. I somehow just fought wolves. Wolves, I will reiterate, who turned into humans. I'm freaking out a little here. I'm also gonna need more than one-word answers from you. You need to explain what is happening. Besides the obvious of what just happened."

"What do you want to know?" he asks, resignation in his voice.

"Why don't you start with everything? What are they? Who are they? What are you? Who are you? Does your mom know what you are? Does Paris know? Why do they think I'm a Siren? What is a Siren? Like a mermaid? How did they find us today? Basically, if you could politely answer, what the fuck?"

"They're shapeshifters, well Werewolves. The only shape they can turn into is wolves. They are what those in The Scath call Omegas."

"The Scath?"

"The Scath is a shadow world of sorts. Kind of like a world that sits on top of the human world. Most humans are none the wiser unless something happens in The Scath that directly affects them."

"Like?" I press on.

"We can get into the history lesson later," Caleb says, his voice steady but low. "Those werewolves that were after you are called Omegas, lone wolves. Paris doesn't know about me, and yes, I'm like them, but not really. I'm a Lycan. Also a shifter, but we're stronger. We can lead packs. Regular Werewolves can't."

He pauses, meeting my gaze as if bracing for disbelief. "This isn't a movie, Kali. I think my mother would notice if her son started turning into a wolf and howling at the full moon. So yes, she knows."

I blink, trying to keep up as my pulse thrums in my ears.

"They think you're a Siren," he continues, quieter now, "because you are. And yes, a Siren is like a mermaid, but not the same. Sirens are older, stronger, bound to the deeper currents. They found us by your scent. One of them must have caught it last night at the pier when he was watching us. Or maybe at The Kill Spot."

"Or he caught it at The Cove," I say softly, realization creeping in like cold water.

"That's what I said," he replies.

"No." I shake my head. "Yesterday I went for a run and met the other one, Heath. He said he was hiking and stumbled onto The Cove."

Caleb's expression hardens as the pieces fall together. He moves to sit on the edge of the bed, elbows resting on his knees, his gaze distant. His face is drawn tight with thought, his mind clearly drowning in it.

For the first time, I really look at him. His eyes, usually striking for their depth, are nearly black, voids that seem to pull light in. But tonight, they aren't the only thing that holds me. His full lips, the faint dusting of freckles across his caramel skin, the sharp line of his nose, and the unruly crown of reddish-brown curls, together, make him look almost too vivid for this dim room.

My gaze drifts lower. The black shirt stretched across his chest and arms reveals more strength than I ever noticed before, every line of him radiating quiet power. Even his still-ness feels charged, as if the air around him recognizes what he is.

"You still didn't answer why they wanted me."

He takes a deep breath, his eyes dropping to his hands. "I really don't know, but I will find out."

"But, they were in a group. How can they be lone wolves in a group?" I encourage him to keep talking, desperate for every bit of information.

"Yeah, that's why they took me by surprise. I've never seen a pack of Omegas. It's unnatural. In most wolf packs, there's an Alpha, someone in charge who takes the lead. Omegas are wolves that either lost their pack or left them. They, in a way, become their own Alpha. Having a group of wolves who all think of themselves as Alphas is dangerous."

"But they all listened to Graybeard."

"Graybeard?"

"Yeah, the older one with the gray beard. I thought the nick-name would have been a dead giveaway. And you? You have a... pack? Because they called you an Alpha. Right?"

"Yeah."

"What can you do? Like, do you have any superpowers?"

"I'm a Lycan, not Superman," he answers with exasperation.

"Right, so you're the most boring Supernatural to exist. Got it."

"Our Lycanism only enhances what we are already capable of, speed, reflexes, smell, strength. Things like that."

"Damn, I was really hoping you had laser eyes or at least mind control," I tease, trying to lighten the mood, despite the gravity of our conversation.

"Well, we do have something like that."

"Why the distinction between Ly-lyci-ism and Werewolf?" I continue, making a mental note to explore the genetics topic later. "Wait, you can read minds?" I ask.

The way he said *we* still echoes in my head, the quiet confidence in it. Was he talking about them or was he talking about *us*?

"Lycanism."

"What does that mean?"

His eyes drop to the floor, and the atmosphere in the room shifts. I can feel his anxiety thickening the air, and I know I've touched on something sensitive.

"It's just a type of wolf. That's all." His answer is evasive, almost dismissive.

"From what I know of history, when there has to be a distinction made, it's definitely more complicated." I move to sit next to him on the bed, sensing that there is more beneath the surface. "Look, you're gonna have to tell me the truth, the whole truth. You can't expect me to trust you or anything you say if you can't offer me that at least."

His demeanor changes instantly, his anxiety evaporating, replaced by an intense energy that fills the room. Desire? It's hard to tell if it is coming from him or if it's my own desire reacting to his proximity. He leans in, slightly tilting his head toward me, inhaling deeply. My breath catches in my throat, my body igniting with an unfamiliar heat.

"Your brother's coming." He abruptly pulls back, breaking

the spell as he stands up and walks to the bedroom door, cutting off our conversation.

"Hey, you left this at the table," Killian's voice comes before he does. He steps into the doorway and tosses my phone onto the bed. It bounces once before settling near Caleb's hand.

His eyes flick between the two of us, reading the room without saying a word. Whatever he sees, he keeps to himself.

"Eli called you so many times without getting an answer that he finally started calling me," Killian says, his tone even but edged with quiet disapproval.

I stare at the phone, the screen lighting up with a string of missed calls. My chest tightens. He must have gone to my apartment and couldn't find me.

"Sorry," I mutter, shooting Killian an apologetic look. My mind is still a swirl of confusion and lingering heat from my conversation with Caleb. Perfect, Eli is just what I need to bring some normalcy back. But, in light of recent events, it has me wondering what everyone knows or is keeping me in the dark about.

"Dad also suggested you spend the night here. Which also means you're spending the night here," Killian says, his tone leaving no room for argument.

"What? Why?" I whine, panic seeping into my voice. If the Omegas had followed my scent from the bar to the woods, what if they follow my scent back here?

"I guess it's my turn to say sorry," he offers his own apologetic look and heads out with Caleb following behind, before I can ask any more questions. "Mom's cooking your favorite. Stir fry."

"I'll be down soon." I wave them off, grabbing my phone. My heart sinks when I see fourteen missed calls and fourteen unread texts to match from Eli. This isn't going to be fun. As I'm about to dial him back, my phone lights up with his name.

"Kali," he says, his voice tense, almost accusatory.

"Babe—"

"Kali," he interrupts, his voice colder now. "I've called you fourteen times."

"I know—"

"—fourteen texts, Kali."

"I know—" I hate when he gets like this. Elijah's anxiety is never a fun time.

"When are you heading back to your place?"

"I'm not. My dad wants me to stay here for the night."

"Good, then I'll see you there," he snaps, hanging up before I can respond.

The pit in my stomach tightens. He didn't even let me get a word in. What about today? I can't tell him what happened.

Sneaking Eli into the house should've felt like a rebellious thrill, but tonight, it's just another complication in a day that has been nothing but chaos. Dad's constant upgrades to the security system mean this is no small feat. Still, staying here tonight is probably for the best. There are too many questions Caleb hasn't answered, and I can't face Paris after everything.

I pause at the top of the stairs, the silence of the house pressing in. Dad has always been indifferent toward Elijah in a way that never quite made sense. It isn't dislike, more like caution, as if there's something about Eli he knows and won't tell me. He's never allowed Elijah to spend the night, not once, even though Liam, Elijah's older brother, is allowed to stay over with Kristina. Different rooms, of course, but still. The double standard has always bothered me. Now, in the wake of everything I've learned, it feels less like parental paranoia and more like knowledge. Like he's been guarding against something all along.

The thought sends a chill through me. Maybe it's just exhaustion warping my logic, or maybe Dad's silence has been a kind of warning all this time.

I make my way downstairs as Caleb is heading out the front

door. "I'll see you tomorrow. Tell your mom I'm sorry she had to leave in a rush. We must do this again," my mom says to him, giving me a meaningful look. Kara Marrinos is nothing if not thorough in her patient care. Perfect. I'll be sure to have a list of questions prewritten for Caleb.

I wave Caleb off at the front door, noticing a woman waiting for him in his Jeep, the same woman I'd seen at the hospital last night with the deep brown bob. The same one who was also at the bar. Who is she? Where did she come from? Why is she driving his car? And why the hell is it bothering me that she's sitting in the front seat of his car like the perfect passenger princess with a smug look on her face? The questions tug at my mind, but I shove them aside as I slip back upstairs, determined to avoid my dad's inevitable interrogation. I have a feeling he's only making me stay home for questioning.

My room hasn't changed much since I last stayed here. All my artwork still adorns the walls, and photos of Paris and me from our college tours, summer camps, swim meets, and even prom are scattered around, capturing moments of a simpler time. I feel a wave of melancholy wash over me, knowing that everything has changed so drastically. The two people I want to confide in the most are the very ones I can't tell.

One photo in particular catches my eye, a picture of Paris, Caleb, Eli, and me at fifteen, all of us grinning like the world would never change. The innocent smiles and carefree laughter frozen in that frame feel like they belong to different people entirely. Back then, none of us could have imagined where life would take us or what it would demand from us.

I climb into bed and pull the heavy comforter over my head, the familiar scent of home clinging faintly to the fabric. I close my eyes, hoping sleep will offer some kind of escape, some silence to the noise in my mind.

It hits me that it's only been six hours since I arrived here today. Yet these six hours already feel like a lifetime.

"Kali, dinner's ready," my mom's voice calls from the bottom of the stairs, pulling me out of a restless nap. I glance at the clock: 7:00 p.m. Just like old times. With a deep breath and squared shoulders, I prepare to face the inevitable conversation.

Downstairs, the dining room feels as familiar as ever, yet there's tension in the air that hasn't been there before. My dad sits at his usual spot at the head of the table, and I take my place to his right. The meal begins with small talk, my mom commenting on the new Asian-inspired chicken recipe she found, and my dad asking Killian a few questions about the bar. But I know it's only a matter of time before the spotlight turns to me.

"You're awfully quiet, Kali," my dad observes, his tone casual, but I can feel the weight behind his words.

"Uh…just eating," I reply, trying to keep my voice steady as I take a bite of food that suddenly feels like ash in my mouth.

"How's school going?" he asks, and so it begins.

"School's good. The semester just ended, so there's nothing much to report," I answer, trying to keep it vague.

"And Elijah?" There it is. The real question.

"Eli's good." I brace myself for what will come next.

"So he's finally declared a major then?" My dad keeps his tone casual, but there's an underlying tension that makes me grip my fork a little tighter.

"Darling, this isn't dinner table talk." My mom tries to intervene, sensing the tension, but my dad's gaze remains fixed on me, unyielding.

"Animal science," I say quietly, knowing it won't be enough to satisfy him.

"Animal science? Huh." He leans back in his chair, his expression unreadable.

"Yeah, he's been volunteering at Dr. Yates's animal clinic," I add.

"Good for him," Dad says, nodding slightly, as if that's the end of it. But I know better. Even though he's dropped the subject, I can feel his disapproval lingering in the air.

The conversation shifts to local news, something about a kid going missing a few days ago. I try to tune it out, but when Dad mentions an influx of wolves in the area, my heart skips a beat.

"Wolves?" I ask, trying to sound casual, but my voice betrays my concern. "Do they know where they're coming from?"

"No, but I want you to stay out of the woods, especially near campus. I know you love your jogs, but safety first," Dad warns, his serious look making it clear this isn't up for discussion.

I nod, my mind already racing back to the events of the day. The image of the wolves, no, the shapeshifters, flashes through my mind. I need to get back to my room and do some research. Yawning, I stretch, setting the scene for my departure.

"Alright, I think I'm gonna head to bed."

"Actually, Kali, would you join me in my study for a few minutes?" Dad interjects, his tone making it clear that this isn't a request.

"Sure," I agree, the pit in my stomach tightening once more.

Dad's study is as imposing as ever, filled with degrees, certificates, and awards that tell the story of his illustrious career as a leading Oceanographer. The walls are lined with photographs of otherworldly creatures he's encountered in the depths of the ocean, translucent fish, sharks with black eyes, and jellyfish that glow from within. These images have always fascinated me, symbols of how we often risk everything to chase what we perceive as beautiful, even at the cost of our safety.

By the time I turn around, Dad has settled into his chair behind his large oak desk, pulling something from his top right-hand drawer.

"I got this for you." He hands me a velvet necklace box. Inside is a delicate gold chain with a teardrop medallion, featuring an intricate maze etching around an aquamarine gemstone that catches the light in a way that makes it seem almost alive.

"I...Uh...Thanks, Dad," I stammer, not surprised by the gesture. Dad often brought me gifts from his explorations, deep-sea rocks, fossils, and even a small shark skull. I sit in one of the armchairs across from his desk.

"The town I bought it from told a story about this stone," Dad begins, his voice taking on that storyteller's cadence I know so well. "They said it helps calm the mind. There's a legend of a captain who went out to sea and got caught in a storm. The crew wanted to abandon ship, but the captain remained suspiciously calm. He steered the ship through the storm safely. In his top shirt pocket was a stone, just like this one." Dad points to the necklace in my hand. "I don't know if the story is true, but I thought of you when I heard it."

"Why me? Kris is the hothead," I deflect.

"Your sister has Krystal and she'll be okay. I want you to be okay, too. I've arguably put more pressure on you than your older siblings. In your academics, extracurriculars, and even in the partner you choose, it all matters to me. I want you to be the best version of you that you can be. But life is going to change, and it will get hard, no matter how much your mother or I try to prevent it. I want you to have something to remind you that even in the storm, a calm mind always wins."

I stare at the necklace, the weight of his words pressing down on me like a physical burden. "Thanks, Dad. I'll try to remember that."

Dad gives me a warm smile, one that makes the years fall away and reminds me of the man who has always been my hero. "I know you will, Kali. You're stronger than you think."

He sits back in his chair, his face etched with lines that mark the passage of time. I can't help but notice the silver streaks in his once jet-black hair, a stark reminder of how much he's aged. Somewhere between becoming a teenager and a young adult,

I've forgotten how much time I used to spend with my dad. We used to watch TV, go for runs, and play chess for hours. But as the years passed, he became the strict authority figure who wouldn't let me do the cool things my friends were doing. Hanging out at the beach or staying out late became forbidden activities.

Despite our differences, nights like these remind me that he's doing his best. Even halfway around the world, when he's conducting multi-million dollar research projects, his mind never stops worrying about his family, about me. The glow of his desk lamp casts a warm light over his weary face as he looks up from his work.

"Thanks, Dad," I say again, standing to leave, my voice cracking, despite my best efforts to stay composed. He stands up, moving around his desk with the same steady grace he always has, and envelopes me in a hug. The familiar scent of his cologne and the strength in his embrace make me feel safe, a feeling I've missed more than I realize.

We stand this way for a few minutes, the silence filled with unspoken words and mutual understanding. Finally, he kisses my forehead, a gesture that speaks volumes, and sends me off to bed. I feel lighter after this, like that one forehead kiss dissolved all my worries.

As I leave his study, a swirl of gratitude, pressure, and frustration follows me into the hallway. Dad's expectations are always high, but his belief in me never wavers. I slip the necklace around my neck, the aquamarine gemstone cool against my skin, its faint shimmer catching the light.

Of course, I love having that moment with him, but the questions pressing at the edges of my mind refuse to fade. I know he has answers, maybe more than he ever lets on, but for now, I'll go to Caleb. Once I understand what I'm caught up in, then I can face my parents. If they even need to be faced at all. Maybe they're like me, still learning what's true. They've always dealt in logic, not emotion, and logic only goes so far in explaining the impossible.

I start up the stairs, the house quiet around me. With every step, the weight in my chest lightens. My fingers brush the aquamarine pendant, and I let myself believe, just for a moment, that it means something more than what it seems.

Once in my room, I take a quick shower, the hot water soothing my tense muscles as I try to wash away the events of the day. The satin robe I slip into afterwards is cool against my skin, a small comfort in the midst of the turmoil swirling in my mind. I open the window to let the crisp fall air saturate the room, the breeze carrying the scent of pine and earth, grounding me in the present. I need that grounding now more than ever.

Sitting on the bed, I unlock my phone and open the short story Paris sent me earlier, *Fatal Perception*. I tell myself I'll read it, lose myself in someone else's darkness for a while. The story follows a woman who leads a mercenary group with six other women and eventually kills her husband. It's sharp and unsettling, the kind of story that usually fascinates me.

But tonight, the words refuse to settle. My eyes skim over the text, but they blur before the sentences can take shape. Every few lines, my mind drifts back to the woods, to the boy's face before everything went wrong. I can still feel the weight of that moment pressing against my chest, the memory sitting just out of reach, too vivid to forget but too heavy to face.

I scroll to the next paragraph, forcing my eyes to focus, but the story's violence feels too close, too familiar. My fingers tighten around the phone, the cool glass suddenly slick against my skin. A faint metallic taste rises in my mouth, and I swallow hard, willing the memory away.

Caleb's eyes flash through my mind again, the red glow and the things he still hasn't told me. The questions twist together with the guilt until I can't tell one from the other. I close the story, the screen going dark, and stare at my reflection in it.

The sound of the window sliding open makes me look up, my heart skipping a beat as Eli climbs through with practiced ease. The sight of him brings a smile to my face, memories of our early days flashing through my mind. Back then, he was clumsier, knocking over everything on the windowsill as he tried to be stealthy. But now, he moves with a quiet grace, slipping inside without a sound.

"Hello, love," he says softly, and before he can say anything else, I run over and jump into his arms, showering him with kisses. It's our ritual, a way of reconnecting after time apart. My kisses are playful, teasing, a way of claiming him as mine. Eli lets me explore, his hands gentle as they hold me close.

Something feels different. There's an urgency in my movements, a need to reassure myself that he's real, that he's here with me. As I touch him, I feel the heat of his skin and the steady thrum of his heartbeat under my fingers. It grounds me, anchoring me in the moment. But there's also a strange clarity, a sharpness to my senses that I can't quite explain. I can feel the blood rushing through his veins, sense the electric charge in the air between us.

As our kisses deepen, the world outside the window fades away. Nothing else matters but the two of us, tangled together on the bed, our bodies moving in sync. Every touch, every kiss, is an affirmation of our love, a way of saying, "I'm here. I'm yours." But beneath the surface, something feels off. A shadow, a lingering doubt that I can't quite shake.

When Eli finally pulls away, I'm breathless, my heart racing. "I love you," he whispers, his voice thick with emotion.

"I love you too." My voice trembles slightly. But even as I say the words, my mind flashes to Caleb, to the way his eyes looked earlier that day. And suddenly, I am filled with a sense of unease. *This isn't right*, a voice in the back of my mind whispers. *This is wrong.*

"What's wrong?" Eli asks, his thumb brushing away a tear I didn't realize had fallen.

"I wish we could stay like this forever," I whisper, trying to hold onto the moment, to push away the doubts that are creeping in.

"That would be fun...but I'm a little hungry," he teases, rolling off me and reaching for his clothes.

"Haha, you're so funny." I throw a pillow at him, trying to lighten the mood. But the tension in my chest won't go away. It only grows stronger as I watch Eli glance toward my desk.

"Doing research?" His tone is casual, but there's an edge to it.

"Uh...kinda." I rush over to the desk to gather the papers. I can't let him see them. I can't let him get mixed up in this mess.

As I sit back down on the chair across from him, exactly how Caleb and I had sat earlier, I can feel the shift in Eli's demeanor. The room grows tense, his questions unspoken but loud in the air between us.

"Was Caleb here today?" he blurts out, catching me off guard.

"Uh, yeah. He did a home visit. My mom wanted to make sure he was okay." I try to keep my voice steady.

Eli rolls his eyes. "Look, Eli, he could have died," I insist.

"Yeah, okay. Well, it would have been his fault for swimming where he shouldn't have. Right?" he challenges.

"That somehow justifies his death?" I shoot back, frustration rising like a tide.

Thunder crashes outside, loud enough to rattle the windows. Rain begins to fall in heavy sheets, the sound deep and relentless.

"Was he in here?" Eli's voice cuts through the storm, sharp and accusing. His eyes narrow as he studies me, searching for something beneath the surface.

"Here...as in my room?" I ask, thrown by the question.

The wind howls, driving the rain harder against the house. Water sprays through the open window, misting across my skin and soaking the sheets. I move to close the window, but the storm seems alive, the air pulsing with a strange energy that prickles along my arms. Eli watches me, rain clinging to his lashes, waiting for an answer I'm not sure I can give.

Eli's gaze locks on mine, sharp and unyielding. He takes a single step nearer, closing the distance between us until I can feel the heat radiating from his body. My pulse stumbles. The air between us hums.

For a moment, the world tilts. My balance wavers, and I reach for the edge of the desk to steady myself. A strange pull grips me, like something is trying to lift me out of my own skin. The edges of my vision blur, and when I blink, the room shifts.

I'm no longer inside my own body. I'm standing across from myself, seeing through Eli's eyes. The perspective is wrong, disorienting. From here, I see the way I move, how my shoulders tense, how my fingers twitch as I reach toward him. Then a scent fills my senses, sharp and familiar. Pine and sea salt. Caleb.

It slams into me, overwhelming. Why can I define his scent so clearly all of a sudden? I've never noticed it before. Questions like what was he doing in here? Why does it smell like him? Swirl in my mind.

The thoughts aren't mine. They vibrate through me, raw and furious. *I will kill him if he got her involved in this.* The anger burns through my chest, hot and foreign. It's Eli's, not mine.

Something inside me resists. This is wrong. I shouldn't be here. I try to pull away, to move back into myself, but the world feels thick, like water closing in around me.

Eli steps forward. From this strange split perspective, I watch as he reaches up, threading his fingers through my hair. His hands are warm, his grip firm as he draws me in. My body responds automatically, leaning toward him even though every instinct tells me to stop.

His lips find mine. The kiss is rough and off balance, lacking the warmth I remember. It feels possessive, a declaration rather than affection. The pressure of his mouth, the strength in his hold, it all feels like a claim.

Somewhere beneath the noise, I hear his voice, but I can't tell if it's spoken aloud or echoing inside my mind. It folds over itself, the same words overlapping in two tones, both his and not his.

Then, as suddenly as it began, he breaks the kiss and steps back, breathing hard. I stumble too, disoriented, gripping the side of the bed to keep my balance. The connection snaps like a stretched cord, and I'm back inside my own body.

The room steadies, but the air feels thick and alive. My pulse won't slow. Eli stands across from me, chest rising and falling, his expression unreadable. Even though I'm back in myself, I can still feel the echo of his thoughts flickering faintly against mine.

"Too much?" I joke, trying to mask the shock rippling through me as I peer at Eli, my heart thudding erratically.

"Just a little," he chuckles into my neck, his voice a low rumble that does little to soothe the growing unease inside me.

What the hell was that? My thoughts are a tangled mess, desperately trying to make sense of what just happened. I was in his head. That can't be right. What other explanation is there? My mind races, replaying the conversation with Caleb earlier. Shit, what did he say? Speed, reflexes, smell, strength. Those words echo ominously as I walk over to the window, the sky outside sparkling with stars. My course of action is already decided.

"Time to go before Dad really uses one of those shotguns," I urge, narrowing my eyes at Eli in a way that masks my inner turmoil.

Eli hesitates, confusion flickering in his gaze before something else takes hold, a sharp realization that changes the air between us. The shift is subtle but unmistakable. My stomach tightens in warning.

He turns toward the window. Rain beats against the glass in steady rhythmic bursts, blurring the world beyond into streaks of silver. His movements are smooth, too sure, as he climbs onto the sill. The stormlight spills over him, outlining his shape against the darkness outside. My instincts scream that something isn't right.

The wind whips into the room, cold and wet, carrying the smell of rain and electricity. Eli crouches on the slick ledge, one hand gripping the frame for balance. He glances back at me. There's something unreadable in his eyes, a mix of regret and resolve. Then he leans in and kisses me.

His lips are warm and familiar, a grounding point in a reality that no longer feels real. My heart pounds so hard it feels like it might break through my ribs. The rain sprays across our faces, cool against the heat of my skin. For a second, I almost believe this could still be normal.

Then instinct takes over. I push him.

He falls backward into the storm, the sound of his body slicing through the rain louder than the thunder. I rush to the window, breath caught in my throat, just in time to see him twist in midair and land on his feet with impossible grace.

My mother insisted on sixteen-foot ceilings downstairs. Elijah shouldn't have been able to make that fall.

He looks up at me through the curtain of rain, his face shadowed by the storm. Then his eyes lift, glowing a deep, unnatural amber. The light burns against the dark, the same color as the wolves' eyes were in the forest.

My breath catches. Neither of us moves. His gaze locks with mine, a silent understanding passing between us that changes everything.

Tears blur my vision. I close the window, shutting him and the storm outside.

I collapse onto the bed, the sobs coming hard and fast until there's nothing left. When the tears finally stop, only silence remains, heavy and suffocating.

The truth presses down on me in waves. Eli has been lying. Caleb has been hiding things. Paris is my only anchor, yet I can't tell her any of this. My life has turned inside out, and everything I thought I knew feels like a story told to someone else.

I didn't stumble into this new world. I'm being swallowed by it.

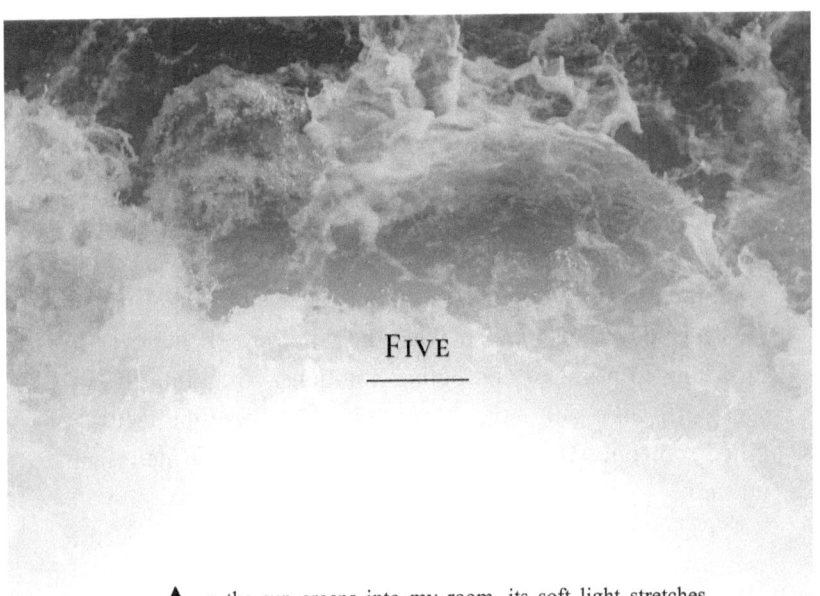

FIVE

As the sun creeps into my room, its soft light stretches across the floor, gentle but insistent, urging me to start the day. The weight in my chest makes every movement feel like an effort. I force myself out of bed, my limbs heavy, my head still clouded from too little sleep.

The shower runs warm, but it doesn't do much to wash away the hollow ache behind my ribs or the questions that circle my thoughts like restless birds. When I step out, I feel cleaner, but not lighter.

I take a deep breath, gather what little energy I can, and head downstairs in search of breakfast, something ordinary, something that might make the world feel normal again.

In the sunroom, I stop short. My mother sits with Caleb and his mother, their voices low, their posture too careful. Sunlight spills through the tall windows, painting everything in soft gold, but it does nothing to ease the tension that clings to the room, humming beneath the polite smiles and half-finished sentences.

"Good morning," I greet, my voice a little too forced as I join them, my heart pounding in my chest.

Mom looks up and gives me a small, weary smile. "Good morning, dear. Did you sleep well?"

"Not really," I admit, my gaze drifting to Caleb, who seems to deliberately avoid my eyes, further fueling my growing unease.

Caleb's mom, sensing the awkwardness, offers a smile that doesn't quite reach her eyes.

I force a smile of my own, but the weight of everything pressing down on me makes the smile feel hollow. I'm drowning in a sea of conflicting emotions, struggling to make sense of it all. I still haven't mentally confronted the fact that I killed someone. The paranoia and guilt eat away at me to make up for it.

"Caleb, can I talk to you for a moment?" I ask, my need for answers overriding any sense of decorum.

He looks at his mom, who gives a slight nod, and then back at me. "Sure," he says, standing up and following me out of the sunroom.

Once we're outside, the walls that had been closing in on me fall away, but the tension remains.

"So, any particular reason your boyfriend tried to bash my head in this morning?" Caleb's tone is laced with dark humor, though his eyes hold a serious edge.

"Maybe because I pushed him out of my window, only to see him land with two unbroken legs," My voice is steady, despite the tempest brewing inside me.

"You what?" Caleb's eyebrows shoot up, genuine surprise breaking through his usual composure.

"I...pushed...him...out...the...win...dow," I emphasize each word, hoping to convey the gravity of what I witnessed, though I'm not sure if I fully grasp it myself.

"Why?"

"Something happened." I try to put the pieces together as we walk over to the gazebo behind the house and sit on the benches under it. "I kissed Eli, and it was like I was able to see what he was seeing, it was like his memories."

"All of them?" Caleb's brows knit together in confusion.

"No, only recent ones, like within the hour, I think. I could feel what he was feeling, smell what he was smelling. It was like I was there, living that moment through him."

"I've never heard of anything like that before. But then again, I don't know any other Sirens besides you." His voice is tinged with frustration at the limits of his knowledge.

"Who's to say that I'm even a Siren?" My frustration mirrors his. Nothing makes sense anymore.

"I'd say those wolves who are hell-bent on getting you."

"They'll be disappointed to learn that I don't even know what being a Siren means."

"I still don't understand why you tried to kill Elijah." Caleb's tone softens, as if he genuinely wants to understand my actions.

"I really hate when I'm lied to. I've always been good at reading people's energy. I can tell when they're lying. But Eli slipped through the cracks. I guess I was more mad at myself than at him."

"What do you mean?" Caleb leans in, his expression a mix of curiosity and concern.

"Through his memory, I could smell you all over my room. I remember you saying Werewolves have heightened senses, but it wasn't just that. At the hospital, he said you weren't going to die if I hadn't saved you, which didn't make sense, until I saw how you healed back at the treehouse."

I turn to face him, my voice trembling with the weight of my realization. "How long have you known about Eli's...secrets? How long has he known about yours?"

Caleb sighs, running a hand through his hair in a gesture that speaks of frustration and resignation. "A while. But it's not what you think. He has his reasons for keeping it from you."

"Reasons?" I echo, feeling my frustration bubble over. "What reasons could possibly justify lying to the person he claims he wants to build a life with?"

"He was trying to protect you," Caleb says quietly, his voice laced with regret. "There are things going on that are bigger than us, things you wouldn't understand."

I take a deep breath, trying to quell the storm raging inside me. "I just don't know who to believe anymore."

"Hey, slow down," Caleb interjects, his voice gentle, trying to ground me.

"It's not just that. He called you an Alpha in his mind, in his memory. He was mad that you told me. This means he knew I was in danger. You knew too. That's why everyone was so worried about the group at the bar that night. You guys knew something was up. Why don't I have a right to know? It's my life."

"You're absolutely right." Caleb rises to his feet so quickly that the bench legs scrape against the floor. His expression hardens, all hesitation gone. "Let's go for a ride."

He extends his hand toward me, his eyes steady and filled with determination.

"The last time I went somewhere with you, I almost got killed." I cross my arms, though my voice betrays a flicker of curiosity.

He doesn't flinch. "Do you want the inside scoop or not?"

The challenge in his tone leaves little room for argument.

We head inside, finding our moms at the kitchen island, eating cheese. "I'll be back soon," I tell her, forcing a small wave. Caleb turns to his mom, saying he'll see her at home. His words are casual, but his jaw is tight.

Outside, the car waits in the long drive, glinting in the morning light. I slide into the passenger seat while Caleb circles around to the driver's side. The door shuts with a solid thud that echoes louder than it should.

As the engine rumbles to life, I can't shake the feeling that whatever this "ride" is, it won't be just another conversation.

"So, where to?" My voice is a fragile veneer over the storm of emotions swirling within.

"You're gonna meet the pack." He smirks, though his eyes are serious. Caleb drives the Jeep with an ease that contrasts sharply with the turmoil in my chest. My mind races with thoughts of what I'll learn, see, and who I'll meet in the pack. What makes Caleb the leader? The jitters I feel stem from the realization of how much I've been blind to.

As always, I am lost in my thoughts when Caleb breaks the silence. "You shouldn't be mad at him."

"You should be the last person giving relationship advice," I shoot back, my voice sharper than intended.

"Paris and I are nothing like you and Elijah."

"How so? You're a lying boyfriend, and she's a gullible girl-friend. Seems the same to me." I emphasize with an eye roll.

"As Alpha, I have the perk of gauging the feelings of my pack. I can feel what they feel. It's how I prevent a mutiny. Elijah has always been cooler towards the pack and me. But when he's around you, talking to you, or even thinking about you…he can't contain the love he feels. It's so much that it even affects my mood. It makes me feel like I have this surplus of love to give. And then I end up…"

"What?" I pry.

"Nothing."

"With Paris?" I ask, my voice trembling with the fear of hearing the answer I dread.

"Yes." His gaze is fixed straight ahead, his knuckles whitening on the steering wheel. The Jeep begins to shake violently as he turns off the road onto a carved-out trail in the forest. As we drive further into the woods, the trees close in around us, their thick branches forming a natural tunnel that feels both protective and suffocating.

"What did you do when she broke up with you? The truth," I press, my voice barely above a whisper, but the weight of the question hangs between us.

"We're here," he says abruptly, pulling the Jeep to a stop.

"Where exactly is 'here?'" I look out at the structure before us. It's like nothing I've ever seen, an architectural marvel that seems to have grown out of the very forest that surrounds it. The building is a seamless blend of natural materials, stone, wood, and moss, combined with sleek modern elements like concrete and glass. The entrance is camouflaged by foliage and rock formations, accessible only, it seems, through a pathway that leads to a door. It's both a fortress and a sanctuary.

In the distance, I can hear the soothing sound of water, perhaps a stream or another mini waterfall. The area around us is tranquil, the air filled with the rustling of leaves, the chirping of birds, and the constant hum of flowing water. It's a place of peace, yet it buzzes with an underlying tension.

"The den," Caleb says simply, his voice carrying a weight that matches the gravity of the moment. He pushes open the door, waving me inside.

As I step cautiously inside, the first thing that strikes me is the air. It's cool, earthy, and tinged with the faint, metallic scent of the wild. The entrance corridor is narrow and dimly lit by faintly glowing moss clinging to the stone walls, casting eerie greenish hues that dance and flicker as if alive. The floor beneath my feet is uneven, a mixture of natural rock and smooth stone pathways, worn by the passage of countless feet, giving the impression of a place as ancient as time itself.

Moving deeper, the corridor widens slightly, revealing intricately carved symbols and ancient runes like carvings etched into the walls. The occasional torch, secured in wrought iron brackets, sputters with a steady flame, providing enough light to navigate the winding path. The flickering shadows create a sense of movement, a creeping unease as though unseen eyes are watching from the dark recesses of the den.

Farther in, the air grows warmer, carrying the faint scent of burning wood and herbs, an odd contrast to the coolness of the outer corridor. My footsteps echo slightly, the sound bouncing off the vaulted ceilings that gradually reveal themselves as the passage opens into a larger space. Here, the walls are adorned with rich, dark tapestries depicting scenes of the hunt, the moon in its various phases, and wolves in majestic, powerful stances. Each piece seems to pulsate with life, capturing the raw energy of the creatures they depict.

As I proceed, I notice alcoves carved into the rock, each housing various objects: ancient artifacts, weapons, and personal items that seem to tell stories of battles fought and lives lost. The occasional glimpse of movement inside them, a glint of eyes, a shadow flitting away, suggests that the den is very much inhabited, its residents ever watchful, ever vigilant.

Finally, the corridor opens up. The space is vast, with a high ceiling supported by thick wooden beams, their surfaces etched with more intricate designs and symbols. The hall is illuminated by a combination of natural light streaming through cleverly hidden skylights and roaring fires in massive stone hearths that line the walls. The floor is a mix of polished stone and thick woven rugs, their patterns echoing the themes seen throughout the den.

At the far end, an imposing throne-like seat stands elevated on a stone dais, clearly the seat of the pack's leader. The sight of it sends a shiver down my spine, a stark reminder of the power dynamics at play here.

As my eyes adjust to the room, familiar faces emerge from the shadows. There's a thick layer of apprehension throughout the space, a tension that's almost palpable.

"Well, I guess the cat's out of the bag, or should I say the wolf's out of the woods," Lucas quips, leaning against the wall to my left. He pushes off it and comes to stand in front of me.

"Get it? Because he's a wolf?" he adds, pointing to Caleb, who's gone to stand next to him.

"I got it," I reply, my voice flat as I try to process everything. With raised eyebrows, I ask, "Are you?"

"Well, yeah. I thought you gathered that. We're a pack of wolves. Not to worry though, you won't be binding with me." He laughs, the sound trailing off as Caleb jabs him in the side with his elbow, silencing his humor.

"What do you mean by 'binding?'" I ask, my curiosity piqued despite the tension in the room.

"These are all questions that can be answered later," Liam interjects, stepping forward from the far corner of the room, his presence commanding attention. I can't believe Elijah and Liam are a part of this world that I had no idea about. I know I shouldn't be mad at Liam, but he's one of the people I also trusted, another friend willing to lie to me.

"Liam," I greet him in a flat tone, my emotions tightly controlled. Sensing my disdain, he raises his hands in a gesture of peace.

"Hey, I have always advocated for you to know. I don't think we should lie to the people we love," he says, his voice sincere.

"Yeah, maybe you should have taught that particular moral value to your brother," I shoot back, the words leaving a bitter taste in my mouth. I regret it the second I say it. I see Liam visibly wince, and Elijah, who sits in the corner next to him, hangs his head in shame, the weight of unspoken guilt in the air.

"Look, Kali, Elijah tells you everything. If he could have told you, he would've." Liam defends his brother, his voice tinged with desperation. What could have possibly been a reason for him not to tell me? Something in the atmosphere of the room has changed. Liam's eyes flick to Caleb, who's behind me, leaning on the wall to the left. I look at him also, noticing he has a wave of guilt rolling off him, as if he's carrying a burden too heavy to bear.

As Liam is about to continue, the doors of the room swing open with a creak that echoes through the hall. Two figures glide in with the grace of predators, their presence commanding immediate attention. One offers me a quick glance before crossing the room to where Liam stands, planting a deep kiss on his lips. The other moves to stand beside me, offering a small, reassuring smile that does little to ease my growing anxiety. Krystal and Kristina Marrinos, my two older twin sisters, identical in every way, tall, athletic, with the same shade of dark skin, thick kinky hair, and piercing moss-green eyes. The only difference is in their personalities and fashion choices, a fact that has always made them seem like two sides of the same coin. They've been MIA recently since they graduated from RU about three years ago.

As the realization sets in, a sharp pain radiates through my chest. Why didn't I think of this before? Kristina and Liam have been dating since high school. Of course she knows. It's a manifestation of what I've always felt, a deep sense of isolation. They can confide in each other and share their secrets, while I'm left on the outskirts, always out of the loop.

"So, the precious baby finally knows, huh?" Kristina says with a smirk, settling next to Liam.

"Kris, stop," Krystal scolds, rubbing my back in a gesture that's meant to be comforting but only serves to deepen the divide between us. I've always hated the dynamic of our relationship. One seems to hate me while the other pities me.

"How long have you guys known?" I finally ask, my voice barely above a whisper, the question that's been gnawing at me, finally finding its way out.

"Well, we've kinda…always known," Krystal admits sheepishly. She's always hated giving me bad news. When our dog died, she didn't tell me for weeks, insisting that he might have run away until I noticed the freshly overturned dirt in the backyard where he used to play.

"Not by choice," Kristina chimes in, her voice dripping with annoyance.

"You don't have to be here, you know. That door works the same way. Just as you enter, so shall you leave," I snap back, my patience wearing thin. Kristina, being older, has always exerted a certain influence over me. But today, I'm done backing down. My anger rises, simmering beneath the surface, and I can feel the tension in the room escalate with every passing second.

"You think you could survive without us, you ungrateful little —" Kristina stops mid-sentence as thunder booms outside, her face contorting in pain, as if she were struck. For a brief moment, fear flashes across her eyes, raw and unguarded, before she masks it with a wicked grimace. I start to calm down, my confusion, along with the sight of her fear, somehow soothing the storm inside me.

She recovers quickly, her gaze narrowing as it locks onto the necklace that lies on my chest. "Where did you get that necklace?" she demands, her tone suddenly sharp. Liam holds her hand in a cute gesture, but I can tell by the death grip he has on her that he's actually holding her back.

"Dad," I answer, confused by her reaction. What does my necklace have to do with anything?

"Of course," she scoffs, settling back down next to Liam. I don't understand how he could stand being with someone like her, someone who seems to take pleasure in being cruel.

"Blink twice if you're being held against your will," I quip at Liam.

"You two need to cut it out. You're wasting time we already don't have," Krystal interjects, her voice laced with frustration.

"She started it," I mutter defensively.

"Well, I'm ending it," Krystal says firmly. "Look, Kal, there is a lot for you to learn here. About what you are, who you are, and where you fit into...all of this." She gestures towards everyone else with a sweep of her hand. "But right now, we're in a time crunch, so you're going to have to get the shortened version."

"Wait, do Mom and Dad know about this? Killian?" The realization that I've been kept in the dark by my entire family hits me like a ton of bricks.

"Oh my God, everyone knows but you," Kristina confirms with an exaggerated eye roll, her tone dripping with disdain. I respond in kind, matching her sarcasm with a dramatic eye roll of my own.

"Wow, the sexual tension in here is ridiculous," Lucas mutters, breaking the thick silence that has settled over the room. His comment prompts everyone to look at him, their expressions ranging from amused to exasperated.

"Did I say that out loud?" he asks sheepishly, looking to Caleb for support, who shakes his head in disbelief.

"Anyway," Krystal continues, regaining control of the conversation, "the cat's clearly out of the bag. You know that you're a Siren. Now, you may not know exactly what that means. Honestly, there are people who can explain it way better than I can and have more knowledge about it. But in a nutshell, you're extremely good at reading emotions. You can control water, or, I guess I should really say fluids, as it can be a conduit of emotional regulation, like blood flow to the cheeks, which can cause a person to get flustered. I don't have the specifics on how it works because we just need to know enough to protect you. We do know you're a special type of Siren because you're part human as well. Dad could probably explain the history behind it more."

"Dad? What are Mom and Dad?" I feel like the ground is shifting beneath my feet.

"I think they should explain that to you themselves. I'm only telling you this because someone has to, and the longer we keep you in the dark, the more danger we put you in. You can't prepare for what you don't know about. We've wanted to tell you for the longest time, but Dad made us swear not to. He wanted you to have a normal life for as long as possible," Krystal explains, her voice softening as she glances at Kristina.

"Yeah, a luxury we weren't afforded," Kristina adds, her tone bitter.

"You guys have known since I was born?" I ask, the sense of betrayal deepening.

"Yes. The day you were born, our lives changed. We weren't just your sisters, we became your protectors. Dad has been training us to be that ever since," Krystal says, her voice heavy with the weight of the responsibility they've borne.

"What about Killian?" I ask, needing to understand where he fits into all of this.

"Where we are from, well, Mom anyway, women are typically the warriors, the protectors," Krystal replies, her voice softening slightly as she looks at me. There's a flicker of pride in her eyes, but it's quickly overshadowed by concern. This is news to me. I knew mom was from Africa, but now I'm even more interested. Why have I never asked her more questions about herself? Shouldn't I know these things too? Shouldn't I have been looking for these things? Shouldn't I have cared at all?

While everyone else talks amongst themselves to figure out the next moves, I find myself zoning out, trying to process everything with a calm mind. The weight of the truth threatens to crush me, and I feel like I'm drowning in a sea of information. Caleb moves from behind me to discuss what happened yesterday with Laim. While everyone else is deep in conversation, Elijah finds his way to me, breaking through the fog of my thoughts.

"You pushed me out of a window," he says with a smirk, his head cocked to one side.

"Really? You look perfectly fine to me," I reply, my voice tinged with sarcasm.

"Can we talk?" The smirk leaves his face and tone, replaced by something more serious, more urgent. I shrug, trying to appear indifferent, even though my heart is pounding in my chest.

"Nothing but time and opportunity," I respond, trying to keep my voice steady.

"Not here." Eli glances over his shoulder toward Caleb, then motions for me to follow. He leads the way toward the front of the den, moving away from prying eyes and listening ears.

I trail behind him, my mind a whirlwind of questions. When did this happen to Eli? How had I not seen the changes in him? Am I so self-centered that I missed what was right in front of me?

As I look at him now, the differences are undeniable. His frame is broader, the lines of his body more defined. Every movement carries a quiet strength, a grace that feels inhuman. His presence fills the space, commanding without effort. How could I have ignored this? Or maybe I did notice, but chose not to. Maybe it was easier not to look too closely.

Without thinking, Eli reaches for my hand, the gesture so familiar that I respond automatically. But his hand feels different, larger, stronger, the skin warmer against mine. Power hums beneath his touch. The realization lands like a stone in my chest. How much have I missed? How much have I refused to see? Can I really blame him for keeping secrets when I've spent so long pretending not to notice?

We step outside, the air cooler and thick with the scent of pine and damp earth. Eli veers to the left, leading us through a patch of trees where a small gazebo waits about a yard ahead. It stands quietly among the greenery, its wooden roof supported by stone columns mottled with moss. The structure is simple yet inviting, a pocket of calm surrounded by the untamed edges of the forest.

The sounds of the den fade behind us, replaced by the steady rhythm of the wind and the rustle of leaves. For a moment, the world feels suspended, as if even nature itself is holding its breath, waiting for whatever comes next.

Eli guides me toward the gazebo, his grip on my hand gentle but firm, as if he's afraid to let go. As we sit down, he raises my hand to his lips, planting soft kisses along the back of it, a familiar gesture meant to soothe, but it does little to calm whatever is brewing inside me.

"Stop stalling…talk," I demand, pulling my hand away and locking my gaze with his. His blue eyes, usually so open and expressive, are clouded with conflict.

"I couldn't tell you," he begins, his voice tinged with regret.

"Really?" My voice is sharp, cutting through the tension between us.

"I wanted to, more than anything. I hate keeping things from you." His frustration is evident.

"And yet you did," I counter, the betrayal still raw in my chest.

"It's not like that, Kals. You were the first person outside of Liam and my dad to know about my mom dying. I confided in you when Dad started the abuse…Look, Kals, I've never hidden anything from you. I didn't do it willingly."

"Okay, why couldn't you tell me?" I need to understand why he'd kept such a monumental secret from me.

He looks like he's fighting with himself, struggling to find the right words. Finally, he lands on the root of it all. "Caleb."

"Caleb told you not to tell me?" My eyes narrow, suspicion flaring.

"Not exactly…it was implied."

"An implication isn't a statement or demand." My frustration bubbles over.

"You're gonna learn there are a lot of politics and nuances in packs. Implications mean something," he explains, his tone heavy with the weight of those unspoken rules.

"I mean, what were you gonna do, Elijah? Where did you see this going? This lie, us? What could have possibly been the endgame here?" My voice trembles with the weight of the realization that our entire relationship has been built on a foundation of secrets.

"Babe, it's more complicated than that," he begins, his voice thick with desperation.

"I mean, we're in college for now. What about the rest of our lives? Did you not think I would've noticed if you were missing a couple of nights out of the month to go howl at the moon? Or would you have figured out a new lie then too? Working late? Business trips? Where was it going to end? How long could you have possibly kept this up?"

"Do you think I chose this? Do you not think those thoughts haven't been haunting me ever since this happened? Since I was fifteen, all I've ever thought about was you. All I've ever felt was for you. All I've ever wanted was you. The only good thing in my life was and has been you. I wasn't gonna lose you to this...because of this," he declares, his voice trembling with intensity. "I needed time to figure it all out," he adds, his head falling into his hands as if the weight of everything is too much to bear.

The raw emotion in his voice breaks through my defenses. He isn't the strong, confident man I know, in this moment, he's the boy I grew up with, the one who always sought refuge with me when the world became too harsh. My heart aches as I remember the countless nights we spent together, him curled up in a ball in the corner of my room, trying to escape the pain of his father's wrath.

Just as I did back then, I get up from where I sit and kneel in front of him, taking his head into my hands, forcing him to look at me. My eyes search his, finding the same vulnerability that has always been beneath the surface.

"You don't keep anything from me ever again. I don't care what it is. I love you. No matter what." My voice is firm but laced with tenderness that only he can bring out in me. And it's true. Despite everything, I know there's almost nothing Elijah could do to make me stop loving him. He's carved out a space in my heart, a place of comfort, safety, and unwavering loyalty.

We sit there in silence for a while, the weight of our shared history and love settling between us once more. My anger begins to fade, replaced by a deep-seated curiosity. I need more answers, specifically about him, about Caleb, about everything that's been kept from me.

I begin to ask Eli all the questions I've been too afraid to ask Caleb, questions about when he became a wolf, how it happened, why Caleb is the Alpha, and how the pack structure works. To my surprise, he answers as best he can, mostly the questions about himself, his voice gentle as he tries not to overwhelm me. But I can sense there are still things he isn't telling me, gaps in his explanations that leave me with more questions than answers.

I learn that Elijah was turned one night with Liam. Even though he doesn't really remember what happened, he is a Werewolf. He can't give me much information on Lycans, except the fact that they can shift to look like any animal while Werewolves can only shift into wolf form and they are born as shifters not turned. But it looks like that is all the information he can give me on that particular subject. Unfortunately for me, like Caleb, he too, has no information about Sirens. He also says he doesn't know what Lucas was talking about when he said he wasn't binding to me.

As the sky turns from light blue to amber, signaling the impending nightfall, Eli and I stand to make our way back to the den. The air is cooler now, the light fading into the deep purples of twilight.

"Make me one promise," he says suddenly, his voice cutting through the stillness.

"That depends on what it is," I reply, glancing down at him, curious.

"Don't join the pack, please." His tone is serious.

"I'm not a wolf or Lycan." I'm confused by his request.

"You don't have to be one. Just don't join, okay?" His blue eyes search mine for understanding.

"Umm…yeah, okay," I confirm, still puzzled by his request. Eli takes my hand, and together we step out of the gazebo into the purple light of dusk, the world around us growing darker, yet our bond feels stronger than ever.

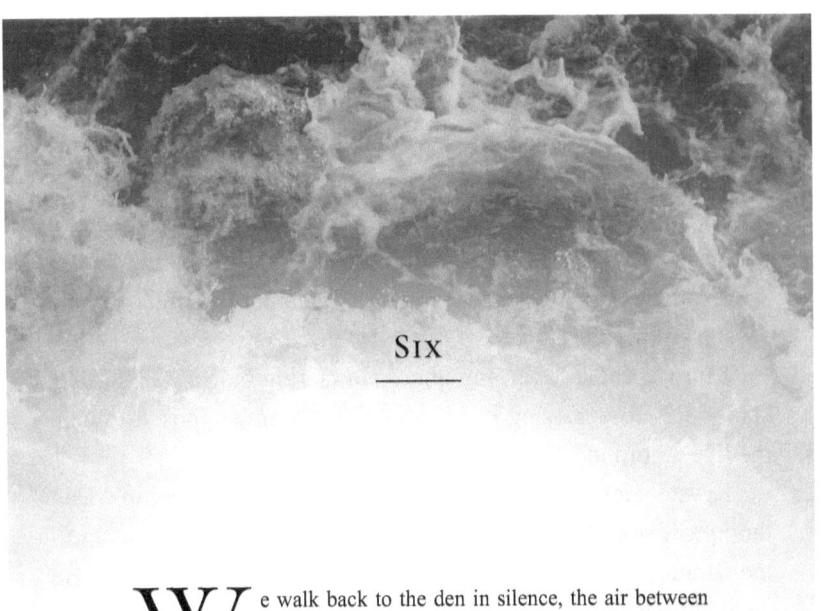

Six

We walk back to the den in silence, the air between us thick with unspoken words. My mind churns as I try to make sense of everything that's happened in the last forty-eight hours. Werewolves are real. I've fought several and survived, and now, it seems, I'm some kind of Supernatural creature too, a Siren, no less. My entire world has been turned upside down, shaken violently like a snow globe. The more I think about it, the angrier I become. How could my dad keep this from me? My mom has always been a little distant, but my dad and I are close. Or at least we used to be. What else are they hiding?

By the time we arrive back at the den, more people have gathered. The space feels different, tense, and charged with energy I don't fully understand yet. I spot my sisters engaged in a heated discussion with the woman who picked up Caleb from my house. When she notices me approaching, she shoots me a glare that can cut glass. Great. Just what I need.

"Which of you is going home?" I ask, ignoring the woman's hostility and directing my question at my sisters.

"I am. You can catch a ride with me," Krystal answers, her

tone neutral. I say a quick goodbye to Elijah and follow Krystal out another exit. We enter a massive underground garage where her new lilac SUV gleams under the fluorescent lights.

We drive in silence, the tension between us a tangible thing. My thoughts spiral, chasing after every lie, every secret that's been kept from me. How can I trust anyone after this? My entire life feels like it's been built on quicksand, and I'm sinking fast.

"You know, he just wanted you to live a normal life," Krystal says, breaking the silence.

I turn to look at her, my anger simmering below the surface. "Normal? How is lying to me about who I am supposed to help me live a normal life?"

Krystal sighs, her grip on the steering wheel tightening. "Dad thought if you didn't know, you wouldn't have to deal with all the dangers and responsibilities that come with being a Siren. He wanted to protect you."

"Protect me?" I scoff, disbelief coloring my voice. "He left me vulnerable and clueless. Do you have any idea how terrifying it is to find out like this? To feel like my whole life is a lie?"

"I don't know," Krystal says softly. "It wasn't easy for any of us. But we did what we thought was best."

"We?" I echo, incredulous. "You mean all of you decided to keep me in the dark?"

"Yes," she admits, her voice barely above a whisper. "It was a family decision. Mom and Dad made the final call, but we all agreed to it."

I stare out the window, watching the trees blur past as my mind struggles to process her words. "I don't know who to trust anymore, Krystal. I feel like everything I believe in is falling apart."

"Kals, we did it because we love you."

Krystal reaches over and squeezes my hand, but I pull away, my anger flaring again. "Love? Keeping secrets and lying isn't love, Krystal. It's betrayal. And now, I'm supposed to just accept that and move on?"

"No," Krystal says, her voice trembling slightly. "We don't expect you to just accept it. We know it's going to take time for you to come to terms with everything. But please understand, we were trying to protect you the only way we knew how."

I take a deep breath, trying to calm the storm inside me. "What else aren't you telling me?"

"There's more you need to know," Krystal admits, her voice steady. "But some of it needs to come from Mom and Dad. They have their own part in this, and they owe you an explanation."

We drive in silence for a while longer, tension thick in the air. Finally, Krystal speaks again. "We're almost home. Just...try to keep an open mind, okay? Give them a chance to explain."

I nod reluctantly. "Fine. But I'm not making any promises. They have a lot of explaining to do."

We pull into the driveway, and I feel a knot form in my stomach. As we get out of the car, I take a deep breath, bracing myself for the confrontation ahead.

"There hasn't been a Siren around for an extremely long time. Keeping you ordinary, kept you off lists." Krystal puts a reassuring hand on my shoulder. "We'll get through this, Kali. Together."

I give her a small, hesitant smile. "I hope so."

We walk up to the front door, and I hesitate for a moment before opening it. The familiar smell of home washes over me, but it feels different, now tainted by the secrets and lies that have been hidden for so long.

As we step inside, I steel myself for the conversation that's about to unfold. It's time to get some answers.

I storm through the house, each step heavy with the weight of everything I've learned. My footsteps echo in the quiet halls as I make my way to Dad's study. Every revelation, every lie that's been unearthed in the past few days seems to pulse within me, a relentless drumbeat of betrayal.

When I reach the heavy oak doors of his office, I hesitate, my hand hovering over the doorknob. Dad has always been more than just a father to me. He's my anchor, the person I look up to more than anyone else. The thought of confronting him, of seeing him in a different light, makes my heart clench with dread. He's the man who built me a treehouse by the waterfall because he knew I loved the sound of rushing water. The man who read to me every night and bandaged my scraped knees. The man who always brought me a piece of the world from his travels. He's always thought of me.

But now, the image of him as a loving, caring father is at odds with the idea that he has kept something so monumental from me. I feel a steely resolve settle over me as I push open the door and step inside.

"Kali?" Dad's voice is calm, but I hear an undercurrent of tension. I find him sitting behind his desk and walk over, not bothering to sit on the chairs in front.

"Father," I reply, my tone colder than I intended. "Well, I'd greet you as my lying overlord, but that might be a bit much. Even for me."

Dad's brow furrows in confusion. "Lying overlord? And what have I lied to you about?"

"I know, Dad," I say, frustration seeping into my words. "I know everything, I think."

His eyes narrow slightly as he studies me. "Like?"

"I never thought I'd see the day you'd speak in anything but a formal sentence," I scoff, deflecting my unease with sarcasm.

"Respect, Kali Marie Marrinos, is still expected," he replies, his tone firm but tinged with warmth.

"I know about Caleb and Elijah." The words rush out. "I know they're Werewolves or Lycans. And they aren't the only ones. I'm not human either. I'm a Siren. And apparently, I'm rare and sought after because someone tried to kidnap me in the past week."

Dad's expression darkens, his eyes flashing with a mix of concern and anger. "Who?" he demands, his voice low and dangerous. He walks around his desk to stand in front of me.

"That's not the point, Dad," I snap, tears stinging my eyes as I stare into his, reflecting the color of my own. "This hurt me, Dad." My voice trembles.

"What do you need?" His gaze softens as he pulls me into a tight embrace.

"I need the truth." My voice is muffled against his chest.

"You're right. How would you like to go on a road trip?" he asks after a long pause, his voice gentle.

"At a time like this?" I look at him incredulously. "Can you repeat the first part?"

"I'm trying to give you answers."

A road trip? It feels like such a mundane suggestion in the wake of everything I've learned.

"Where to?" I ask, my voice barely above a whisper.

He simply raises his eyebrows and kisses the top of my head.

For the first time in days, I feel a flicker of hope. The tension eases at the mundane affection. Maybe this trip will give me the answers I need, or at the very least, the space to figure out what those answers are.

Turns out, the road trip isn't much of a trip at all. We leave the next afternoon and drive about thirty minutes outside of Rysen. Still, the moment the city fades behind us, everything changes. The outskirts stretch into a landscape of rugged, haunting beauty. Pines tower on either side of the road, their branches tangling like skeletal fingers against the sky. The air feels thicker here, heavier with secrets.

Each turn winds deeper into dense forest, the occasional cliff edge flashing by like a warning that this isn't an ordinary place.

It is fascinating to listen as my dad points out details along the drive, his voice carrying a mix of nostalgia and curiosity. Each landmark seems to spark a story or memory, turning the journey into a tapestry of anecdotes and observations. His passion for the little things, like the way the trees arch over the road or how a building has changed over the years, makes the drive feel less like a trip and more like a glimpse into his world.

He tells me we're headed to a school hidden deep within the wilderness, a place kept secret from the public eye. Few know it exists. Fewer still have ever seen it. It only reveals itself to those who are meant to find it.

The drive feels like a test. It's as if the road itself is deciding whether we belong. Shadows flicker through the trees, and the hum of the tires seems to sync with my heartbeat. By the time the forest begins to thin, I'm not sure if it's nerves or something else that makes my chest feel so tight.

Nestled in the heart of the wild is Wraithstone University. The sight steals the air from my lungs. The buildings rise from the ground as if grown from the dark stone itself, veins of silver threading through the walls like captured lightning. The campus blends seamlessly into the mountainside, ancient and alive, as though it's always been here, waiting for someone to remember it.

He points toward the jagged peak in the distance, Obsidian Crag. Even from here, the mountain seems to pulse with energy. Rumor says it's an active volcano, its molten heart still beating below the surface. Locals whisper about strange lights that dance across the cliffs, about shadows that move when the wind is still. Most people stay away, too afraid to disturb what sleeps beneath the stone.

As we climb the last stretch of road, the air grows electric.

Every hair on my body stands on end. The moment the gates appear between the trees, something shifts inside me. A jolt, raw and thrilling, races under my skin like lightning caught in my veins.

This place feels alive. Wild. Ancient. A school for Supernaturals.

The architecture of Wraithstone University is a blend of old-world charm and modern innovation. Ivy-covered buildings stand side by side with sleek glass structures, towers rising against the skyline, casting shadows that dance across the manicured lawns. Stark in contrast against the dark stone of the mountain it's built into. The entire campus feels alive, as if it's a living, breathing entity that has witnessed centuries of secrets and is now inviting me to be part of its story.

As we drive deeper into the heart of the university, glimpses of its many buildings come into view, each one more captivating than the last. The architecture shifts from ancient to modern, a seamless blend of eras and energy. Massive stone archways mark the entrance to the library, its facade dark and regal, with veins of silver light running through the stone as if the building itself is alive. A few turns later, a glass structure gleams in the sunlight, sleek and angular, the words *Science Center* etched across its entrance.

I can't help but wonder what a Supernatural science class even looks like. Do they study the anatomy of Supernaturals?

Despite the movement around us, the campus feels peaceful. Students walk in groups or alone, their laughter mingling with the steady rhythm of the wind that flows down from the mountains.

For the first time in a long while, I feel something stirring inside me. A sense of belonging.

With the rugged peaks of the mountain rising above us, we step out of the car and take in the view. Wraithstone stands like a secret carved from shadow and stone, its presence both beautiful and intimidating. The air tastes different here, thin and sharp with the scent of minerals.

Students move across the grounds, their voices carrying softly through the cool wind. Some of them wear light cloak-like coverings, unlike any I've ever seen, the fabric shifting in color from charcoal to silver when it catches the sunlight. He tells me they're called Emblematic Cloaks, each one representing not only the school but the wearer's resilience and identity. The material is coarse yet elegant, the kind of weave that looks born from the mountain itself.

My gaze drifts to the circular pins and patches fastened to their cloaks. Every student has one, though from this distance, I can't make out what it depicts. The designs glint faintly when they turn.

He explains that the cloaks are woven from fibers found deep within the Obsidian Crag, strong enough to withstand more than the mountain's volatile weather. They protect against wind, ash, and other things he only hints at with a knowing look. Apparently, everything made here, clothing, gear, even the fabric lining the dorms, is threaded with traces of that same mineral essence.

The academic administration building of Wraithstone University stands as a beacon of knowledge and authority amidst the rugged landscape. Constructed from the same dark stone as the rest of the campus, intricate carvings and symbols are etched into the stone walls, hinting at the magical heritage of the university. Turrets adorn the rooftop, reaching toward the sky like fingers stretching toward the heavens.

As my father and I approach the entrance, we're greeted by

the sight of towering columns flanking the massive oak doors, each one bearing the university's emblem.

The moment we step inside, I'm struck by the sheer scale of the foyer. The ceiling soars high above us, supported by elegantly carved arches etched with symbols that shimmer faintly in the light. Sunlight pours through the stained glass windows on the doors behind us, scattering pools of color across the polished marble floor. The air smells faintly of parchment, rain, and something older that hums quietly beneath the surface.

Portraits line the walls in perfect symmetry. Former deans and professors, I assume. Their eyes seem to follow us as we move deeper into the hall. It feels as if the building itself is aware of our presence, as if it recognizes every step that crosses its floor.

A soft, melodic voice fills the air through the overhead speakers.

Wraithstone University prides itself on fostering individualism and pursuing personal goals. We offer specialized disciplines tailored to each student's unique abilities and aspirations. Among these are Shapeshifting Mastery, Elemental Mastery, and Astral Projection. Each discipline invites students to explore their innate talents and push the limits of what they believe possible.

I exchange a glance with my father, who gives me a reassuring nod. This is why we're here.

We approach the door to the dean's office where a secretary with vibrant red curls sits behind a desk, her sharp eyes barely lifting to acknowledge our presence. Her lips are set in a tight line. She directs us to the main office with a perfunctory nod, her gaze already returning to her work, as if we're mere nuisances in her carefully controlled environment.

Inside, the space is both grand and imposing. The large windows frame the rugged landscape outside, and a polished mahogany desk dominates the room. Bookshelves line the walls, filled with leather-bound volumes that speak of a lifetime of knowledge and power. The air is thick with the scent of aged paper and polished wood.

Behind the desk stands a man I've known all my life: Quinn, my father's best friend and my godfather. His tall frame is as commanding as ever, his silver hair lending him an air of authority that's only grown with time. He greets my dad with their customary half-hug, the camaraderie between them palpable. But there's something different in the way they hold onto each other, something unsaid lingering in the space between them.

When Quinn turns to me, his usual warmth is there, but it's tempered by an undercurrent of seriousness that I haven't noticed before. His kiss on my forehead, though familiar, feels heavier with the weight of his unspoken words.

"I was wondering when you would finally be joining us," Quinn says as he settles back into his chair. His voice is calm, but there's a gravity to it that makes me feel like a chess piece being moved into place.

"Finally?" my dad echoes, raising an eyebrow in mild surprise. "I thought you had enough troublesome students on your hands?" His tone is light, almost teasing, but I can sense the sharpness beneath his words, testing the waters.

"Troublesome can often be confused with restlessness," Quinn replies, his gaze steady as he meets my dad's eyes. There's a quiet intensity in the room, an exchange that seems to hold more than just words. I feel like an outsider looking in, unable to grasp the full extent of what's happening between them.

Quinn finally turns his attention to me, breaking the tension that's been simmering in the room.

"Kali, the library is right across from this building. Why don't you head there for a little while? I'm sure you have plenty of questions. You'll find we have a range of information, larger than any library at Rysen University. Fenrir is amazing. Tell him what you're looking for, and he'll point you in the right direction."

"Okay," I say, though my eyes linger on my dad and Quinn. They're already back in another quiet exchange, their words low and unreadable. My dad looks like he wants to stop me, but I meet his gaze and hold it. This is why we came here. We need answers, and I intend to find them.

When I step out of the office, the air feels different. Heavier. The polished floor beneath my boots echoes faintly with each step as I move down the hall. The sense of foreboding that's been pressing against me since we arrived sharpens into something I can't ignore.

What are they discussing that I'm not meant to hear?

And why does it feel like everything I know is balanced on the edge of something about to break?

As I walk towards the library, my thoughts are a tangled mess of confusion and frustration. How have I gone so long without knowing any of this?

The library's grand entrance looms before me, the intricate carvings on the stone columns drawing my eyes. Pushing open one of the heavy oak doors, I step into a world that seems to be as much a sanctuary as it is a labyrinth.

Rows upon rows of towering bookshelves stretch into the distance, each one crammed with volumes. Similar to the administration building, the stained glass windows here cast a kaleidoscope of colors across the marble floors, and the air is thick with the scent of old parchment and leather. It's a place that demands reverence, and I feel a shiver of anticipation as I walk deeper into its depths.

At the center of the room, sitting behind a grand oak desk, is the librarian Fenrir, I'm guessing. His silver hair is pulled back into a loose ponytail, and his gray eyes, though clouded with age, sparkle with an intensity that speaks of lifetimes spent guarding the secrets of this place. As I approach, he looks up, and for a brief moment, I see something wild and untamed flicker in his gaze.

"Welcome to the Library of Wraithstone, young one," the librarian greets me, his voice a deep rumble that seems to resonate through the very stone of the building. "I'm Fenrir, guardian of these halls and keeper of the knowledge within."

His presence is almost otherworldly, as if he's more a part of the library itself than a mere librarian. I find myself drawn to him, captivated by the ancient wisdom that seems to emanate from his very being.

"Hi...I'm Kali," I say, feeling small and out of place in this vast, mystical setting. My voice seems to echo in the silence that follows, as if the library itself is listening.

"What is it you seek, young one?" Fenrir asks, his tone formal and almost archaic, as if he's been speaking this way for centuries.

"I'm looking for information on Werewolves, Lycans, and... Sirens," I begin, watching his expression for any sign of reaction. His face remains perfectly still, carved from something colder than stone. The silence stretches, but his lack of response only encourages me to continue.

"And also anything you have on Omegas."

That gets a reaction. It's small, a flicker in his eyes, gone almost as quickly as it appears, but it's enough. The way his gaze lingers for half a second longer than necessary tells me I've touched on something important. I make a mental note to start there.

"You may take a seat over there," Fenrir says, his voice even and measured as he gestures toward a secluded desk tucked into the far corner of the room. "I'll bring you the necessary materials."

"Thank you," I reply, hesitating for a moment. "Are you sure I can't help—"

"You wouldn't know where to begin," he says, his interruption smooth and unbothered. A faint smile touches his lips, softening the precision of his tone. "But I admire the offer."

I nod and move toward the desk, my thoughts already spinning. The faint rustle of his movements behind me feels deliberate, practiced. There's something about him, something quiet and knowing that makes me wonder just how much he already understands about what I'm looking for.

When Fenrir returns with a stack of books, a spark of anticipation shoots through me. He places them carefully on the desk, the scent of aged paper and ink rising between us. Each book looks older than the last, their bindings worn smooth by centuries of hands that once searched for the same answers I'm seeking now.

The first volume is heavy, its cover marked with a faint silver insignia. I open it, and the pages whisper as they turn. It's a detailed account of Lycans, their bloodlines, their complex hierarchies, and the fragile balance that governs their packs. The section on Omegas catches my attention. It describes them as the outliers, wolves who exist on the fringe of pack life, untethered yet essential. Some are cast out. Others choose exile.

Then a name begins to repeat across the pages, standing out like a stain on clean parchment. *Varros.*

I stare at it, my chest tightening as I trace the word with my fingertip. The name feels familiar, like smoke curling through the edges of memory that's present, but impossible to grasp. I try to remember where I've heard it before, but it slips through my mind before I can hold on.

The more I read, the more that name seems to follow me from page to page.

The second book is thinner than I expected. Its title promises a comprehensive guide on Sirens, but it isn't even ten pages long. Most of it reads like recycled mermaid folklore, full of sailors' myths and romanticized tales of song and shipwrecks. I flip through the pages, disappointment settling in my chest.

Maybe they're wrong, I think. Maybe Sirens and mermaids have always been the same, mislabeled and misunderstood by humans who never learned the difference.

The few credible sections mention their gifts, their ability to manipulate emotion, to sway the will of others, and to command water with a single thought. It's unsettling to see my own reflection in the text, written in faded ink centuries before I existed. The realization that I belong to this ancient lineage of rare beings sends a shiver down my spine.

The last book in the stack catches me by surprise. I don't remember asking for it. Its cover is bound in dark leather, embossed with the word *Amoraks*. The pages are heavy and smell faintly of smoke and iron. The text describes them as powerful, solitary wolves who roam the edges of civilization. They're said to appear when great change is coming, like omens rather than allies.

I glance toward Fenrir across the room. He doesn't look up. Maybe he included it for a reason.

Still, my attention drifts back to the volume on Lycan hierarchies. The name *Varros* stands out again, bolder now that I've seen it before. According to the text, the Varros pack is the oldest and most powerful of all. Their bloodline is said to hold access to abilities beyond any other Lycan, though the pages never explain why. They're written as heroes, defenders of balance and order.

But something about the way their name repeats across every account unsettles me. The more I read, the more it feels wrong. I can't explain it, but I get the distinct feeling that they aren't the heroes history made them out to be.

As I try to process everything I've read, a familiar voice cuts through my thoughts.

"Kali?"

I look up to see Qora, Quinn's daughter, standing beside me. Her expression is calm, almost unreadable, but there's a flicker of recognition in her eyes.

"Long time no see," she says, giving me a quick hug. It's brief but steady, enough to pull me back from the chaos spinning in my head.

"Qora," I say, managing a small smile. "What are you doing here? I mean, in the library." I haven't seen her since my first semester at Rysen U, and the question slips out before I can stop it.

"Dad said I'd find you here," she replies simply. "Wanna grab something to eat?"

Her tone isn't warm exactly, but it's not unkind either. She speaks with the same evenness she always has, a quiet certainty that doesn't need embellishment.

"Sure," I say, even though my stomach twists with everything I've learned. I need a break, a moment to think without the weight of all those pages pressing on me.

I close the book carefully, tracing the name *Varros* one last time before following Qora toward the doors. The library's quiet hum fades behind us as we step into the open hallway. The weight of the knowledge I've uncovered lingers like a shadow, but Qora's presence pulls me forward.

The walk to the student center feels longer than it should. The air outside carries the scent of pine and rain, a cool contrast to the weight still pressing against my chest.

"So, what kind of classes do you take here?" I ask.

"Last semester I took Advanced Elemental Studies and a focus elective in Water Manipulation," she says. "It's a lot of fieldwork, but honestly, it's kind of fun. There combat courses too, though those are intense."

I glance at her, watching how her cloak moves with the wind, the faint shimmer of its threads catching the fading light. "You make it sound like normal college classes."

She laughs softly. "That's the point. Wraithstone tries to keep things balanced. Every student has a core discipline they're trained in, but we still take general courses too. Like, Languages of Power, Supernatural Law, and things like that. You'll figure it out once you settle in."

"I'm not taking courses here," I say. "My dad brought me here for answers to a lot of questions."

"Oh." She blinks, then gives me a small, curious smile. "I thought he finally told you what you were and that you were coming here to train." Even she knew.

The path curves toward the student center, its glass walls glowing softly in the fading light. Music drifts through the open doors, mixing with laughter and the low hum of conversation.

Qora bumps my shoulder playfully. "It's not all serious, you know. You'll like it here, Kali. People actually want to understand what they are instead of hiding it."

Her words stay with me as we reach the door. Maybe that's what I want as well, to understand who I am before someone else decides for me.

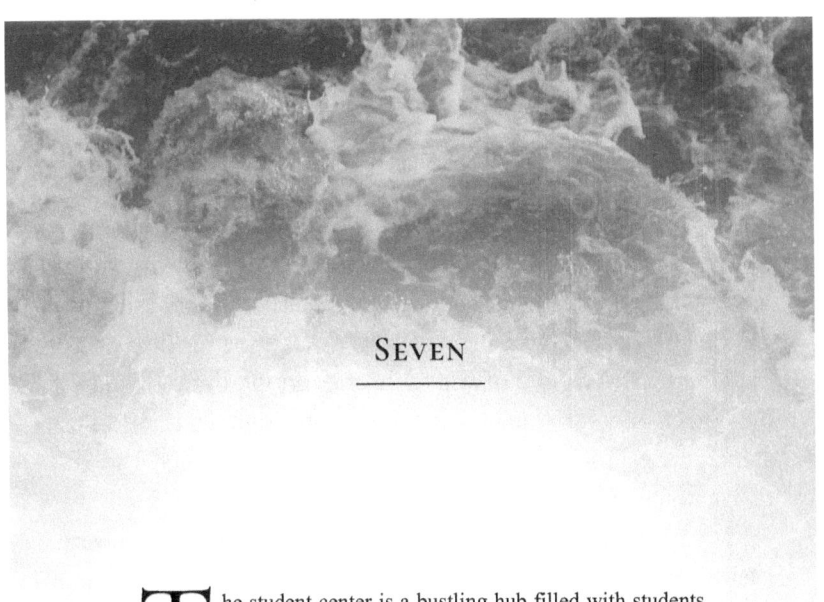

SEVEN

The student center is a bustling hub filled with students. As we enter the dining hall, the noise and activity feel almost overwhelming after the quiet of the library. I grab an apple and follow Qora to a table in the back.

There, I'm introduced to what I assume is Qora's friend group.

"Noah," she says, pointing to a guy with a lopsided smile. His eyes are completely black, and for a moment, they remind me faintly of Caleb. There's a calmness in him that feels disarming, a quiet confidence that makes it easy to look his way.

Then she gestures to another. "That's Duke."

Duke's presence is harder to take in. His eyes are the opposite of Noah's. His white irises and pupils make it impossible to tell where he's actually looking. Every time his gaze flicks toward me, a strange unease settles low in my stomach. It feels like he's searching for something beneath my skin, and I can't decide if I want to look away or keep watching to make sure he doesn't vanish.

"And this is Zori," Qora adds.

Zori smiles, and the tension in my shoulders eases a little.

She looks ethereal, almost otherworldly, with her curly dreads threaded with charms and tiny gold beads that chime softly when she moves. Her waist is lined with colorful strands that glint in the light, each one catching the rhythm of her laughter.

Unlike most of the students I've seen, the three of them aren't wearing cloaks. They stand out effortlessly, comfortable in a way I can't quite grasp. Their conversation flows easily, full of teasing and quiet humor, and they include me without hesitation.

But as I sit among them, I can't shake the feeling of not belonging. The weight of what I learned in the library clings to me like a second skin, setting me apart from their effortless camaraderie. They seem so sure of who they are, and I'm still trying to understand what that means for me.

My phone buzzes in my pocket, pulling me from my reverie. I take it out and see it's Elijah. Duke looks down at my phone in my hand. He doesn't look away before inspecting every surface of my face, and I want to know what question he's trying to answer without asking. I'm also annoyed because I know I tend to wear my emotions on my face, so what exactly is he seeing right now?

I excuse myself and step outside to take the call, needing the fresh air to clear my head.

"Where are you?" Elijah's voice is sharp, his tone accusatory.

"Hello to you too," I reply, my irritation flaring.

"Are you with Caleb?" His words are laced with suspicion.

"What?" I'm taken aback by the accusation.

"Are you?" he demands, his voice tense.

"Are you going to assume every time I'm not in your line of sight that I'm with Caleb?" I snap, my frustration boiling over.

"Why aren't you answering the question?" His voice is hard.

"Because it's not a question. It's an accusation, you dick," I hang up on him.

I stand there, fuming, the fresh air doing little to cool my anger. How has everything gotten so messed up? As I'm trying to calm down, Qora and the others emerge from the dining hall.

"Everything okay?" Qora asks, her tone calm but her eyes searching.

"Yeah, just...yeah," I say, brushing it off. The truth burns in my chest, too tangled to explain. The nerve of Eli, lying to me, then accusing me of lying about being with Caleb. I saved his life. That doesn't mean I want to orbit his every move.

"Let's go," Qora says, turning down the path. She doesn't pry, which I'm grateful for.

We all walk in silence until the administrative building comes into view. The sun has dipped low, painting the stone walls in muted gold. My dad and Quinn stand on the steps outside, their voices low and serious. Whatever they're discussing, it looks heavy.

Quinn notices us first. He smiles faintly at his daughter, then at me. "Kali and her father will be spending the night," he says.

"Really?" I ask, glancing between them.

"You can room with me," Zori offers quickly, stepping forward with a bright smile that feels a little too eager.

"I think she deserves to see what life is like here," Quinn continues. "What it could be like."

My dad's jaw tightens, his expression unreadable. The tension between him and Quinn is sharp enough to taste.

"Okay," I say finally, my voice careful. I meet my dad's gaze, waiting for his reaction. He gives a slow, reluctant nod.

The evening air feels heavy as the decision settles. I'm not sure what tomorrow will bring, but as the sky deepens into twilight, one thing feels certain, Wraithstone isn't done with me yet.

Quinn's gaze shifts from my dad to Qora, his expression sharpening. "We've had reports of packs passing through," he says, his tone all business now. "Double the patrol on the north flank and inform Holsten's team."

Qora doesn't hesitate. "I already sent a notice to the gate wardens," she replies. "I'll have them run a secondary sweep before nightfall." Her voice is calm, confident. The quiet authority in it makes me realize this isn't new for her. She's used to being part of the decision-making.

"Good," Quinn says with a nod, his approval quick but unmistakable.

"Senator Holsten?" I ask, my surprise slipping through before I can stop it. "He's involved in this?" I gesture to the buildings, to everything that makes Wraithstone what it is.

"Yes," Quinn replies, his voice measured. "We work closely with the human government to maintain the secrecy of our world. Cooperation prevents unnecessary panic."

That word—*secrecy*—lingers in the air, heavier than before. I think of the hidden campus, the unmarked roads that lead here, the quiet power that hums beneath every stone.

"We were just about to take Kali to the gym," Qora says, breaking the tension. Her tone is composed, but I can sense the quiet push behind it.

Quinn studies her for a moment, and there's something in his expression that feels like pride. "Good idea," he says, exchanging a glance with my dad. "We'll join you."

For a heartbeat, Qora's shoulders straighten, and I can almost see the weight of his approval settle on her like armor. She doesn't smile, but there's purpose in the way she turns toward the path.

As we step into the gym, I'm struck by the size of it. The air hums faintly, charged with energy that feels more alive than electric. The ceiling arches high overhead, lined with crystal lights that flicker in shades of blue and silver. Every corner of the space seems to shift with movement, weights that gleam faintly with enchantment, treadmills that hover inches off the ground, and sparring mats that ripple like water when touched.

The place hums with life. The rhythmic clang of metal, the

pulse of footsteps against treadmills, and the echo of sparring calls blend into something almost musical. There's no mistaking this is training, but it's not the kind I'm used to. The energy here feels wild, contained only by willpower and control.

"Come on, I'll show you around," Qora says, her tone even as she gestures for me to follow. She leads me toward the cardio section, her stride confident and unhurried. My dad and Quinn trail a few paces behind, their quiet conversation lost in the gym's steady rhythm.

"These treadmills adjust to your stamina level," Qora explains. "They read your energy signature and match your pace. The weights do the same, adapting resistance based on your strength. It keeps training efficient and fair."

I nod, though my focus drifts. The air seems thicker here, vibrating faintly against my skin, as if the building itself recognizes power when it enters.

She points out the far corner, where students are sparring in a ring surrounded by glowing runes. The movements are sharp, fluid, and faster than human eyes should be able to track. "Combat training," Qora says. "Elemental channeling is allowed, but within limits. The mats absorb most of the damage."

Her calm voice grounds me, but my thoughts wander back to Elijah. His accusations, his lies, the mess that still knots in my chest. The weight of everything I've learned presses harder with each breath.

As we walk, Zori joins us, her enthusiasm infectious. "This place is amazing, isn't it? You'll get used to it in no time," she says, her playful nudge pulling me back to the present.

"Zori must like you," the guy introduced as Noah says.

"Zori likes everyone," Duke replies, disdain dripping from his tone. I begin to wonder whether I've unknowingly offended him. But my mind filters back to what was said earlier, and I don't have time to think about Duke. What does she mean by I'll get used to it here? Of course, my dad and Quinn are back in their own conversation. It isn't the time to ask questions, but he's definitely going to explain.

"She's just hoping you visit again," Qora tries to change the subject. "She gets attached quickly," she continues.

"I sure hope you visit again, Kali. Maybe you'll even be able to stay longer than just one night," Zori states. Turning to my dad, who now finds the windows very interesting, I see his eyes fall back to Zori, and my attention peaks. They've been discussing my place here. I don't even know where my place is, much less to consider whether or not here is where I'll find it.

"It's just an option," my dad finally says as his eyes fall to mine.

"I hope so," I reply, the weight of everything pressing down on me like a physical burden. I force a smile, but it feels thin and brittle.

We eventually make our way to a quieter corner of the gym where a few students are stretching and cooling down. The contrast between this serene area and the rest of the bustling facility mirrors the turmoil inside me. I take a deep breath, trying to absorb the atmosphere, letting the vibrant energy of the place lift some of the heaviness from my shoulders.

"So, what do you think?" Qora asks, her eyes searching mine for any sign of reassurance.

"It's a lot to take in," I admit, my voice heavy with understatement.

"I figured it would be," Zori says softly, her tone gentle. "No worries. We'll answer any questions you have," she promises, while the others nod in agreement.

"Why don't we go for a walk?" my dad suggests, his voice steady but edged with something urgent beneath the calm. The concern in his tone makes my palms sweat. I realize my face must be saying everything I haven't managed to put into words, the confusion, the exhaustion, the weight of too much truth all at once.

I nod, eager to escape the crowded gym. We walk out and follow a cobblestone path that eventually gives way to a trail leading into the woods. The silence between us is thick, laden with the unspoken questions and doubts swirling in my mind. How much of my life has been a lie? Do I even know the man walking beside me? The trees close in around us, their towering forms offering both comfort and claustrophobia.

We walk the trail for about ten minutes before the questions boiling inside me become too much to contain.

"Why can't I remember?" I ask, my voice trembling slightly as I break the silence.

"Remember?" he echoes, as if the question itself is foreign, his gaze fixed straight ahead.

"Yes, remember anything. There's no way you're all...wait, I don't even know what you are. What anyone in my family is." The realization hits me like a cold slap. I feel like I'm drowning in a sea of unknowns, desperately grasping for something solid. The world I've known is rapidly disintegrating, leaving me stranded in unfamiliar territory.

We find a moss-covered log to sit on, and I try to hold myself together as my dad settles next to me. "You've noticed things, Kalabunga," he says, using the nickname that usually brings comfort but now feels like a threadbare blanket against a winter storm. "The reason you don't remember is because I took your memories of anything associated with the Scath away."

"How?" I press, my voice cracking under the weight of my emotions. "Why was keeping me in the dark better than letting me know the truth? Everyone else knows, and I feel like an idiot."

"Why would you feel like an idiot?" His confusion is almost genuine, as if he truly doesn't understand the depth of my betrayal.

"Because I don't know anything," I snap, the words slipping out before I can stop them. My frustration boils over, burning in my throat. "It's like I'm starting over, but I'm not a child. There's this whole world that exists around me, and I was completely oblivious to it. Werewolves, creatures I thought were just folklore, are real. They have hierarchies. And what I am, what you kept from me, is real too."

My voice wavers, but I don't stop. "How can you not understand why I feel this way? What was the plan? Were you ever going to tell me?"

The questions spill out one after another, sharp and heavy, cutting through the fragile space between us. Each word feels like it chips away at the trust I thought we had. I can see the hurt flicker across his face, but right now, I can't bring myself to care.

He pauses, his voice quieting. "You've always been strong-minded." He glances sideways at me. "I wanted you to live as just Kali for a while. To choose your life without the weight of what you are. You're attuned to others' emotions in ways most people can't understand. That kind of sensitivity can make your own emotions volatile. From what little I know about Sirens, that's part of it. I don't even know how powerful you'll become. I just wanted you to have a normal life for as long as possible. I wanted you to have autonomy."

"Why exactly wouldn't I have autonomy?" I ask, my pulse quickening. The word feels sharp in my mouth, cutting through the quiet between us. "From what you're saying, being a Siren means I feel things deeply, maybe too deeply. But I'd still be in control, right? I'd still get to make my own choices, be with whoever I want?"

The thought of my argument with Elijah rushes back, a wave of dread rising in my chest. The accusations. The unspoken fear.

"Right, Dad?" I ask again, my voice smaller this time. I need him to say yes. I need something solid to hold on to in a world that keeps shifting under my feet.

"We should head back," he says quietly, pushing to his feet.

His voice sounds steady, but there's something beneath it, something tired and heavy. He keeps his gaze on the ground, not on me, as if meeting my eyes would make it harder to hold himself together.

He exhales slowly, his shoulders tightening before he answers. "A storm's coming."

He turns toward the path, and I know he's not talking about the weather. Still, thunder rolls in the distance, low and warning. His avoidance should make me angry and it does, but underneath that anger, I see it. The way his jaw tightens. The way he swallows hard before saying nothing at all. He's still trying to protect me, even if it means carrying the weight of things he won't explain.

Raindrops begin to fall, light at first, tapping against the leaves above us. He moves ahead, his hand brushing my shoulder briefly, guiding me forward. The small gesture says what his words don't.

By the time we reach the administration building, the rain is coming down in sheets. I walk up the stairs to the figures waiting under the Portico, Quinn, Qora, and the others from earlier. My dad pauses at the bottom of the steps, water streaking down his face, and for a moment, he looks like a man caught between love and fear.

Then he straightens, the mask of calm sliding back into place.

"Why don't we head to the dorms?" Zori suggests, her voice a lifeline pulling me out of the storm that's both outside and within.

"Yeah, let's," I agree, not sparing my dad another glance as I follow Zori deeper into the building. My dad is still keeping things from me, something important. Even after dragging me here under the guise of getting answers. The dread in my stomach grows. Why can't I have autonomy? Why can't I choose my own path?

Lost in thought, I barely notice where we're headed until I ask, "I thought this was the admin building?"

"It is," Zori confirms as we descend a couple of flights of stairs into a long underground corridor. I'm so lost in thought I don't even know how we made it this far. "When the school was built, they constructed these tunnels to connect the buildings. They were useful during the Underground Railroad period," she adds in a matter-of-fact tone. We climb another set of stairs and walk down a hallway to a door labeled "Zori." "We don't use the tunnels frequently, but I don't want to get wet," she adds.

As I step into her room, I notice the walls are adorned with tapestries bursting with intricate patterns and rich colors, creating a warm, inviting space. A cozy, oversized rug covers the wooden floor, its design a blend of earthy tones and bold hues.

There's a large, well-worn leather armchair nestled in one corner, surrounded by an assortment of plush cushions in various textures. Nearby, a low wooden coffee table holds a collection of well-loved books, an antique brass lamp, and a few potted plants that add a touch of greenery.

"So, this is my room." Zori spins in the middle with a playful grin.

"It's nice." I take in the cozy space. The room is a stark contrast to the rest of the day's chaos, offering a brief respite from the storm raging in my mind.

"Why don't you get cleaned up? The bathroom's at the end of the hall." She hands me a pair of pajamas and some toiletries. "These should fit you just fine."

The bathroom is functional and unremarkable, a standard dorm bathroom. I take a long shower, trying to make sense of everything that's happened, but my thoughts continue to swirl in confusion. The storm outside beats violently against the building, mirroring the turmoil inside me. I let the sound of the rain and the rush of water drown out my thoughts until I feel numb.

When I return to the room, Zori is already washed up and

ready for bed. As I settle onto the bed, a knock comes at the door. I look at her, questioning.

"I hope you don't mind. I invited Qora over. It seems like you have a lot on your mind, and we really want to help answer any questions you might have." She opens the door to reveal Qora in striped pajamas.

"Hey," she says, her voice gentle and filled with concern.

"Hey," I manage to say, my shoulders slumping. I'm always so strong, so confident, but this entire situation has thrown me. I hate that I feel pitiful, but I can't deny that I do.

"We know you have questions," Qora says gently.

"I do," I admit, feeling a lump form in my throat. "I just don't know where to start."

"Well, start with what you want to know most. We'll see if we can answer it," Qora offers, sitting down beside me and giving my hand a reassuring squeeze.

I look at each of them, seeing the sincerity in their eyes. Despite the chaos, there's a small comfort in knowing I have them by my side. "Thank you," I whisper, feeling a tear slip down my cheek.

I take a deep breath, trying to steady my thoughts. "What do you know about Caleb's family?" I ask.

"Who's Caleb?" Zori asks, tilting her head.

"He's the leader of the Carwell pack," Qora answers before I can respond. "Although we don't know too much about Lycans. Maybe Noah could offer more insight. We mostly learned the basics, like how to recognize different species, and how not to die at their hands." Her voice is even, almost clinical, though her tone softens a little as she adds, "Most of our classes are customized to what we are. Similar to what human colleges call electives." She gives an apologetic shrug.

"Okay," I say slowly. "That means you're not Werewolves, right?"

Zori frowns. "Carwell pack as in the Varros pack?"

"That's right," Qora replies.

The name hits me like a spark. "Wait," I say, my voice catching. "What's the Varros pack?" My mind flashes back to the pages I spent the afternoon studying. The name that kept surfacing. The one that felt like smoke in my memory.

Qora's expression hardens slightly. "I'm what you would call a Nix," she says. "And the Varros pack is nothing good. Stay away from them at all costs."

"A Nix?" I repeat, raising an eyebrow. The word feels unfamiliar and heavy on my tongue. "What exactly does that mean?"

"Yeah," Qora says, nodding slightly. "A Nix is a kind of water spirit. We're tied to lakes, rivers, sometimes even waterfalls. We can shift between forms kinda, human or something closer to what we really are."

"Which is what exactly?" I ask, leaning in.

She gives a faint smile. "Alluring, apparently. At least that's what the stories say. That whole mystical-creature thing. Don't worry, I don't have webbed feet. And shifting is preferred by specific supernaturals, we can utilize our full power in our human form."

Zori laughs softly. "She's leaving out the part where Nixes are supposed to charm people with music and drag them underwater."

Qora rolls her eyes. "Those are mostly old legends. Though...there's some truth to them. Our strength depends on how pure our bloodline is, and some of us channel power through music. It's part of how we manipulate water and emotion."

"And you're all Nixes?" I ask, glancing between them.

"No," Qora says, shaking her head. "Just me, my dad, and a few others here. There's actually a separate academy for Nixes. Most of them go there instead." She looks toward Zori expectantly.

Zori grins, the beads at her waist chiming softly. "I'm something else entirely. I'm an Asrai. We're a type of water nymph. Most of us come from the lakes and ponds." She smiles faintly, her voice carrying a soft lilt that makes me think of rain.

She tucks one of her curls behind her ear as she continues. "We're connected to water like Sirens are, though not nearly as powerful. We can stir ripples, call up mist, sometimes purify water or heal minor wounds. It's all about balance. The more peace we hold inside, the stronger our control."

Her tone softens. "We're not as tied to emotion as Sirens, but a few of us can sense when someone's overwhelmed. That's how I knew you needed answers."

I blink, still trying to catch up with everything she's said. "Oh," I manage. My voice sounds small even to me. "Do you know anything about my family?"

Zori's expression shifts, the easy smile fading into something more thoughtful.

"They didn't tell you?" Qora asks, her brow creasing.

I shake my head. Whatever expression I'm wearing makes both her and Zori exchange a look I can't quite read, something between pity and hesitation.

"From what we know," Qora begins carefully, "everyone in your immediate family, aside from your mom, is a Kelpie."

"A Kelpie? So my dad and my siblings are?" The word feels strange in my mouth.

"Yes," Zori explains, her voice softer now, almost cautious. "Kelpie's a creature from Scottish folkloreA shape-shifting water spirit that usually appears near rivers or lakes. Most stories describe them as horses, beautiful, wet-coated, impossible to resist. They lure people close, either out of curiosity or enchantment."

My chest tightens. I can picture it, too clearly: a creature standing in the mist by a lake, its eyes gleaming with something not entirely kind.

Zori continues, "Kelpies can shift into human form. Sometimes they appear as a man or woman so beautiful it's hard to look away. But once someone touches them, or rides them while they're in horse form, they're bound to it. The stories say the Kelpie too drags its victims into the water to drown.

"Of course," Zori adds quickly, sensing my unease, "those tales are exaggerated. Humans always dramatize what they don't understand. The truth is, Kelpies are powerful, fast, and fiercely protective of their own. Their allure isn't just physical, it's instinctual. It's what keeps them alive."

"And my mom?" I ask quietly. My voice feels smaller than I want it to. Part of me already knows the answer will change everything

"Your mom's a Selkie," Qora says.

She studies my face before continuing, "Selkies are shapeshifters. They move between sea and land by shedding their seal skin. That skin is tied to their power and it's what lets them change. Most keep a small piece of it with them, usually as a necklace or charm. If someone steals it, the Selkie is trapped on land until they can get it back."

Zori listens quietly, her expression soft. Qora's voice takes on a quieter note. "In human form, they're beautiful, but it's more than that. There's an energy to them, a pull. They fall in love with humans sometimes, but they never stop longing for the ocean."

The image sits heavy in my chest. My mom, standing at the edge of the water, staring out like she's waiting for something, or someone, to call her back.

All of this information helps, but it still doesn't explain why I exist or what my place is in all of this. The question forms before I can stop it. "And what do you know about Sirens?"

Zori hesitates. Her expression softens as she searches for the right words. "Sirens are the balance between beauty and danger," she says finally. "They used to live near the ocean, usually on cliffs or hidden islands where their voices could carry. Their power comes from their song."

I sit a little straighter, my pulse quickening.

"A Siren's song isn't just music," Zori continues. "It's alive. It reaches inside you, takes hold of your emotions, and makes you forget everything else. People describe it as irresistible, something that pulls you in no matter how much you fight it. That's their main gift, the power to enchant, to control through emotion."

She glances down, as if realizing how intense that sounds. "But it's not only their song that's dangerous. Sirens are naturally clever and intuitive. They can read people in a way that's almost unnatural. Sometimes they use that understanding to deceive, sometimes to survive."

Zori gives a shy smile. "Sorry if that sounded like a lecture. I have a photographic memory. It's kind of my thing."

I manage a faint laugh. "I can tell."

The sound feels foreign in my throat, but it breaks the heaviness between us for a moment. Still, her words cling to me. The way she described Sirens feels too close to what I've felt under my own skin. The pull, the power, the fear of what might happen if I lose control. And for the first time, I realize I might not be afraid of others finding out what I am. I might be afraid of finding out myself.

"Why do you guys work with the government?" I ask, curious about the connection.

"For survival," Qora states bluntly. "Well, it's more of a symbiotic relationship than that." She notices my puzzled expression.

"They help us keep our existence hidden from the general public, and we assist in keeping Supernaturals from taking over the government," Zori explains.

"So, you offer protection for their silence? Why would you care?" I ask, trying to piece everything together.

"Well, yeah. I mean, for the most part, earthbound Supernaturals don't want to be known by humans. Everything is created from the earth, so everything to heal you and kill you can be found here as well. The last thing we need is some scientist trying to discover something to take us out," Zori explains.

"Earth Supernaturals? So there are others?" I ask.

"Aquatic Supernaturals, like us. We help because we're also earthbound most of the time. But there are deep-Aquatic Supernaturals that don't necessarily take kindly to humans. There are also multi-dimensional Supernaturals like Duke," Zori continues.

"Okay, I think that's enough sharing for tonight," Qora says, sensing my exhaustion.

"I just have one more question," I say.

"Go for it," Qora encourages.

"Why exactly don't the deep-Aquatic Supernaturals like humans?" I watch the two exchange glances.

"Apparently, they violated some treaty hundreds of years ago," Qora says, making her way to the door, signaling the end of the conversation. Based on the glance they exchanged, I can tell that they're keeping something from me too. But what and why?

"Get some sleep, Kali," she says as she leaves the room.

"I definitely could use some," Zori says, turning out the lights. I lay back in bed, my mind spinning with everything I've learned today. As the rain continues to beat against the window, I find myself forming a new list of research requests for Fenrir tomorrow. There's still so much more I need to understand.

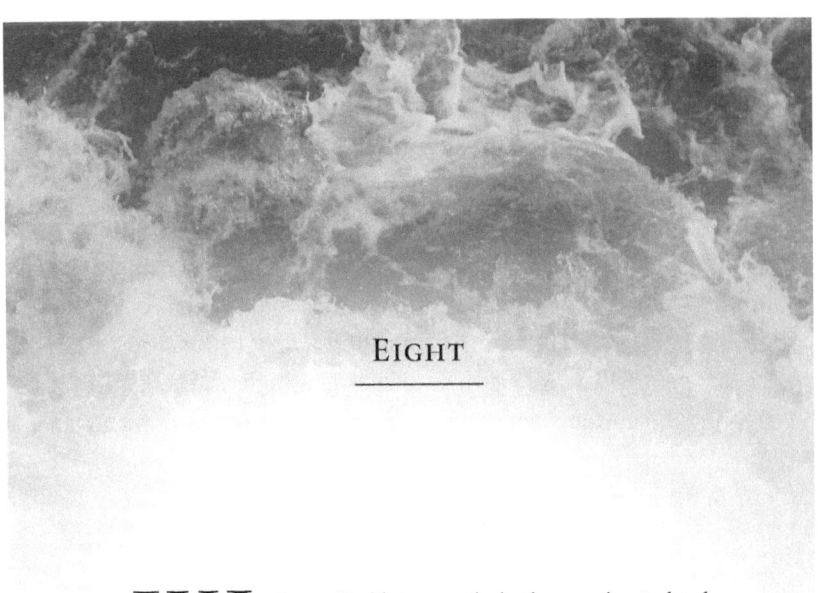

EIGHT

We leave Wraithstone early in the morning to head back to Rysen. I wake up feeling somewhat renewed, buoyed by the knowledge that, even though this journey will be hard, I have more allies in my corner than I think. Before we leave, I have enough time to ask Fenrir for some additional information since I can't stay to continue my research. I give him my number, hoping he can help me piece some of this together, although I don't truly know when or if I'll be back.

The ride back is filled with a heavy, uncomfortable silence. My dad and I barely speak, except for the occasional, random facts he offers about the animals we see on the short ride. He's avoiding the real conversation that needs to be had.

I'm not sure I'm ready for the truth anyway. Still, the need for it clings to me like a leech, draining reason from every thought. Psychology 101 taught me that the mind can't process trauma all at once. Maybe that's why I keep staring out the passenger window, watching the blur of trees and wishing the wind would carry my thoughts away with them.

About forty minutes later, we finally pull into the driveway.

The familiar sight of home brings a rush of mixed emotions. I practically run from the car to my room. I'm avoiding the campus at all costs. I can't look Paris in the eyes and lie to her the way I've been lied to. Despite the distance I now feel from my family, this is still home. It will always be home.

Inside my room, I collapse onto my bed, drained from the emotional toll of the past few days. The familiar surroundings offer a faint sense of comfort, but the unanswered questions press heavily on my mind. At some point, exhaustion wins. I fall asleep and don't wake again until sunlight, high in the sky, filters through the curtains and paints a bright sliver across the wooden floor. My alarm clock on the nightstand to my left reads just after one in the afternoon.

The urgency to confront my family presses down on me like a weight. I can't let this go on any longer. I head downstairs, finding my mom and Killian in the kitchen, talking in hushed tones. When they see me, their conversation halts abruptly, and their eyes fill with concern and something else I can't quite place.

"Hi," I say, trying to keep my voice steady.

"Good afternoon, Kali," my mom replies. She's looking at me the way someone looks at a stray kitten they're afraid to move too quickly around, as if one wrong step might send me running.

"I need to talk to you," I say, taking a deep breath. "I need answers."

They exchange a worried glance but she nods anyway. "Of course, honey. Let's sit down." Mom gestures to the island while Killian finds somewhere else to be.

As we sit down at the large kitchen island, the tension in the air is thick enough to taste. I glance at her, trying to gather the courage to ask the questions that have been haunting me.

"Why didn't you tell me about our family's true nature? Why keep me in the dark?" My voice trembles slightly.

My mom reaches out and takes my hand. "We wanted to protect you, Kali. We thought that if you had a normal life for as long as possible, it would be easier for you."

"But it hasn't been easier." I pull my hand away. "It's been confusing and terrifying. I need to know everything. No more secrets."

She nods, her expression tightening with guilt. "You're right. You deserve to know the truth. I'm so sorry, Kali. We should have told you sooner. It's just…complicated."

"What does Caleb have to do with any of this?" I ask, still trying to make sense of everything.

She spends the next hour explaining what little she knows about our family's Supernatural heritage. It turns out she knows almost nothing, and even less about Caleb's role in it. She admits she's unaware of the true nature of his involvement, and the uncertainty in her voice only makes the silence that follows feel heavier.

A small voice in the back of my mind whispers that I came to the wrong parent for information. It hurts to even think it. I want to believe she would tell me everything if she could, but the hesitation in her eyes says otherwise. She's guarding something, or maybe she's afraid of what the truth might do to me. Either way, I'm left sitting across from her, realizing that love and honesty don't always live in the same place.

"So, Caleb is a descendant of a large Lycan pack, and for some reason, our families are connected?" I'm still struggling to grasp the full picture.

"Yes."

"I still don't understand what that has to do with me, though." I feel a mix of frustration and curiosity.

"Well—" The doorbell rings before she can finish. We both freeze, tension crackling in the air. I stand up, and make my way to the door. A man in a tuxedo stands there, holding out a letter on a silver platter. I open it to find it isn't a letter but an invitation to dinner at Caleb's house, signed by a Carwell Varros.

Caleb's grandfather?

My mom reaches over my shoulder to grab the invitation, her face growing more tense as she reads it, paling visibly as her eyes scan the page. She hands the invitation to my dad who seems to have joined us hearing the bell ringing.

The invitation reads:

> *"Dear Marrinos Family,*
> *You are cordially invited to dine with the head of the Varros pack this evening. We can't wait to meet you and witness in person the things that bind our families. We look forward to hosting you.*
> *-Carwell Varros."*

"What does he mean by 'the things that bind our families'?" I ask, but my parents exchange a look of silent agreement and quickly retreat to my dad's study without a word. I try to eavesdrop, pressing my ear against the door, but all I can hear are hushed, urgent tones. Frustration bubbles inside me. I'm already overwhelmed with information, and the secrecy only makes it worse. Whatever is going to happen tonight seems unavoidable, and I'm not sure if knowing more will change anything. I need to clear my head.

So I decide to visit Nox, my horse. Since I'm supposed to be staying out of the woods, running isn't an option, and he always has a way of calming me down. As I walk to the stable, the familiar sounds and smells of the horses bring a small sense of normalcy. Nox neighs softly when he sees me, and I feel a wave of relief wash over me.

"Hey, buddy," I murmur, running my fingers through his mane. "I missed you."

Nox nudges me gently, as if he can sense the storm brewing inside me. I spend the next hour brushing him and talking about everything and nothing, letting the steady rhythm of the brush and his quiet presence calm my frayed nerves.

"Can I just be a horse like you?" I ask, half-laughing at the absurdity of it. He simply neighs in my direction, and somehow, that feels like an answer. For now, I take comfort in the simple, steady companionship of my horse.

As I prepare to head back to the house, the weight of the upcoming dinner settles on me again. Tonight, I'll face the Varros pack, whatever that means, and hopefully, I'll get some of the answers I desperately need.

The wrought iron gate creaks open, allowing our car to glide up the long driveway, flanked by ancient oaks. Solar lights dot the path, though the moon's gentle glow renders them almost unnecessary. My parents and I step out of the car, my attention immediately drawn to the fountain at the roundabout, a true masterpiece of craftsmanship. Four men, their backs turned, bear a platform upon which a majestic wolf stands, its head raised in a haunting howl. Water cascades through the intricately carved fur, catching the moonlight and creating an ethereal glisten.

Elizabeth emerges from the house in a modest red gown that accentuates her curves. A cape draped over her shoulders, held together by a delicate gold chain, gives her a commanding presence that's impossible to ignore. I've hardly ever seen her this dressed up. With a nod from my father, we ascend the steps, Elizabeth leading us through the sleek modern interiors of the house and into the backyard.

As I step into the house, the polished marble floors and minimalist décor speaks of wealth and refinement. The walls, painted in shades of charcoal and ivory, serve as a backdrop for striking modern art. The living area, with its plush furniture and floor-to-ceiling windows, offers a panoramic view of the moonlit garden outside, a tranquil oasis bathed in silver light. But tonight, the calm exterior feels like a thin veneer, barely concealing the tension simmering beneath.

Unlike our backyard, which was built for quiet family evenings, this space feels designed for spectacle. An elegant table stretches across the patio, set with fine china and crystal glassware that glimmer beneath the soft glow of pendant lights. To the right, a polished dance floor waits, ready for what I guess to be the evening's celebration to begin.

Caleb and a few others are waiting for us in the backyard. I notice several members of the pack have gathered as well, along with the black-haired girl who keeps appearing everywhere. Who is she, and why does she always seem to be wherever Caleb is?

Caleb, the pack leader, stands tall, his presence impossible to ignore. He wears a perfectly tailored three-piece suit that fits him like it was made to command attention. My heart quickens the instant I see Caleb. His eyes find mine, searching, until I drop my gaze and pretend to be interested in anything else.

I take my seat, my father pressing a gentle kiss to my forehead, a small gesture of reassurance. Directly across from me sits Caleb, his intense gaze tracing over my skin like a line of heat. I look away, but not before a flash of memory hits, Caleb and I in a cave, a closeness too vivid to be imagined. Yet the faint curl of his lips hints that it might not have been a dream after all.

Caleb and I in a cave? The thought is ridiculous, but the image refuses to fade. Whether it was a memory or a dream, it leaves me rattled. I can't fall apart now. Maybe my mind is fracturing under the weight of everything I've learned.

I force myself to return my gaze to him, fixating on his lips, their fullness invoking a strange longing. Another flicker, a sensation of closeness, of intimate exploration. The boundary between dream and reality is blurred as I'm drawn deeper into the fragmented memories. His touch, his whispered claims of "MINE," the possessiveness in his voice—it all feels so real. My body remembers even if my mind struggles to comprehend.

The reverie shatters as heavy footsteps approach from behind me. I rise with everyone else, turning to see who's arrived. A chill crawls down my spine when I recognize the man leading the group. Caleb's grandfather, or at least, I think it's him. I've only seen his face once, in a faded photograph buried in one of the books I read at Wraithstone. Seeing him in person feels like watching that image step out of history and into my world, solid and far more menacing.

He moves with slow authority, flanked by an entourage dressed in black suits that seem to absorb the light around them. Something about his presence presses down on the air itself, heavy and cold, and my heart beats faster, instinctively warning me to stay small, to stay quiet.

The moon hangs above us like a pale pearl against the indigo sky, its glow spilling across the backyard and catching on the glassware and silver. The table is laid out beneath it, candles flickering beside delicate flowers that tremble in the night breeze. It should feel beautiful, but instead it feels like a stage set for something I can't name.

Caleb's grandfather takes his seat at the head of the table, his movements deliberate and cold. He greets no one, his sharp eyes sweeping over the group with open disgust. The silence that follows feels suffocating, as if the entire pack is holding its breath, waiting for permission to move.

I glance toward Caleb's father, desperate to ease the awkward quiet. "It's a beautiful night," I say softly, forcing a small smile. He turns to me with a look that makes my stomach tighten.

"When the highest-ranking member of the pack arrives, he decides when and if we speak," Caleb's grandfather says, his tone clipped and cold. "You would do well to remember that."

"Who would that be?" I ask, refusing to back down, my heart running a mile a minute.

"Me," his grandfather says with what I can only describe as a wicked smile plastered across his face.

Heat floods my face, and I nod quickly, lowering my eyes to my plate. My attempt at small talk dies instantly. Around me, the others remain silent, their heads slightly bowed. The air feels thick, heavy.

Then Caleb begins to move. He circles the table with quiet confidence, every step measured. My pulse stutters. I know he's coming toward me, and part of me wants to run. Another part, the one I can't explain, is drawn to him all the same. When he reaches me and extends his hand, our eyes meet, and something deep inside me stirs, an invisible thread pulling tight. I'm too nervous to take his hand, yet too curious not to.

As soft music fills the air, I place my hand in his. Caleb's gaze, filled with longing, meets mine, and we step onto the improvised dance floor. My gown, the one my mother insisted I wear, shimmers beneath the moonlight, blue layers cascading like waves around me. Caleb moves with a grace that seems to contradict his usual ruggedness, his steps aligning perfectly with mine, as if we've done this a thousand times before. Technically, we have—just a few years earlier.

Under the watchful eyes of the stars, we begin to waltz. Our movements flow as if in a dream, each turn and dip whispering of a connection older than memory. Time seems to hold its breath, and the rest of the world fades away until only Caleb and I remain, suspended in the music and the moonlight.

As we move, something begins to change. At first, it's barely noticeable, a flicker deep within his gaze, like shadows rippling across still water. Caleb's black eyes shift, the color bleeding into molten amber. My breath catches as the transformation deepens, the amber brightening before it cools into a piercing blue that gleams under the light. His presence seems to grow with it, commanding and powerful.

My body stiffens. My chest rises and falls too quickly, a rush of fear threading through my veins. He leans close, his voice low and steady as we turn. "Each color means something," he says. "Amber for Omega. We all start as lone wolves." He spins me outward, then draws me back, his eyes now glowing blue. "Gamma," he continues. "They're the protectors of the pack. You have to be willing to put your life on the line for every member." He dips me lightly, his voice reverent, his gaze fierce.

Though I've never been attuned to the rhythm of magic, I feel it now, humming through the air between us, a pulse that matches my own heartbeat. When I meet his eyes again, something inside me shifts in answer. Understanding. Recognition. The pull between us tightens until it feels like fate itself is holding its breath. With each step of the dance, the connection deepens, and the yearning within me grows, as if the world is being rewritten. One turn, one heartbeat, one look at a time.

The music swells, and Caleb's eyes begin to change again. The golden hue melts into a fiery crimson that burns with the intensity of a storm contained behind his gaze. My breath catches, not from fear but from awe. Whatever he is, whatever I'm standing before, I know I'm not afraid of him.

He leans closer as we turn, his voice low enough that only I can hear. "Red is for the Alpha," he says. "The leader. The one who carries the weight of the pack." His hand tightens gently around mine. "An Alpha protects, commands, and unites. It's both an honor and a burden."

As he speaks, I can feel the truth of his words in the air itself, humming through the space between us. Caleb is more than a title, more than strength or power. He feels like a force of nature, something ancient and unyielding, something that exists to protect.

Then, as if responding to a thought I've not yet spoken, the crimson fades. In its place blooms a delicate violet that glows faintly in the moonlight, an impossible color that seems to hold the night within it.

"What's violet?" I ask, my voice barely more than a whisper.

Caleb blinks, confusion flickering across his face. "I don't know," he says, and there's no pretense in his tone. Only truth.

The music carries us through the final steps of the waltz, our bodies moving together as though guided by something beyond us both. The night feels suspended around us, the stars watching in silence. Whatever this is between us, this strange connection, this pull, I know it won't fade when the song ends.

The final notes drift into the air, soft and lingering. Caleb releases me when the last echo fades. He leads me back to my seat, his hand warm against mine until the last moment. His eyes, still that mesmerizing shade of violet, catch the light and hold it as he takes his place across from me.

"Are you now the highest-ranking member at the table?" I ask, one eyebrow lifting despite the quiet warning voice in my head. The courage that danced through me still lingers, emboldening me in a way I've never felt before. Subconsciously, I knew it was true. Whatever happened between Caleb and me on the dancefloor had some effect on the ranking system in the Lycan world.

"It appears so," he replies succinctly, his gaze unwavering as our eyes lock in an unspoken exchange. I wasn't exactly sure what just happened as we were dancing. But something in the air gave me the indication I needed to know that dynamics were changing. Before we sat down, Caleb's eyes glowed an amber color, and now his eyes are red, while every other wolf's eyes at the table glow amber. I remember one of the books I read at the library confirms what Caleb shared about how Alpha's eyes glow red, signifying the highest rank in the pack. But would that logic be the same across multiple packs? I mean, they're all technically related.

"Mr. Carwell," I address Caleb's father, "It's been so long, how is everything going? The business?" I redirect the conversation, offering a fleeting glance at Caleb's extended family before focusing my attention solely on his father, purposefully disregarding the patriarch's presence.

"It's doing well. I'm actually—"

"Are you fucking kidding me?" A guy suddenly erupts, jumping to his feet. "Are you gonna sit here and let this happen?" His voice shakes with rage.

"Everyone, this is my half-brother Cebastian," Caleb's dad says, shaking his head.

"She's supposed to be Cedric's, or at the very least mine. Not that fucking mutt's. We've been cheated!" he continues, glaring at his father.

"They bonded. You can see it. What do you want me to do?" Carwell replies coolly.

What does he mean we bonded? His demeanor and stance give nothing away, but I can sense the undercurrent of emotion, the irritation, the hatred, the displeasure. But what stands out most is his fear. He levels Caleb's dad with a look that could wither a flower.

"The bond isn't specific. If he isn't alive, it'll be rerouted to the right side of the family," he spits in Caleb's direction.

"Bond?" I ask, looking quizzically at Caleb. Confusion laces my face as much as my mind.

"Sit down and shut the fuck up," Caleb spits back at his uncle. To my surprise, his uncle does exactly that. I can see the strain on his face and the tension lining his body as he tries to resist the order.

"Explain," I say quietly, forcing my voice to stay steady even though my body feels wound too tight to breathe. The air between us hums with pressure, thick like a storm about to break. My gaze locks with Caleb's, and I see it, the deep red swirling in his eyes, rimmed by a faint violet glow that pulses like a heartbeat.

Realization slams into me. This is what they've been hiding from me all along. We're not just connected, we're bound. Somehow, in some way, I still don't understand, our lives are threaded together. A bond that cannot be broken, redirected, or stolen.

I glance toward my parents. Both sit rigid, avoiding my eyes, their silence cutting deeper than any explanation could. The rage that rises inside me is raw, burning hotter than anything I've ever felt. My pulse thunders in my ears. My hands curl into fists against my lap. The edges of my vision begin to blur with red, the world narrowing to shapes and shadows.

Caleb's jaw tightens. A muscle ticks beneath his skin as he closes his mouth, his eyes darkening even further. He shakes his head once, slow and deliberate, refusing to speak. The motion sends a chill through me, a warning that whatever truth lies beneath this moment is something I may not be ready to face.

"Fine," I say, the word laced with the fury building inside me. "You tell me!" I demand, turning to the young girl who was earlier introduced as one of Caleb's cousins. Cecil, I think her name is.

"Gladly," she responds, her eyebrows lifting in excitement. Though there's a struggle, as if she's trying to open her mouth to let the words out, but can't find the right way to unhinge her jaw. It's a jarring sight to see.

"I sai—"

"I don't care what you said," I interrupt Caleb with venom in my voice. "Speak," I command with an authority I didn't know I had, turning back to the girl.

Eyes widen around the table as a devilish smile creeps across her face, and she begins to speak freely, the vocal constraints from earlier all but gone.

"The bond, simply put, is a contract made by your ancestors and mine," she says matter-of-factly.

"What's the contract for?" I ask, my eyes returning to Caleb, who sits sulking across from me.

"For you, of course," she continues.

"Would someone who has a better grasp of storytelling like to take over?" I ask exasperatedly.

"Of course, they wouldn't have told you," Cebastian murmurs.

"The bond is a contract between our two families. Many years ago, your ancestor strayed a little too far from the ocean, and something terrible happened to her at the hands of a human. My ancestor stepped in and saved yours. They entered into a contract, stating that my ancestors would keep yours safe as long as once a pure Siren was born, they would be bonded by blood to a member of our family," a younger guy says with a voice of indifference. His cropped blue-black hair is a stark contrast against his pale skin under the backyard lights.

"How could they have known a Siren would be born?" I ask.

"Not sure. The contract was never kept by either family, so no one could go messing with the terms. It's not even in this dimension. Cedric, by the way," he continues, wiggling his eyebrows at me.

"I don't care who you are. What does 'bonded' mean?" I ask, dread lining my stomach at the answer I somehow know is coming.

"Well—"

"Not you," I cut him off, staring directly into Caleb's now fully red eyes. "What does this mean…Caleb?"

"We bonded…it…it means…you belong to me." He's struggling to find the words.

"When?"

"The night of prom," he admits, his head bowed.

And there it is, the javelin that's been hanging over my head comes crashing down. Everything I've ever known is about to change. The only thing I keep thinking as I look from Caleb's eyes to my mother's and father's, is that they know. They all know. I've been in the dark this entire time. The more I think about what Caleb said to me, the more my anger rises. I must be visibly shaking.

"Yours?" Caleb's uncle narrows his eyes and lets out a low growl that vibrates through the air. Before I can react, two of the bodyguards leap over the table toward Caleb. Everything happens in an instant. They crouch mid-air, claws extending, eyes blazing with intent.

Instinct takes over. I raise my hands, not to fight but to stop them. "Wait!" I cry, though my voice is swallowed by the chaos. The moment my palms face them, the world shudders.

They don't hit the ground. They dissolve.

A sickening burst of mist fills the air where they should have landed. Blood, hot and metallic, sprays across the table, staining the white linens and splattering the plates, glasses, and faces of everyone around me. The scent of iron invades my lungs. Gasps ripple through the crowd. Every eye turns toward me.

Caleb's grandfather watches with one eyebrow raised, a look of mild surprise and something far more unsettling, amusement. Cedric's expression twists with envy, as does Caleb's father's. His younger cousin studies me with the same hunger, her gaze sharp and unblinking.

My hands tremble. My head feels light, spinning. At first, I think it's nausea, but then I feel something wet sliding from my nose. I touch it. When I pull my fingers away, they're red. My blood, thick and still warm.

The world tilts. My body is heavy, but my mind refuses to stop racing. What did I just do?

"Well, if anyone was wondering whether she is the Siren,"

one of the men in a black suit says, his voice cutting through the silence, "I think we have our answer."

I don't care who he is. My body feels weak, my vision swimming in and out of focus as I fight to stay upright. The air tastes like metal and fear, and I know, deep down, nothing will ever be the same again.

"There is one more thing to discuss," Caleb's grandfather says, his voice carrying a weight that settles over the room like thick fog. He leans on his cane, eyes gleaming with a mix of authority and menace. "This is a blood binding. If either party doesn't honor it or tries to break it, the bloodline dissipates," he continues, his tone unwavering.

"Dissipates?" I echo, through my fog, a chill running down my spine.

"Both bloodlines will cease to exist. That includes the entire bloodline. Present company included," he clarifies, his gaze sweeping over us, lingering on each face. "I'd say I rather like being alive. You wouldn't want to be the reason young Lila here doesn't make it to eighteen, would you?" His eyes fix on Caleb's younger sister, her innocent face pale with fear. "You also have a younger brother…Knox, correct?" he adds, looking at me, his threat and expectations unmistakable.

His words hang in the air, heavy and oppressive. The realization of the gravity of the situation settles into my bones. The entire room seems to hold its breath, the only sound the ticking of an unseen clock counting down the moments.

Caleb's grandfather taps his cane on the ground, the sharp sound echoing through the silence. "I trust you understand the seriousness of this bond," he says, his eyes boring into mine with a steely intensity. "You will honor it, or everyone you love will pay the price."

With that, he stands, signaling the end of the dinner. The room slowly comes back to life as chairs scrape back and murmured conversations resume, but the weight of his words lingers, casting a long shadow over the evening.

"It will be interesting to see how you manage what is shared through your bond," his grandfather says, his eyes glinting with something dark as he looks back at us.

"This isn't over," Caleb's uncle states as everyone else gets up in unison to leave, no doubt to go get their buddies' blood off of them.

"That's sounding more and more like my new catchphrase," Caleb says, now staring at me sheepishly in awe. With them gone, the tension around the room reduces, but not the tension between Caleb and me.

"That was interesting," Caleb's dad says. When my eyes swing over to him, he holds his blood-soaked hands up in defense, as if he thinks I'll turn him to mist too. As if I could. I have no idea how I did that.

"We should get going," my mom says.

"I need to talk to Caleb," I respond.

"I'll take her home later, Mrs. Marrinos," he says, running his own blood-soaked hand down his face.

"Why don't we get you all cleaned up?" Elizabeth suggests.

Everyone else who remains at the table stands, leaving Caleb and me staring at each other. I can't pinpoint one feeling. It's like they're all a jumbled mess. I'm angry and want to rip his face off. But there's something else there, below the surface. In his eyes, the way he's looking at me, it's like he could devour me right here. It's the exact look he had on prom night...

The air between us crackled with an electric tension. We had found a secluded spot where he pulled me into a passionate kiss. His hands roamed over my body, and I felt a primal desire surge within me. We'd found ourselves in a cave, but I don't know how we got here, our bodies pressed together, his whispered promises mingling with the sound of the crashing water.

I jump out of the memory, back to the present, where that

same look flickers in Caleb's eyes, but my mind is a chaotic storm. Where are these memories coming from? My anger is snuffed out, replaced by a desperate need. In the back of my head, a nagging voice whispers that I need him, need Caleb's lips on me, everywhere, and his hands roaming over every accessible piece of skin. I crave his weight on me again, his devotion, his attention...his everything. The look in his eyes reflects that he feels the same way.

Before either of us can say anything, he stands from the dining table and walks out, casting me a glance, a silent indication to follow him. I scramble to my feet, not really thinking about the consequences. My entire being is captivated by the thought of Caleb. His touch, his presence, the way he smells. Stumbling, I follow him to the side of the guest house where he sweeps me into an earth-shattering kiss.

He holds my head firmly in place, not allowing me to move. A million stars explode across the back of my eyelids. My brain splinters into a thousand tiny pieces, only to be reassembled by one word: Caleb. His tongue claims every surface of my mouth. Every place his hands touch my skin ignites a fire within me.

I'm pinned against the side wall of their guest house under Caleb's watchful gaze.

"Caleb," I whimper. Something in the back of my mind is screaming for me to stop. But right now, it's hidden behind pure lust. I don't even know if it's coming from me or Caleb. Is this what his grandfather meant? How much of this is him? How much of this is me?

"Shhhh," he responds, stepping back up to me, closing the gap. He wraps my hair in his hands, pulling my head taut to one side as he begins to devour my neck. My breath quickens at the devastation he's committing on my skin, and my hips instinctively buck into him.

He breaks the kiss and takes me by the hand as we enter the guest house. He tilts his head from side to side, studying me like a predator weighing its options. Finally, he opts to rip my dress straight down the middle, revealing my body and lacy undergarments to him. His eyes darken, and a low rumble erupts from his chest.

He pushes the remnants of my dress, now hanging off my shoulders, onto the floor. Then, sweeping me into his arms, he leads us into the shower. He turns it on, leaving behind a slick floor and remnants of blood. Once he's washed us both clean, he carries me, as if I'm weightless, to the bedroom and lays me on my back on the bed, dragging me to the edge so my knees bend, and the soles of my feet rest on the edge of the bed, my core exposed by the thinnest piece of lace.

Energy courses through me, ping-ponging from the top of my head to the soles of my feet. Caleb stands there staring, as if he doesn't know where to begin. He lowers himself to his knees before me, and I have to prop my head up to see him as he lowers himself closer to my core, his nose brushing against my sensitive nub. He inhales deeply.

"So perfect," he murmurs to himself. My body is taut with desire. One touch and I'll unravel right here for him. He plants a kiss on my lower belly.

"Mine," he claims, one kiss replacing the other. "Mine." One kiss on my upper pelvic area. "Mine."

"Caleb," is all I can manage, a silent plea. I squirm under him, craving more. I can't help but think in the back of my mind that I'm forgetting something or someone. But overwhelmingly, my senses start and stop with Caleb. He lowers himself further, bowing his head to kiss the spot I've been waiting for...off in the distance, we hear a howl. It's filled with pain and anguish. I recognize that anguish. I've felt it before. Suddenly, I remember what I've been forgetting. Elijah. Snapping out of whatever trance I'm in, I sit up as Caleb sits back on his heels, looking annoyed.

The realization of what I've done, what we've almost done,

begins to dawn on me. The weight of our actions crashes down like a tidal wave, and I feel the gravity of the situation settle in. I turn to Caleb, my heart racing. "Take me home, please," I manage to whisper.

Caleb's expression softens, and without a word, he rises and helps me to my feet. He takes a towel from a nearby chair and wraps it around my shoulders with careful hands, his touch steady and grounding. Then he disappears into a closet and returns with a pair of boxers and an oversized hoodie, the fabric worn and warm from his grasp.

I dress in silence, still trembling, and he waits patiently, saying nothing. When I'm ready, he opens the door and guides me outside. The cool night air hits my damp skin, sending a shiver down my spine. The scent of rain and pine drifts through the darkness, crisp and clean, a sharp contrast to the metallic tang that still lingers in my memory.

We walk to the car without speaking. The silence between us feels heavy, but not empty. It hums with everything we can't yet say. When we finally drive away from the guest house, the night seems to swallow the road ahead, and I can feel the weight of what happened settling deeper into my chest.

We arrive at my family's home, and Caleb walks me halfway to the door, then turns to face me. His eyes are back to their normal gray hue, filled with a mix of regret and determination.

"I'm sorry," he says quietly. "I didn't mean for any of this to happen."

"But it did. And now we have to figure out what to do next," I reply, my voice barely above a whisper.

He nods, and for a moment, we stand there, staring at each other. There's so much I want to say, so many questions I have, but now isn't the time. I don't have the mental capacity or the strength.

"I'll see you tomorrow," I say finally, turning to walk towards the door.

"Goodnight," he replies softly.

I step inside, closing the door behind me. All I can think about is the bond, the contract, and the mess my life has become. I have no idea what the future holds, but one thing is certain: nothing will ever be the same again.

NINE

I wake up to a harsh buzzing erupting from my phone. The sound drills straight into my skull. Squinting against the glow of the screen, my eyes finally focus on a text.

CALEB

My place. 12:30

I groan and glance over at my ancient alarm clock. It reads 8:30 a.m. Why the hell is he up this early, and why is he texting me now?

I swipe through my messages, hoping, no, needing, to see something from Eli. Nothing. Not a single word. My stomach twists. How did everything get so completely, hopelessly messed up? I had a plan, a real, clean plan. College. Med school. Marry Elijah. Have stupidly cute babies. Grow old and die together. That was supposed to be my life.

Now all I can see is blood.

It flashes behind my eyelids every time I blink, the dinner table, the smell of iron. Two people, gone because of me. I can still feel the warmth of their blood on my hands, even though

I've scrubbed them raw. I've never been particularly emotional, and I'm aware of how convenient this is right now. This kind of thing seems to happen in the Scath more often than I want to dwell on. I've killed several people, and Caleb hasn't batted an eye. I don't know whether I'm refusing to process it or if my senses are simply overwhelmed by the whiplash of everything that's happened. Either way, I recognize the irony in how easily I've relegated my mental health to the bottom of the list, somewhere beneath survival and far beneath the consequences of murder.

My thoughts make my skin crawl as they plague me. I can't tell where my fear ends and the paranoia begins. What if Eli suspects something? What if they're both pretending, watching me? What if he can see it in my eyes? What if he looks at me and knows?

Rolling over, I bury my face in my pillow and scream until my throat burns. How could my family keep so many secrets? How could they let me walk into this blind? And why do I keep seeing flashes of Caleb, his hands, his mouth, my body betraying me in memories I'm not even sure are real?

The worst part is not what I've done. It's what I might do next.

Because for the first time in my life, I'm scared of myself.

I really don't want to see Caleb or Elijah. Hell, I'd be fulfilled hiding in a cave somewhere, never to be disturbed by anyone currently in my life again. The only thing that dinner did was create more questions and establish that Caleb's extended family doesn't like him or his dad. And now there's a 'bind' situation.

I scream into my pillow once more as thunder rumbles in the distance. The sound feels like the world agreeing with me, shaking in anger. I'm so tired of everyone lying to me, treating me like I don't deserve to know the truth. As if this isn't my life hanging in the balance. As if the blood on my hands isn't real.

And now, as if that isn't enough, I have all these other lives I'm somehow responsible for.

Tears spill down my face before I can stop them. The realization hits hard and deep, stealing the air from my lungs. I'm going to lose Elijah to this bind, and I'm going to lose Paris too. How could I ever begin to tell her what's happening? What has already happened? If I lie to her, I become the very thing I hate in everyone else.

I get up to wash last night off again. The water runs hot, but I still feel like some of that blood is somewhere I can't see, hiding beneath my skin. When I finally pull on clean clothes and head downstairs, the morning feels too still, like the house is pretending everything is normal.

In the kitchen, I stop short. Knox, my younger brother and the youngest Marrinos, is sitting at the island, a bowl of cereal in front of him, his curls sticking out in every direction. He looks bigger than I remember, broader through the shoulders, his face older and sharper. When did that happen? His focus is fixed completely on the small gaming device in his hands, thumbs moving in quick bursts of motion.

For a second, I almost smile and reach out to ruffle his hair like I used to. But my hand hovers in the air before I pull it back. The thought hits me like cold water. What if I touch him and something happens? What if I lose control again? What if I hurt him too?

"You know that's for eating," I say instead, nodding at the untouched cereal as I cross to the fridge and grab a yogurt.

"I'm eating," he says around a mouthful, shoveling in one big spoonful before returning to his game.

"Why are you up so early?" I ask, glancing at my watch. Only an hour has passed since I woke up. "Where have you been? I haven't really seen you since I got here."

He shrugs, eyes never leaving the screen. "Summer camp," he mutters.

I study him for a moment, searching his face for any sign that he knows. About the bind. About me. Surely they would tell me before they told Knox. Wouldn't they? He seems different, not just older but...heavier somehow. The air around him feels charged. I wonder what he is. Could he be a Kelpie like Dad, a Selkie like Mom, or something else entirely? Could he be like me? The thought makes my heart beat faster in fear.

"Why are you?" he replies simply, paying more attention to the game than our conversation. I watch him, thinking about all the time we've spent together. I've always loved hanging out with Knox. He never seems to feel anything but peace and happiness, which makes me feel the same way. At peace. I miss him. The one person who most likely isn't lying to me.

"I'm going to see Nox," I say after realizing I never responded. "Might even get in a little ride. Wanna join?"

"Yeah right. As if I wanna go near your demon horse. Every time anyone else tries to ride him, he tosses them off," he says. "And if I go to the ER one more time, Mom is gonna cover me in bubble wrap," he continues, still staring at the screen.

"Oh, come on. He's not that bad," I answer sheepishly. The first time I tried to let Elijah ride Nox, he threw him off immediately. The horse truly only lets me ride him.

"I can't believe I'm named after your horse," he says.

"Hey, Nox is a purebred and super strong. Just like you," I say, winking for comedic effect, which is lost on my brother, who's still staring at the screen in front of him. "Also, Nox is named after you."

We've always been the closest. Even though I have a couple of years on him, we did everything together growing up. Of course, the others are older and don't want to bother with us, but we have each other. Then I went to college and had to start thinking about life, and Knox somehow became a second thought. I was so obsessed with him when Mom and Dad brought him home from the hospital. They wouldn't let me hold him for too long because he was a newborn and weak. So I named my new horse after him, a bigger, stronger version of him that I couldn't hurt.

"Join me! It'll be fun," I say, walking around the island, holding his head in place with one hand as I plant a big wet kiss on his cheek, which he swiftly tries to move away from.

"Kals, stop!" he squirms, only for me to plant more kisses. He may be growing like a beanstalk, but I still have him beat in the strength department, for now. I spin away as he tries to get a jab in.

Heading to the stables, I call out, "Heya, buddy," as I reach Nox's stall. He neighs at me, rubbing his head against my shoulder. The smell of hay and the soft nickering of horses fills the air, a comforting reminder of simpler times.

Nox's eyes seem to understand my turmoil as he nuzzles my hand. "At least you're not hiding anything from me," I murmur, stroking his sleek coat. I saddle him, feeling the tension in my muscles ease with the familiar routine. Knox follows at a distance, still engrossed in his game but occasionally glancing up, his curiosity piqued.

"Ready for a ride?" I ask, mounting Nox with ease. Knox shakes his head, a slight smile playing on his lips.

"I'll just watch. You and your demon horse have fun," he says, leaning against the fence.

He studies me for a second longer, like he wants to say something else, then sighs. "I'll be here when you get back."

"Promise?" I ask, half teasing, half serious.

He nods, stepping aside as I click my tongue and guide Nox forward. The gate creaks shut behind us.

As Nox and I step out of the stables, the morning sun breaks through the clouds, spilling gold across the paddock. The air smells like hay and rain, sharp and clean. Knox is waiting by the gate, leaning against the fence with his usual slouch. He looks up when he hears Nox's hooves and jogs over, pushing the heavy gate open.

The riding circle is still damp from last night's rain. Nox moves easily through it, his black coat shining where the light touches. The rhythmic sound of his hooves against the packed dirt calms me, steady and sure. For a little while, it's just the two of us, the world narrowing to the sound of breathing and the shifting of leather.

I know what my father said. Stay out of the woods. Too dangerous, too unpredictable, too many things that don't belong to us anymore. But he also said a lot of things I was supposed to listen to, and look where that's gotten me.

When we reach the edge of the circle, I pull gently on the reins, turning Nox toward the narrow path that leads into the mountains. He flicks his ears, almost as if he knows where I want to go. This trail has always been his favorite, and maybe mine too. It feels wild and secret, like a place the world has forgotten.

"Alright, boy," I whisper. "Let's go."

We slip into the trees, the light dimming around us as the canopy closes overhead. The sounds of the ranch fade behind me until there's only the creak of the saddle and the soft thud of Nox's hooves on the forest floor. The deeper we go, the more the air seems to hum.

We ride for about an hour, the path winding higher through the mountain. The scent of pine and damp earth fills the air, and the world feels suspended, caught between calm and something darker. For a while, I let myself forget everything else. It's just me, Nox, and the woods that my father told me to avoid.

And for the first time in days, I can breathe.

Eventually, I turn back towards the stables. Knox is still there, waiting patiently. He looks up as we approach, his face breaking into a grin.

"Feel better?" he asks.

"A bit," I admit, dismounting and giving Nox a final pat. My shirt and pants are soaked from the rain. "Thanks for not asking too many questions."

Knox shrugs. "Figured you'd tell me when you're ready."

I smile, grateful for his understanding. Is this the reaction my parents wanted from me? To be understanding and not ask any questions.

As we walk back to the house, Knox stays close, his presence a comforting reminder that not everything in my life is falling apart.

We re-enter the kitchen, and Knox resumes his place at the island. I lean against the opposite counter, watching him for a moment, appreciating the normalcy of the scene. I wish I could stay here, like this. But I know I can't avoid Caleb forever.

I check my phone again to see it's almost time to head to his place. I sigh, tossing the empty yogurt cup I left on the island in the trash. "I guess it's time," I say, more to myself than to Knox.

"For?" he asks.

"Heading over to the Carwell's."

"Want me to come with you?" Knox looks up from his game.

I hesitate, then nod. "Yeah, actually, I'd like that."

"Good. Because I was coming anyway," he says with a grin.

We grab our jackets and head for the door. The drive to Caleb's place is a mix of silence and small talk, with Knox occasionally glancing at me, as if to gauge my mood.

Caleb's house looms ahead, my stomach threatening to bring up my yogurt at the sight of it, last night's memories still fresh in my mind. I park the car and take a deep breath before stepping out. The sun is high now, casting stark shadows that seem to mirror the turmoil inside me.

We walk up to the door, and I knock. After a moment, it swings open to reveal Caleb. His expression is unreadable, but his eyes soften slightly when he sees me and then widen in surprise when he sees Knox.

"Thanks for coming," he says, stepping aside to let us in. Knox, knowing the house well, leaves to find Caleb's sister. They're the same age, just like Caleb and me.

I walk past him into the familiar hallway, the memories of last night's dinner still fresh in my mind. "We need to talk," I say, my voice firm.

"I know," he replies, leading me to the living room. We sit on opposite ends of the couch, the silence between us heavy.

"Why didn't you tell me?" I'm unable to keep the accusation out of my voice.

"I wanted to, but there's so much you don't know. So much that I wasn't sure how to explain." Caleb sighs, running a hand through his hair. "I have a pack to protect. Although I do want you to know, I want you to trust me. But there are some secrets that aren't mine to share. That's why I've been telling you to ask your parents. They have fewer…limitations."

"Try me," I challenge.

He looks at me, his eyes full of frustration and regret. "The blood bind…it's ancient magic. It's not something you can just break or ignore. If either of us tries, it will destroy our families. Literally."

"Yeah, I got that last night. Why let me walk in there blind?" My voice rises, the anger I've been holding back all morning finally spilling over.

"Because I didn't know how to protect you," he admits, his voice cracking. "I thought…I thought if you didn't know, maybe you'd be safe."

"Safe?" I echo incredulously. "How exactly is keeping me in the dark supposed to keep me safe?"

Caleb's face hardens. "Because knowledge can be dangerous, Kali."

I shake my head, feeling my frustration build. "You don't get to make that decision for me. I deserve to know the truth, all of it."

"I know," he says quietly.

The sincerity in his voice takes me by surprise. For a moment, the tension between us eases, replaced by a mutual understanding of the impossible situation we're in.

"What now?" My voice is barely above a whisper.

"Now, we figure out how to navigate this together." He reaches out to take my hand. "We protect our families, but we also find a way to live our lives."

His touch is warm and reassuring, a stark contrast to the cold fear that gripped me earlier. For the first time since this nightmare began, I feel a glimmer of hope.

"How have you been?" he asks.

"What do you mean?"

"I know what it means to take someone's life, Little Bird. Intentional or not."

"I'm fine. I was defending myself."

"Yes. You were," he says gently. "And I need you to hear this. There is no guilt or shame in protecting yourself, or the people you love, from those who would rather see you erased from the world."

His eyes stay on mine, steady and unyielding, like he's anchoring me in place.

"We have to tell Paris...and Elijah." Just the thought of doing that has my stomach in knots. How can I tell two of the most important people in my life about this mess?

"I don't think that's a good idea." Caleb's tone is flat.

"Just because you're comfortable lying doesn't mean I am. We owe them the truth. I owe Elijah the truth," I insist. He doesn't deserve this.

"Neither of them deserve this," I continue.

"I could maybe agree about Paris, but Elijah can go fuck himself, and he knows why." Caleb's eyes are hard.

"What's your problem with him?" I ask, exasperated.

"You're the one who tried to sleep with his girlfriend, and I know this isn't only on you. I participated too. I'm not blaming you. I just don't understand."

"Like I said, he knows why." Caleb effectively ends the conversation. We sit there in silence for a while, the tension between us palpable.

"I have a real problem when people keep things from me," I clarify, narrowing my eyes at him.

"I can tell." He sighs.

"So you're really not going to tell me?"

"What?"

"What the hell happened with Elijah," I clarify. "We also need to find a way to break this bind," I say, hoping he won't call my bluff.

"Did you happen to miss the part where they said both of our families could die?" he asks sarcastically, still ignoring my first question.

I look out to the backyard where Knox and Lila, Caleb's younger sister, sit, heads down, both playing a handheld game. "I know what they said. Did you happen to miss where I said I won't be attached to someone who can't trust me enough to tell me the damn truth about anything?" I eye him, raising a single brow.

"Why can't you just trust me?"

"When have you done anything to earn my trust?"

I know I shouldn't be blaming him. I'm out of my depth, and I honestly don't know if I can handle the whole truth. But I need it. I feel like a fish out of water, like I'm back on the beach, and the tide is rising. Instead of pulling me out of the water, Caleb is helping hold me down while it washes over me until I'm submerged. How can I be okay with being attached to someone who won't tell me the truth about anything? How can he be okay sleeping with someone he doesn't trust? We eye each other, never breaking eye contact. The more I try looking indifferent, the deeper the lines between his brows grow.

"Have you heard about the missing teenagers?" he asks, throwing me for a loop.

"Yes?" Why would he be asking me about a bunch of kids?

"I think they're being collected for something."

"Something like?"

"Something like you."

"Me?" I ask, incredulous. "Why the hell would they have anything to do with me?"

"Well, Omegas show up trying to get you and they try to take us out, only to end up with a dead wolf," he says, in a tone that indicates I should've put this together myself. "They underestimated you. I doubt that will happen again. Look, it's just a theory right now, but somehow my theories always end up being correct."

"So how do you plan on knowing whether or not the theory is a theory or a fact?"

"Some of the pack elders have a theory about why they're picking teenagers to turn. Young werewolves can be volatile, reckless and aggressive, but strong. The only recent change is the rumor that I binded to you. My theory is that they're gathering in the shadows, building a guerrilla pack to challenge my position as Alpha."

"What exactly does that have to do with the bind?"

"No one really knows the statutes of the original contract. Lycans are egotistical, I wouldn't be surprised if they thought replacing me as Alpha means they can replace me in the bind? Technically, you have been with another werewolf this entire time," he says.

"Dating, not binded to him, or whatever the hell this is," I clarify.

"We could try to go after Graybeard?" He ponders, rubbing his chin.

"Yeah, I don't think so," I say sarcastically. "He handed your ass to you last time you came in contact with him, if I remember correctly."

"Excuse me for being a little occupied trying to make sure the other three didn't kill you. I'll make sure to focus on myself next time." Irritation seeps into his voice.

"When is the next time? If it's anything like the last time or last night, you should know that I'm able to handle myself now, right?"

"Right," Caleb says, his tone now playful, but the seriousness of the situation still hangs heavy in the air.

"Getting a little cocky, aren't we?" he asks. "How's your nose bleed from last night?"

"Wouldn't this be the pot calling the kettle black?" I scoff, the words slipping out before I can stop them. Then what he's saying really sinks in, and my stomach twists.

He's right. Whatever it is that I do, whatever this thing inside me is, it takes something out of me every time. The first night in the woods, once the adrenaline faded, I could barely stand. My whole body felt drained, like my bones had turned to water. Last night was the same, only worse. When it was over, I could taste metal as my nose bled.

"No worries, Little Bird. We're both pots in this scenario." He ends the conversation with a smile.

If I'm being honest, being in this room with Caleb is stifling. The room itself is massive, but everything about Caleb is as massive. His aura stretches from where he's planted across from me to every corner of the room. As we sit in silence, he tilts his head to the side, studying me as a predator studies its prey. I'm more aware of every nerve in my body. My skin heats where his gaze sweeps over me. The only thought in my head is how over-whelming everything about him is.

I hate myself for the thoughts crossing my mind. The way I'm drawn to Caleb, how his smallest movement captures my attention. The way his eyes trace my lips, the deep breaths he takes in my direction. The way he balls his fists inward, straining as if he's holding himself back from doing something stupid, which he probably is. I hate myself for how I react to him, for how my body screams for him not to restrain himself, even when, deep in my mind, I know he should. This shouldn't happen. This can't happen.

"Were we ever in a cave…you know…together?" My voice is smaller than I mean it to be. I'm praying he understands without me having to say more.

Caleb's mouth tightens, his gaze flicking to mine. He looks like he's about to say something that will ruin me or save me, I can't tell which. He stands, slow and deliberate, closing the distance between us—

"Hey." Knox's voice cuts through the air behind me.

I turn, startled. "Are you ready to go?" he asks casually, like he hasn't shattered the moment. Maybe it was on purpose.

For a second, I can only stare. I thought he would still be with Lila, dragging the hanging out longer, the way he always does when she's around. What made him come find me now, of all times?

"Yeah," I say quickly, finding my voice.

Caleb leans back in his chair, the muscles in his jaw tightening. His eyes narrow. "It happened…It was prom night." One more puzzle piece clicks into place.

With Knox there, the fog around me starts to thin. Shame and reason come rushing back, heavy and cold. I stand, mumble a quick goodbye to Caleb, and follow Knox from the room before I can change my mind.

"You should focus less on Elijah and Paris and more on learning about yourself," Caleb says. I rush to get out of the house, only to be blocked at the front door by Caleb's dad.

Caleb's father, tall and imposing, looks down at me with a mix of curiosity and concern. "Leaving so soon?" he asks, his voice a deep rumble.

"Yes, we were just heading out," I reply, trying to keep my voice steady.

He glances at Caleb, who has come to stand beside him, then back at me.

Caleb's eyes dart between his father and me. Knox, sensing the importance of the moment, squeezes my hand reassuringly before stepping back to give us some space.

"Knox, why don't you stay here with Caleb for a moment? I'm sure Lila will also join soon," Cal suggests, his tone leaving no room for argument.

Knox looks at me, then back at Cal, and nods reluctantly. "Okay."

Cal gestures for me to follow him into a small quiet study off the main hallway. The room is filled with bookshelves and mementos of a life lived fully. He closes the door behind us, the noise of the household fading into a distant hum.

"Please, have a seat," he offers, motioning to a leather armchair. I sit down, my hands clasped tightly in my lap. Cal takes the seat opposite mine, his eyes studying me intently.

"I know you have many questions," he begins. "And I understand that you feel overwhelmed. This world, our world, isn't an easy one to navigate."

"Why didn't anyone tell me?" I blurt out, unable to contain my frustration. "Why keep me in the dark?"

Cal sighs deeply, leaning back in his chair. "It wasn't our intention to hurt you, Kali. The truth is, we were all trying to protect you. I know everyone is probably saying that right now, but there are forces at play here that are beyond our control. And Caleb…Caleb has always felt the weight of that responsibility."

"But why Caleb?" I ask. "Why is he the Alpha? And why does your family seem to resent him?"

Cal's expression softens, a hint of sadness in his eyes. "Caleb is the Alpha because he was born to lead. It's not just about strength or dominance. It's about the ability to make the hard decisions, to put the needs of the pack above his own. He inherited that burden."

He pauses, as if choosing his next words carefully. "Caleb has faced challenges that most can't even imagine. Being the Alpha means constantly being tested, both by our enemies and by those within our own ranks. There are those who believe they could do a better job, who think they deserve the power and respect that comes with the title. But Caleb has proven himself time and time again. He's earned his place, even if others refuse to see it."

"I saw how they treated him," I say softly. "At the dinner, it was like they were waiting for him to fail."

"Yes," Cal agrees. "There are those who would see him fall. But Caleb is stronger than they know. And he has you now."

"Me?" I ask, surprised.

"You're more important than you realize, Kali. Your presence, your strength, it gives Caleb something to fight for. It's about the bond you share. And that bond makes you both stronger."

I look down, the weight of his words sinking in. "I just want to understand. I feel like I'm drowning in all of this."

Cal reaches across, placing a reassuring hand on mine. "You'll understand in time. And you won't have to face this alone. We're family now, whether you like it or not. And family stands together."

I nod, a small glimmer of hope igniting within me. "Thank you," I whisper. "Why are your names different?" I blurt out before I can lose my nerve.

"What do you mean?"

"Why is your last name, your father's first name, and his last name different from yours altogether?

"My father had an affair with my mother. Well, we'll call it that for now. He thought she was a Werewolf, and Werewolves can only procreate with other Werewolves or humans, Lycans only with Lycans. Much like how a frog and bird can only procreate within their respective species, although werewolves can be made from a bite by a Lycan as well. I won't get into the complications of that too much." He says.

"If I hadn't been born, there would be no one else to claim the bind, because there shouldn't have been any other offspring besides those between my father and his wife. It wasn't until I came along that he realized he'd made a mistake.

"My mother...she came from a Lycan bloodline. He just didn't care to check. He thought she was just another werewolf that he could use and toss to the side. When she gave birth to me, it split his bloodline and created new openings for the bind to take hold elsewhere, openings he never intended. She hid me until it was too late for him to do anything about it.

"The real problem is that he was so focused on tracing your family's lineage to find the next Siren that he forgot to look at his own. If he had, he would've seen it years ago, that there were others the bind could claim."

"Claim?"

"It's a contract based on the bloodline. Most of his predecessors were disciplined, but my father wasn't. Having extramarital affairs can split the bloodline. He assumed you or whoever the Siren was would bind to the son he claimed, or one of the grandchildren he claimed, not Caleb," he confirms.

"Why? What's so special about the bind?"

"From what I've heard, one of the main reasons our ancestors signed the contract was the mutual use of each other's abilities. Sirens are so rare that we barely understand the extent of their power. We do know they're formidable, especially when trained. It's said they can harness the strength of the deep sea even in the heart of the desert. Wouldn't you want to be bound to that?"

For a moment, I can't breathe. The room tilts slightly, like the floor's been pulled out from under me. My heart beats so hard it hurts.

I press a hand against my chest, trying to steady myself, but it doesn't help. The bind traces back to me. To my blood. To my name.

As Caleb's father watches me, I can tell he knows it too.

"That didn't really answer my question," I say.

"Isn't it obvious?" he asks, his eyebrows burrowing in confusion. "She hid me so he couldn't find me and kill me, but she made his first name my last name as a fuck you to him." He chuckles at the thought, shrugging and squeezing my hand gently before releasing it. "Talk to Caleb. The two of you have a lot to figure out. And remember, we're here for you."

I stand up, feeling a renewed sense of determination. As I walk back to the living room, I catch Caleb's eye. He's watching me, a mix of apprehension and hope in his gaze.

"We should go," I say to Knox, who's waiting patiently. "But I'll be back."

Caleb nods, understanding the unspoken promise in my words. As we leave the house, I know that this is the beginning of a long and difficult journey.

As we drive away from Caleb's house, the tension of the day begins to ebb, replaced by the comforting presence of Knox beside me. The trees blur past the windows, their green leaves shimmering in the late afternoon sun. I glance over at Knox, staring out the window, lost in thought.

"Thanks for coming with me," I say softly, breaking the silence.

He turns to me, a small smile on his face. "Always, sis. You know I've got your back."

I reach over and ruffle his curly hair, earning a playful swat at my hand. "I missed you, you know. College and everything... it feels like we've drifted apart."

Knox shrugs, but his eyes are warm. "You've been busy. It's okay. I always know you'll come back."

His words tug at my heart. "I'm here now," I promise. "And I'm not going anywhere."

For a while, we drive in comfortable silence, the hum of the engine and the rhythmic thud of the tires on the road creating a soothing backdrop. As we near the edge of town, Knox turns to me, a thoughtful expression on his face.

"Can I tell you something?" he asks hesitantly.

"Of course." I glance at him with curiosity.

"I've always liked Caleb better than Eli." He looks a bit sheepish.

I raise an eyebrow. "Really? Why?"

"Caleb's real, you know? He's straightforward, and he's always seemed to care about you. I mean, I know Eli does too, but...there's just something about Caleb. He's always been there, even when you weren't looking."

I'm taken aback by Knox's insight. "You really think so?"

"Yeah," he says with conviction. "I know Eli's your plan and all, but Caleb...Caleb's the guy who'll fight for you, no matter what."

I sigh, gripping the steering wheel a bit tighter. "It's all so much more complicated than that, Knox."

He reaches over and squeezes my shoulder. "Well, whatever happens, you've got me. Always."

A lump forms in my throat at his unwavering support. "Thanks, Knox."

He grins, his eyes twinkling with mischief. "Besides, I get the feeling Caleb's pretty much head over heels for you. It's kind of obvious."

I laugh, the tension in my chest easing a bit. "Is it that obvious?"

"Totally," he says, leaning back in his seat. "And honestly, I think you're pretty head over heels for him too."

I don't respond immediately, mulling over his words. Maybe he's right. Maybe the reason I'm so angry and frustrated is that, deep down, I care more about Caleb than I want to admit.

As we pull into our driveway, I feel a sense of calm wash over me. Knox is right. I have people who love and support me, no matter how messy things get.

Inside, the house feels warm and welcoming. I know there are still many challenges ahead, but I feel confident that whatever comes next, I won't be facing it alone.

TEN

I t's been several days since my talk with Caleb's dad. I've practically been living here, trying to avoid Paris and the inevitable confrontation. Just thinking about telling her what happened with Caleb makes my insides churn, about the kiss or the fact that Caleb and I have slept together. There's no way to come out of this unscathed. I can't tell her about the Supernatural side of things either, which means I'll end up looking like a conniving bitch regardless.

Part of me knows I'm justifying not telling her. I keep telling myself that the less she knows, the safer she'll be. But isn't that what everyone else has been doing to me? Making decisions on my behalf, as if I don't have the sense to understand what's happening? The hypocrisy of my actions makes me uneasy. And then there's Elijah. I can try to justify lying to Paris, but Elijah already knows about the Supernatural world. Yet, I still haven't told him what happened between Caleb and me. I owe him that much at least. But I'm avoiding him too. I feel trapped in a web of lies, unable to break free and save myself or anyone else.

I'm unsure how long I sit in my car, lost in my thoughts, until a light tap on my passenger-side window startles me. I turn to see my dad, signaling for me to get out of my car and follow him. I step out, meeting him on the passenger-side of the car.

"Are you wearing sweatpants?" I ask in disbelief. My dad, Kadir Marrinos, never wears laid-back attire. The most relaxed outfit I've ever seen him in was a linen suit when we vacationed in Jamaica.

"Yes, it's what someone wears to work out," he replies with playful sarcasm.

"I've never seen you work out a day in my life," I answer, matching his tone. Now that I think about it, he's always been fit, taller than most men, broad-shouldered and toned. I never realized I've never seen him exercise. Are all Supernatural creatures naturally adept to be in peak physical condition?

"Yes," he answers my unspoken question.

"How…" Did he just read my mind?

"No, I didn't read your mind. I would need to be touching you for that. However, you're my daughter. I can read you with all of my senses."

"For someone who can't read my mind, you're hitting the nail on the head."

"Yeah, well, since my particular sense of sight still works, it's not that hard to tell what you're thinking. We definitely need to work on you being less expressive with your face." He chuckles, pulling me into a tight hug. "I've missed you, Kalabunga."

"I've been here almost every day, Dad."

"Your body's been here. Not your mind," he clarifies knowingly. "I think we should work on that today." He kisses my forehead before releasing me from his bear hug. I instantly miss the warmth of his embrace. I used to be attached to my dad at the hip, but when I went to college, our dynamic shifted. The older I got, the more restrictive he became. I felt like I was wrapped in a line that tightened the more I struggled. Then I decided to move into the dorm for some semblance of freedom. But there were times when I missed this, just us being together. He would tell me about his adventures surveying the deep waters of the ocean, and I would hang onto his every word like it was the most important thing I'd ever heard.

"How so?" I ask apprehensively.

"Don't you trust me?"

"You kept a secret from me my entire life, Dad." "You still are." My voice drips with disdain.

"I protected your innocence," he corrects. "And I'll protect you now, just as I always have. Omitting information isn't lying, Kali."

"You think that would hold up in court?" I ask with a smirk.

"If your lawyer's good enough." He raises an eyebrow in challenge.

"I'll agree to disagree." I sigh. "So how does one get their mind back after learning they're some rare, mystical creature who can blow people up?"

"Well, how do you control everything else in your body?" His tone indicates I should already know the answer. "You train the muscle." He takes my keys from me and walks around to the driver's side of my car.

"Where are we going?" I ask, settling into the passenger side.

"To train." He leans over to plant a kiss on my forehead.

He reverses the car, heading toward the southwest corner of the property where a trail for a vehicle has been carved out. As we drive along the trail, a feeling of déjà vu washes over me. It's like I've been here before, but I can't remember running on this trail. I can feel a phantom memory trying to surface.

"There's a fallen tree up here. The car's not gonna get past," I say as my dad makes a sharp right turn with the car. I'm more confused. How did I know about the tree being down? There it is, a huge white oak that's fallen but is stopped by two smaller trees, leaning on them in a way that the car won't be able to go under. Unfortunately, the trees in this area are so dense that there's no going around. We'll have to proceed on foot from here.

I step out of the car, my dad following behind me. We push through the thick underbrush, the forest around us dense and teeming with life. Towering trees reach up to the sky, their canopies forming a natural roof that filters the sunlight into a mosaic of greens and golds. The air is heavy with the scent of moss and damp earth, and the faint sound of a nearby stream adds a soothing melody to the silence.

I know we're close when the foliage starts to change. Vines and moss thicken, cloaking the ground in a lush, green carpet. The entrance to the facility is almost invisible, a seamless blend of nature and human ingenuity. Moss-covered stone blends perfectly with the surrounding forest, and only a keen eye can spot the faint outline of the concealed doorway.

Taking a deep breath, I reach out and press my hand against a specific section of the stone. With a soft hiss, the door slides open, revealing a stark contrast to the natural beauty outside. I shouldn't know this is here or how to open it.

Inside, the environment is completely different. As I step through the doorway, I'm greeted by a cool, crisp atmosphere, a welcome relief from the humid forest air. The walls, made of reinforced glass and polished steel, gleam under the soft ambient lighting that fills the space. Data flickers on holographic displays, casting an ethereal glow.

"Your memory may be a little off for now. I'll give you a quick refresher," my dad says as we step inside.

I follow him in, the air cooler here, tinged with salt and metal. The space opens up around me, a strange blend of high-tech precision and natural calm. It's beautiful, but in the way a weapon can be beautiful, polished, intentional, a little too sharp.

"This is your combat training room," he says.

I move farther in, my boots echoing against the floor that shifts beneath me. It's gravel one second, smooth stone the next.

It's disorienting, like walking through a memory that doesn't quite belong to me. Holographic landscapes flicker to life: a city street, a jungle, crashing waves. Each one feels both distant and familiar, like I've stood in them before, fighting something I can't remember.

"Here, we have the water manipulation training pool."

The pool dominates the room, its surface glowing softly under the lights. The scent of chlorine mixes with something clean and electric, almost oceanic. I stare at the rippling surface, at the floating targets that rise and sink like they're alive. My chest tightens. I don't know why, but it feels like the water is waiting for me.

Dad keeps talking, his tone even, almost rehearsed. "Here, we have the meditation and focus chamber."

The next room feels worlds away. The air is warm and still. A shallow pool mirrors the dim light overhead, so quiet that my heartbeat sounds too loud.

"Finally, the healing and recovery zone."

He gestures toward a space that looks like it belongs in another world entirely, soft lights, the scent of lavender and sea breeze, a low hum of water features in the background.

I glance at my dad, but his expression gives nothing away. He's watching me too closely, like he's measuring every breath, every flicker of recognition.

The room hums quietly around us, and I can't shake the feeling that I've been here before. Only back then, it wasn't a tour. It was training.

I turn to my dad behind me. "How did I know this was here?"

Instead of answering, he walks up and kisses me on the forehead again.

"Dad, what is this—" My question is cut off as a flood of memories begin to infiltrate my brain. Memories of me being here, training here.

The first memory that surfaces is from years ago. I'm much younger, perhaps around ten, and my dad is leading me through the same dense forest. My small hand is clutching his, my eyes wide with curiosity and a touch of fear. The forest seemed darker then, the shadows longer and more menacing. I remember him reassuring me, his voice calm and steady.

"Don't be afraid, Kalabunga. This is our special place. You're safe with me."

He leads me to the same hidden entrance, and I remember the awe I felt as the stone door slides open. Inside, the facility looks as it does now, but to my young eyes, it's a magical, futuristic wonderland. The gleaming walls, the holographic displays, the sophisticated training areas, it's all so new and exciting.

In another memory, I'm older, maybe around fifteen. Standing in the combat training area, my fists are clenched as I face a holographic opponent. My dad is beside me, guiding me through a series of defensive moves. His voice is firm but encouraging.

"Focus, Kali. Control your breathing. Use your opponent's energy against them."

I remember the sweat dripping down my face, the strain in my muscles, and the surge of satisfaction when I finally manage to disarm the hologram. My dad's approval is palpable, a proud smile lighting up his face.

"You did well. You're a natural."

Another memory flashes through my mind, this one more recent. I'm in the water manipulation training pool, standing on a floating platform. My dad is in the water, demonstrating how to move the liquid with a flick of his wrist. The water obeys his command, forming intricate shapes and patterns.

"Water is an extension of your will, Kali. Feel it, guide it. It's a part of you."

I recall the sensation of the water responding to my touch, the thrill of controlling something so powerful. My dad's encouragement echoes in my ears as I practice, my movements becoming more fluid and confident.

There are memories of the meditation and focus chamber, too. I sit cross-legged in the center of the room, my eyes closed, the soft light reflecting off the shallow pool. My dad's voice is a soothing guide as he teaches me to center my thoughts, to find calm amidst chaos.

"Meditation is key, Kali. It will help you harness your powers and maintain control."

I pause by the edge of the pool, the faint ripples turning my reflection into something half-real. The glowing water shimmers against my face, and for a second, I almost don't recognize the person staring back. Then I see it, my hair, the same way I wore it on prom night.

My chest tightens.

I was here. I was *training* here. Two years ago? That can't be right. But the image in the water doesn't lie. The memory slips through me like cold water, and suddenly the space feels smaller, heavier.

The memories keep tugging at me even as we leave the facility. They settle slowly, like silt in water, clouding everything I think I know.

My dad leads the way back to the car and is silent for most of the drive. When we finally step into the foyer, the shift in atmosphere hits me, the stillness, the warmth, the faint hum of something familiar.

He turns to me then, his expression caught somewhere between pride and concern.

"You kissed me on the forehead the other night before the dinner," I say, my voice sharper than I intend.

"I did," he answers carefully.

"What I saw today…those were memories, weren't they?"

"They were," he says, slow, cautious.

"How?"

"Memory blocking is one of my abilities."

I stare at him, the words sinking in. "So you weren't just leaving things out," I say, my voice rising. "You were actively blocking me? My memories of The Scath too?"

His silence tells me everything.

"You've been deciding what I get to remember? What I'm allowed to know about myself?" My throat tightens, anger burning hot behind my ribs. "Do you have any idea what that's done to me? What it *feels* like to not even know who I am?"

He doesn't flinch. "Remember, Kali, you're stronger than you think. You always have been. Trust in yourself, and you'll find your way."

I laugh once, bitter and breathless. "Right. Trust in myself. After you've been rewiring my mind?"

He starts to say something else, but I cut him off with a sharp nod. "Save it. I get it. I was just another part of the plan."

The air feels too tight around me. My whole body hums with restless energy, the kind that makes me want to hit something or drown.

I don't wait for him to say anything else. I turn on my heel and storm down the hallway and upstairs, the sound of my boots echoing off the walls. My chest burns, my vision blurs, and I don't even realize I'm holding my breath until I slam my door shut behind me.

I press my back against the door, hands trembling. How long has he been doing this to me? Blocking my memories, deciding what I'm allowed to know? The thought makes something in my chest twist, hot and ugly.

I pace the length of my room, trying to breathe past the knot in my throat. I want to scream. I want to hit something. I want to *understand.*

My body is still on fire from the session we just finished. I thought he was going to show me around, maybe ease me back in. Nope. He threw me right into it. My muscles ache in ways I forgot they could, but at least it helped clear my head a little. I haven't been able to run in so long that this might be the next best thing.

Even though I still don't know exactly how I killed that kid in the woods, what we did today gave me a small piece of comfort. Proof that I can control what's happening inside me, even if not completely.

I rub my sore shoulder, letting the memory of those last few hours replay.

I'm standing in the center of the training room, panting, hands raw from gripping weapons, my muscles screaming from hours of drills. My dad, a towering figure, circles me like a predator.

"Again," he barks, tossing me a wooden staff. I barely catch it before he lunges, giving me no time to prepare. My instincts kick in, and I block his swing with a grunt, but the impact rattles my bones.

"You're holding back," he says, his voice a low growl. "Power comes from the core, not just your arms. Channel it."

He strikes again, forcing me to sidestep and swing the staff around in a desperate arc. I can feel his eyes on me, measuring, judging.

I drop my stance lower, my muscles coiling as I steady myself. I meet his next blow with a firm block, surprising myself as much as him. For a heartbeat, his gaze shifts into something almost approving.

"Better," he says. "Now put it to work."

As we continue sparring, sweat beads along my brow and slides down my spine. But in those relentless, punishing hours, something shifts inside me. Each clash of wood, each strike and counter-strike, is honing my instincts, chipping away at the soft edges until only steel remains.

"Channel the current." His voice echoes across the room. "This isn't just about control, it's about power. Show me what you can do."

I take a slow, steadying breath and raise my hand. The water stirs, faint ripples spreading from my fingertips. For a moment, I feel it—the pull, the connection, like a heartbeat syncing with my own. But then it slips. The rhythm falters. The water surges too fast, then collapses flat, refusing to obey.

"Focus." The word is sharp enough to cut.

"I *am*," I snap, trying again, forcing the energy to move, to *listen*. The surface shivers, then stills, mocking me.

My chest tightens. I can feel the power coiling inside me, begging to be released, but no matter how I try to shape it, it twists away, wild and unpredictable. I reach deeper, but the harder I push, the less it responds. A low vibration builds in the air, and before I can pull back, the water lashes upward and then drops, splattering against me in a cold, humiliating wave.

"That's enough," he says quietly, his expression unreadable.

I lower my hand, teeth clenched, shame burning hot under my skin. The pool goes still again, as if nothing ever happened.

The memory shatters, and I'm back in my room. My heart is pounding, my palms slick with sweat. I can almost hear the water still moving beneath my skin, restless, waiting.

I sink onto the edge of my bed, pressing a hand to my face. My breath comes in shallow bursts.

If I can't control this now...what happens if the Omegas come again?

The thought terrifies me.

My phone buzzes in my hand, cutting through the thick, lazy hum of summer air. For a heartbeat, I think it might be Eli, but the flicker of hope dies as soon as I see the name on the screen.

The message is short, almost demanding.

CALEB

Den. Thirty minutes.

I stare at it, my thumb hovering over the screen. The last thing I want right now is to see him, but the part of me that needs answers, the part that's tired of being lied to, won't let me ignore it.

I slip the phone into my pocket and grab my keys. I don't tell my dad I'm leaving. I can't. Not when the anger is still simmering under my skin, not when I can still taste the truth he kept from me. If I stay another minute, I might say something I can't take back.

Outside, the air is heavy with heat, clinging to my skin and slowing everything down. The sun glares off the hood of the car as I climb in. My hands stick to the steering wheel, but I barely feel it over the weight in my chest.

Will I ever be able to trust any of them again? What other pieces of me are still locked away in my mind? And why keep that knowledge from me, especially if we are bound together?

With everything I've learned, everything I've remembered, it's clear Caleb and I haven't just been circling each other all this time. We were together once. It was real. It was just buried.

And he acted like it never happened.

The memory flashes, his mouth near my ear, the warmth of

his breath when he whispered, "*Mine.*" He kept saying it that night after dinner. *Mine.*

By the time I pull up to the den, the drive has done nothing to untangle the storm in my head. Maybe this will help. Maybe it will just make everything worse. I'm not sure why Caleb called me here, but he'd better be ready to talk about the memories that won't stay buried.

As I approach the entrance, the massive wooden door swings open before I can knock. Allie stands there, her hair catching the sunlight, a soft smile on her lips. Her eyes are kind but searching, like she already knows I'm not okay.

"Allie," I breathe, the cool air of the den washing over me as she steps aside to let me in.

"Kali, come in," she says, her tone warm but cautious. The heavy summer air is replaced by the cool, pine-scented calm inside. The scent of cedar wood and dried herbs wraps around me, grounding and familiar, like a forest after rain.

We walk together through the sparring hall, the rhythmic sounds of training echoing faintly behind us, the clashing of weapons, shouted commands, the dull thud of fists on mats. The polished floor gleams beneath the overhead lights, and the walls are lined with old weapons, each one marked by use.

Allie leads me through a side door into a quieter section of the den. The air here feels different, softer, warmer. A wide hearth dominates one wall, flames licking lazily at stacked logs. Shelves of worn books and small charms fill the corners, and a low table sits between two deep armchairs facing the fire. It should be sweltering because of the fire, but it's not.

"I can tell something's weighing heavily on you," Allie says, motioning toward one of the chairs.

I sink into it, the plush fabric swallowing me whole. The firelight flickers across the floor, dancing over the dark wood and scattering shadows against the walls. Allie settles into the chair opposite me, crossing one leg over the other with quiet grace.

"Yeah," I admit, my voice catching. "Everything feels like it's falling apart. I've learned things about myself...about Caleb. I don't even know what's real anymore."

The confession feels too loud in the stillness. I glance around, half expecting someone to be listening from behind the shelves. The den is full of people with sharp senses and I doubt there's no such thing as privacy here. But Allie doesn't seem to care. She leans forward slightly, her attention steady, her presence enough to make the noise in my head slow down.

She reaches across the table, her hand light on mine. "Take a deep breath, Kali. One thing at a time. What do you want to know? How can I help?"

Her touch is cool and steady. I know she has limits, bound by the same restrictions that hold Elijah and Caleb. But, she isn't trying to defend them or justify the things they've done. She just wants to help. And that, right now, feels like the safest thing in the world.

"I hope I'm not overstepping," she says gently, her eyes searching mine.

I shake my head. "No. You're fine."

The words start spilling out before I can stop them. I tell her about the memories that won't stay buried, my father's confession about blocking my mind, the power that feels too big for my body. I keep the kiss with Caleb to myself, the last thing I need is for Eli or Liam to be eavesdropping and overhear.

Allie listens without interrupting. The only sound in the room is the soft pop of burning wood and the faint hum of voices from the hall beyond the door. When I finally stop, my throat is tight, and my hands are trembling, but I feel lighter somehow, as if saying it out loud made it real.

Allie sits back in her chair, her expression thoughtful, eyes reflecting the firelight. She doesn't rush to fill the silence, and for once, I'm grateful. For the first time all day, I don't feel like I'm drowning. I know I'm supposed to be meeting Caleb, but

Allie makes me feel like I can turn my brain off. She feels warm and sisterly, andI'm missing from my life right now. With everything that's happened with Paris, there's no way I'm walking out of this with my best friend after essentially stealing her boyfriend, fated mates or not.

I realize I didn't need her to have the answers. I just needed someone to listen. Someone to let me exist in the space between questions without trying to fix it.

Most days, it feels like I'm screaming into a black hole, heard by no one, my voice swallowed whole as my atoms pull apart under the weight of it. But sitting here, with Allie watching me like I'm still a whole person, it's the first time in a long while I don't feel like I'm disappearing.

Allie is quiet for a long time, the firelight flickering across her face. Then she leans forward, elbows resting on her knees, eyes soft with memory.

"You know," she says quietly, "I wasn't always this calm about things. The first time I shifted during a full moon, I thought I was dying."

I look up, startled. The pack doesn't usually shift. Caleb carries that burden for them. Everyone knows it's painful, dangerous even.

Allie smiles faintly, but it doesn't reach her eyes. "I begged him to let me. I wanted to know what it felt like, to really be what we are. He warned me, told me it hurt in ways I wouldn't forget. But I wouldn't let it go."

Her voice catches for a second. "It was agony. Every bone, every nerve, every heartbeat felt like I was tearing myself apart. I remember screaming until I couldn't make a sound. When it was finally over, I wasn't me anymore."

She looks into the fire, and I realize her hands are trembling. "That night, a hunter came for us. I didn't think. I just reacted. I tore him apart before I even knew what I was doing."

The air in the room feels heavier, pressed down by her words.

"I couldn't live with it," she says softly. "The guilt was like poison. I wanted to run until I disappeared, but Caleb wouldn't let me. He helped me through it. Made me understand that survival and violence sometimes look the same. That what we are isn't something to hate, it's something to control."

She meets my eyes, her expression full of quiet strength. "He isn't perfect, Kali. None of us are. But give him grace. Not to forget. Just to let go. Forgiving someone you're stuck with forever is a lot easier than hating them for the same amount of time."

I swallow hard, her words cutting deeper than I expected.

She exhales slowly, sitting back again, and for a moment, the silence feels fragile, like the world itself is waiting to exhale.

Then her tone shifts. "There's something else you need to know."

The warmth in her voice cools, turning cautious. "There's a group of people. They've been a threat to our kind for generations. Hunters. Skilled in tracking and killing Supernaturals, especially Werewolves."

My stomach tightens. "Hunters?" The word sounds wrong coming out of my mouth, like it doesn't belong in this room. "Why are you telling me this now?"

Allie's gaze flickers toward the fire. "Because you deserve to know what we're up against. Hunters operate in the shadows. Their presence is hidden from most humans, and even from some of us. They're patient. Strategic. When they move, they leave nothing behind."

"Who are they?"

"They go by the Maylards," she responds, a knowing look crossing her eyes.

The name echoes in my head like a warning. "Maylards? As in Paris Maylard?" My voice cracks on her name.

A chill spreads through me despite the heat of the fire.

Allie's expression turns grave. "It's possible, Kali. Their reach is wide, and their methods are cruel. They'll use anyone or anything to get what they want. Even people we care about."

Before I can respond, the air shifts. I feel it before I see him.

Caleb stands in the doorway, his face carved into something unreadable. His eyes meet mine for only a moment before he tips his chin toward the far door, the message clear.

I stand, the chair creaking softly beneath me. Allie gives me a small knowing nod. Her eyes hold understanding and a warning.

"Thank you," I whisper.

She gives me a faint smile. "Just remember what I said."

Then I turn and follow Caleb, my heart hammering like a warning drum in my chest.

Once I'm close enough, Caleb guides me toward a side door that opens into another room. It looks like a personal library, though the space feels more deliberate than cozy. Shelves line the walls, filled with worn books and faint traces of old parchment and cedar. A massive desk sits in the center of the room, papers scattered across its polished surface. Beyond the floor-to-ceiling windows, a small pond glitters in the fading light, the soft splash of a fountain breaking the stillness.

Caleb rests his hand lightly on my lower back as he leads me inside. My body tenses at the touch, and he notices, pulling away immediately, as if my skin burned him.

We sit on a plush sectional next to each other near the fireplace, our bodies slightly angled towards each other, the tension in the air an electric zap in the small space between our bodies pliable. The flames cast a warm glow across the room, flickering against the glass and making the air between us feel too close, too personal.

"We've confirmed that three more teenagers have been kidnapped," he says, his tone clipped but tense. "This is escalating faster than we anticipated. We need to figure out who's behind this and how to stop them."

He runs a hand through his curls, tugging at the ends in frustration. My heart sinks as the weight of his words settles in. The danger is no longer abstract. It's here and real.

"Why do I keep seeing us in a cave together?" I ask quietly.

He doesn't answer, at least not directly. "We need to act quickly," he continues, voice firm. "Each minute these kids are missing, the danger to them increases."

"Why are you telling me this?"

"You don't want to be left in the dark," he says simply. Then, after a beat, he continues, "And I think whoever is behind this is trying to build something. A makeshift pack, maybe."

"Or an army," I murmur, the words tasting bitter. My conversation with Allie echoes in the back of my mind, the hunters, the disappearances.

"Have you spoken to Paris? Or Eli?" I didn't see him on my way in.

"Kali, that's not exactly important to me right now." He exhales sharply, rubbing the bridge of his nose.

"It's not important to *you*," I repeat, leaning forward, my voice low and tight. "But it is to me."

His eyes flick up to meet mine, but he doesn't respond. The silence stretches thin between us.

Then something clicks in my mind. "What's an Amorak?"

The question lands like a stone dropped into still water. Caleb's eyes widen slightly before he looks away, jaw tightening. His lips press into a hard, thin line.

He's hiding something.

The realization ignites the frustration already simmering in my chest. "You know what it is, don't you?" My voice turns sharper now. "Fenrir put that book in the pile for a reason. Why won't you tell me what it means?"

"Who's Fenrir?" Caleb's voice drops, a low growl rumbling

in his chest. The sound sends a shiver down my spine, awakening feelings I definitely shouldn't be having.

"If you can only speak to me in half-truths, then you won't be speaking to me at all." I rise from my chair.

"I'm an Amorak," he blurts out. "I think. I don't know what it is or what it means. My grandfather called my dad about it after the dinner the other night. Said it had something to do with my eyes turning violet."

He lowers his head, shoulders slumping under the weight of the admission.

"So you're just as rare as me," I murmur. The memory of what I read floods back, sharp and clear. When his black eyes lift to meet mine, I can see the strain written all over him. He might lie to me, but I can tell this part isn't easy for him. I don't want to add to that weight, even if I should.

"Tell me something true." I watch him closely.

He rubs his jaw, the movement slow, thoughtful. "The truth," he murmurs, like he's testing the word in his mouth. "I've argued with your parents and mine every day since we...since prom, to let me tell you everything. And now that you finally want the truth, I don't know what I can say that won't make you run."

The air thickens between us, filled with things neither of us are saying. His voice is low, almost broken, when he finally looks up.

"Not a day goes by that I don't think about you saving me on that beach. I might have survived on my own, but you risked your life for me. Did you know I took over an established Lycan pack just to have enough power behind me to protect and defend you? And still, you were the one who saved me. Before that, I was only drifting in the idea of you, but that moment pulled me under, dragged me into your depths. There is nothing I wouldn't do for you."

I can see it now, the burden he's been carrying. It's etched into the lines of his face, the tension in his shoulders, the exhaustion in his eyes. The pack, his family, his friends, me...it's all taken its toll.

I want to reach out, to touch his hand, to tell him he doesn't have to carry it alone. But the room feels too close, the moment too intimate, and I don't trust what will happen if I let myself get any nearer.

Then there's Eli. And Paris.

The heat in the air turns stifling, pressing against my skin. I can't stay here.

"I should head out," I say finally, forcing my voice to stay steady.

Caleb doesn't stop me. He nods once, eyes shadowed by something that feels like regret.

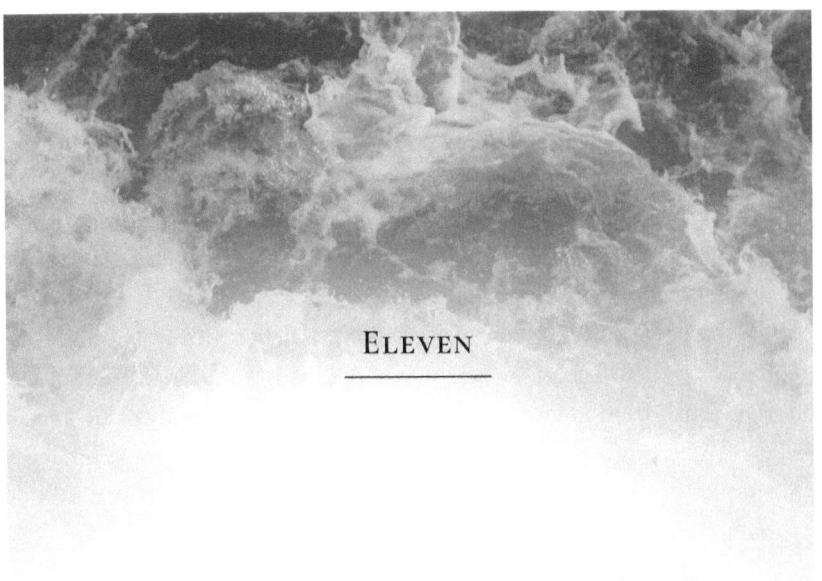

ELEVEN

I walk out of the room, nearly colliding with a familiar body. I look up into the navy eyes I've known almost my entire life. Eli's gaze meets Caleb's above my head, and the tension between them is palpable as I stand awkwardly between them. Elijah gently takes my hand and leads me out of the den, my heart pounding in my chest. Without a word, he guides me to his black sports car, opening the passenger side door, and waits for me to get in. Once I'm settled, he enters on the driver's side, still silent.

"Ummm...Hi," I say tentatively, breaking the uncomfortable quiet.

"Hi," he responds, his tone strained.

"That's it?" I ask, unsure of what I want him to say. I'm now the one with secrets that are changing the dynamic of our relationship. I'm now eternally connected to another person. What can he possibly say to make things right?

"You didn't call...or text." I try to keep the hurt out of my voice.

"What would I have said?" His voice is thick with emotion. "What could I have said?"

"You could have started with 'hi.'" The words leave a faint sting behind them, and I hate that it's still there. I understand why he stayed silent, but a bruised part of me wishes he had reached out anyway.

"Hi," he echoes. A faint smirk touches his lips, but it falters before it can brighten his eyes. His whole posture is tense, shoulders tight, his grip on the steering wheel so firm it looks as if it might crack beneath his hands.

I stare at my fingers, twisting them together in my lap until they ache. My heart is heavy with guilt, but it carries a thin thread of irritation too, and I am ashamed of both feelings.

"Where are we going?" I ask at last, expecting something simple or familiar. Something that fits into the versions of ourselves we left behind.

"I thought we could take a little time away. That small bed and breakfast outside town. The one we planned to go to after prom. Do you remember?"

I remember too well, the memory dropping into my stomach like a stone. If he knew what happened after he broke up with me on the drive to prom, he's never said it. He walked away, and I went straight into Caleb's arms, careless and hurting, and ended up, metaphorically, in his bed before the night was even over. And now, with the bond I share with Caleb, a bond that will tie us together for life, the weight of that night feels even heavier.

My head sinks lower, hair sliding forward, and I press my hands together to stop them from trembling. I force the tears back, holding them tight behind my lashes.

"I just thought you might need a break from everything. I grabbed a few things from yours and Paris's place. I can't imagine how overwhelming all of this must be. I'm sorry I haven't been present." His eyes soften as they meet mine. "I'm trying to figure out how to navigate this."

"Me too," I whisper. I'm not sure he even hears me, but his hand finds my knee and gives it a gentle squeeze. I turn toward the backseat and spot my weekender bag. I wonder what he packed, what pieces of my life he collected without asking.

"Let's not think about it then. This weekend, we focus on us. No talk about any of it."

"I don't think that will help," I say quietly, though a part of me aches for exactly that escape. "There are things we need to talk about."

"We both need a break, Kals. We deserve one. You didn't ask for any of this." His gaze holds steady, warm and earnest in a way that makes my chest tighten.

Do I deserve a break? I can hardly believe that. Some part of me feels responsible for everything that's happened, for the lies and the secrets, for the choices I made out of hurt, now knowing what binds Caleb and me in ways Elijah can't begin to imagine.

Yet, selfishly, I want this. A weekend with Elijah, where we get to be ourselves again, even if only for a little while. No chaos. No Supernatural politics. No impossible truths hanging over us. Just two young people trying to hold on to whatever's left between them, even if it's fragile and fading. Finally, I see what my dad was trying to protect.

An hour later, Elijah pulls into the bed and breakfast, and he walks around the car to open my door. He grabs a duffle bag from the back and takes my hand. The quaint B&B has a small gazebo and a pond nearby, its peaceful exterior contrasting with the turmoil inside me.

The place exudes a serene charm, its rustic façade and well-tended gardens offering a comforting contrast to the chaos swirling in my mind. Elijah leads me up the steps to the front door, his touch gentle. Inside, the reception area is cozy, with warm lighting and a welcoming atmosphere that immediately puts me at ease.

A friendly, elderly woman greets us from behind the counter, her smile genuine as she hands us the room keys. Elijah exchanges a few pleasantries with her, seamlessly navigating the check-in process while I remain lost in my thoughts. It feels surreal to be here with him, away from the familiar surroundings that now feel suffocatingly laden with secrets and complications.

As we walk down the hall to our room, Elijah's hand never leaving mine, I can't help but steal glances at him. His profile is etched with concern, his brow slightly furrowed, as if he's trying to decipher a puzzle. I know I owe him an explanation, but the words stick in my throat, tangled in a web of guilt and fear.

The room itself is quaint yet comfortable, adorned with floral curtains and a cozy queen-sized bed. Elijah places our bags on a nearby chair and turns to face me, his expression softening.

"Kali," he begins, his voice gentle yet firm, "I know things have been…complicated. But we're here now, and I want us to try to forget about everything else, just for this weekend."

I nod, appreciating his repeated effort to shield us both from the storm brewing outside these walls. Sitting down on the edge of the bed, I finally meet his gaze.

"I want that too, Elijah," I admit quietly.

We decide to venture out for dinner after settling into our room. The evening air is crisp as we stroll hand in hand down the charming main street lined with small shops and cozy restaurants. The town seems frozen in time, its historic architecture bathed in the warm glow of street lamps.

A cozy Italian restaurant with checkered tablecloths and soft candlelight draws us in. The atmosphere inside is intimate, the aroma of garlic and herbs wafting from the kitchen. We order our favorite dishes, and as we wait for our food, Elijah leans across the table, his gaze soft yet questioning.

"Are you okay?" he asks, his voice barely above a whisper.

I nod, grateful for the dim lighting that hides the tears threatening to spill over. "I'm trying to be," I admit. "Thank you for bringing me here, Elijah. I needed this."

His smile is tender. "I wanted us to have a chance to just… be."

As we settle into a comfortable silence, our food arrives, and we begin to eat, savoring each bite. The tension between us loosens with every passing moment in each other's presence. Elijah's nearness is a balm on my frayed spirit, his steady support a lifeline woven through the chaos in my mind. It makes me wonder if I've always felt this, or if everything that happened in the last few weeks has sharpened my awareness of it.

My ride with Knox flashes through my thoughts, his blunt little voice declaring that he liked Caleb for me better. Knox, perceptive in a way that borders on unsettling. What is he seeing that I'm not? What truth is sitting right in front of me that I keep refusing to look at?

After dinner, we walk on the main street hand in hand beneath a sky scattered with stars. The night feels quiet and generous, as if it's willing to lend us a bit of peace we don't deserve. Elijah suggests a late-night movie at the tiny theater nearby, and I agree without hesitation. I want more time like this. More moments where the world feels simple, where responsibilities and secrets fade into the background for one small stretch of time, and it's just him and me.

The theater is quaint, with velvet seats and vintage posters lining the walls like relics from another era. We settle into the back row, sharing popcorn and whispering comments to each other as the movie plays. In the darkness, something in me loosens. For a brief moment, I feel normal again, like the version of myself I used to recognize before everything became complicated.

When the credits begin to roll, Elijah turns toward me, his eyes warm and searching.

"How are you feeling?" he asks quietly.

"Better," I admit, surprised by the honesty in my own voice. I truly do feel lighter, as if some of the pressure has slipped from my chest. "Being away…it's helped."

He smiles, and his fingers graze mine with a tenderness that sends a flutter through me.

"I'm glad," he whispers.

Outside, the night air is cool and crisp. We linger on the sidewalk, neither of us ready to break the fragile peace we've found. Elijah drapes his arm around my shoulders, pulling me close as we walk back toward the bed and breakfast. The path is dim, lit only by the occasional lamp, and the quiet between us feels soothing rather than awkward.

He presses a gentle kiss to the top of my head. The affection in the gesture is unmistakable, and even though it's soft, I still feel my body tense for a heartbeat before I can relax again. By the time we reach the steps of the bed and breakfast, a sense of calm begins to settle over me once more.

Inside the room, the atmosphere shifts. It isn't uncomfortable, but charged, delicate, as if one wrong breath might tip the balance. I decide to shower, hoping the warm water will help clear my mind. When I emerge in my pajamas, steam follows me like a veil, and I head toward the bed.

Elijah moves behind me with quiet steps. His presence is familiar, comforting, and yet tinged with something deeper, something hesitant. His arm slides around my waist, drawing me gently back against his chest. Soft kisses trail from the nape of my neck to the shell of my ear, and despite everything weighing on my heart, a playful giggle escapes me.

His fingers trace the curves of my body with a restraint I've always admired about him. Every touch feels intentional, careful, as if he's holding something fragile and precious. And maybe he is. Maybe we both are.

"Miss me?" His voice is low and husky, filled with anticipation that sends a shiver racing down my spine.

"No," I tease, even though my body betrays the lie. I arch into him, seeking more of his warmth, more of his touch. His hand slips beneath my shirt, tracing slow, sinful patterns across my skin, while his other hand slides into my sleep shorts. With deliberate patience, he moves beneath my panties, fingertips circling my most sensitive spot. Each touch sends heat rippling through me, my breath catching as I press closer, wanting more, needing more.

"It sure feels like you missed me," he murmurs, his lips brushing my earlobe. The brief contact is enough to spark a deep, aching need low in my belly.

"Eli..." I gasp. My thoughts dissolve into a fog of desire, every coherent word slipping away. I only know I need him, desperately.

"Hmm?" he answers, fingers continuing their slow, devastating rhythm. "What do you need, Kals?"

"I need..." The words falter, torn apart by the sensations he draws from me. His fingers slip inside me, moving in steady, purposeful circles that push me toward the edge. My composure is unraveling, thread by trembling thread.

"Please..." I breathe, arching toward him, chasing the climax hovering just out of reach.

"What do you need, Little Bird?" His whisper is soft and coaxing, yet edged with something that pulls me deeper into the haze.

At once, everything shifts. His touch, warm and sure only moments ago, changes. A cold tremor slips through me, settling deep in my bones. I freeze, his words replaying in my mind with perfect clarity.

Little Bird.

My heart stutters.

"What did you just call me?" I turn toward him slowly, dread pooling low in my stomach. I know the answer, but part of me still hopes I'm wrong.

"You flew so far, so fast, my Little Bird." Elijah's voice asks the question softly, but the familiarity is all wrong. "Did you know wolves love the chase?"

I spin fully to face him. The sight steals the breath from my lungs.

It's Elijah. His tousled hair. His strong jaw. His piercing navy eyes locked on mine. His body, his scent, his presence. All of it unmistakably him.

But the words, every single one of them—are Caleb's.

"You should know I'm not fond of sharing." His tone is cool, controlled, but his eyes betray a storm. A flicker. A truth.

And then I see it.

The navy irises I know so well are rimmed with a deep unmistakable violet.

Not Elijah.

Not entirely.

Caleb.

I step back to the edge of the bed, not shrinking but creating space so I can think. My arms wrap around my waist on instinct, grounding me rather than protecting me. All I wanted was a single night, one moment to breathe outside the mess we now live in. But this is no longer something I can avoid.

"Hey, everything okay?" Elijah kneels beside me, concern etched across his face.

I rake my fingers through my hair, gripping the roots of my braids as I steady myself.

"Kals, what's wrong?" he asks again. And I finally accept that time is up. I have to tell him.

"After prom…" My voice wavers, but I hold his gaze. "I ended up with Caleb. We—" I inhale sharply, refusing to look away. "We kissed. And more. I thought I could handle what happened, but things have spiraled so fast. And yes, I'm scared, Elijah."

His jaw tightens, emotion flickering in his eyes. "Scared?" His voice drops to a low, wounded rasp. "After everything we had, you went to him?"

"You broke up with me," I say, steady and direct. No whisper, no apology. "You ended it on prom night, and then apologized a week later. Then you acted like nothing happened."

"I didn't tell you because I couldn't remember." My voice is firm even as the confession stings. "I only just found out. Apparently, my dad can block memories."

For a heartbeat, something dark passes through his eyes. Then, too quickly, too easily, he nods.

The acceptance lands wrong, unsettling. He doesn't question it. Doesn't react with confusion or disbelief. He simply…accepts it all.

Something inside me twists. It should reassure me. Instead, it feels like missing a step on a staircase, a sudden drop in my stomach, a whisper that something isn't right. It almost sounds like he expected this answer.

"Elijah," I say slowly, searching his face, "did you…already know something happened that night?"

His jaw works, a flicker of something unreadable crossing his features. "I knew something was off," he says, carefully neutral. "That's all."

But the way he says it, the way he avoids my eyes for half a second…I can't shake the feeling that he isn't telling me everything.

A small seed of unease lands in my chest.

Silence settles between us, heavy and suffocating, thick with everything we said and everything we avoided. Elijah stands a few feet away, shoulders sagging under the weight of his own guilt, while I sit on the bed, trying to make sense of the ruins of what we once were. The space between us feels like a canyon too wide to cross, carved by truths we were never ready to face.

That night, he chooses the couch without a word. The gesture isn't dramatic, but resigned, a quiet acknowledgment of how far we've drifted. I stay in the bed, staring at the ceiling, the ache in my chest sharp and relentless. Sleep refuses to come. My mind replays every part of our conversation in jagged fragments, each one cutting deeper than the last. Tears slip down my temples, silent and unwelcome, but I don't crumble. I let them fall, let them burn, let them remind me I'm still here.

Morning finds us both hollowed out mentally and emotionally.

The drive home is suffocating, every second filled with a silence that feels like its own kind of accusation. Elijah sits rigid behind the wheel, his hands gripping it too tightly, his jaw clenched. He doesn't look at me. Not once. It's as if speaking might shatter him, or maybe shatter whatever fragile thing is left between us.

I sit with my hands clasped in my lap, not because I'm afraid, but because I need to hold myself together. I can feel questions bubbling beneath my skin, sharp and insistent. Questions he still hasn't answered. Questions he avoided with careful phrasing the night before.Is that what Caleb's issue with him is?

When we reach my house, he pulls up in front of the gate. The engine hums in the stillness. Neither of us moves.

The air between us is thick with everything unsaid.

With the version of us we can no longer pretend to be.

With growing suspicion twisting quietly in my gut.

He inhales, as if preparing to speak.

I wait.

The moment stretches, taut and fragile, threatening to snap.

"There's something else," I say, finally cutting through the silence. My voice is steady, but my fingers betray me, twisting together in my lap. I keep my gaze lowered until I hear Elijah exhale, long and heavy.

"Caleb's grandfather invited me to dinner. At Caleb's house."

I lift my eyes to him. He doesn't look at me. His stare is fixed straight ahead, jaw tight.

"And?" His single word is clipped, his grip on the steering wheel tightening until his knuckles pale.

This is it. The last piece. The truth I've dreaded but refuse to hide.

"And…Caleb and I kissed."

The confession hangs in the air between us, stark and undeniable. If I want honesty from him, I owe him the same. I won't build a relationship on half-truths or hidden pieces, not anymore. Whatever happens next, I'll respect his decision. I won't beg, and I won't shrink.

Elijah finally turns toward me. His eyes sweep across my face, searching, hurting, regretting. But there's something else beneath it all too. Something unreadable. Something I can't name.

"I'll call you," he murmurs.

The words are soft, almost tender, but they feel hollow. Thin. Like he's offering a door he's already begun to close.

He looks away before I can reply.

In the quiet that follows, the distrust settling in my chest deepens, cold and quiet, like a truth waiting to be unearthed.

I nod, unable to trust my voice as I reach for the handle. The cool morning air hits me as I step out, crisp and unforgiving. Elijah drives away without looking back. I watch the car shrink down the street, a lump forming in my throat as the truth of our brokenness settles inside me like a stone.

Inside the house, I close the door and press my back against it, the click sounding too final. The tears I've been holding back finally spill over, hot and relentless. My legs give out, and I slide down the door until I'm sitting on the cold floor. I bury my face in my hands as sobs shake through me, raw and unrestrained.

Images of Elijah flash through my mind, the way he laughed with me, the warmth in his eyes, the promises we whispered into each other's skin. All of it feels fragile now, brittle enough to crumble at the slightest touch. Memories that once brought comfort now sting like open wounds.

Soft footsteps approach. I don't have to look up to know it's Knox.

In a small, almost embarrassed voice, he murmurs, "I read that physical touch helps sad people feel better. It, um…it tricks the brain a little."

A wet laugh escapes me, broken around the edges. "Is that so?"

"Yeah," he says, nudging his head a little closer against my shoulder, like he's doubling down on his commitment. "So…I'm here. Tricking your brain."

After a couple of minutes, I pull in a shaky breath and stand. I kiss his cheek before he can say anything, then nod toward the hallway. I don't want to traumatize my twelve-year-old brother with the hurricane inside me.

In the quiet of my room, the weight crashes back. I sink to the floor again, the grief hitting hard and fast. I mourn what I've lost, what slipped through my fingers no matter how desperately I tried to hold on. Tears fall freely, washing away the last fragile remnants of hope that maybe Elijah and I could fix what we broke.

For now, there's only the ache. Only the hollow quiet where his presence used to be.

Eventually, I force myself to rise, wipe my face with the back of my hand, and breath uneven but determined. The room feels unsteady, spinning around me, but I stay upright.

Picking up my phone, I see a missed call from Caleb. A knot tightens in my stomach.

What does he want?

Does he know about Elijah?

Guilt stirs, sharp and unwelcome, and I hate that it has a place inside me at all. But I know I have to call him back. Too much is tangled between us to ignore.

I take a breath, trying to gather the pieces of myself, then dial his number. The ring barely lasts a second.

"Hey, it's me," I say, forcing steadiness into my voice.

"Where are you?" Caleb's voice comes through immediately, firm with concern, like he's been pacing.

"I'm home. Just…needed some time."

"Are you okay? I've been worried."

The tension in my chest tightens. "Just processing everything." I can't unpack the mess of Elijah and heartbreak and memory blocks right now.

There's a pause.

"Can we meet up? There's something we need to discuss."

"No." The word escapes me harsher than intended, but I don't take it back. "Not today. I barely slept last night, and… Caleb, I'm exhausted. My body feels like it got hit by a truck. I need rest."

He hesitates, like he wants to argue but thinks better of it. "Alright. But call me later."

"I will," I say, because I know I have to. Avoiding him won't make any of this disappear.

When I hang up, I set the phone down like it weighs a hundred pounds. I can feel the exhaustion in my bones, a deep ache that feels too heavy to be only emotions.

I head to the bathroom, turn on the shower, and let the steam fill the room. I need the heat, the quiet, the momentary escape before I have to face whatever comes next.

I take a deep breath, drawing strength from the lessons my father drilled into me. I need to move forward. What's done is done. My life may be a tangle of secrets and pain and mistakes, but I won't make myself a victim. Not for Elijah. Not for Caleb. Not for anyone.

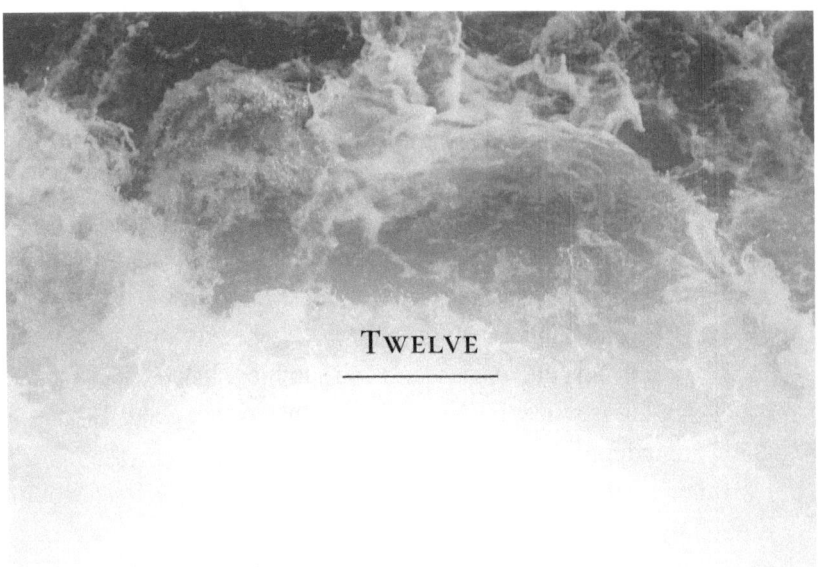

TWELVE

The next evening, I decide to go for a run to clear my head. The house has been empty all day, and I don't know what to do with myself. I know I shouldn't be going into the woods, but this is the only thing that ever helps me breathe. With no one in the house to stop me, I slip out and follow the familiar trail.

My feet eventually lead me to the mini waterfall. This place usually brings peace, but today, the moment I see it, the memories hit me hard. The boy who died here because of me. His dehydrated skin. The way blood seeped through his pores like his body was unraveling from the inside out. The image crashes into me, and bile rises in my throat.

I can't stay here.

I turn away and make my way toward the treehouse. By the time I reach it, I feel wrung out, exhausted in a way that's both physical and emotional. I step inside, toss my phone onto the coffee table, and head straight toward the bathroom. I need water. It's always been my refuge, the closest thing to quiet my mind ever finds.

As I turn on the shower, Elijah comes back into my thoughts.

He's understandably upset about Caleb and me. He has every right to be. But it was years ago. I never intended to hurt him, and I certainly never meant to end up with Caleb. It happened in a moment when I was young and hurting and convinced nothing could touch me. I wanted my first time to be with Elijah. For four years, I believed it was.

And now Caleb is here again. In my life. In my memories. In places inside me I can't seem to untangle. I don't even know how to act around him anymore.

The steam fills the room, warm and soothing. I step under the water, hoping it will wash away the confusion that keeps tightening around me.

I thought the trip to the bed and breakfast would have ended differently. I wanted us to spend time together and maybe remember how we worked in the first place. Instead, everything fell apart the moment we started arguing. After that, all I wanted was to scroll through social media, shop, research, anything at all to avoid fighting with Eli again.

The sputtering showerhead snaps me out of my sad thoughts. I finish washing up and dress in a fitted T-shirt and cheeky boy shorts. My headache has eased a little, and I know exactly what will help next. Tea.

The sun has almost set now. I walk to the kitchen, turning on the lights as I go. I switch on the electric kettle, and the faint smell of Chinese food reaches me. That's strange. I didn't order anything. I assume it must be something leftover, but it still prickles at the back of my mind.

I decide to put on something in the background while I wait for the water to heat.

The scent hits me first. Pine. Sea salt. Wild and unmistakable.

A hand covers my mouth. A second locks firmly around my waist.

Then a scream tears out of me before I register what's happening.

Caleb.

His breath is warm against my ear as he whispers, "Shh. Don't forget we're in the woods. You never know who could be out there."

His voice is low, calm, too calm for how violently my heart is pounding. My breathing is erratic, sharp and uneven. I can't tell if the fear is from the intrusion or from everything that's been building between us.

"Caleb," I manage to say once he loosens his grip enough for me to speak. "What are you doing here?"

He turns me to face him, forcing me to meet his eyes. He's tall enough that I have to tilt my chin up, so instead I stare at his chest for a moment, trying to steady my breathing. I don't owe him an explanation, but I also know I have no real understanding of how the pack structure works. I only know one thing. It can't be good if anyone finds out that the Alpha's bind has been sleeping with another pack member, even if Elijah is still technically my boyfriend.

I'm not giving Eli up. Not when I don't fully understand this bindi. Eli wouldn't tell me what could happen to him either. He kept saying he was working on it. I still have no idea what that means.

Caleb leans back slightly and studies my face with quiet intensity.

"You think you're the only one affected by all this?" His tone softens a little. "It affects me too, Little Bird."

"Eli called me that," I say. "Little Bird." The words fall out of me before I can think them through. I'm not even sure what I'm asking him. I just know something is wrong. I need to know how he spoke through Elijah. There's no other explanation for what happened. He did say it, didn't he? My thoughts start spiraling. Was I imagining it? Making connections where none existed?

Caleb raises an eyebrow at my words, slow and deliberate, then crosses his arms over his chest without answering.

"How, Caleb?" I press.

He remains silent.

Frustration surges like a wave. "You don't understand." My voice shakes with anger and exhaustion. "This, whatever it is, is tearing me apart. My relationship with Paris is strained because of you. And Eli…I don't even know where to begin with Eli. He broke up with me on prom night without any explanation, then acted like it never happened the next day. That's how I ended up with you that night. I was so hurt and confused."

Tears spill down my cheeks, hot and unrelenting, but I don't look away from him. I let him see all of it.

"I wanted my first time to be with Eli." My voice trembles. "For years, I believed it was. And now, with everything happening, I can't navigate any of this. I feel pulled in every direction, and I don't know what's real anymore."

The words hang in the air between us, raw and painful, but honest.

Caleb's expression softens as he listens. For a moment, he almost looks vulnerable.

"Kali, you think I don't feel this too? You think it's easy for me? I'm not some heartless monster. I care about you. But I can't let you go. You mean too much to me."

"Let me go?" I laugh, sharp and bitter. "You never had me. You can't even tell me what's happening or why you keep showing up in my life. You can't even tell me—"

His voice cuts in, calm and steady. "The bind allows me to briefly control others who are around you. You have this ability too. Somewhere in you. I noticed it at dinner. The guy you blew up had been trying to come at you all night. He couldn't because I was controlling him. It wasn't until you got mad at me and I became distracted that everything went wrong. You know the rest."

My stomach twists. "So we can share powers?"

He shrugs, almost casual. "Sometimes."

He studies me for a long moment. "When you get mad, what do you see?"

"Besides me punching someone in the face?" I try to keep my voice steady, but my pulse betrays me.

"I mean your vision. At dinner, or in the woods. Did it go red?"

"Yes," I whisper. "How did you know?"

"Did I know?" he repeats, tipping his head slightly as if examining me. "Because you get that bloodlust from me."

My breath catches. Bloodlust. The word feels cold, corrosive.

I force air back into my lungs and ask, "But what if this destroys us both? What if it destroys everything we care about?"

Caleb steps closer, his movements slow and deliberate. He cups my face gently, his thumbs brushing away the tears I didn't realize had fallen.

"Then we deal with it," he says. "Whatever comes, we face it. Together. But I'm not letting you go, Little Bird. Not now. Not ever."

His words settle over me like a vow. Heavy and Unyielding. Frightening in a way I don't want to name.

I open my mouth to ask him why he calls me that, why the name Little Bird sounds different every time it leaves his lips. Before I can speak, a sharp, piercing beep cuts through the room. My phone vibrates in my hand, and the sound makes my heart jump.

An Amber Alert lights up the screen.

AMBER ALERT

Missing child. Sheriff's daughter. Last seen
near town square.

Caleb leans forward to read it. I watch the shift happen in him. His breathing changes first, shallow and sharp. His jaw tightens, his shoulders stiffen, and something cold and focused settles over his expression.

Not fear for himself. Fear for Lucas too.

"This isn't good." His voice carries an edge I've never heard before. His instincts have snapped into place. Alpha first. Everything else second. "We need to find her."

I wipe my face and force my own tangled emotions down. "Let's go. We don't have time."

Caleb grabs his jacket quickly, already moving with purpose. I pull on jeans and shoes with trembling hands. There's no room left for confusion or heartbreak. A child is missing, not just any child.

Lucas's sister. She's a member of Caleb's pack.

The moment we step outside, Caleb moves like a man with the weight of an entire pack on his shoulders, because he is. We run to my house in the dark, and I dash inside, grabbing my keys. He takes the driver's seat without question, his movements clipped and controlled. As we pull onto the road, the world outside feels strangely still, as if even the forest is waiting for what happens next.

The drive to the town square is silent, but full. I keep glancing at him. In profile, he looks carved from something solid and unbreakable, but I can see the tension in the way he grips the steering wheel. He's trying to stay composed. Trying not to panic. But losing a member of the pack, especially a child, is a nightmare no Alpha wants to imagine.

"Do you have any idea where she might be?" I ask quietly.

Caleb shakes his head, eyes trained on the road. "No. But we'll find her. We have to." His voice cracks on the last word.

This isn't only a duty for him. This is personal. Lucas is his Beta, his right hand, the person he trusts most in the world.

Losing Lucas's sister wouldn't just break him as an Alpha, but Lucas as well.

For the first time since I found him that night at The Cove, I see the truth. For all his strength and power, Caleb is terrified.

By the time we reach the town square, night has already settled over everything. Streetlamps cast long, shaky circles of light across the pavement, and the darkness between them feels heavier than it should. Red and blue flashes from patrol cars strobe against buildings, turning people's worried faces into quick snapshots of fear.

I feel the weight of it before I even step out of the car.

The sheriff stands at the center of everything, barking orders while trying not to fall apart. His eyes are red, his jaw clenched hard enough to crack a tooth. Seeing him like that twists something sharp in my chest. No parent should ever look that desperate.

Caleb steps ahead of me, shoulders squared. There's a steadiness in him that seems to anchor the chaos around us.

"We'll find her," he tells the sheriff. His voice is calm, confident, the kind that makes people breathe a little easier without knowing why. "Whatever it takes."

The sheriff nods once, tightly, as if that promise is the only thing holding him upright.

We join one of the search teams moving toward the woods. The deeper we walk, the more the night swallows sound. Crickets fade. Wind quiets. Even the branches seem to hold their breath.

My boots crunch over leaves and twigs, each step sounding too loud in the silence. I pull my jacket tighter against a sudden chill. The air smells like damp earth and pine, but beneath it lingers something sour with fear. My fear. The sheriff's. The pack's. Caleb's.

Caleb strides a few paces ahead of me, his posture rigid with focus. In the faint light, I watch the subtle shifts in him. The way his nostrils flare, the way his eyes flick from shadow to shadow, and the way the muscles along his spine coil tight.

This is Caleb as Alpha.

Not only powerful. Not only protective but frighteningly alert, every sense tuned to danger.

A low hum fills my ears, something like tension building under my skin. Maybe it's the bind responding to his emotions. Maybe it's my own fear rising. I can't tell anymore.

The forest thickens as we move deeper. Cold air brushes my cheeks, and the smell of wet leaves climbs higher until it's all I can breathe. Every tree feels like it's watching us. The night presses close, heavy with the wrongness of a missing child.

Caleb stops.

So suddenly I almost run into him.

His head tilts slightly, eyes narrowed, body still in a way that makes my pulse spike. He crouches low, brushing his fingers across the ground. I can hear his breathing change, slow and controlled, as if he's listening to something I can't hear.

My stomach twists.

"Over here," he says, his voice low and tight.

I hurry to Caleb's side, my heart pounding so hard it feels like it might shake loose. The forest seems to darken around us as I push through the underbrush.

I see it.

A tiny shoe, half-buried in leaves and dirt. Pink fabric smeared with mud.

Beside it, lying in the grass like a cruel offering, is a severed wolf's tail. Thick fur matted with blood that glistens wet and fresh under the beams of the flashlights' glow.

My hand flies to my mouth as a choked gasp escapes me. The metallic scent of blood mixes with the damp earth, sharp enough to sting my throat.

"Is that…" I whisper, unable to finish the sentence.

Caleb crouches beside the tail, his jaw tight. "We don't know if the shoe belongs to her yet," he says, though his voice sounds like he already fears the answer. "But the tail is a message."

A cold shiver races down my spine. "A message to you."

He nods, eyes hardening in a way that makes him look older, more dangerous. "It's a warning. Someone is challenging me. Using her to get to me."

Before I can respond, footsteps crunch through the leaves behind us. The sheriff appears, flashlight trembling in his hand. His face is washed pale beneath its beam, his eyes wild with dread.

"Did you find something?" His voice cracks on the last word.

Caleb hesitates for a heartbeat, then steps aside so the sheriff can see.

The man's breath catches as his gaze lands on the shoe. His knees almost buckle.

"That's her shoe." His whisper is broken. He steps forward with shaking hands, as if afraid that touching it will make it real. "That's my daughter's shoe."

My chest tightens painfully.

Caleb stands and places a steadying hand on his shoulder. "We'll find her. I promise you." The sheriff nods, fighting for control, and swipes at his eyes before stumbling back toward the search team to call in the discovery.

Caleb watches him go, his expression grim, his whole body tense.

"We need answers," he says, turning to me. "Someone did this to provoke me. If they're targeting the Alpha, they won't stop until they've made their point."

The woods feel heavier around us, the darkness thicker, as if the trees themselves are listening.

I swallow hard. The shoe. The tail. The blood. It's too much.

The missing girl is no longer just a frightened child lost somewhere in the night.

She's a pawn. A warning. A symbol in a game of power and dominance that I barely understand.

We move deeper into the woods, the darkness pressing in around us, as the truth settles over me like cold water. My senses feel stretched thin, tuned to every sound. The rustle of leaves behind us. The snap of a twig somewhere to our right. Even my own breathing sounds too loud. My heart races so fast it feels like it might give out.

Caleb walks beside me, close enough that I can feel the heat of him even in the cold night air. His presence steadies me, but it also reminds me how serious this is. If Caleb is this tense, this focused, we're in real danger.

"Caleb," I say quietly, the words barely more than breath. "What if this is just the beginning? What if they have more planned?"

My mind spirals. More children. More traps. More bodies. More challenges to his leadership. The possibilities twist my stomach into knots.

He glances at me, and something fierce and unshakeable burns in his eyes. "Then we'll be ready for whatever comes. I won't let them tear us apart, Little Bird. Not you. Not the pack. Not anyone."

Before I can respond, a faint sound floats through the trees.

A cry.

Small, high-pitched, and desperate.

We both freeze. I hold my breath. The woods quiet. The cry comes again, breaking like glass in the dark.

Caleb's eyes snap to mine. He doesn't need to speak.

We run.

Caleb shoots ahead of me instantly, his speed inhuman, his feet barely touching the ground. I push myself to keep up, lungs burning, legs aching. The trees blur past me, branches scratching my arms. The cries grow louder, clearer, more frantic. My heart slams against my ribs.

I reach a dense thicket as Caleb tears through it with sheer force. Branches crack and split under his hands.

I see her.

Huddled in the dirt, shaking so hard it looks painful, sits the sheriff's daughter. Her little face is streaked with tears, her clothes dirty and ripped. She looks so small, so broken, but alive.

"Thank God," I whisper. Relief crashes through me so fast my knees almost give out.

Caleb drops to one knee beside her. His voice shifts instantly, soft and calming, so different from the Alpha command he's been using all night.

"You're safe now," he murmurs, brushing her hair with his hand. "We're going to take you home."

The girl's tiny fingers clutch his arm like he's the only thing in the world that can protect her.

And the awful truth hits me like a punch.

Someone wanted to hurt her.

To deliver a message.

The woods around us feel darker than ever, and not because of the night.

She nods, tears streaking down her dirt-smudged cheeks. Caleb gathers her into his arms with surprising gentleness, cradling her close as we make our way through the trees and back toward the glow of the town square.

The moment we step into the clearing, the sheriff sees us. His entire body jerks forward as he rushes to us with a raw sound caught in his throat, something between a sob and a prayer.

"Daddy!" the girl cries, reaching out for him with trembling hands.

The sheriff scoops her up, clutching her so tightly it looks painful, but she buries her face against his chest without complaint. Relief breaks across his features in waves, washing away the terror that had carved lines into his face.

"Oh, thank God," he breathes, rocking her as if afraid she'll disappear again. "Thank you, Caleb. Thank you so much. Thank you, everyone." His voice cracks, and he leans back against the hood of his vehicle, pressing kiss after kiss to the top of his daughter's head.

The sight hits me harder than I expected. Something deep inside me twists as I watch him hold her. Fathers really will do anything for their children. No hesitation. No limits.

Caleb nods, but his expression stays grim. He turns to Lucas, who's been hovering nearby, eyes blazing with barely controlled fury.

"We need to find out who did this," Caleb says quietly. "We need to make sure it never happens again."

Lucas gives a rigid nod. His jaw is clenched tightly, and I can see his muscles twitching. He doesn't need to say anything. Both of them know what comes next. An attack on the pack isn't something they can ignore.

As I stand there, watching the sheriff rock his daughter as if he never wants to let go, a sense of resolve settles over me. Heavy. Solid. Unmistakable.

The threat is real, the danger is growing, and the stakes are higher than any of us are ready to admit.

But we're not powerless.

I walk into the meeting room at the den the next morning. The air feels tight the moment I step inside. Everyone is gathered around the long table, waiting for updates about what Caleb and I found in the woods. Conversations are hushed, tension hanging in the room like humidity before a storm.

Caleb's been trying to include me, and he can't skirt around the truth if I'm here.

He stands near the far end, shadows under his eyes. He's worn that haunted expression since last night, the severed wolf tail weighing on him like a silent accusation. It's not just a threat to him as Alpha. It's a warning to the entire pack.

Lucas spots me the moment I enter. He strides over with stiff shoulders and worry still etched into his face. Without hesitation, he pulls me into a crushing bear hug.

"Thank you," he says as he sets me back on my feet, his voice thick with emotion. He turns to Caleb and pulls him in too, holding him tighter than I've ever seen the two of them embrace.

I leave them to their quiet exchange and walk over to Allie. She gives me a soft smile and squeezes my hand. I can only imagine how terrified she was for Lucas's sister. We both were.

"Let's begin," a tall, slender woman announces from the side of the table. Her black hair falls in precise, sharp lines that match her tone. She must be one of the older Lycans in the pack.

Caleb reaches for my hand. His grip is warm, grounding, and he guides me to the head of the table, placing me in the seat to his right. The gesture makes several people glance our way, their expressions unreadable.

Allie slips into the chair beside me, her presence a comforting weight against the rising tension in the room.

Caleb takes his place at the head of the table. He looks relaxed, at least on the surface, and sits with that calm Alpha posture that commands attention. But I know better. The tension is there, just buried deep.

Liam sits on Caleb's other side. He pointedly avoids looking at me, staring straight ahead as if I'm invisible. His jaw is tight, and I can practically feel the anger radiating from him. Or maybe it's disappointment. I'm not sure which hurts more.

I slide a little lower in my seat, the guilt and shame settling across my shoulders. I shouldn't feel this exposed or feel like I need to shrink.

But I do.

Every choice I've made in the last few days has consequences. For Caleb. For the pack. For all of us.

"Well then, let's begin," Caleb says, his voice steady and controlled.

"She shouldn't be here," the girl with the bob from the hospital cuts in, turning her glare on me like a blade. "She doesn't belong." The disdain rolling off her is sharp enough to taste.

Allie straightens beside me. "She has every right to be here, Moyra. In case you've forgotten, she's bound to our Alpha." Her voice is firm and unwavering.

My head snaps toward Allie. Bound. She said it like it's common knowledge. I glance around the table, searching for shock, curiosity, anything. But every single person keeps their gaze steady or carefully neutral.

They knew. All of them knew.

Heat rushes up my neck, fury curling in my gut.

"She's not a wolf," Moyra spits, leaning forward as if I'm something foul she has to look at. "A stupid little contract tying her to our Alpha doesn't make her worthy of this meeting, or of him."

"Allie," I begin, wanting to defend myself, wanting someone to explain why this woman thinks she can tear me apart in front of everyone.

But Allie opens her mouth at the same time, and Moyra sneers, "Allie, you're outranked here. Sit down and be quiet."

My pulse spikes. I turn toward Caleb, silently begging him to say something, anything. He sits perfectly still, eyes fixed forward, face unreadable.

Nothing. Not a word. Not a single sign he heard what Moyra said.

Blood roars in my ears. The edges of my vision flicker with red. I try to breathe, but each inhale tastes like rust. I didn't ask for the bind. I didn't ask for Caleb. Or for Moyra to look at me like I'm the problem, like I'm the stain on their precious hierarchy. It's too much.

Who does she think she is?

My fists knot tightly in my lap, curling my nails into my palms until it hurts. Anything to keep the rising rage from spilling out. All I can think about is blood. Moyra's blood. The violent urge frightens me in a distant, detached way.

"Does your jaw get tired of sucking Caleb off every imaginable way possible?" Liam asks lazily from across the table, his voice cutting through the tension like a blade dipped in poison.

His gaze flicks to mine for half a second. For the briefest moment, his eyes soften.

Moyra turns toward him slowly. "My jaw will get tired of it when he does," she replies with a smug smile that makes bile rise in my throat.

The room seems to tilt for a moment, nausea twisting through me. I drag in a sharp breath, reaching for the mental exercises my father taught me years ago. Clinging to them, I force myself to hold on to the smallest sliver of control.

The truth is painfully clear. Only a few people here know what will happen if I lose control, and I can't afford to kill a high-ranking wolf in front of every pack member waiting to see if I belong.

Though every part of me wants to.

Caleb sits there for a moment, gaze distant, jaw tight. Whatever has him preoccupied pulls him far away from the room, far away from me. His silence stretches long enough for people to exchange uneasy glances.

Then he blinks hard, like shaking off a trance, and straightens in his seat.

"Begin," Caleb says again, his tone leaving no room for more snapping between pack members.

The tall, slender woman at the side of the table speaks up. "We have several theories. One: the Omegas may be building an army. Two: the Varros pack might be trying to expose us to the humans. And three: there may be another player involved that we aren't yet aware of. We considered the Maylards, but that seems unlikely. They hide behind a platform of human protection."

"Right," Lucas mutters. "Because humans don't kill enough of their own that the Maylards need to step in and keep the numbers balanced."

A few heads turn, but no one laughs.

"Focus," Caleb says quietly. He extends his hand across the table, tracing invisible patterns on my forearm. The touch is gentle, almost absentminded, a silent attempt to soothe me or keep me grounded.

I pull my arm back slowly and place my hands in my lap. The message is clear. I stare straight ahead, trying to ignore the heat creeping up my neck, as I feel the weight of his gaze pressing into the side of my face.

"Technically, we don't know if anyone is killing the humans," Liam says after a brief silence. "We only know there have been kidnappings."

Caleb straightens. "Look into the Omegas and the Maylards. I'll handle the Varros pack." His tone signals the end of the meeting.

Chairs push back. Conversations swell. I stand and gather myself, ready to slip out quickly before someone else decides to take a shot at me.

Moyra steps into my path and stops, looking me up and down in a slow, deliberate assessment, then walks around me without a word, her lips curling in satisfaction.

I turn in time to see her reach Caleb. She drapes herself

around him, fingers sliding into his curls as if she belongs there. I can't hear what she says, but the way she leans into him speaks volumes.

Caleb lifts his gaze to mine. His eyes have gone dark, unreadable, hard.

A spark of fury ignites deep inside me, burning hot and fast, climbing through my chest like a lit fuse.

Without giving either of them another second of my time, I spin on my heels and walk out of the room. My footsteps are steady, but inside, everything feels like it's shaking loose.

If Moyra wanted to remind me I don't belong, she's succeeded.

But if Caleb wanted me to stay by his side, he shouldn't have stayed silent when it mattered.

As I step into the hallway, my phone buzzes loudly in my pocket. Paris's name lights up the screen as I pull it out. A wave of anxiety washes over me, but I answer anyway. At least she's a distraction from everything I want to scream about.

"Hey, Paris." I try to sound normal.

"Kali! I miss you." Warmth and sunshine pour through her voice. Hearing her makes something tight inside me loosen a little. "Can we have lunch today? I feel like we haven't caught up in forever."

"I miss you too," I answer, and this time the smile that rises is real. "Lunch sounds perfect. How about one at our usual spot?"

"Perfect. See you then," she sings before hanging up.

I tuck my phone back into my pocket and take a breath, only to freeze when I turn around.

Moyra stands far too close to Caleb, laughing at something I know isn't funny, leaning in with her hand resting on his arm. She touches him like she has the right, like she owned the space beside him long before I ever stepped into it.

Caleb doesn't pull away, but he also doesn't seem particularly interested. His expression is neutral, unreadable, as if he's somewhere else entirely, but the image still twists in my chest like a knife.

My jaw tightens. The anger is instant and hot.

Caleb glances up at that exact moment, and our eyes lock. Something shifts in his expression, something I can't read. He steps away from Moyra and walks toward me. She watches him go with a smirk, smug and satisfied, as if my anger is exactly what she wanted.

When Caleb reaches me, his face is blank, guarded. "Kali—"

I cut him off before he could continue, by taking a step backward. I don't trust myself to speak. The fury pressing against my ribs feels too sharp, too volatile.

Arguing with him right now will only make things worse. It won't solve Moyra. It won't solve the bind. And it won't fix the part of me that's still shaking from being humiliated in front of his pack.

I turn on my heel and walk away.

I don't look at Moyra again or give Caleb a chance to follow or explain. The only thing keeping me together is distance.

Distance from this place.

Distance from him.

Distance from the version of me that almost lost control in that room.

THIRTEEN

I arrive at the café a few minutes early, hoping the familiar setting and a good friend will steady me. The warm lighting, the soft hum of conversations, and the smell of espresso feel like a lifeline after the chaos of the past few days.

Paris shows up moments later, her smile as bright as ever. She spots me and practically bounces over, her energy a sharp contrast to the storm in my chest.

"Kali!" she exclaims, pulling me into a tight hug. "I've missed you so much."

"I've missed you too." Some of the tension in my shoulders loosens as I breathe her in. Her warmth works like a balm, not fixing anything, but softening the edges.

We order and settle into a booth by the window. Paris slips easily into her usual chatter about work, her latest projects, and a pottery class she's obsessed with. I let her voice wash over me, grateful to anchor myself in something normal, if only for a moment.

"So," Paris says eventually, her tone turning gentle. "How are things with you? You all but moved out of the apartment.

Was it something I did?" She fidgets with the edge of her napkin, not meeting my eyes.

The question lands harder than it should. I stare into my drink, searching for words that won't drag her into the mess. "It's complicated. Things with the people around me are intense."

"People around you?" she echoes, head tilting.

"Yeah." It's all I can manage without lying outright. I force myself not to retreat, but I still can't quite meet her gaze.

Paris reaches across the table, her fingers wrapping around mine. "You don't have to tell me everything. Just don't shut me out, okay? I miss you." There's a plea in her eyes that twists something in my chest.

"Thanks," I say softly. "I really needed that."

As we talk, her bracelet snags my sleeve. It's a braided leather band threaded with fine silver wire. "New?" I ask before I can stop myself.

Paris pulls her hand back a little too quickly. "Gift," she says lightly, but the answer comes a beat too fast.

A faint prickle creeps up my spine. I shake it off. I'm tired and probably reading into things too much.

My guilt scrapes deeper than suspicion. How can I sit here, smiling and pretending, after everything that's happened with Caleb?

I've never claimed to be the nicest person, but I always believed I was at least good. Now I'm not sure I can claim either.

Paris gives me a reassuring smile, completely unaware of the internal battle I'm fighting. "We should do this again," she says, her tone hopeful.

The café around us hums with its usual rhythm. The smell of roasted beans clings to the air, warm and earthy. Cups clink. A milk steamer hisses. Someone laughs too loudly near the counter. The place feels safe, familiar, almost peaceful. Almost.

I nod and force a small smile. "Definitely. I'll make more time. I promise."

"Come with me to the game tonight?"

"Oh, come on, Paris, it's not even a real game. It's just the team split into two sides and playing each other." Summer is the off-season, and the players treat these scrimmages like practice more than anything else.

We finish our meal as the bell over the café door jingles. Two tall men walk in, both watching the room like they're searching for someone. One of them spots me first, his eyes snagging on mine for a second too long. The other looks me over with a slow, assessing sweep.

Once again, a cold prickle crawls up my spine.

Paris doesn't notice. She's busy pulling a mint from her bag, humming softly.

My phone buzzes. Caleb asking me to come back to the den. My irritation spikes, hot and sharp. Why does it bother me so much that he let Moyra drape herself all over him? Especially when I'm sitting across from his current situation-ship and my best friend.

I shove the thought away and glance back at the door. The two men have taken a table near the entrance, both angled toward me. Both pretending not to stare.

Paris notices the tension in my shoulders. "Everything okay?" she asks, tilting her head.

I slip my phone into my bag and force another smile. "Yeah. Just some things I need to sort out."

She studies me carefully this time. "You know you can always talk to me. Even if I don't understand everything, I'm here for you."

Her sincerity cuts deeper than it should. Guilt swells, thick and uncomfortable. She has no idea about the world I'm sliding into, or the things that stalk its edges. She has no idea why men watching me make my pulse spike.

"Thanks, Paris," I say quietly. "I really appreciate it."

We pay the bill and move outside. The cool-ish evening air wraps around me, clean and calming after the cramped warmth inside. Paris hugs me tightly and whispers, "Take care of yourself, okay?"

"I will," I promise, holding her for an extra heartbeat before letting go.

When I pull back, my eyes drift to the café windows. The two men are still there, one watching me through the glass.

My stomach dips.

"I should get going," I tell Paris, keeping my voice steady. "Long day."

She nods and walks toward her car. I wait until she pulls out of the lot before heading down the sidewalk myself. My senses stay tuned to every small sound behind me. Footsteps. Breath. The shift of gravel.

Nothing follows. Still, the unease clings.

I head home first, but my feet pull me toward the forest trail before I think it through. I need space, movement, something sharp enough to cut through the weight in my chest. The moment I step beneath the trees, the scent of pine and damp earth settles around me. The woods feel like they inhale with me, a familiar embrace that steadies the parts of me still shaking.

I run harder than I should. The burn in my legs matches the pressure building behind my ribs. The path winds deeper into the trees, guiding me toward the training center. It has become a sanctuary, the only place where the noise in my head quiets, even for a moment.

A small voice inside warns me that this is a bad idea. I drown it without hesitation.

The trees begin to blur at the edges of my vision. Caleb. Eli. Paris. The way the two men stared in the café. Everything smears together until my thoughts feel tangled enough to choke me.

I glance up again.

Someone stands in the middle of the trail.

I skid to a halt, dirt scattering under my shoes. My heart leaps into my throat, pounding from the run and the shock. The woods around us are silent in a way they never are. Even the insects seem to hold their breath.

The man is tall, motionless, as if he's always been there. His striking green eyes catch what little light slips through the canopy, and his dark hair frames sharp, almost carved features. Something about him pulls at the air, thinning it. My skin prickles.

He watches me with a calm, knowing smile. It feels rehearsed. Expected. As if he has been waiting for me.

"Who are you?" My voice comes out steady despite the way my pulse hammers. I force my breathing to slow as I scan the trees around him, checking for movement, for anything. The last time I was alone out here, it ended badly. I still barely understand my own abilities, and I don't trust myself to rely on them if this turns into something dangerous.

The air shifts. For a heartbeat, the pressure drops, almost like a sudden change in weather.

"I am someone who knows more about your situation than you might think," he says. His tone is calm, but something underneath it coils, waiting.

His pupils narrow to thin slits for a blink before returning to normal.

I frown and shift my weight back, keeping a safe distance. "What do you mean?"

He steps closer, deliberate and unhurried, his gaze unwavering. "You are bound to that Alpha, are you not? Caleb, is it?" His tone carries a light tease, but the focus in his eyes is sharp enough to cut through any hint of humor.

My heart stutters once. "How do you know that?"

A slow smile curves his mouth, touched with something that

feels like mischief but tastes wrong. "I have my ways. My name is Aleron, and I am here to offer you clarity about your bond."

"Aleron," I repeat quietly. "How can you offer clarity? Who are you really?"

I take another subtle step back, but a sudden wave of calm washes through me. My pulse slows. My shoulders loosen. My muscles unclench without my permission. The shift is too smooth to be natural.

My mind screams at me to run.

My body stays rooted.

What is he?

"I just told you who I am," Aleron says, already sounding bored with the conversation. He tilts his head, studying me like he's reading a book. "The bond you share with Caleb isn't a simple contract. It's a binding. It ties your fates together far more deeply than you realize."

I force air into my lungs. "What does that mean exactly?" I don't trust him, but I'm not going to pretend I don't need answers.

He begins to circle me slowly, not close enough to touch, but close enough that the air seems to move with him. "It means the bond is anchored to more than the two of you. It's tied into the balance between worlds. The human realm. The Scath. The old places between them."

His eyes catch the fading light and seem to burn brighter. "If this bond is broken carelessly, it could unravel that balance. It could be the beginning of the undoing of both worlds."

A chill settles in my bones. "You're saying if I break this bond, I could destroy *everything*?" The words feel ridiculous and heavy at the same time.

"I'm saying that forces older than his pack, older than your hunters, chose to bind you in this way." His voice deepens, almost resonant. "They don't move lightly. When they tie lives together, it isn't a game."

I swallow hard. "How do you know any of this? And if the bond is so powerful, can it be broken or not?"

"That is the question, is it not?" For a moment, something like respect flickers in his eyes. "There are always ways to cut a knot, but every method leaves a mark. On the string. On the hand that holds the knife. On everything tied to it."

My frustration spikes. "So that's a yes, it can be broken, or a no, it can't?"

His lips curve again, not quite a smile. "You shouldn't trust anyone who offers you an easy answer to that."

He pauses in front of me, looking straight into my eyes. The air tightens between us, thin and sharp.

"Listen carefully, Kali," he says. "Do not trust anyone. Not Caleb's pack. Not the hunters. Not your enemies. Not even me." His voice becomes softer. "For now, the safest thing you can do is stay close to your wolf."

My wolf.

The words snag in my chest. Caleb's face flashes in my mind. Then Elijah's. Both of them are wolves. Both of them are tangled in this whether I like it or not.

Before I can push for more, he turns away. His outline blurs for a heartbeat, as if the forest itself bends to let him pass, and then he disappears between the trees.

The false calm snaps off like a switch. My heart slams back into a frantic pace. My skin is damp, my hands shaking, but I stay on my feet. I'm not broken or running away.

I stand there a moment longer, his words circling like vultures. Undoing of both worlds. Stay close to your wolf. Don't trust anyone.

Then I force my legs to move and push into a run again, heading toward home. The trail blurs beneath me as my thoughts race faster than my feet.

Back home, I find Killian stretched out on the couch, scrolling through his phone with lazy intensity. He glances up as

I walk in, a grin tugging at his mouth. "Hey, stranger. You look like you've seen a ghost."

"Just tired from the run. I forgot my water," I say lightly as I drop onto the couch beside him. My body feels steady enough now, but my mind is still replaying what happened in the woods. I have no idea what Aleron is, and even less what telling Killian would mean.

Killian studies me for a second too long, concern flickering behind his usual casual expression. Before he can ask anything, I force out, "Things have been a little crazy lately. You know. Sirens. Being bound to an Alpha whose pack seems like they would rather see him bound to a hyena."

I gesture vaguely to myself, trying to keep it playful even though frustration crushes my words.

Killian's grin fades. His face softens with quiet understanding. "Yeah. I know it can be rough. But it will be okay."

A tired scoff escapes before I can stop it. "You don't know that." I lean against the couch. "They don't like me because I'm not like them. I'm different, not a wolf."

"Different isn't so bad. Rita isn't like us either. She's human," he says, rubbing the back of his neck with a sheepish look.

I turn to stare at him, disbelief sharpening my voice. "Does she know? About you? About our family? Any of it?"

He sighs and runs a hand through his hair. "Yeah, she does actually."

"Great. So your human girlfriend got an invite to the family secrets before I did." The irritation slips out before I can rein it in. "I really don't understand how you all justified lying to me for years."

"I never lied. I just didn't tell you." He gives a guilty shrug. "I'm starting to realize that keeping secrets isn't the way to handle things."

"Yeah, apparently ignorance is the best protection. Alert the judicial branch." The sarcasm tastes sharp on my tongue.

"Hey, I admitted I was wrong. No need to shank and twist." He nudges me with his shoulder, trying to lighten the mood.

Despite everything, the corner of my mouth twitches. I've missed my brothers. My sisters are always off doing their own things, too busy to want a younger sibling around. But Killian has never minded. Even with our ten-year age gap, he's always made space for me. Same with Knox. They never make me feel like the odd one out.

I exhale and look at him. "How did she even find out about all this?"

His phone buzzes in his hand. He glances at the screen and winces. "That is a story for another time." He pushes up from the couch as the phone buzzes again. "I have to take this."

"I want that story," I call after him as he waves me off and slips down the hall.

My own phone vibrates in my hand. When I check it, Paris's text appears on the screen.

PARIS

See you tonight?

My stomach tightens. *Tonight.* The scrimmage. Caleb and Elijah are captaining opposite sides. Great. Exactly what I need. Both of them stare each other down from opposing fields like the universe is trying to make a point.

I sigh and type back a simple.

Can't wait.

The words look stiff on the screen, like they know I'm lying.

What am I going to do? Paris and I know each other almost too well. She'll smell the truth on me sooner or later, even without Supernatural senses.

I lean back into the couch, fingers tightening around my phone. I feel stretched thin at the edges, pulled in directions I can't name. I want everything to stop spinning. I just want to not think for a little while.

Before the game, I find Eli near the locker rooms. "Eli, we need to talk. Meet me after the game?" I ask, hoping he'll at least hear me out. I owe him closure, if nothing else.

He looks at me with an expression I can't read. "Sure," he says, though something in his tone feels distant.

The entire school gathers for the summer scrimmage. Even though it's off-season, these split-squad games always draw a crowd. Football is the town's heartbeat, and everyone treats these practices like real matches.

Caleb has drafted one team.

Eli, as captain of the other side, has drafted the opposing squad.

The rivalry between them simmers beneath the surface, the air crackling with it.

Paris sits beside me on the bleachers. "Wow, they're really going at it, aren't they?"

"I can't take my eyes off the field," I admit. Something feels off. The tension in the air has teeth.

As the scrimmage progresses, it becomes obvious that something is wrong. Eli's team moves with eerie precision, every play designed to corner Caleb. They keep forcing hits on him, ignoring the ball and the rhythm of the game. It looks less like a strategy and more like they're trying to take him out.

The refs just stand there. No whistles. No flags.

"Do you not have eyes?" I shout at the ref, my frustration snapping loose. He looks right at me and gives a smug smirk. My stomach twists. That isn't incompetence. It's deliberate.

Paris blinks at me, confused, but I keep my gaze locked on

the field. Caleb may be infuriating, but he's their quarterback. Their season depends on him. No sane captain would risk injuring him right before preseason… unless something else is pushing this.

Another player from Eli's team lunges at Caleb. Caleb reacts fast, dodging and taking the attacker to the ground with clean, effortless strength.

The moment they hit the turf, chaos explodes.

Benches clear. Eli's team surges forward. Caleb's squad rushes to meet them. A full fight breaks out, bodies colliding, fists flying, helmets being ripped off. I search frantically for Caleb, spotting him standing firm in the center of it all, breathing hard but unhurt.

Against my will, relief floods me.

I shouldn't care. He's impossible. But seeing him attacked like that twists something in my chest.

A quieter thought reminds me Eli is in the fight too.

A louder one reminds me *he's the one who started it.*

Coaches and staff eventually drag players apart. Multiple guys get benched. Caleb is sent off the field.

Eli, somehow, is not.

He wipes sweat and blood from his mouth, steps into the quarterback position, and leads his team to a narrow victory. The crowd loses its mind.

I stare down at him, stunned. I've seen Eli angry before, but never like this. There's a ruthlessness in him I don't recognize.

After the game, I call him. Once. Twice. Again.

Straight to voicemail every time.

Frustration and hurt coil together in my chest until breathing feels heavy.

"Wanna head to The Kill Spot?" Paris asks as we make our way across the parking lot. She shortens the name automatically, her voice hopeful but thin around the edges.

I shake my head. "No. I think I'm going to head home." My

voice comes out flat with exhaustion. There's too much noise in my head already. Adding alcohol to it feels like a promise to spill something I'm not ready to explain. And right now, I can only handle one best friend hating me, not two.

Paris nods, but her shoulders dip slightly. She's trying to keep her expression casual, but I catch the flicker in her eyes. She noticed how I reacted during the game. How I yelled at the ref. How I couldn't look away from Caleb. She must suspect something.

But she doesn't mention it, just waits.

"We definitely need to do this again," I say, pulling her in for a hug. I squeeze her tightly, pressing a kiss to her forehead before letting go.

Her smile returns, a little brighter, but I can still feel the question she isn't asking.

The moment the door shuts behind me at home, anger and betrayal rise like a tide. I throw my bag onto the couch and pace the living room. Caleb. Eli. Aleron. Paris watching me like she knows something is wrong. Everything feels tangled, and I can't find the ends.

I sit on the edge of the couch and stare at my phone, waiting for Eli to text or call or give me anything. The silence feels heavier with every minute.

Then my phone buzzes.

When I open the message, my stomach drops.

UNKNOWN

A picture of Eli at The Kill Spot. His arm around a girl I've never seen before.

My breath catches.

Why is he there?

And who is she?

My phone vibrates again.

Stay away from Eli if you know what's good
for you.

The words freeze me in place. The cold rush in my chest turns quickly into anger, sharp and hot.

Fine. He can go to hell.

I walk down to my parents' wine cellar and grab one of my mom's bottles. I drink one glass and then another, finishing both faster than I should, the edges of the day blurring, but not enough to numb anything. I pour another, guzzling it down just as fast, making the room soften at the corners. Not drunk, but fogged enough to stop thinking.

Then a brilliant idea forms.

The Kill spot.

Before I can talk myself out of it, I call a taxi. My heart pounds the entire way, matching the storm grinding through my mind.

When I push open the doors to TKS, the familiar rush of noise, sweat, and cheap perfume hits me. I scan the room, breath tight in my chest.

I see him immediately.

Eli. At the bar. Kissing the girl from the photo.

Something in me tears and flares all at once. Hurt. Anger. Pride. All of it ignites.

Before I can think, I walk straight toward the dance floor. A group of people crowd the center, laughing under pulsing lights. I spot a guy who looks harmless enough and lean in to kiss his cheek. My smile turns flirty, practiced, a shield I know how to wear.

If Eli wants to play games, fine.

I can play too.

"Dance with me?" I ask, not really waiting for an answer.

He grins and pulls me into the crush of bodies on the dance floor. The music vibrates through the room, heavy and relentless, each beat thudding in my chest. For a moment, the noise wipes my thoughts clean, and I let myself move, allowing the rhythm to blur the edges of everything hurting inside me.

I glance toward the bar.

Elijah is staring straight at me.

His eyes meet mine, sharp with something between surprise and anger. The heat of that look sends a jolt through me, quick and undeniable.

Then a hand closes around my arm.

Firm. Strong. Not painful, but absolute.

I turn, expecting Eli.

It's Caleb.

His eyes blaze with fury, controlled only by the thinnest thread. The music's strobe-lights flash across his face, catching the red rimming his irises.

"Hey," I say, breathless.

Caleb's jaw locks. For a second, he looks like he might snap. Instead, he forces his voice low.

"Kali," he says in a tight whisper, "come outside with me. Now."

Not an order. A plea wrapped in urgency.

I yank my arm free on instinct. "Don't command me."

He flinches slightly. Then he steps closer, lowering his voice even more, the anger in his eyes shifting into something almost frightened.

"Please. Outside."

I hate that the word softens me.

I hate that it hits somewhere deep.

But I choose to go.

Angry. Hurt. Still choosing.

He walks beside me out of TKS, shoulders tight, fists clenched at his sides. The door shuts behind us, muffling the music.

The ride home is thick with a heavy silence. Caleb grips the steering wheel too tightly, knuckles pale against the leather. His jaw works like he's chewing back words he can't say without exploding.

The air feels charged.

Maybe it's the cramped space. Maybe the wine. Maybe the adrenaline still pulsing through me. I drift closer and let my hand slide over his chest.

He turns rigid at the touch.

"I'm not Eli's substitute," he says, voice cutting through the quiet. "I'm not his replacement, and I'm not your distraction."

The words hit me like a slap. I pull my hand back quickly, heat rising in my cheeks.

When we finally pull up to my house, he turns toward me, eyes still bright with anger. "What were you thinking, Kali?"

I stare out the windshield, suddenly exhausted. "I don't know, Caleb. I just wanted to forget."

Some of the tension leaves his shoulders, but not enough. "This isn't the way to handle it."

I turn to look at him. His eyes are rimmed in red. He's furious. Scared. Something else I can't name.

My head is splitting, my thoughts a mess. Why does he even care? Hooking up with Eli wouldn't break the bond, so why is he acting like this?

Has he been messing around with Moyra? The thought sparks hot irritation, and I scoff.

"How exactly should I handle it?" I ask bitterly. "My boyfriend had his tongue down another girl's throat."

The word boyfriend feels wrong and uncertain.

At this point, I don't even know if it still applies.

"Also, how did you even find me? And why did you drag me out like I'm your lost dog?" The words come out sharper than I intend, the wine fuzzing the edges of my restraint. I know I'm half-picking a fight. I want to argue, and Caleb is standing right there, breathing steady and calm like he always does. It makes something messy in me want to push harder.

"I guess you wouldn't understand," I go on, my voice dipping into a taunt I can't pull back. "Maybe I should become Alpha, then I can sleep with my pack members too. Since monogamy clearly isn't your thing."

Caleb recoils as if I slapped him.

The moment hits me through the wine haze, enough to make my stomach dip. He turns away slowly, shoulders tight.

"Goodnight," he says.

The word lands like a brick. My anger fizzles out in one breath, leaving guilt crawling across my skin. He's not the one I'm furious at. And we both know it.

I stare at my hands. They feel too warm. Too heavy. "Goodnight," I whisper, pushing the door open and climbing out.

He waits until I get inside before driving away. The Jeep's taillights smear red across my vision, and I blink harder than I should have to.

I stand in the foyer for a moment, swaying a little, letting the quiet house steady me. The warmth in my blood buzzes and softens everything, making the silence feel too loud. When I see the living room light on, I drift toward it because facing Krystal feels easier than facing my own thoughts.

She looks up from her book, eyes widening. "Kali. What happened? You look exhausted."

I drop onto the couch beside her, the cushions swallowing me.

"You went out with Caleb?" she asks.

"How did you know?" I mumble, rubbing at my forehead. The room tilts for a second, and I blink it back into place.

She holds up her phone. "Cameras. We get alerts when someone arrives." Her voice softens. "Kali…do you think maybe you should address your feelings for Caleb?"

"What feelings?" The embarrassment stings more because

I'm buzzed, and my chest feels too warm and exposed. Caleb's rejection flashes through my mind, sharper than it should after two bottles of wine and a terrible decision.

Krystal sighs, shifting closer. "You asked us to be honest, so I'm being honest." She hesitates, choosing her words carefully. "You're angry at Elijah and Caleb for the same reason. Different girls. But the emotion is the same. It's not about Paris. It's about Moyra."

I stare at the fireplace because my eyes feel too bright. The wine makes the truth sting worse, stripping away my defenses.

"You should be mad for Paris. But it feels like you're also mad at Caleb for yourself. As if he's wronged you."

"He dragged me out of a bar," I protest, but my voice sounds softer than I want.

"What were you doing at the bar?"

"Dancing."

"With whom?"

I suck in a breath. "Look, that doesn't matter."

"It does matter," she says gently but firmly. "His bind was grinding on a stranger to make her ex jealous. Kali, that matters. Especially now."

I close my eyes as she gives me one of Mom's looks. The kind that sees right through me.

"There are a lot of politics in packs," she continues, her voice steady. "And you're in the center of it now. There are wolves after you. And whatever has happened, you can't be reckless. You need to think about yourself first."

She squeezes my hand.

"Caleb has to think about everyone else. You only have to think about you. But you've also put a target on him. Not just from other packs." She pauses. "From essentially everyone."

The words settle in my chest. The wine cushions them, but it does nothing to dull their weight.

It might be the alcohol, but suddenly, everything feels too big. Too tangled and true.

"That isn't my fault. I didn't make or sign the stupid contract," I mutter, hugging my arms around myself. The wine softens my voice, but the frustration underneath stays sharp.

Krystal tilts her head. "Did he?" she asks gently. "All I'm saying is try to look at this from a different angle. You might see something you didn't expect."

My eyes drift to the fireplace. The logs crackle softly, flames twisting in bright ribbons. The room glows with heat, but I don't feel any of it. My skin stays cold, like the warmth stops three feet in front of me and refuses to reach.

For a moment, I wish I could let the fire swallow everything weighing inside my chest.

Krystal sets her book aside and pulls me into a hug, slow and careful. "It's okay to feel overwhelmed," she murmurs. "You've been through a lot. But you're strong, Kali. Stronger than you realize."

The words hit too close. The tears I've been swallowing start to spill. I press my face into her shoulder, the wine lowering whatever walls I usually keep in place.

"It's just…everything," I whisper. "Caleb. Eli. The pack. I feel like things are slipping out of my hands. I feel like I'm losing control."

I pull back and wipe beneath my eyes, noticing how the firelight reflects off my damp fingertips. "How do you keep it together?" My voice is tired and unsteady.

Krystal gives a soft smile. "I don't keep it together all the time. But I focus on what I can control and try to let go of what I can't. And I lean on the people who care about me."

I nod, the motion heavy from the buzz still clouding my head. "Thanks. I needed that."

"Anytime, little sister." She squeezes my hand. "You're not alone in this."

I push to my feet, swaying a little before I steady. The house feels too quiet, the warmth of the fire still not reaching me.

I start toward the stairs when Krystal calls after me.

"Oh, and Kali?"

I pause, my hand on the railing.

"Caleb isn't sleeping with Moyra."

My heart thuds once, hard.

She continues lightly, but the meaning underneath is unmistakable. "Maybe you're not the only one trying to make someone jealous."

I turn my head enough to catch the small smirk on her lips.

For the first time that night, the fire flickers against my skin in a way I can feel.

The next morning, a text pops up on my phone.

ALLIE

Meet me at the den.

I groan into my pillow. My head feels like it's packed with cotton and static. Those glasses of wine were a terrible idea, and my body is making sure I fully understand that.

Still, I drag myself up and throw on training clothes.

Dad suggested I train with the pack regularly so I can learn how their bodies move, how they fight, how they think. So here I am, hungover and cranky, trudging toward the den like a sacrificial lamb.

The air outside is crisp and painfully bright. Every footstep crunches against fallen leaves. The familiar sounds of the forest bring a small sense of normalcy, even if my stomach rolls every few steps.

When I reach the training grounds, I see Allie already

stretching near the mats, her blonde hair pulled back tightly, her expression focused.

"Hey, Allie," I say, joining her.

"Kali. How are you holding up?" Concern flashes in her eyes.

"I'm managing," I answer, which is a generous interpretation of how I feel.

She gives me a supportive smile. "Good. Ready?"

I nod even though I have no idea what I'm getting myself into.

Allie begins circling me, her steps light and predatory. Her pupils thin slightly, wolf instincts pushing to the surface. "You're thinking too much, Kali," she says with a smirk. "In a fight, hesitation will kill you. Werewolves are instinct. You hesitate, you lose."

Before I can respond, she lunges, her claws aimed directly for my shoulder.

I duck just in time, her swipe slicing the air above my head. I drop low and spring backward, the motion jarring my skull. I force myself to keep moving, but another wolf is already closing in behind me, hemming me in.

"Move, Kali," Allie snaps, her voice sharp enough to cut through the haze. "React. Don't think. Feel. Trust your senses, not your eyes."

Frustration bubbles up, hot and dizzying. My hangover throbs behind my right eye. I squeeze my eyes shut for a single heartbeat and steady my breathing.

When I open my eyes again, I stop looking at where Allie is and focus on where she will be. My senses widen, letting in more than sight. The sharp tang of sweat. The shift of air as someone pivots. The faint vibration of a foot hitting the dirt.

Allie is fast, but this time, I feel her coming. The air shifts, subtle but definite, a coiling pressure that telegraphs her next move. I roll to the side an instant before she pounces, her claws slicing through the space I held a moment ago.

A spark of adrenaline flares through me, but there's no time to savor it.

Another werewolf charges from the left. I spin, drop into a crouch, and sweep my leg out. My heel connects, knocking them off balance. They stumble, surprised, and I push to my feet, repositioning before the next strike.

Allie chuckles lowly. "Not bad. But you're still moving like a human."

The words sting, sharper because she isn't wrong. The wolves circle around me, their low growls vibrating the ground beneath my feet. My nerves jump, but I dig my nails into my palms, grounding myself. If I want to survive, I have to stop hesitating.

I need to move like one of them.

Another shift of air behind me. A heavier weight. A fast approach.

I pivot cleanly this time. No fear. No thinking. Only instinct.

The wolf barrels toward me, and instead of flinching or retreating, I step into the attack, redirecting their momentum with a twist of my hips. It feels fluid. Natural. My body moves faster than my thoughts.

For a heartbeat, everything inside me aligns.

Allie huffs a breath. "Good. Now keep up."

She moves faster, claws flashing, footwork tightening. Feints blend into strikes, her pace doubling until the world blurs at the edges. My muscles scream in protest. Sweat drips down my spine. My head throbs viciously, the last remnants of wine pounding behind my eye.

I adapt. I react. I stop trying to predict and start trusting that my body already knows where to go. I weave through their rhythm, letting instinct carry me where logic is too slow.

By the time Allie calls a halt, my body aches in a hundred

places. My breaths come in ragged pulls, and my skin feels too hot.

When I look up, the wolves around me are watching with something I've not seen from them before.

Respect.

Allie wipes sweat from her brow, a grin tugging at her mouth. "You're getting there. Fast."

A fierce sense of accomplishment rises in my chest, cutting through the headache and the bruises and the exhaustion. I may not have their strength or their speed yet, but I'm learning how to move with them.

Throughout training, I can't ignore Moyra's constant hovering around Caleb. Every time I look over, she's brushing against him, her hand drifting to his arm, her laugh too bright and deliberate. Her eyes never leave him, and every touch lingers a little longer than it should. Caleb doesn't exactly encourage her, but he doesn't push her away either. His attention keeps flicking toward me when he thinks I'm not looking, which only makes everything worse.

Heat coils in my chest. Jealousy, sharp and humiliating. I try to swallow it, but it sticks.

Allie steps close during a water break, lowering her voice. "Don't let her get to you. She's doing it on purpose."

I grit my teeth. "I know. It's just pissing me off."

"Good. Use it. But don't let her control you."

I nod, though the anger still simmers beneath my ribs. Moyra laughs loudly at something Caleb says, leaning into him again, and my jaw tightens. I swear she looks at me over his shoulder, checking to see if I noticed.

Allie squeezes my shoulder.

By the time training is over, my muscles ache, and my patience is frayed. Sweat drips into my eyes. My head throbs. But the worst ache is the fury curling in my chest every time I remember Moyra's hand on Caleb.

He's walking toward me.

"Kali," he says quietly. "Can we talk?"

I glance at Allie, who gives an encouraging nod. Fine.

"Sure."

We walk a few steps away from the others, stopping under the trees. Caleb looks tense, shoulders stiff, expression guarded. I can still see Moyra in my peripheral vision, pretending not to stare at us.

That fuels the anger all over again.

Caleb draws in a long breath. "I'm sorry about last night." His voice holds a thread of regret. "I shouldn't have dragged you out like that."

"And?" I ask, lifting a brow. He owes me more than that.

He hesitates. "There's a lot going on. More than you know. I know it's overwhelming, but we need to stick together."

I scoff lightly. "Like you stick with Moyra?"

His jaw twitches. The storm under his expression cracks for a second, revealing frustration and something else I can't place. "That isn't what this is."

"Really? Because she seems pretty comfortable hanging all over you."

He looks away for a second, exhaling hard. "Kali, I'm trying to talk to you."

I fold my arms. "Then talk."

He steps closer. "I mean it. Things are getting worse. We can't afford to be divided."

The words settle, though they don't erase the image of Moyra clinging to him all morning. I inhale slowly. "Thanks for the apology," I say at last. "And for the ride."

A small smile tugs at his mouth. "Anytime."

As we walk back toward the others, I catch Moyra watching us. Her glare slides from Caleb to me with clear irritation.

Good. She can be annoyed too.

For the first time since training began, determination replaces the jealousy twisting in my chest. I may not be a wolf, but I'm not rolling over for her or anyone else.

Later that evening, my phone buzzes with a message from an unknown number. When I open it, my stomach drops. It's a picture of Elijah at TKS with the same girl tucked under his arm. They look comfortable. Too comfortable. A second message arrives, then another picture, closer than the first. Questions slam into me. Who is she? Why is someone sending me these? Why now?

This isn't the Eli I know. Maybe I never really knew the version of him who's not orbiting me, or chasing me, or obsessing over whatever twisted dynamic sits between us.

Either way, I know one thing with absolute certainty: The stakes are getting higher by the hour, and the danger circling me is becoming impossible to ignore. I can't afford to drop my guard. Not now. Not ever.

Fourteen

The next day, I arrive at the den early for training, still replaying that photo of Elijah in my mind, though I'm trying to shove it aside. The moment I walk into the clearing, my stomach tightens. Moyra is already paired with Caleb for warm-ups, her hands on him far more than the drill requires. She adjusts his stance, ignoring that he doesn't need the help, trailing her fingers along his spine as she corrects his posture. When they switch to partner drills, she circles him like she owns the place, showing him "techniques" that somehow always involve touching his chest or guiding his arm longer than necessary. Every move comes with a flirty smile, a soft laugh, or her brushing her body too close to his.

Caleb doesn't flirt back. He keeps his expression tight and focused. He doesn't move away either, which is enough to make something hot and unpleasant flare in my chest. My jaw aches from clenching it. Krystal is right. I need to figure out whatever this is between Caleb and me. If I don't, Moyra is going to make me lose my mind.

Caleb works with more force than usual, almost aggressively in the way he executes each move. His brow is furrowed, his jaw locked, and I can't tell if he's angry, distracted, or pretending not to notice Moyra's hands lingering on him. A part of me wonders if he knows about Elijah. Another part wonders if it bothers him that I care. I hate that I wonder at all.

During a break, Allie slides up beside me. "You look like you're about to snap someone in half," she murmurs.

I sigh and push a strand of hair from my face. "Just a lot going on."

"Want to talk about it?"

"Maybe later," I mutter, my eyes flicking toward Caleb and Moyra. She stands behind him now, helping him stretch as if her hands belong on his shoulders. "I just need to get through training without punching her in the throat."

Allie snorts. "Understandable."

When training finally wraps up, Caleb calls everyone into a circle. Moyra stays close to him, hovering like his shadow. Caleb begins outlining plans for the next few days: searches along the edges of pack land, daily check-ins, headcounts, and everyone moving in pairs. Moyra glances at me over Caleb's shoulder with a smug expression, as if she's won something.

Caleb's gaze sweeps over the group, landing on me a moment longer than it should. "Remember, we're a team," he says. "We need to trust each other. There's no room for distractions."

The word 'distractions' hits hard, and I swallow back the heat rising in my chest. Something is going on here. Something bigger than Elijah's photo and Moyra's theatrics. Something Caleb isn't saying.

As the meeting breaks up, I walk toward Allie. She gives me a steady, reassuring look, the kind that makes it clear she sees everything I'm trying to hide. The tension in the air is thick enough to choke on, and I can feel the stakes rising again. Whatever is coming, whatever puzzle piece I'm still missing, it's close.

Too close.

"What's that about?" I ask as casually as I can, trying not to let the tension in my chest show.

Allie's expression softens with something like worry. "Well, with all the teenagers going missing from the neighboring towns, the severed wolf tail we found, the attack on Lucas's sister, and the fact that none of us have seen any of the Omegas lately, Caleb is being protective." She hesitates, her gaze flicking to the ground. "And..."

"And?" I prompt, wanting the truth, even if I'm not sure I'll like it.

She lets out a slow, reluctant breath. "And with you being here, things are different. You're a Siren. It's not only wolves that might come after you. There are other things out there. Things older than the packs or hunters. We all have to be more mindful of protection now."

Her eyes lift to meet mine, full of quiet loyalty. She doesn't say it, but I can feel the weight of what she's not voicing. The pack is at risk simply because they choose to stand beside me.

The next morning comes too quickly, but I'm grateful for the change of scenery. Today marks the first official day of my summer shadowing at the hospital. Despite everything happening in my life, the familiar smell of antiseptic and the steady hum of fluorescent lights are strangely comforting. After days filled with pack drama, training, and emotional chaos, stepping into the hospital feels like crossing into a different world. Here, things make sense. Here, there are rules and routines and problems I can actually solve.

I fall into step beside Dr. Evans as he leads me through the halls, reviewing charts and explaining the cases for the day. The rhythmic beeping of machines and soft murmurs of nurses moving between rooms calms something raw inside me. For the first time in days, my heartbeat begins to match the hospital's steady rhythm instead of the frantic pace of pack politics and personal turmoil.

We start our rounds, and I take notes while Dr. Evans examines an elderly woman with his usual calm, reassuring tone. I watch closely, absorbing every detail. I've only been shadowing for a few weeks, but I already feel more at home here than anywhere else. The hospital gives me something I desperately need: focus.

As we finish up with the patient, movement in the hallway catches my attention. Two men linger outside the room. They're dressed in casual clothes, but something about them is off. Their presence carries a quiet menace that immediately puts me on edge.

Dr. Evans heads to the next room, but the unease twisting in my stomach refuses to let go. I step out into the hall, forcing my voice to remain steady. "Can I help you?"

The taller man smirks, eyes sharp with something that isn't friendly. "Kali, right?"

My pulse spikes. "Yes. Who are you?"

The shorter one leans in slightly, tone casual but gaze cold enough to make my skin crawl. "We're Caleb's cousins. Sort of. And we've been meaning to have a little chat with you."

"What do you want?" Every instinct tells me the answer is nothing good.

The taller man invades my space so aggressively that the fluorescent lights catch on the edge of his smile. "You need to find a way to break the bind between you and Caleb."

The words hit me like a slap. I frown, confusion mixing with a creeping sense of dread. "Why would I do that?"

Instead of answering, the shorter cousin pulls out his phone and scrolls through several images. He holds the screen up to my face. My breath catches in my throat. Knox. My little brother. In one photo, he's laughing at soccer practice. In another, he's leaving the house with his backpack slung over his shoulder. The last picture turns my blood to ice: Knox walking alone down a dim street, shadows stretching behind him, completely unaware he's being followed.

"If you don't," the taller cousin says, his voice low and thick with malice, "your brother here may not have a happy ending."

My heart slams against my ribs. Panic surges through me like a rising tide, but anger hits harder, spiking through my veins until my hands tremble. "You wouldn't dare."

As if the sky itself responds, a low rumble of thunder rolls outside, deep and distant, shaking the windowpanes. The sound vibrates through the floor tiles, mirroring the pressure building inside me.

The shorter cousin leans in close, his breath cold against my cheek, his expression deadly serious. "Try us. We don't mind getting our hands dirty. Caleb's been making choices that weaken the family. Sometimes consequences need a reminder." His eyes glint as he studies me. "You're the perfect leverage."

My mind races, clawing for a way out. "I can't break the bind," I say sharply. "It's not something you undo. It's unbreakable."

The taller cousin gives a small shrug, amused by my panic. "Figure it out. You have one week."

Another growl of thunder echoes above us, louder this time, as if punctuating the threat with a warning of its own.

I glare at them, fighting to keep my voice steady despite the storm boiling inside me. These men aren't just pack troublemakers. Caleb has warned me about what his cousins are capable of. Their bloodline gives them status, but their hunger for power makes them reckless. They thrive on chaos and intimidation, pushing boundaries because fear is the only language they respect.

Now they're using my brother to get to me.

Before I can respond, the cousins turn and walk away, leaving me frozen in the hallway, shaken and furious and terrified all at once. The threat hangs in the air long after their footsteps fade. Knox's face flashes through my mind, and a sickening weight settles in my chest. I need to protect him. No matter what. The responsibility presses on me so heavily that for a moment, it's hard to breathe, and I understand something I've never truly grasped before. This is what Caleb feels. Every day. For everyone. The pressure of being responsible for lives that don't belong to him but depend on him anyway.

I draw in a slow breath, trying to steady the chaos twisting inside me. I won't let those thugs hurt my brother. I won't let them hurt anyone close to me. As I make my way back toward Dr. Evans, something fierce settles inside me, threading through my veins like steel. I'll find a way to keep Knox safe.

Later, after my shift ends, I try pushing the encounter from my mind, but the fear keeps crawling back. I head to the only place where I might find answers. The sleek, modern library inside the Werewolves' den is quieter than usual when I slip inside, and the contrast hits me immediately. The tension from earlier clings to my skin, but the library feels like a sanctuary carved out of stone and silence. Shelves stretch high along the walls, filled with old texts, pack records, and histories that trace bloodlines back centuries.

I stand in the center of the room for a moment, taking it in. Wraithstone's archives are far more extensive, but this place still holds secrets. Maybe something here can tell me more about Caleb's family. Maybe I can find something to use against the men who cornered me at the hospital. Something to protect Knox. Maybe even something about the bind they think I can break.

The library exudes an aura of sophistication and intellect, seamlessly blending contemporary design with elements of the mystical and ancient. As I step into the expansive space, I'm immediately struck by the juxtaposition of clean lines and organic textures. The walls, adorned with rich, dark wood paneling, rise to meet a vaulted ceiling intricately carved with Celtic-like knots and runic symbols, hinting at the library's connection to the Supernatural world.

Floor-to-ceiling windows bathe the room in natural light during the day, offering sweeping views of the surrounding wilderness. After dusk, strategically placed sconces illuminate the space with a warm, inviting glow. Rows of sleek, minimalist bookshelves line the walls, their polished surfaces displaying a vast collection of tomes and scrolls spanning centuries of Werewolf lore, arcane knowledge, and literary classics.

In the center of the room, a reading area beckons with plush leather armchairs and chaise lounges. A low-slung coffee table, crafted from polished marble and adorned with intricate etchings, provides a convenient surface for books, tablets, and other reading materials. The air is filled with the captivating blend of natural and earthy aromas, aged parchment, leather-bound books, and a touch of lavender, sage, and cedarwood.

I take a deep breath, letting the scents wash over me as I observe, who I guess is, the librarian, moving gracefully among the towering shelves. Luna, tall and imposing with an air of quiet confidence, has more silver streaks than black in her hair, which is swept back in a neat bun. Her piercing blue eyes miss nothing as she surveys the room, though her warmth and gentleness belie her formidable presence. I've seen her in the pack meetings before.

"Welcome to our library. I'm Luna. How may I assist you today?" She greets me with a warm smile, her tone friendly and inviting, reminding me of another librarian for Supernatural books.

"Just looking for now," I reply, matching her smile with one of my own. "Would you happen to have something on mystical contracts? Also, Lycan bloodlines?"

Light filters through stained glass windows, casting ethereal patterns on the polished marble floor. The shelves, lined with leather-bound volumes and scrolls of forgotten lore, seem to beckon me forward.

Despite my earlier fears, I can't shake the feeling that Caleb, burdened with the weight of our shared destiny, might have concealed the key to our liberation within these sacred confines. As my fingers brush against the weathered spines of ancient tomes, they come to rest upon a set of old, dusty volumes bearing the title *Contracts of Nature*. My heart quickens with anticipation. Could this be the key? Is this what Fernir alluded to, the elusive answer to our plight?

Before I can ponder further, a voice, both gentle and firm, breaks through the silence of the library. "Seeking answers, are we?" I turn to find Luna standing before me. Her eyes gleaming with wisdom born of centuries spent safeguarding the secrets of the pack.

"Yes," I reply, meeting her gaze with determination. "I'm trying to figure out this bind thing," I say, hoping I'm selling that I just want knowledge.

Luna nods, her expression thoughtful.

With her guidance, I delve deeper into the repository of knowledge, scouring ancient texts and forgotten manuscripts for any clue that might lead us to salvation. Each volume I peruse, each inscription I decipher, brings me no closer to the truth.

As I survey the array of ancient tomes spread across the table, titles such as: *Binding Spells and Pacts*, *Covenants with Otherworldly Entities*, *Laws of the Shifting World*, and *Forbidden Knowledge* seem to whisper promises of hidden knowledge and arcane secrets. With a mixture of hope and trepidation, I reach for the first volume, *Binding Spells and Pacts*, hoping it might offer some clue or loophole in our Supernatural entanglement.

As I delve into the pages, a sudden thud on the table startles me. Looking up, I meet Caleb's enigmatic gaze, his presence a silent interruption to my solitary quest for answers. His casual attire, a plain T-shirt and dress slacks, exhibits the effortless authority.

"Light reading?" he inquires, his tone betraying a hint of amusement as he surveys the scholarly disarray before him.

"Something like that." My focus returns to the book in my hands, though his unexpected appearance leaves my thoughts in disarray.

"Being bonded to me is that bad, huh?" His voice, tinged with curiosity and something deeper, draws my attention once more.

"Isn't it for you?" I counter, meeting his gaze with a blend of defiance and vulnerability.

"You won't find anything in there," he remarks cryptically, his words casting doubt on the efficacy of my search.

"You already checked?" A pang of disappointment tugs at my heart. I'm unsure if it stems from the fruitlessness of my efforts or the possibility that he already sought release from our bond.

"Not recently." He evades my gaze. "But knowledge of such matters was ingrained in me from childhood. As an Alpha, understanding the laws of nature is essential."

"Was that a segue to proclaim yourself a great leader?" I quip, a faint smile playing at the corners of my lips.

"Oh, I excel in all things," he retorts with a wink, his charm momentarily disarming me.

"Didn't you just lose your pre-season game, Captain?" I tease, a playful challenge in my tone.

"A great leader knows when to conceal their true strength," he counters, his response veiled in layers of unspoken meaning.

"Did you need something, other than to brag?" I sense a shift in the conversation as Luna approaches, her presence commanding attention with an aura of quiet wisdom and authority.

"I need more information on Omegas," Caleb reveals, his request laden with implications that pique my curiosity.

"Why?" My eyebrows draw together.

"Omegas are elusive by nature," Luna explains, her voice resonating with the weight of centuries of knowledge. "Securing information on them won't be easy, but I can endeavor to seek out alternative sources."

"Why not speak to one directly?" I interject, a spark of realization igniting within me. This could be my chance to get more information.

"They prefer to remain unbound by pack affiliations," Luna clarifies, her words shedding light on the intricacies of Omega dynamics.

"Today might be your lucky day," I chime in, excitement bubbling within me as I reveal a potential lead. "I happen to know an Omega."

"How?" Luna asks.

"A trip then?" Caleb proposes, his smirk hinting at the adventure that lies ahead. I cock an eyebrow with a smirk of my own playing on my lips. This probably won't help the bind problem or the problem I have with Caleb's cousins, but it could give us a leg up on the Omega. I might run into Quinn, and maybe he'll tell me what he and my dad were silently arguing about or give me a hint at least. "Are you guys busy tomorrow?" he asks.

I wake up with the threat of Caleb's cousins' voices still echoing in my head, sitting heavy in my chest. One week. That was yesterday, which means I only have six days left to figure out the impossible. Six days to protect Knox.

My footsteps echo alongside Caleb's and Luna's as we walk across the marble floor of the Wraithstone library, the sun dancing across the tiles and creating a kaleidoscope of colors through the stained glass windows.

Caleb glances at me, his brows drawn together with mild concern. "This librarian of yours. Fenrir. He's not exactly... conventional, is he?"

I smirk. "You'll see. He grows on you. Or he doesn't."

Towering shelves stretch to a ceiling so high it vanishes into darkness. The air smells of old parchment, binding glue, wax, and secrets.

"Fenrir!" I greet him when we reach the desk.

The figure turns at the sound of my voice. Luna stiffens beside me, like she's bracing herself. I catch the subtle shift in her posture.

Fenrir steps into view, tall and lean, his silver hair tied loosely back. His face is sharp and elegant in a way that makes him look both ageless and impossibly old. His pale gray eyes sweep over us, seeing far too much with a single glance.

"Kali," he greets, his voice smooth and quiet, like a blade sliding from its sheath. His gaze moves to Caleb, weighing him without a word, then shifts to Luna. Something passes between them quickly. Familiarity. History. Maybe even a hint of unresolved tension.

"Luna," he says, inclining his head. "Back again."

Luna crosses her arms. "I didn't exactly have a choice in the assignment."

"That's usually how fate works," Fenrir replies with a faint smile. "It drags us to the places we least want to revisit."

Caleb looks between them, clearly sensing something deeper but not sure what to make of it. I file that away for later.

Fenrir steps closer, the dim light catching in his pale eyes. "The three of you didn't come all this way for pleasure reading. What is it you need from me this time?"

"We-re…" I want to steer us away from whatever history is simmering between them.

Caleb clears his throat, interrupting me. "I think some of it might be better suited for Luna and Fenrir to discuss directly." His tone is careful, but the way he glances at me isn't. It's questioning. Suspicious. Like he's trying to connect dots he's never been allowed to see.

I lift an eyebrow at him, silently asking what exactly he thinks they need to talk about that we can't hear. He doesn't offer an answer, only presses his lips into a thin line. I can practically feel the questions burning under his skin.

Luna and Fenrir exchange a look, quiet, familiar, and layered with old understanding, confirming everything Caleb is afraid to ask outright. They have history. They have answers. And whatever those answers are, they don't want to share them with us just yet.

To break the tension, I say, "Caleb and I can go to the dining hall while you two talk." I offer Luna a reassuring nod, letting her know she's safe to speak freely.

She gives me a faint smile, her shoulders loosening. "Thank you, Kali."

Fenrir inclines his head in approval. His gaze lingers on me for a heartbeat longer than expected, like he's evaluating me, almost protective, before he turns and guides Luna toward a secluded corner of the library. Their voices drop to a murmur, swallowed by the endless rows of books as Caleb and I slip out through the heavy doors.

We walk in silence for a while, our footsteps echoing through the winding stone corridors. The oppressive quiet of the library fades behind us, but a different tension settles between us now. Thick, unspoken, and too heavy to ignore.

"Hey, there they are," I say, nodding toward the table where Qora, Zori, Duke, and Noah are gathered. The four of them sit like an oddly mismatched but surprisingly functional family, plates scattered in front of them, the easy murmur of conversation drifting through the mess hall.

Caleb follows my gaze, and I see a flicker of something shift in his expression. Curiosity first. Then caution. Then mild concern when his eyes land on Duke, who looks like the kind of guy who could break a wall just by leaning on it.

"They," Caleb repeats slowly. "Are they all friendly?"

"Friendly enough," I reply with a shrug, keeping my voice light. "Just…different."

As we approach, Qora looks up, her posture straightening with the kind of confidence only she can pull off. There's warmth in her smile, but I can still see the tension in her shoulders, the way her eyes flick over Caleb with quick, assessing precision. Zori sits beside her, quieter and softer, her gentle smile easing some of the tightness in my chest.

"Hey, Kali," Zori greets, her voice instantly brightening the table's energy. "Who's your friend?"

"This is Caleb." I gesture toward him. "He's a newbie."

Caleb offers a polite smile and extends his hand to Zori. "Nice to meet you."

He barely gets the words out before Duke, sitting across from them, leans forward, his eyes narrowing. His jaw tightens as he locks onto Caleb like he's analyzing every potential threat he could pose.

"New doesn't mean trustworthy," Duke mutters, crossing his arms over his massive chest.

The tension around the table tightens instantly, sharp enough to cut. I can feel Caleb stiffen beside me, the shift of his breathing, the subtle tensing in his shoulders. His polite expression falters for a heartbeat before he forces it back into place.

Qora and Noah exchange a look, both of them wearing the same wary expression, though Noah tries to hide it behind his usual laid-back shrug. "Everyone is new at some point, right?" He attempts to keep the mood light, but the flicker of apprehension in his eyes tells a different story. They're assessing Caleb, measuring him against standards he doesn't know exist.

Zori is the only one who seems genuinely warm. Her smile is soft, steady and disarming in the way only she can manage. "It's nice to meet you, Caleb. I hope you're finding the place okay."

Caleb inclines his head, some of the tension in his shoulders easing. "Thanks. I am."

Duke rolls his eyes at the exchange, but at least he doesn't add another jab. The air still feels thick, heavy with unspoken judgments, as the group settles into a loose semi-circle. Conversation bumps awkwardly from one topic to another, never quite finding a rhythm.

Zori breaks the silence with a burst of enthusiasm. "Have any of you been to the new lounge near Rysen yet? It's supposed to be great for hanging out and meeting new people."

My brow lifts, curiosity nudging aside some of the tension. "Not yet. What's it like?"

Zori leans forward, eyes bright. "It's cozy, really atmospheric. Live music on weekends. And I heard the drinks are incredible. I think we should go. It would be good to relax."

The idea sparks a flicker of interest in my chest. I glance at Caleb, wondering if he's up for it. His mouth tugs into the beginning of a smile, small but real.

"Sounds good to me," he says, sounding more confident than before.

"Great." Zori beams. "Let's head over tonight."

The lounge is a short drive from the campus and pulses with life as we enter. Qora wears a striking leather dress, which hugs her figure. Noah looks polished in chinos and a button-down, sleeves rolled up to reveal toned forearms. Zori wears a flowy, black skirt paired with a crocheted bralette.

Thankfully, we're about the same size, and I sifted through her closet, pulling together flared jeans and a crop top that felt comfortable enough to wear but still reflected my style.

Duke, by far, looks the most out of place in his three-piece suit. I stifle a giggle at his outfit as he hands me the dirty martini he'd ordered me, since I didn't know if they would card. It settles warmly in my stomach when I take a sip. As we step further into the lounge, I notice the atmosphere shift. The thumping music and swirling lights fill me with a mix of excitement and nerves.

I'm surprised by how different this is from The Kill Spot, even though it's only about thirty minutes away.

"Something funny?" Duke leans over, whispering in my ear.

"I just think we must be a sight to behold." I laugh, though my heart is still heavy from earlier.

"We're all dressed for what seems to be different occasions," I add, unable to shake the feeling that something is off.

"It's Duke," Zori chimes in from my other side. I raise my eyebrows, surprised.

"On the grounds of the various campuses, Supernatural powers aren't allowed to be used unless we're training, so we can't influence our fellow students negatively," she explains, making it sound all too casual. "So he's just stretching his muscles, so to speak."

"His muscles?" I echo, incredulous, a hint of laughter escaping me.

"Yeah, I could make you feel things you've only dreamed of," he whispers, his breath warm against my ear. My heart races at the unexpected tension that dances in the air, especially considering Caleb being here. He opted to stay in what he wore earlier.

I freeze at his brazenness. The last time I was here, he looked like he wanted nothing to do with me. I reach up and playfully shove his head away. Looking at Caleb, I see his lips thin and wonder if he heard what Duke said over the thumping base.

"You've probably already been influenced, you just don't know it." Duke wiggles his eyebrows at me.

"Zori," I say, trying to steer the conversation back, "what do you mean by campuses?" She looks confused.

"Earlier, you said campuses. You meant on campus, right? At Wraithstone?" I'm genuinely curious.

"Nope. There are five schools for Supernaturals, which focus on cultivating different abilities. My sister is the dean at one, and Noah's brother is the dean at another. Well, really, there are four schools now after one shut down a long time ago," she continues, swaying to the beat.

Other schools? I hadn't even known this one existed. Now I have more questions swirling in my mind: What do they teach? Where are they? Why did one shut down?

"You can ask your questions later. Let's dance," Qora urges, pulling me up from my seat and leading me to the dance floor.

As I dance, I let the music wash over me as each beat loosens the knots that have been tightening in my chest for days. For a little while, everything else fades. Zori moves with fluid grace, her smile gentle and bright. Noah dances like he's made of pure chaos, limbs everywhere, laughter spilling out of him. Qora sways beside me and then spins behind me, grinding playfully against my back until I burst into laughter. Even Duke surprises me, stepping close and taking my hands, guiding me through a formal, almost old-fashioned, dance that leaves me feeling light and breathless.

For the first time in ages, I feel free. Untangled. Alive.

Caleb joins me for a moment, his eyes warm, his movements easy. He smiles, and something in my chest stirs, but I push it away and let myself enjoy the moment.

It takes me a minute to notice a group of guys edging closer to our circle. Their movements are too stiff, their eyes lingering too long. They give off a bad vibe, like they're waiting for something. Watching us. Watching me. But I'm having too much fun to care, so I force myself to ignore the creeping unease.

A sudden commotion shatters the rhythm. Shouting erupts near our table. We rush over, and I freeze as I see a thin, pinched-faced kid upend a drink all over Zori. The liquid splashes across her shirt, dripping down her arms. She stands stunned, silent, hurt blooming on her face like someone slapped her.

My heart drops, then spikes. A surge of protectiveness hits me so fast my vision blurs.

I grab a napkin and step in front of Zori, gently wiping the drink from her cheeks, my fingers soft against her skin. I lean down and press a kiss to her forehead, a quiet promise that she's not alone.

Behind me, the jerk snickers.

I turn slowly, pinning him with a stare so sharp it could cut glass. "Something funny?" My voice is quiet, low, and ice-cold.

At this point, I don't care what started it. I don't care what excuse he thinks he has. Zori could have poured the drink on herself, and I still wouldn't tolerate him humiliating her.

Anger pulses through me, hot and heavy. The bass from the speakers thuds through my chest, syncing with the pounding of my heart. The room seems to tilt. Edges blur.

Before I can stop it, I start seeing red.

He opens his mouth to respond, but I'm already moving. I drive my knee into his groin, folding him instantly, but before he can hit the floor, I kick up, the heel of my boot connecting with his face. The crack is sickening. His nose shatters, blood spraying across the table and down his shirt as he crumples.

I snatch the half-bottle of Jack Daniel's that Duke had been nursing, take a burning swig, then pour the rest over the pathetic lowlife writhing at my feet. The whiskey splashes across his ruined nose and soaked shirt. Now he's the one humiliated.

"It was a rhetorical question, dick," I say, crouching over him. His eyes are wide, full of pain and panic, and his friends are frozen behind him, unsure whether to run or try something stupid. Three of my people tower behind me, and I know the sight of them is enough to keep the cowards still.

"Time to go," Noah urges, spotting club security pushing through the crowd.

We all bolt for the exit and sprint two blocks back to where we parked, breathless with adrenaline.

The moment we reach the cars, the tension shatters. I bend forward, laughter bursting out of me uncontrollably. I feel light, wild, alive in a way I've not felt in years.

"You're a fucking beast," Noah crows, catching me around the waist and lifting me off my feet. He spins me once, and I laugh helplessly, giddy from the liquor, the rush, and the pure freedom of the moment.

But the joy dies in an instant.

A sharp pop echoes down the street. Noah's body jerks violently in front of me, his breath catching in a strangled sound. I blink, stunned, before I see it: the jerk's friend standing several yards away, a gun shaking in his hands, pointed directly at Noah's back.

Rage floods me so quickly it feels like my blood boils. The red haze surges stronger than ever, swallowing my vision, drowning out every other sound. My power rises, raw and instinctive, reacting before I can think.

No one even has time to scream before I lift my hand toward the shooter, willing the blood in his body to answer me.

And it does.

Blood begins to stream down his face, first from the corners of his eyes, then from his nose and mouth. It pours thick and dark, like someone wringing a soaked rag. His hands claw at his throat as if that will stop it, but nothing slows the flow. Panic twists his features, his body trembling violently. Only when he collapses to his knees do I feel a hand clamp gently around mine, something cold slithering invisibly across my entire body.

Duke.

The contact snaps me out of the trance so abruptly that my breath shakes. My fingers uncurl, and the invisible pull on the man's blood breaks. He slumps forward in a silent heap.

"Get them back," Duke orders, his voice steady and calm in a way that tells me he's done this before. He jerks his chin at Zori and Qora, who move instantly. "We'll clean this up," he adds, gesturing between himself and Caleb.

My stomach flips at the realization that Caleb saw everything. He saw what he's attached to forever.

Qora pulls out her keys before anyone argues and drives us back toward campus with Zori in the passenger seat, her knuckles white around the handle above the door. Noah lies stretched across the back seat, his head resting in my lap. I brush his wavy hair away from his forehead, checking him for injuries even though he keeps insisting he's fine.

"No one has ever killed someone for me before," Noah murmurs, voice low and astonished.

A lazy smile tugs at his lips. "You're vicious. I like it."

I let out a soft breath, half laugh, half disbelief. "Yeah, well, let's hope you're never on the receiving end of it." I lean my head against the seat. A small smile tugs at the corner of my mouth, but inside, my thoughts spiral. The weight of what I did presses down on me, heavy and cold, humming with power.

Exhaustion tugs at my eyelids. I try to fight it, but by the time we reach the school gates, my body gives in. The world blurs. My head lolls back.

Sleep pulls me under fast.

But the dreams that come feel more like drowning than resting.

I see Caleb.

No.

I am Caleb.

Lost in a whirlpool of confusion and desire, his senses fold into mine, and mine into his. The boundaries of our minds blur until I can't tell where I end and he begins. His pulse becomes the rhythm of my dream. His pleasure ripples through me. His pain stings my nerves. The bind twists tighter, wrapping around us in a way that feels both intimate and terrifying.

I sink deeper, unable to wake, caught in a mind that's not entirely my own.

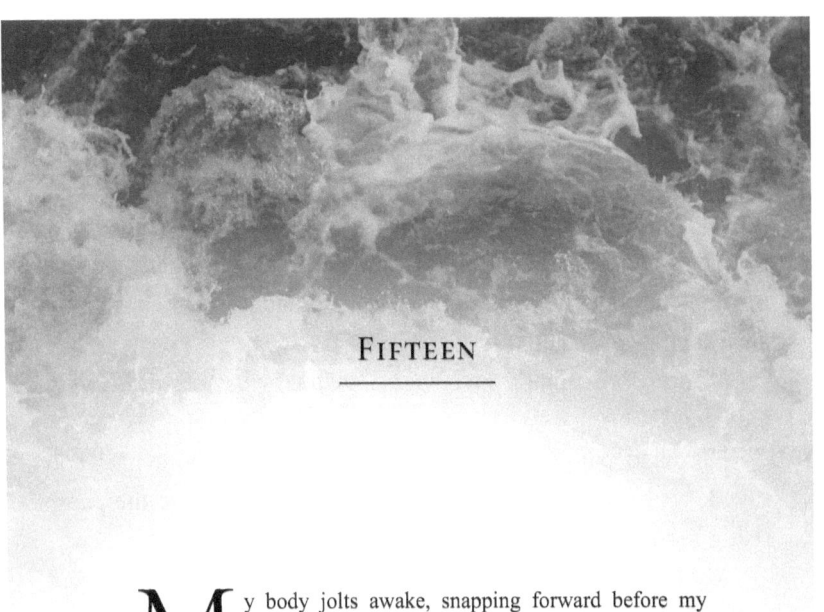

FIFTEEN

My body jolts awake, snapping forward before my mind has time to understand where I am. A sharp breath tears out of me, and for a moment, I expect to see the boho looking walls of Zori's room or the blood that had coated my hands. Instead, I find myself staring at the familiar wood-paneled ceiling of my treehouse. My pulse spikes so fast it hurts. I'm home. Somehow I'm home. The last thing I remember is Noah bleeding out and the man collapsing at my feet. The memory hits me hard, forcing the air from my lungs. I try to sit up, but a sudden wave of dizziness forces me back down.

"Drink this," Caleb says from beside me. His voice is calm but firm, and when he leans into view, his face is set in a serious expression.

"How did I get h—"

"Questions later. Energy first."

My hands tremble as I take the green drink, nearly spilling some, but I manage to get it down despite its bitter taste. My breathing is uneven, and I press a hand to my chest, trying to steady the racing inside. Caleb reaches out and gently brushes my braids away from my face. The kindness almost makes my eyes sting.

"When you're ready," he says quietly, "we have a lot to talk about."

I nod, though the motion feels heavy. Everything crashes down on me at once. Caleb, the strange pull between us, my brother's danger, Noah's blood, and the man who died because of me. The thought coils tight in my stomach until I can barely swallow.

"Caleb," I finally whisper. "After what I did...what happened?"

His hand pauses in my hair for the briefest moment. "You saved Noah," he says with certainty, like he can sense the panic rising in me.

My breath shakes. "I killed him, Caleb. I didn't mean to, but I still did it. I reacted, and then he was just...gone." Shame burns through me, but underneath it, there's a stubborn refusal to fall apart. "I didn't want to kill him."

"It was self-defense. Your instincts took over."

"That's the problem," I mutter, rubbing my forehead. "I feel like I'm walking around with something dangerous inside me, and I don't even know how to control it."

His expression shifts, the warmth fading into something more serious. "You'll learn. All of us had to figure it out. But you need to be careful. That level of exertion clearly has effects."

I force myself to sit up despite the lingering dizziness, determined to meet his eyes.

"You've been out for two days." He sighs, the tension in his shoulders obvious. "We're all trying to figure out our roles in this world, and it's complicated. The pack dynamics, the other Supernaturals, all of it is a balancing act. The bond adds pressure on top of everything. It becomes a minefield."

The silence that follows is thick and uncomfortable. Caleb's gaze drops to the floor, and I can see the conflict twisting through him. "I know I made mistakes," he finally says. "I didn't want to drag you into this mess. I wanted to shield you from the dangers that come with being part of this world."

"Shield me," I repeat with a scoff. "Or shield yourself from the guilt of potentially putting me in danger. I have a right to make my own choices, Caleb. You don't get to decide what's best for me."

He looks up, pain etched across his face. "I know. I just thought if I could handle it, you wouldn't have to."

His vulnerability hits a soft place inside me, and for a moment, I let some of the anger go. "I understand the urge to protect me, but I need to know what I'm facing. If we're going to get through this, we have to be honest."

Caleb nods slowly.

I want to believe him, but another thought rises before I can stop it. My stomach knots with sudden anxiety. "Caleb...what did you tell my parents?"

He blinks, taken off guard. For a moment, I swear guilt flickers across his face before he masks it. "They know you were hurt. I told them you needed time to rest. I didn't tell them anything...else."

That isn't as reassuring as he thinks it is. A dozen worries swirl inside me. What did they ask? What did he avoid saying? Do they know more than he's admitting? The uncertainty makes my pulse spike again, and my mind spirals back to the man I killed. If my parents ever found out what really happened...

Before I can push further, my phone buzzes on the coffee table. The sharp sound cuts through the air, and I grab it quickly, desperate for something else to focus on. A text from an unknown number appears on the screen.

Tick Tock, Tick Tock.

My breath stutters. The words feel like a threat, a clock already counting down.

"What is it," Caleb asks, concern shadowing his voice.

"Nothing." The lie is thin, but I can't make anything else come out. Unease curls low in my stomach, tightening every second. The message isn't random. It's intentional, a constant reminder that someone is watching.

Caleb leans forward, his eyes narrowing. "Kali, you can't keep things from me."

"Oh, you mean the way you've been keeping things from me?" The moment I say it, he stiffens. I expect the tension to push me into another argument, but I'm too exhausted to keep fighting. The weight of everything presses down on my shoulders until I feel like I could collapse.

I sigh and let myself fall back against the cushions.

Caleb looks at me for a long moment, and something fragile passes between us. For now, neither of us speaks. The air feels heavy with everything we have yet to say.

I hesitate, my fingers tightening around the phone. Part of me wants to tell him everything, but another part freezes. If he knows who threatened me, who cornered me, he'll do something reckless. He'll go after them. And if he goes after them, they'll retaliate, and Knox will be the one who pays for it. The thought makes my stomach twist.

"It's just a text," I finally say, forcing the words out as calmly as I can. "Someone trying to intimidate me."

"Who?" he presses. His voice sharpens, and the protective tension in his posture makes my pulse jump.

"I don't know," I lie, frustration creeping in. "But it isn't important right now. We need to focus on what's ahead of us."

Caleb watches me in a way that feels like he's peeling back layers, and I see the storm forming behind his eyes,the red creeping up around the black. "Don't brush this off."

"I know," I say, letting out a long, unsteady breath. "But right now I need a plan. I need to figure out how to deal with the bind and keep Knox safe." It rushes out of my mouth before I can catch it.

His expression hardens instantly. "What do you mean? Keep Knox safe?"

"Caleb...please."

"From whom?" he asks again. His voice is too calm, too controlled, the kind of quiet that comes before something breaks. He isn't used to being kept out of anything, and it shows.

"Kali," he snaps, louder this time, making me flinch.

My shoulders sink as I finally tell him what happened with his extended family—if they even are his actual cousins. The veiled threats. Their expectations. Their interest in me, in the bind, in Knox. As the words leave my lips, I can feel his fury building, thick and electric, layer by layer. When I look up, his eyes are blood red and his leg is shaking like he's fighting the urge to destroy something.

"I'll handle it," he says suddenly, standing to get me a bottle of water.

"How?" My voice is barely steady.

"I said I will handle it."

"He's my brother," I fire back, my irritation rising to match his. "And if you go after them without thinking, he's the one who could get hurt."

That hits him. His shoulders stiffen, and for a moment, he has no answer.

He sighs and sits back down next to me, placing the bottle in my hand, jaw still tight. "If you can break the bind with me, there's a slight possibility you can rebind. At least that's what they're hoping. I was never supposed to exist because my father was never supposed to exist. Theoretically, you could bind to someone else in the bloodline."

My mind flashes back to the dinner. The stares. The questions. The sudden, unsettling interest in me. Everything clicks into place, cold and heavy. I shake my head, trying to push away the dread crawling under my skin.

This is exactly what I feared. Telling him the truth was

necessary, but now the danger feels even closer. Closer to me. Closer to Knox. Closer to all of us.

"We'll find a way. I promise," he reassures me.

"How?" I whisper, understanding the weight of what I've been dragged into. I didn't want to be Caleb's, but I definitely don't want to bind to anyone else in his family.

"Can you trust me?"

"Can I?"

"No one is going to hurt anyone in your family. I promise."

"Don't make promises you can't keep," I say.

"I'll take care of it."

"And who takes care of you?" I don't know why I ask. It seems like a lot for him to have on his plate. I don't want him to have to worry about my family too.

"Position is open," he says, looking at me. I feel my face heat at his gaze and look away.

"I should go to the den. See what I can do." He clears his throat at my rejection. Is it even really a rejection? My head is so foggy. It feels like every time I gain my sense of direction, the world's axis tilts, and I'm as confused as I was in the beginning.

"Okay," I say, my voice steadier now. As we settle into a quiet understanding, the atmosphere shifts. The tension begins to ease, and I can feel a sense of determination building between us.

We walk back to the house on high alert. Every sound feels sharper, every movement at the edge of my vision making my body tense. I feel unmoored, like the ground under me is shifting. I don't know who I can trust, who might try to kidnap or kill me, or what to do with the mess of feelings I have about Caleb. The only concrete information I have from this entire trip is something I already knew: a bond like ours typically can't be broken except by the one who created it in the first place.

My phone buzzes. I glance down, barely paying attention, and see Eli's name.

Eli has been attacked.

The words from Paris's text swim in front of my eyes. For a moment, I don't fully register them, like my brain refuses to accept what I'm reading. Then my heart stops and slams back to life in my chest.

Meet me at the hospital.

My fingers tighten around the phone. I look up and see Caleb staring at his own screen, his expression darkening. I'm sure he's reading the same message. I understand why Paris sent it to me, but something twists inside when I realize she sent it to him too.

I don't think. I move, spinning on my heel and sprinting for my car, my mind racing ahead of me. The hospital is about thirty minutes away. Every second feels like too much time. Panic surges through me in a hot wave. What happened to Eli? He's a wolf, like Caleb, someone I've watched heal from injuries in front of my eyes. What kind of attack puts him in a hospital bed instead of letting his body repair itself on its own?

"Wait," Caleb calls. His hand clamps around my upper arm and yanks me to a stop. "Little Bird." His voice is caught between concern and frustration.

"Let go of me, and stop calling me that," I snap, twisting against his grip. The nickname scrapes against the raw edges of my nerves.

"What are you going to do?" he demands. "Think about this. You want to walk straight into what could be a trap?"

"He's part of your pack," I shout back, my anger bursting through the fear as I struggle to pull free. "And he's my...friend. I'm not going to stand here while he's lying in the hospital."

"What happened to all that loyalty you spouted about?" I ask.

Caleb counters, his voice sharp. "I have hundreds of pack

members to worry about. Not just who you've seen. You couldn't even begin to understand the network I'm in charge of. When I'm not worried about my pack, I have to worry about other packs trying to hurt my members, kill them, fuck, even kill me. Excuse me if I don't pine away over one member who willingly left."

His words hang in the air, heavy with unspoken tension and the words he won't say—now he has to worry about me as well. I feel the heat of his gaze on me, the intensity snuffing out my fight.

"He left?" My eyebrows pull together in question. I don't have time for this. "I'm going to that hospital, trap or not!" I stare defiantly into his black eyes, seeing the weariness and red rimmed around them. His Alpha side wants to surface to assert dominance, but I refuse to back down.

"And if I don't let you?"

"Excuse me?" I shoot back, incredulous.

"You heard what I said." He tilts his head, studying me with a mix of frustration and something softer beneath the surface.

"You can't make me do anything! If you want to keep your fingers, I suggest you remove them from my personal space." My voice is steady.

"Make me," he replies, his eyes hardening as he steps closer.

"We don't have time for this!" I snap. "Do you want all the others in your pack to think you're willing to let them be hurt or even die for petty reasons?"

Caleb finally releases my arm, and I bolt toward the car without looking back, though I can feel the heat of his gaze burning into my spine. He catches up and slides into the driver's seat before I can argue, and I'm too frantic to fight him. The drive to the hospital should take thirty minutes, but we make it in fifteen. Caleb's knuckles are white on the steering wheel as he weaves through traffic, and we nearly crash into the front security booth when he pulls in a little too quickly.

"Sir, you can't park here," the guard says firmly. "Emergency vehicles only. You need to move to the visitor lot."

Caleb's jaw clenches. "We're here for a family member. Someone is hurt. I just need to get her inside."

"Rules are rules," the guard says, unmoved. "You can drop her, but you can't leave your car here."

Caleb turns to me. "Kali, wait for me. I mean it."

I hear him, but the words barely register. The moment my feet hit the pavement, instinct takes over. Eli's name is still flashing behind my eyes as I take off through the sliding doors before Caleb can finish whatever he's saying.

"Kali! Wait!" he shouts, but the guard steps in front of him again, forcing him back toward the car.

I don't stop. I can't.

The hospital lobby feels cold and familiar, a place I've walked through countless times while with my mother. Today it feels completely foreign. Heavy. Dangerous. My heart thunders as I approach the front desk.

"Can I help you, miss?" the young man behind the counter asks. His warm smile barely dents my panic.

"I'm here to see Eli," I manage through my trembling voice.

"Oh, yes. He's on the ninth floor, room 908, at the end of the hall to the right." His expression shifts into mild sympathy, making the dread in my stomach twist harder.

"Thank you," I whisper before rushing toward the elevators. My thoughts trip over each other as I ride up, replaying every moment I shared with Eli and imagining what state he might be in.

When I step into Elijah's room, my breath catches. He lies motionless on the bed, his usually warm skin pale and slick with sweat. A tight ache spreads through my chest. Memories rush in all at once: Eli sneaking into my house to escape his stepfather's drunken rage, curling up on my floor with tear-streaked cheeks, trusting me with every piece of his broken childhood. It's too much.

The room shines from the afternoon sun washing everything in its golden hue. I step forward and press my forehead gently against his. My eyes drift to the drip attached to his arm. The bag hangs heavy with a cloudy yellow substance I don't recognize.

The door opens behind me. I lift my head and turn to see a young nurse entering the room. Her eyes flick between Eli and me, and something about her face feels oddly familiar, though I can't place where I've seen her before.

"I didn't realize his family had arrived," she says with a pleasant tone. "I'll get the doctor." She offers a small, almost knowing smile before spinning on her heel and leaving the room, her expression lingering in my mind long after she disappears.

Family?

The word hits me like a punch. Liam should already be here. Eli's entire pack should be here. Why hasn't anyone come?

Then it clicks. Fear grips me again.

I never gave the kid at the front desk Eli's last name. I never mentioned family. I walked in here blind, desperate, stupid. Panic spikes through me. This is wrong. All of it is wrong. Come to think of it, both he and the girl seem entirely too young to be working at the hospital.

The door opens behind me again.

Graybeard steps inside with the same casual confidence of someone walking into their living room. Behind him stand the front desk guy and the nurse, their warm smiles replaced with empty, obedient stares.

My stomach plummets.

Caleb was right. I walked straight into their trap.

"Well. This is a pleasant surprise," Graybeard says, voice smooth with mockery.

"I wouldn't call this pleasant," I snap, forcing strength into my voice even as my pulse hammers.

"It looks like you swam a little too far from home." His eyes gleam with amusement. "Do you know what destroys humans more than anything else?" He taps a finger to his temple, pretending to ponder. "Love. It makes you stupid. Reckless. Willing to die for someone who can't even save you."

"Do you always talk this much?" I fire back, more to steady myself than to insult him.

His smile widens. "What's the rush? You came here. Alone. For him."

His gaze flicks to Eli, then back to me. So they don't know Caleb is with me.

Movement behind him draws my eye. The two teenagers step forward, their faces blank but familiar. Missing persons. The ones from two towns over. They're standing here, silent and controlled.

My blood runs cold. At least one theory is confirmed. Omegas are kidnapping the teenagers.

"Do your new friends know I'll paint the walls with their insides like I did to your other young friend?" I ask, buying time, keeping my voice steady even as fear edges my vision.

"You will do no such thing." His tone drops, cold and final.

He steps to Eli's bedside and adjusts the drip. My heart jumps as I get a closer look at the bag. The liquid is thick, yellow, wrong.

"I'm pumping him with Lunashard," Graybeard says, almost conversational. "Enough to keep him barely alive. If I increase this by even one milliliter, his organs will shut down faster than his healing abilities can repair them. The toxin will eat him alive."

He smiles then. A twisted, delighted smile.

"And you, Siren, will get to watch."

"What do you want?" I ask, the desperation in my voice impossible to hide. Graybeard's grin stretches wider, savage with victory.

"You're going to walk out of this hospital with us. Willingly. Or he dies."

"I'll go," I say immediately. My mind is already clawing for alternatives, escape routes, anything.

Graybeard lifts his phone, tilting it so I can see the screen. "And don't try anything clever. The drip is connected to an app. One press and his veins flood with Lunashard. He won't last fifteen seconds."

I don't know what Lunashard is, but Eli's condition speaks for itself. Graybeard isn't bluffing. And if I stay frozen, Eli will pay for it. I need to pull them away from him, even if I can't see the path out yet.

"Follow me, please." The girl's voice is sugar-sweet as she gestures toward the door.

I look back at Elijah, his still form, the sweat on his brow, the rapid beeping of the monitor.

They move around me like they've done this before. The nurse walks ahead of me, her steps quick and confident. Graybeard lingers a pace behind, close enough that I can feel his breath on my neck. Another young boy joins the group. The two teens flank either side, making a perfect cage. A rhombus formation.

I swallow down panic and force myself to think. Training. Instinct. Strategy. Anything.

But dread keeps fogging my thoughts. I've only ever used my powers on one to two people at a time. Even if I could drop two of them, the others would overpower me in seconds. And if I push too hard, I could pass out again, leaving me completely vulnerable. I can't risk that.

We step into the elevator. The descent feels like an anchor tightening around my chest. No alarms. No witnesses. No one who will realize what's happening until long after we're gone.

The doors slide open into the basement parking garage, dimly lit and quiet. The perfect place to disappear someone.

They guide me toward a black Escalade tucked in the far corner, the windows tinted so dark they look like mirrors. One of the teens pulls the door open.

"This way," the girl murmurs.

I hesitate for the briefest moment, heart pounding, scanning the shadows, the cars, the exit ramps, searching desperately for a chance.

As I go to climb into the SUV, a low snarl erupts behind me. I whirl around in time to see Graybeard's body drop to the concrete. For a split second, stunned silence hangs in the air, then adrenaline floods my veins.

I dive out of the car for the phone that slips from his hand. Before my fingers can close around it, pain rockets through my scalp. The girl to my left jerks my braids hard, slamming my head against the SUV door. My skull rings like a struck bell. Spots burst across my vision.

I stagger but force myself to stay upright. Instinct finally claws its way to the surface.

I pivot and punch one boy squarely in the stomach, then strike lower, sending him folding to the ground with a choked gasp. I swing toward the girl and throw all my weight into her, knocking her back. She hisses, and her claws rake across my side, slicing through skin. Hot blood spills down my ribs, and a sudden burning spreads under the wound.

At first, I think it's just pain. But no, this is different. Too hot. Too fast. Too wrong.

A strange numbness begins to crawl up my side, eating at the edges of my strength.

I push through it, fueled by rage. I grab the girl by the neck, squeezing as she thrashes beneath me. My fingers tighten, clenching hard, and I feel the life drain from her. The only part of her that shifted are her claws. Scraping weakly against my arms, then slipping away, she loses consciousness.

For a heartbeat, the thrill of it pulses inside me. A wave of savage satisfaction, thick and dangerous.

"Get them back!" Caleb's voice thunders from somewhere behind me. The sound is both distant and sharp, cutting through the haze like a blade.

But the burning in my side suddenly flares, twisting deep into my muscles. My breath catches as the concrete beneath me seems to tilt.

"Little Bird!" Caleb's voice snaps me back, and then his arms are around me, pulling me away from the girl's limp body. His scent, his presence, anchors me in place when everything else feels like it's sliding out from under me.

"Eli...the phone...he...he..." The words tangle on my tongue. My lips feel wrong. Heavy.

"I know. I know," he murmurs, pushing my braids out of my face. "We've got him. You're safe."

We? No. Something's wrong. Something's very wrong.

The burning in my side sharpens into a cold, creeping numbness. My limbs go sluggish. My heartbeat thuds unevenly, too slow, then too fast. The air feels thick, too thick to breathe.

My knees buckle.

"Caleb..." I whisper, the taste of metal filling my mouth. "Something's...in me..."

My vision tunnels. The world smears at the edges, colors blending, collapsing.

Caleb's face blurs as he grabs me tighter. I think he's shouting my name.

Then everything goes black.

I wake to bright light bleeding through thin curtains, the smell of antiseptic stinging my nose. My body feels heavy, like something thick and cold is still clinging to my veins. When I turn my head, I jolt slightly at the sight of Paris standing in the doorway.

Her arms are crossed.

Her expression is a cocktail of anger, confusion, and something that looks painfully close to betrayal.

"Hey," I rasp. My throat feels scraped raw.

"Hey," she answers, and the venom threaded through that single word slices sharper than her expression.

"What's wrong?" I ask, even though I already know. I can feel her emotions rolling off her like heat. Hurt. Confusion. Fury.

"Caleb has been here all day. All night," she says, stepping further into the room. "He looked like hell. Like he was going to die if you didn't wake up." Her jaw tightens. "Why would my ex-boyfriend care whether you wake up? And why were the two of you together to begin with?"

Guilt slams into me. I open my mouth, but nothing comes out.

"I didn't mean—"

"You slept with him?" she snaps, too loud in the quiet room.

The accusation freezes me. I swallow hard, searching her eyes for any softness left in them. There is none. Only pain.

Before I can answer, the door opens behind her.

Caleb enters, looking nothing like the man I'm used to seeing. His hair is messy, his eyes are bloodshot, and a shadow darkens his jaw. He looks like he hasn't slept in days, like someone who's been losing his mind.

"Hey," he murmurs, voice low and hoarse.

"Hey," I whisper back, not sure where to look between him and Paris.

"So this is the complication you mentioned?" Paris says to him, voice ice-cold.

Caleb exhales, and something in him snaps into place. He stops hiding. Stops pretending.

"I slept with her," he says flatly.

My breath catches as Paris's face crumples before twisting into fury.

"You're both disgusting," she spits. "You deserve each other."

She storms out, slamming the door so hard my monitors tremble.

I sink back into the pillow, suddenly exhausted. The room feels too big without her, but too small with Caleb standing in it.

He crosses to me slowly, like he's afraid I might shatter.

"Graybeard?" I ask, needing to anchor myself.

"Dead," he says. "I snapped his spine. But the others are out there. We're tracking their scent, the missing teens, but not being tied down to a pack helps them vanish."

I nod weakly, but the thought of Eli nearly dying because of me makes my stomach lurch.

Caleb sits on the edge of the bed, his expression tightening as he watches me struggle to breathe through the guilt.

"Caleb—" I begin.

"No," he cuts me off softly but firmly. "I'm not hiding this anymore."

His eyes burn with something raw and unfiltered.

"You have no idea what the past two days have been like. What it did to me when I found you." His voice cracks. "I've been tortured before. To become Alpha, everyone in the pack cuts into you. It's one of the rituals. I can handle pain. I can handle blood." He shakes his head, jaw trembling. "None of that compares to what I felt when I realized they'd almost taken you. When the poison reached your nervous system, I couldn't feel you. Then I thought you were gone."

His hands hover near me before he finally reaches out, brushing his fingers gently along my cheek. Poison? So that's why everything was going numb.

"You're mine now, Little Bird. I'm not hiding it anymore. I'm not sharing you. And I'm not letting you go."

He lowers his forehead until it rests against mine, grounding me with the warmth of his breath and the steady pulse under his skin.

His voice drops to a whisper.

"You're the only thing that's ever terrified me."

"Caleb," I begin again, but the words stick in my throat. With him looking at me like I'm the only thing anchoring him to the earth, I finally understand something I've been avoiding for far too long.

There is no me and Eli anymore.

There can't be.

They used him to get to me. They hurt him because of me. They saw me slipping between them, torn and unsure, and they used that vulnerability to trap me. My uncertainty made him a target. My refusal to face what was happening put him in danger.

If I keep running from whatever Caleb and I are, people I care about will continue to pay the price.

Our lives have been tangled since the beginning, whether I wanted them to be or not. Every time I tried to pull away, fate only tied us closer. Caleb has been the one constant through the chaos, showing up even when I pushed him away, even when I didn't want him to care.

And after everything that happened, after the poison, the trap, and almost dying, I feel unbearably alone. Except for him. He's the only one who's stayed.

Maybe it's that loneliness. Maybe it's the way his eyes hold mine like he can't breathe without seeing me awake. Maybe it's the truth I've been choking on for weeks. I don't know which reason breaks me, but I lean forward until our lips are almost touching. Our breaths mingle, warm and shaky.

"Then take what's yours," I whisper.

His eyes widen, caught between surprise and hunger.

He closes the distance with a kiss that ignites something

fierce inside me. Energy rushes between us, sliding beneath my skin, filling every part of me that feels hollow. It's heat and light-ning and something ancient I don't have a name for. My heart aches for everything I'm letting go of, especially Eli, but Caleb's hands cradle my face with a tenderness that steadies the storm inside me.

"Mine," he breathes against my mouth, both of us struggling to catch our breath.

"Say it," he murmurs, his voice low, gaze locked on mine. There's no demand, only truth and a challenge he already knows the answer to.

My pulse races. I meet his violet-glowing eyes and finally stop fighting what's been obvious from the beginning.

"Yours," I whisper, my lips brushing his as I say it.

Something loosens in him at the sound of the word. A tension I didn't realize he'd carried melts from his expression. Then the corner of his mouth lifts in that familiar smirk, the one that feels like trouble and comfort at the same time.

"This might not be a good time," he says softly, "but will you go to a party with me?"

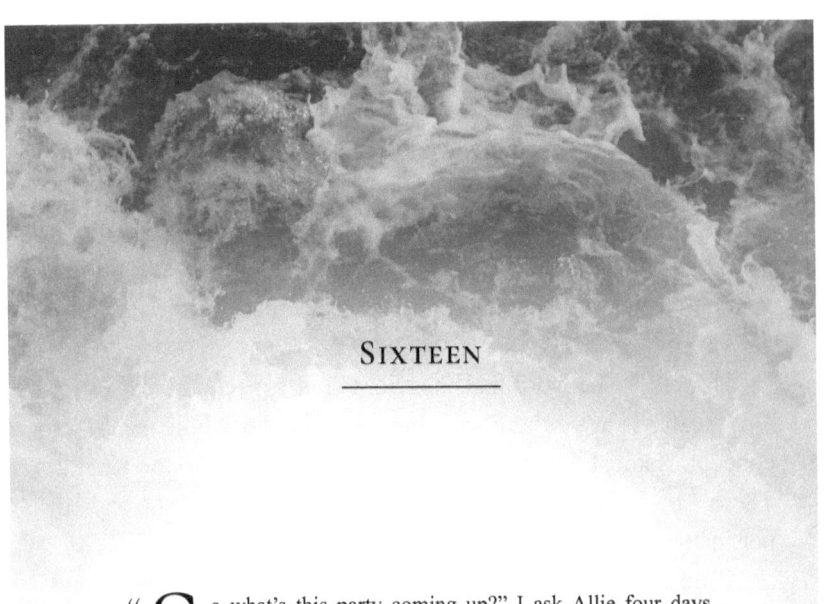

Sixteen

"So what's this party coming up?" I ask Allie four days later as we stretch on the mats in the sparring room.

I'm still taking it easy. I've been home resting and feel pretty good, but I'm definitely not back to normal. My muscles are sore, tender in places I didn't even know could hurt. During my fight with that girl, she raked her claws across me, claws tipped with Lunashard, which is poisonous to both Lycans and Werewolves. Caleb's pack elders and my parents are still trying to figure out why it affects me at all, but at least I wasn't pumped full of it like Eli was.

So far, the damage seems minimal, although there's no way to know for sure. I'm lucky my dad even let me out of the house. He hates how slowly I'm healing. He drove me here himself and refused to leave until Caleb promised on his own life that I would be safe.

"Party?" she repeats, eyebrows pulling together as if the word itself confuses her.

"Caleb asked me to go to a party with him."

Her face lights up. "Oh, the mating festival!"

"Excuse me?"

"Not like that." She giggles, already shaking her head. "It's not some giant orgy." The giggle explodes into real, uncontrollable laughter.

"Glad I'm entertaining you," I mumble, pushing myself up from the floor and brushing imaginary dust from my leggings.

"Sorry," she says between fading laughs. "I forget you didn't grow up with this stuff. It's a tradition. We hold it every three years to celebrate the mates in the pack and honor the ones we've lost."

"Mates?" The word feels heavier than I expect.

"Yeah. That's where you humans get the whole soulmate concept. Except humans can't actually mate the way we do. There's no instinct in your biology that calls for it," she says in her matter-of-fact way.

I press a hand dramatically to my chest. "What? There's no Romeo to my Juliet?" I ask.

"Trust me, Juliet. You don't want the kind of tragic romance humans write poetry about." Allie snorts in response. "I said the human species," she continues, giving me a pointed look.

"What exactly does being mated entail?" I ask.

"No idea. No one in the pack is currently mated. The only person who ever was is Moyra."

"Was?" My curiosity is sparked.

"Different story for a different day." Her eyes flick toward Moyra, who's on the other side of the gym, calmly throwing knives at a target like it personally offended her.

"Wait, so no one in this entire pack of hundreds is mated?"

"Well, there is no pair so perfect for each other that nature needs to declare it to the world. Mating isn't only about love. It's about hate and everything in between. It's protecting someone even when you don't love them in the moment. It's showing them kindness even when you want to claw their eyes out. It's knowing them on a level their parents never could. It's changing from one person into something new, something shared. You don't belong only to yourself anymore."

"That sounds like a lot," I admit, glancing toward Caleb. He's pretending to read a book, although with Lycans and their enhanced senses, I have no idea if he's listening or not.

"No worries," Allie says, following my gaze. "Interspecies mating isn't a thing."

I let out a small laugh, trying to shake off the sudden knot in my stomach. "I wasn't thinking. I just meant...I know I'm not exactly the ideal choice for all this. Someone like Moyra would probably make a better mate anyway."

As soon as the words leave my mouth, I regret how loud they sound.

"Unfortunately for her, you only get one." Allie's voice is tighter than before. "Ready?"

I breathe out, nod, and move into the wolf fighting techniques she's been teaching me. "Damn, you want to take it easy?" I ask as I stretch, trying to loosen the pull in my ribs.

"Actually, I don't."

She sweeps my legs out from under me before I can react. My back smacks the mat, and she's already walking away, leaving the room like a storm in motion.

"What the hell, Allie?" I call after her, pushing myself up and following at a slower pace thanks to her hit.

"No, what the hell is wrong with you?" she fires back the moment we're in the meeting room, shutting the door and wheeling on me.

"Excuse me—"

"I get it. You don't want to be bound to Caleb. Fine. But do you honestly think you two are the only ones dealing with this? We have an Alpha who's basically at the mercy of someone we know nothing about. He's on an emotional rollercoaster every day he's around you, which affects the entire pack."

"Where is this coming from, Allie?"

She takes a breath, steadying herself. "Kali, it wasn't just his ancestors who made the deal. He's not some villain ruining your life. His life is being ripped apart too."

"I don't think he's a villain. I never have," I say quietly. "It's just…a lot. I'm not a wolf, like Moyra reminded me earlier. I'm trying to figure out where I fit into any of this."

Her expression softens. "I'm sorry. I think you've convinced yourself you don't belong here, and I know the thing with Eli makes everything messier. But the pack is a system. If one organ fails, the whole body suffers. Try looking at this from another angle. You might be surprised by what you see."

"Can they hear us?" I blurt, suddenly paranoid. Her eyebrows draw together.

"The room is soundproof," she says. "But yes, we do have amplified hearing." A small smile tugs at her mouth.

"Oh." Is all I manage. I accepted the bind, and she's right. If interspecies mating has never been a thing, why would it start now?

"No one here is judging you, Kali." Allie heads for the door.

Her words hit something deep in me. My insecurities are suddenly louder than the room around us. I didn't choose this. Neither did Caleb. Yet somehow, we're both carrying the weight of it. My life has already been shaped by lies and secrets. This bond feels different. Bigger. And I don't know what to do with that.

Still, it feels good to have a friend here. I didn't realize how I've been holding myself at a distance.

I step out of the meeting room and make my way toward Caleb. Stopping in front of him, I clear my throat. "Can you drive me home?"

Back in the sanctuary of my room, I try to calm down, but I've worked myself up thinking about all of this. Fixation has always been a huge problem for me. But it's who I'm fixated on right now that's the problem. I can still smell him, even though he left twenty minutes ago. What the hell is happening? My body starts to vibrate from my adrenaline searching for a way out. I pace around for a while, trying to dispel my energy, but it barely helps. I need to do something quick. The only thing I can think of is to run. I make my way out the front door onto the trail that leads to the waterfall, just to end up by the edge, pacing once more. The more I think about everything, the more antsy I become, and the hotter I feel. I need to not be in control

I jump, dive, really, where the waterfall cascades down and meets the river. The water is crystal clear, and I can see every rock on the bottom, as if they're an arm's length away. But I know better, the deepest part of the ravine is about twenty feet. The cool water and the crisp fall air cause me to shiver but also clear my head. The waves push and pull me gently, caressing me as I swim, coaxing out the stress and tension that's riddled my body.

I swim under the falls, the water pounding the surface of the cavern that sits directly behind the cascading water. Out of the water, I feel a chill run through me. I brush it off, attributing it to the cold air, but then the coldness on my backside is replaced with warmth. The smell of pine and sea salt infiltrate my nostrils. I realize then that those are my favorite scents. Trees and the sea. His hand wraps around my waist, his fingers splaying across my lower abdomen, pulling me back to him.

"Rough day?" He nuzzles his nose into my neck.

"What are you doing here?" I ask, breathlessly. There will be no fighting today. No resistance. There's no way out of this. Caleb is my destiny, whether I want him to be or not.

"Maybe I missed you. Maybe I think you're trying to run away from me."

"You just saw me," I answer.

"There's no scapegoat for you or me this time, Little Bird. No flying off you can do, no forest far enough for either of us to run away to."

"Would you?" I ask. "Run?"

"I thought about it," he says truthfully.

"And?" I turn myself into his arms.

He steps back from me, allowing cold air to rush up my front, leaving me shivering. He raises his hand over his head, taking off his shirt.

"I'm not having sex with you here," I say.

"One, we've already had sex in here. Two, I'm showing you something."

"That something wouldn't happen to be your penis, right? Because you taking off your shirt after that conversation is kinda making me feel like you see me as a hole to be used." Sarcasm drips from each word.

"Any preference?" he asks, raising a cheeky eyebrow.

"On?" I narrow my eyes at him.

"Which hole gets used?" He cocks his head to the side questioningly.

"What did you need to show me?" Annoyance creeps into my tone. He pulls a bandage from his left pectoral muscle to reveal a tattoo, an intricate design with crisp lines drawn with circles overlapping each other. The most alluring part is the center, where a wolf howls with a chain around its neck. The other end of the chain is connected to a small bird's leg.

I walk up to him, running my hands over the fresh ink.

"Is this your way of telling me I'm trapped with you forever?" I ask, my eyebrows raised, trying to lighten the mood. But the feeling is gone before I can catch it.

"Perspective, Little Bird." He steps into me, his hands cradling either side of my face as he rests his forehead against mine. "It's not you being chained to me. It's me who's chained to you. You're the one who could fly away, drag me anywhere you want, and I'll go. I'm chained to you, for this life and the next. And all the others after that. Where you drag me, I'll go. Even if it's at the bottom of the ocean. I'm yours, now and forever."

"So, it's a leash?" I whisper against his lips, trying to keep the mood light, but my heart feels anything but. It feels full, not in a bad way, but in a way I've never experienced before.

"A leash would have been a little degrading to ask Lucas for," he says, making me burst into hysterical laughter.

"Why are you telling me this?"

"Because you need to hear it," he says. "And I know I haven't exactly been understanding of how all this is affecting you."

"I guess we're both guilty of that—wait, Lucas does tattoos?" My curiosity is piqued.

"Focus, Little Bird," he says, his voice lowering to a serious tone.

"Focus on what?" My eyes trail over his body, unashamed for the first time. He says he's mine, so I can look at what is mine. I take in his height, towering over most, and how his arms are covered from wrist to shoulder in tattoos, with no interruptions, save for the many veins that run along them down to his untattooed hands. There are none anywhere else, just the brand new one for me, which sits right above his heart on his incredibly built pecs. My eyes roam over his wide chest. He honestly looks like a Greek statue, chiseled from stone.

My hands explore their own path. He takes in a sharp breath at my boldness, and that's all the encouragement I need. I trail my fingers across his chest and down his stomach, feeling the hardness of each ab under my nails. Eight, to be exact. Stopping above the hem of his slacks, I look up into his eyes to find them glowing a soft violet. I can feel something string-like pulling us in, wrapping us together. He lets out a low growl as I dip my fingers below the hem of his slacks, moving them back and forth across his abdomen, close to where he wants my hand but just out of reach.

"Focus," I say, looking back up into his eyes and cocking my head to the side.

He reaches behind me, gripping the base of my neck and pulling my body flush against his. "Don't take my kindness for weakness, Little Bird. I'm still a wolf, and you can still be devoured." He once again presses his forehead to mine. The blood rushes to my ears, and my body feels hot and cold all over, like I'm in free fall.

"Promise," I whisper, looking into his eyes, which darken at the plea. "Why do you call me that...Little Bird?" I know he explained it at some point before, I just can't remember when he looks at me like that. As though I commanded him to die right here before me, he would fall to my feet, the breath fighting to rush from his body.

"Do you remember how we used to have classes in the same studio? I was doing karate, and we were like six?" he asks as I nod my head. "Well before I started dancing with you, sometimes I'd watch you as you did ballet. You would spend so long on your tippy toes like you weren't even touching the ground. You were so little, it's like you were spinning around, like you were flying, like a—"

"Bird," I finish the sentence for him and glance down at our feet as I let the weight of his words settle.

"Unfortunately, you have to wait until after the festival to be devoured," he says jokingly, stepping away and pulling me back to the present, holding my hand to guide me from the other end of the alcove behind the waterfall where he must have come in.

"What's the big deal with this festival anyway?"

"It's tradition. We keep the festival every three years to signify that sometimes there are forces greater than us that know our destinies before we do." He throws a look of longing in my direction.

"What's the difference between a contractual binding and a mating bond?"

"For me, with the bind, it feels more like a dance of energies. It's as if our powers intertwine and amplify one another. It's an exchange of abilities and feelings that goes beyond mere attraction. It's almost like our souls are intertwined, allowing us to share our strengths and vulnerabilities.

"In contrast, from what Moyra has told me, a mating bond feels much more intimate and grounded in the physical. It's that undeniable pull that draws us together, almost like gravity. I've heard that when mates are near, they can feel this intense warmth radiating from each other. It's a bond that suggests permanence, like they're meant to be together, destined souls entwined for eternity, not just a lifetime. There's a sense of protectiveness that comes with it.

"So, while both bonds are powerful, they serve different purposes."

"Oh, so not everyone has some ancient contract binding them?"

"A mate is a binding contract, sort of," he answers as we make our way out of the cave. He helps me back up the steep hill from where I jumped. The little time swimming and with Caleb has eased away some of my stress.

"A car will pick you up at six for the party."

"Okay," I reply, not really knowing what to expect.

With a gentle squeeze of my hand, he leads me back toward the house.

"Oh, and I also got you some assistance for the evening," he says, a small smirk playing on his lips.

Two hours later, I stand before my floor-length mirror, almost not recognizing myself. The women have worked around me like an efficient army, and the result is nothing short of breathtaking.

The dress is a deep gold that seems to hold its own light, the beadwork woven so precisely it looks enchanted. The fabric clings and flows in all the right places, and the thigh-high slit reveals the delicate gold heels that make me feel taller, sharper, almost regal.

But my hair and makeup are what steal my breath. My skin glows softly, as if lit from within, and my braids are shaped into a circular crown that feels ceremonial, ancient, like something worn by priestesses in old stories. For a moment, I feel like I belong in those stories too.

My parents do well, but nothing in my life has ever hinted at this level of luxury. Caleb's family lives comfortably, sure, but not lavishly. His mother works double shifts at the hospital, and his father spends long days at the mechanic shop. None of that screams the kind of wealth that sends stylists and designers to your doorstep.

A whisper of curiosity curls through me. Where does all of this come from?

"One more thing," my hairstylist says. Caleb booked her for the evening. She settles a golden spiked headpiece onto my braided crown and fastens it with careful fingers. The weight is solid, almost symbolic. The thoughtfulness of it tightens my chest in a way I'm not prepared to examine.

"You look fit for a king," Mrs. Charty says. She's the Carwells' clothier, and her keen eyes gleam with satisfaction. Caleb sent six gowns with her, each more extravagant than the last, so we could choose the one that suited me best. He didn't miss a single detail.

Krystal, who usually handles my makeup for special events, happened to be home and swooped in before rushing out again. Thank the gods for her. If I'd been left alone with eyeshadow, I wouldn't be looking at the glowing goddess in the mirror right now.

I inhale slowly, letting the unfamiliar weight of beauty, expectation, and something dangerously close to hope settle over me.

Tonight, everything shifts. I can feel it.

"I feel like a queen," I whisper, unable to pull my eyes away from my reflection.

A familiar voice drifts in from the doorway. "Well, this is a pleasant surprise."

I turn to see my dad leaning against the frame, wearing the kind of soft smile that always makes my chest loosen a little.

"I can't thank you ladies enough for what you've done." He addresses the stylists. "And excuse my manners, but may I have a moment alone with my daughter?"

The two women share a knowing look before gathering their things.

"High heads hold crowns up," Mrs. McGrath says with a smile as she slips out the door.

When it clicks shut, my dad steps farther into the room. "I got you something." The tone of his voice pulls my attention to him immediately.

"Dad—"

"You look as beautiful as I look handsome," he cuts in, giving me the line he used backstage before dance competitions, the one that used to unravel every knot in my stomach.

I let out a breath I didn't know I was holding. "Well, I must be the most beautiful girl in the world," I say, picking up the familiar joke.

His smile widens, soft and proud, like I'm still his little girl…but also someone entirely new.

"That you are," we say together, finishing the line the way we always have.

He takes my hand gently and fastens a golden cuff around

my wrist. Waves are etched into the metal, curling like currents frozen in time. "Something old," he says, lifting an eyebrow.

"It's a party, Dad. I'm not getting married."

"I'm not proud of the path I took to get us here," he says, brushing a kiss against my forehead. The touch melts the tension sitting between my shoulder blades. "But I am proud of how you're carrying it."

I lean back to study his face, half teasing and half desperate for confirmation. "I'm not getting married, right? This isn't some kind of arranged marriage situation?"

"No, Kali. I would tell you if it were. What kind of monster do you think I am?"

I raise my eyebrows, the unspoken memories of withheld truths hanging between us.

He sighs. "All right. Yes, I did leave things out when you were growing up. But I wouldn't keep something like that from you now."

"You sound like a lawyer," I say, giving him a small shove with my shoulder.

"I'm pleading my case," he replies, smiling.

"There's no case to plead. None of us could have stopped this." My voice softens. "I'm just glad it was Caleb and not one of his cousins."

"He's a good kid," my dad says, though his gaze drifts around the room as if he's searching for something he can't quite name.

"And you're a good dad," I say, pulling his attention back to me. I'm not sure why I say it or why it suddenly feels important, but I want him to hear it.

The world quiets, leaving only the two of us, the cuff warm on my wrist, and the heavy, uncertain future waiting on the other side of the door.

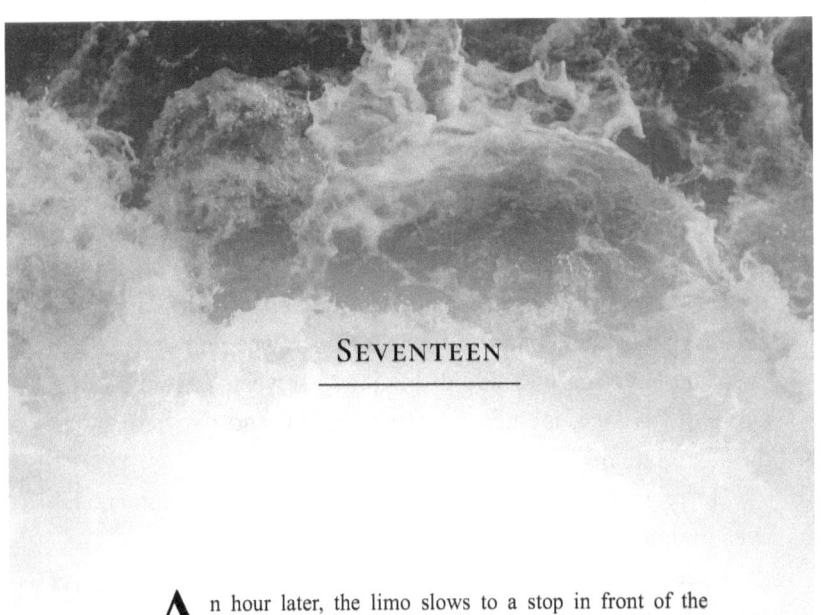

Seventeen

An hour later, the limo slows to a stop in front of the Carwell estate, its engine purring like some sleek, well-fed creature. The door swings open, and an attendant in a sharp black uniform offers his hand. I step out carefully, the gold of my dress gleaming beneath the soft glow of lanterns lining the walkway.

The Carwell house, if it can even be called a house, is lit like a castle preparing for a coronation. Warm light spills from tall windows, music hums from somewhere inside, and laughter drifts into the night air. Even from the outside, the place vibrates with energy.

Inside is a whirlwind. Guests flood the entrance hall in vibrant fabrics and layers of perfume, exchanging greetings and weaving through one another with practiced ease. But the detail that hits me immediately is the masks.

Every single person is wearing a masquerade mask.

Every single person except me.

Why did Caleb not tell me this was a masquerade?

I move deeper inside, slipping between clusters of chattering guests. My heels tap sharply against polished marble as I follow the music toward the back of the estate. The space opens into a grand hall draped with gold banners and strands of shimmering light. Round tables frame a long dance floor that glows like still water.

At each end of the floor sit two thrones on raised platforms, carved from dark wood and trimmed in gold.

In one of them, Caleb lounges.

My breath catches.

He wears a fitted three-piece suit tailored to perfection. His mask is gold, matching the room's glow, sweeping across both eyes and covering one side of his jaw. It reveals only the lower curve of his face, including his mouth, full and dangerous, and the sharp line of one jawbone.

He reclines with an air of disinterest, but the moment his eyes find mine, something in him sharpens.

I feel the weight of his gaze before it fully settles. Heat crawls across my skin, deliberate and lingering. My heart stutters violently in my chest, and warmth coils low in my stomach. My thighs press together as the memory of his earlier comment, his promise to devour me, flashes through my mind.

His scent reaches me even from across the room, pine threaded with salt and warmth. It curls around me, familiar and intoxicating, and my pulse quickens in response.

I'm completely undone before he even stands.

A sudden shoulder bump pulls me out of my thoughts, snapping the charged moment in half.

"Hey, girly," Allie says, lowering the mask she's holding to her face, and grins at me over the edge of it.

"Hey," I reply, bumping her shoulder playfully. "Why did you not tell me I needed a mask?"

"Not telling you was Caleb's choice," she says, waggling her eyebrows. "Maybe he didn't want anything getting in the way when he kisses you later." She puckers her lips and makes obnoxious smooching sounds.

I roll my eyes at her. "Seriously."

"Besides, no Alpha of mine needs to hide their face," she adds, sending a pointed look toward Caleb. He still lounges in his throne as if he hasn't a single care in the world.

"He's literally wearing a mask," I say. But now that I'm standing closer, I notice the tension in his jaw, the way his hands clench and unclench against the armrests. He's pretending to be relaxed, but something is bothering him.

"He isn't the Alpha who needs to be seen tonight," Allie says. Her tone shifts into something steadier, more purposeful. She points toward the second throne on the opposite side of the dance floor. "You sit over there."

"Is that really necessary?" I ask.

"It's a comfy chair," she says with a shrug, already grabbing my hand and pulling me toward it.

As I walk, I can feel Caleb watching me. The pressure of his stare slides over my skin like warm hands. He looks relaxed, legs spread in a posture that should be casual, yet I can sense the tension coiled beneath it. The way he sits feels like an invitation. Or a warning. Maybe both.

"Ready to party?" Allie asks beside me, her attention flicking toward the dance floor as the music rises.

As the festivities surge into motion, I let myself sink into the energy of it all. Music pulses through the hall like a living heartbeat, and laughter ripples across the room in bright waves. People dance, mingle, drift from group to group in shimmering masks and glittering fabrics.

Even with all of that noise and movement, I can't escape the steady pull of Caleb's stare from across the dance floor. It clings to me like warmth, like pressure, like a tether.

I slip my phone out of my clutch.

You know I have been to parties before, right?

I type.

His reply flashes almost instantly.

> Not a party like this.

My hazel eyes flick up in instinct, searching for his, but the gold mask hides them from me.

> You could have at least gotten me a mask.

I tease.

His lips curl into a small, unmistakable smile.

> Your face is the only one here I want to see.

Heat spreads across my cheeks, and I look away, pretending to focus on the small plate of finger sandwiches Allie insisted I try. After a few more bites and two glasses of champagne, Allie turns to me with a grin that borders on feral.

"It's beginning," she says, vibrating with excitement.

A deep drumbeat echoes from somewhere outside the hall. The sound is rhythmic and slow, a steady thump that sinks into my bones and makes the edges of everything feel soft and dreamlike. Maybe it's the champagne, or maybe it's something in the air.

Several broad-shouldered men enter carrying a massive iron fire pit. They set it in the center of the room, and the crowd opens like a living sea. Flames roar to life inside the bowl, and guests begin tossing long, veiny plants into it. The smell is sharp and earthy, almost metallic.

"What is that?" I ask, leaning toward Allie.

"Wolfsbane," she says quietly, her expression losing all traces of playfulness.

"In English, please." I lift one eyebrow.

"It's a plant deadly to Werewolves and Lycans. It weakens us."

My heart jumps. "Then why is it here? Why are they holding it?"

"To gain something, you must sacrifice," Allie explains, watching the fire with reverence. "Nature gifts us strength, but it values weakness. In weakness we're shaped, molded, able to fit one another. It's the only way the next part works."

A shiver runs down my spine, not entirely from fear. The room feels different now, charged, ancient, expectant.

Something is about to happen.

A torch is touched to the fire pit, and the flames swell high and bright. The heat rolls across the room in a thick wave. Caleb rises from his throne, steps down from the platform, and walks toward the fire with the unhurried confidence of someone approaching destiny rather than danger.

He leans over the flames.

The drumming stops. The music fades. The entire hall goes silent in a way that feels wrong.

Then Caleb starts to vomit.

Hard. Violently. Over and over, into the fire.

I jerk upright, horror punching through my chest. "No. Are you crazy?" I shout, already pushing myself from my seat. My pulse hammers in my ears as I rush toward him.

Allie grabs my wrist and yanks me back into the throne. "Kali, stop."

"Let me go. What's happening?" My voice cracks with panic.

"He has to ingest the fumes," she says, her grip tightening.

"Why?" The word scrapes out of me.

"We all have to do that." Her voice is thin, and when I look at her, fear sits sharp in her eyes. She glances toward Lucas for a fraction of a second, and the look makes my stomach drop.

"That didn't answer my question."

Allie swallows hard. "Lycans, and those like them, are controlled by nature. The fumes weaken us so nature, or destiny if you want to call it that, can decide the path instead. It's the only way the ritual works."

I stare at her and the way her hands shake slightly in her lap. "If this is so normal, why do you look terrified?"

She exhales slowly, her gaze drifting again to where Lucas stands at the edge of the crowd. "Because when nature takes over, you don't get to choose," she says quietly.

Suddenly it hits me. Allie is a Lycan. Lucas is not.

They care about each other, maybe more than either is ready to admit.

But the ritual doesn't care.

The fumes don't care.

Nature will choose for them.

A cold weight settles in my chest. What if destiny pulls them apart? What if they're not meant for each other?

What if this ritual takes away the one thing they both want?

"Good thing mating is rare, right?" I try to pull Allie back toward something that feels hopeful.

She gives a tight, almost absent nod, but her attention is still divided, flicking toward Lucas like she's preparing herself for heartbreak.

I want to reassure her again, but something tugs at me. A pull in my chest, sharp and wrong. My focus drifts back to Caleb.

At first, it feels like nerves or maybe the champagne catching up with me. Then it intensifies. My lungs ache, like every breath strains against invisible pressure, and heat blooms beneath my skin. It spreads fast, curling up my spine, licking at my ribs.

It feels like fire.

Too real. Too alive.

For one terrifying second, I think I'm burning.

Then I understand.

It isn't me.

It's him.

His pain slams into me like a wave, and I almost double over. The world tilts slightly, the music becoming a distant, underwater hum. My pulse races wildly, and the air feels too thin to breathe.

Caleb isn't just suffering. He's hurting in a way that steals air and thought and sense.

I grip the arm of the throne, fingers trembling, and force myself to look at him.

He's dry-heaving into the fire pit now, his body shaking with each violent convulsion. The flames throw uneven light across his face, carving harsh shadows into features that are usually so steady, so controlled. Sweat beads along his temples. His skin looks too pale, stretched too tight.

Something inside me twists painfully at the sight.

My chest tightens, my breath stutters, and panic threatens to climb up my throat. I want to run to him, to drag him away from the flames, to scream at whoever decided this ritual was necessary. But my legs refuse to move, locked between fear, instinct, and the overwhelming weight of whatever bond is tying his pain to my body.

I've never felt anything like this.

I've never felt anyone like this.

He's hurting, and I feel every flicker of it.

Every echo.

Every burn.

All can do is watch.

Suddenly, someone steps forward, his movement cutting through the tense air like a blade. He's tall, broad-shouldered, and carries an aura of barely restrained fury. The anger coming off him is suffocating, thick enough to taste, and it prickles across my skin in sharp, cold bursts. I've never seen him before. I don't know all the people who orbit Caleb's world, but something about this man feels wrong. His presence hums like distant thunder, a storm waiting for the right moment to break.

"What's happening?" I whisper to Allie. My voice trembles, thin and frayed.

She looks at me with an uneasy stiffness in her posture. "It must be the bind. You're feeling what Caleb is. We'll all feel it soon enough."

Her words hit me hard. "What do you mean?" The question escapes in a raw, ragged scrape. My throat burns as if I've swallowed something sharp.

"It goes by succession," she says quietly. Her voice sounds far away, hollow. "The Alpha first, then the elders, then the advisors, then the inner circle, and then everyone else. The younglings are the only ones spared."

My stomach twists violently. My knees wobble beneath me, and I fold forward slightly, clutching my middle as waves of nausea crash through my body. Bitter bile rises in my throat, scorching hot, but I force it down. I refuse to fall apart. Not here. Not now.

"Why is no one doing anything?" I choke out, scanning the crowd with wide, frantic eyes.

Everyone looks stricken, pale, tense. Their hands are clenched at their sides, breathing unevenly. Their bodies look as if they want to move, need to, but something unseen holds them in place. They're watching. Waiting. It feels like they're bracing for the sky to rip open.

"It's the night of the mating festival," Allie murmurs. Her eyes drop to the floor, her voice almost reverent. "If you disrespect the traditions, some believe you'll never find your mate. It's meant to be a celebration of love, not hate."

But all I feel is pain.

Caleb's pain tearing through me.

The crowd's fear closing in.

And the heavy truth settling in my bones.

There is no turning back from whatever's coming.

The truth hits me so hard it knocks the breath from my lungs. This is it.

Caleb is vulnerable. The bind is still intact. I didn't break it in the week they said I had. Now they'll try to kill him, even if it risks destroying both bloodlines in the process.

The irony slices deeper than I expect. All this talk of tradition, of destiny, of nature choosing, yet they're willing to stain the night meant for mates with murder.

A massive figure steps forward, and the entire hall seems to shrink beneath his presence. His posture is rigid and commanding, as if he's already claimed victory. Caleb straightens with visible effort, dragging himself upright despite the tremors wracking his body.

"There is no bloodshed on the night of the mating ritual." His voice rings out clear, but the strain beneath it betrays how weakened he is.

The stranger laughs, sharp and cruel. "Do you really think anyone here cares about your pathetic traditions?"

He takes another step toward Caleb, and several more figures emerge from the edges of the crowd, forming a loose circle, their faces shadowed by masks, their intent written in the way they advance.

My heart spikes, lurching painfully. Fear slams into me, but fury rises just as fast and burns hotter.

Why is no one stepping in?

Why is everyone watching him collapse?

He's their Alpha.

Caleb sways, his power flickering around him like a dying flame fighting for air. He tries to square his shoulders, tries to stand tall, but the ritual has drained him, leaving him exposed.

Too exposed.

A crushing tension settles over the room. It feels like the air itself is bracing for violence.

Allie shifts beside me, her attention darting toward Lucas, and in that tiny heartbeat of distraction, instinct takes over.

I wrench my arm free from her hold and launch myself toward Caleb. I don't think, don't plan. My body moves on something primal and unyielding, something deeper than fear.

Caleb sees me instantly. His head snaps up, his eyes locking onto mine through the golden mask.

"Kali, don't," he warns. The words scrape out of him, low and pleading.

But it's already too late.

I'm running straight toward the danger.

Straight toward him.

Straight toward whatever comes next.

But I can't stop.

Something inside me won't let me.

"You think I'm going to let you do this alone?" I say, stepping in front of Caleb. My body moves on instinct, pure and unfiltered. The figures keep advancing, shadows stretching across the floor like reaching hands.

Caleb's breath catches behind me. "You have to respect the traditions." His voice shakes, and the look in his eyes is a plea.

"They clearly aren't," I fire back, fury shuddering through me. "I'm not going to stand here and watch you die."

Two sensations slam into me at once.

The first is pain. His pain. His suffering slams into my chest as if we share the same ribcage. My lungs contract and my vision flashes white. It's like the ritual has cracked something open between us.

The second is heat. Not from the fire, but from something deeper. A burning thread snaps taut inside me. It coils, tightens, pulls. My body trembles from the pressure. Power floods my limbs until my fingertips buzz. My veins feel too full, too sharp, too hot. Caleb sees it. I hear it in the panic in his voice.

"Kali, don't."

Too late.

Too far.

Too much.

The men lunge forward.

The bond snaps into place with a savage, blistering clarity. I feel Caleb's fear, his protectiveness, his determination to shield me even while weakened. His emotions slam into me with violent intimacy.

My own power surges outward.

"Get away from him!" I scream, my voice raw and monstrous.

Something inside me tears wide open.

A wave of invisible force bursts from my body, a cold rush that rips through the hall. The advancing men jerk mid-step. Their eyes widen. Their veins rise beneath their skin like dark ropes.

And then the blood moves.

I feel it respond to me.

I feel it obey.

It pulls through them like water drawn through a sieve, rushing toward me in violent streams. The air fills with the metallic sting of it. Their bodies crumple before they can even scream. The crowd cries out, stumbling back, but the world narrows to white heat and rushing blood and Caleb behind me shouting my name.

His voice is in my mind, clear and terrified.

Kali, stop. Kali, please. You're going to burn yourself out. Please stop. I can't lose you.

My breath stutters.

His thoughts flood into me. His fear. His desperation. His love, even if he's not spoken it aloud. It crashes through my senses so fast my knees buckle.

The power drains from me in an instant, leaving nothing but ringing exhaustion. The room tilts, colors draining to gray.

Caleb's voice shouts through my mind again, fierce and broken.

Kali, hold on.

But I can't.

The darkness pulls me under with cold, gentle hands.

And everything goes still.

I wake without knowing where I am or how long I've been unconscious. The room is dark and still, lit only by a thin slice of sunlight slipping through the heavy curtains. My body feels weighted, as if something is pressing me into the mattress, and my mind drags with a thick fog that refuses to lift. Every attempt to remember what happened feels like struggling upward through deep water with stones tied to my limbs. The harder I try to reach the surface, the more the memories scatter. Slowly, faint fragments begin to float back into place: the festival, the rising panic, the men stepping forward, the sharp heat of my power, and the terrible, instinctive violence of what I did. My breath catches, and I push myself upright as the fog begins to thin just enough for clarity to hurt. I remember killing them without hesitation, without control, drawn by something primal inside me.

A soft groan sounds to my right, pulling my attention to the shadows beside me, but I can't make out who it is. For a fleeting second, I cling to the desperate hope that everything was a nightmare. Maybe there was no mating festival. Maybe I didn't lose control again. Maybe I didn't kill anyone. I sink back down and turn toward the warmth beside me, needing something grounding. The body next to mine shifts, and a strong hand closes around my waist, pulling me closer with a familiarity that sends a tremor through me. I drape my arm over his neck, seeking comfort, until a scent rises to meet me and shatters the fragile illusion. Pine trees. Sea salt. Caleb. In that instant, the truth crashes back with unmistakable force.

My hand travels up the back of his neck, twisting in the curly hair I recognize all too well. This is Caleb. I try to pull away, but the more I struggle, the tighter he clamps his arm around me. Looking up into glowing violet eyes, I watch memories flood back: the first time he saw me dance, our first dance together, the day we met in kindergarten, and more recently, our shared intimacy. But they're wrong, or at least not mine. They're his memories. From his perspective.

I suck in a breath and jerk upright again, heart pounding. He sits up with me, one hand steady at my lower back as he rubs small circles meant to soothe me.

Caleb exhales slowly, as if preparing himself. Then he stretches out an arm and fumbles along the nightstand. A soft click fills the silence.

The bedside lamp flicks on, flooding the room with warm, golden light.

"What am I wearing?" I ask, my voice sounding like it is being dragged over glass. My eyes narrow on him.

"A T-shirt." His morning voice is smooth and deep like aged scotch.

"Whose T-shirt?" I feel the chill of uncertainty creep in.

"You're top of our class. I think you can figure it out."

"Why am I wearing your T-shirt with no pants?" A hint of indignation creeps into my tone. "And where the hell is my dress?"

"I couldn't undo the corset, so I got impatient and ripped it open."

"You ripped that dress?" I gasp, horrified.

"I bought the dress," he says defensively.

"So that gives you the right to rip it?"

"You passed out!" A smirk plays on his lips.

"Not from the dress, you dick."

"I'll buy you a newer, prettier, more gold dress if that will make you happy."

"What would make me happy is to know where I am, and why I'm not in my room at my parents'."

"They tried to take you home." His expression turns serious.

"Who?"

"Your parents came after you…" He struggles to say what I know I did.

"And?"

"And I shifted into a wolf and guarded you like my favorite toy." His embarrassment is evident.

"Excuse me?"

"They tried to take you from me."

"They're my parents!"

"And you're my mate, so I don't really give a fuck." The intensity in his eyes is unwavering.

"What?"

"I said I don't care."

"Before that, Chihuahua." My tone is teasing as he growls audibly in response.

"I said you're my mate."

"Allie said there hasn't been a mating in decades. Not to mention I'm not a Werewolf."

"Neither am I, smart ass," he snorts. His chest is now on full display as he has one arm bent behind his head, the other playing with the ends of my hair.

"I'm not a Lycan either."

"Yeah, I know."

"So?"

"So what?"

"So how are we mates? And what does that even mean?"

"It means I'm not letting anyone near you again," he replies, the finality in his tone making my heart race.

"First of all, my parents are not a threat. Second of all, if I remember correctly, I saved your ass at that mating ceremony. I definitely don't need your protection. Thirdly, you can't hide me from my parents."

"As your mate, I can do whatever the fuck I want with or to you. And you'll let me because, as mates, our inherent nature is to please each other, protect each other, and care for each other at a depth most can't begin to comprehend."

"And because of this, you couldn't let my parents take me home?"

"You're lucky if I let anyone see you again."

"You're the one who literally inhaled poison. Do you realize how incredibly idiotic that was?"

"I had to."

"You almost got killed."

"It's not usually like that. The full moon mating festival is always the worst," he says, fidgeting with something behind him as the curtains begin to part, flooding the room with early morning sunlight.

"There are different mating festivals?"

"No, just one."

"I'm confused."

"One mating festival, but we have a festival every three years around the same time at different phases of the moon. They all represent different things. The full moon is always the worst," he explains, sitting up and leaning back against the plush headboard.

"Why?" I ask, mirroring his posture.

"Because I'm the Alpha."

"So?"

"The reason I'm the Alpha is that my dad gave up the position for me. But the reason the pack protects me and respects me is that they don't have to shift."

"In English, please," I reply, exasperated.

"Werewolves and Lycans alike usually have to shift on a full moon. I take on the shift for everyone in the pack so they don't have to suffer through the pain."

"When you say take on?"

"I feel it, so they don't have to."

"Every full moon?"

"Yes."

"Why?" I sense the weight of what he's about to say.

He gives me a knowing look, and I brace myself.

"I knew you were the Siren. I knew I would have to protect you. I needed the resources of the pack to do that, without having to ask someone for it. As the Alpha, I can control the pack and ensure your protection. It was a no-brainer."

"You did it for me?" I relent, the words heavy in the air. He sits up, looking down at his hands. "All this suffering for someone who barely spared you two glances? That's stupid," I say, tears welling in my eyes.

"I know."

"Absolutely idiotic." A single tear slips down my cheek.

"I know," he says, wiping it away gently.

"How bad is it?"

"Bearable."

"I felt what you felt last night. Wait, was it last night? What day is it?"

"You've been out for four days this time. It seems the more you use your powers, the weaker you get."

"How bad is it, really?"

"Bearable."

"Why can't you just be straightforward with me?"

"Excuse me? You're a Siren, and the one thing I do know about Sirens is that whether they want to or not, they take on others' emotions and feelings. I won't have you responsible for mine."

"You've been responsible for me for years, even when I didn't know it. I don't want you to be," I argue.

"We're mates. There's nothing you can do about it now." He narrows his eyes.

"Then tell me the truth, mate. Did you know?"

"Know what?"

"That we were mates?"

"I had a feeling, but I wasn't sure."

"A feeling?"

"Yeah. I figured it could just be the bind, but you tend to have the same level of bloodlust and wrath when it comes to people you care about."

"That's from you?"

He shrugs. "Honestly, I don't know what's the bind and what's the mating. I don't know if the bind influenced the mating. I'm feeling around in the dark with this crap just as much as you are."

"Wait. I've been here four days?" I jump out of bed, frantically looking for my phone.

"Why do you need your phone?"

"I have to call—" I stop, realizing what I was about to say.

"Who do you need to call?" he asks, tilting his head to the side, curious.

"I need to go home," I say, my voice firm.

"Why?"

"Because I do."

"Who do you need to call?" he presses.

"I'm not doing this."

"Doing what?"

"Fighting with you. Take me home."

"No."

"Then I'll walk."

"You have on a T-shirt, panties, and no bra. You don't even know where you are, Little Bird. Go ahead."

"Take me home," I demand.

"Nope," he says, popping his lips on the 'p.'

"He deserves closure," I insist, my shoulders slumping in defeat. "He deserves to hear that we're mates from me."

"That's a waste of time. He's already heard."

"You?"

"No. I doubt he would answer my call, even if I did want to tell him. His brother happens to be in my pack and was at the festival. You don't know what you were feeling when we were mating, but everybody else knew you felt what I felt."

"What? They could feel it too?" I ask, stunned. He gives a single nod. "I still need to speak to him." I stand, crossing my arms in defiance. "Could he feel it too?"

"He left the pack, Kali. He's an Omega now. He can't feel anything related to the pack."

"Take me home, please," I repeat, feeling defeated. I never meant to run Elijah away from his pack.

He rises from the bed and crosses to his dresser, pulling open the top drawer. He grabs a clean T-shirt and a pair of soft joggers, then walks back and sets them gently beside me. "Here. Put these on."

As I stand, my gaze drifts toward his dresser. A collection of leather cords hangs there, each holding a single carved stone. My breath catches.

They look exactly like the necklace resting against my chest now, the one I've worn for years.

"Caleb," I say softly.

He turns, and the moment he sees where I'm looking, something in his expression cracks.

"Those," I murmur. "They look like mine."

He's silent for a long moment, then walks to the dresser,

picks up one of the stones, and rolls it between his fingers. "I made them," he says. "All of them."

My pulse stutters. "You made mine too."

His jaw tenses. "Yes."

I swallow hard, the truth pressing close enough to choke me.

His shoulders rise with a slow inhale. "The letter you found in your window freshman year...the one you thought was from Elijah." His eyes lift to mine, unbearably raw. "I wrote it. I put it there. I gave you the necklace."

My hands go cold. The room tilts.

I clutch the fabric of his shirt against my chest. "I only started dating Elijah because I thought it was him," I whisper, the realization cutting deeper than I expect. "I thought he saw me. I thought he understood me."

Caleb's throat works. "I know."

Tears burn behind my eyes, but I force them back.

We walk to his car together in tense silence. He opens the passenger door of his Jeep and waits as I climb in. He closes it gently, walks around to his side, and slides behind the wheel.

The ride to my parents' house is quiet, thick with everything neither of us is ready to say. My thoughts churn, heavier than the air between us.

As usual, I'm trapped in my own head.

But this time, the truth is sitting right beside me.

As we pull through the wrought iron gate at the end of the driveway, dread floods my system. He pulls up in front of my parents' house.

"I—" I begin as he grabs my face, cupping my cheeks with his large hands, tilting my head to the side as his lips slant over mine, pulling me into a deep kiss. I feel like I can't breathe. He infiltrates all of my senses, his smell, the feel of him, the growl he makes as he pulls me in, and his taste. He tastes like everything I've ever wanted. My head begins to feel light as we break the kiss. Taking deep breaths as we regain our composure, I turn to say something, anything really, but I can't formulate a coherent sentence.

"Go let your parents know you're still alive before I do what I want and turn this car around." His eyes plead with me. Is it bad that I want to go back with him?

"I'll call you," I say, shaking my head to clear it.

"I'll see you later," he declares as he licks his lips like a starving man. And maybe it's just me, but that declaration seems to have a suggestive, hidden promise.

I take a deep breath and step out of his Jeep, realizing I can only deal with one thing at a time.

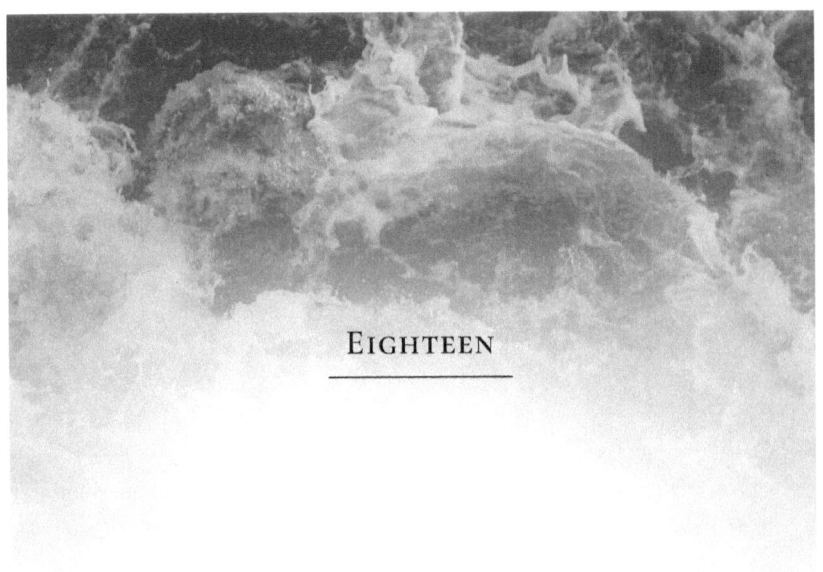

Eighteen

I make my way into the house, which seems empty, and head to my room. I mean to call Elijah, at least to make sure he's okay. I'm still furious that he lied to me. He didn't even flinch when I confronted him with the letter and the necklace. All that time, it was Caleb. Elijah manipulated me, but I keep wondering how much of it was him and how much was my own abilities twisting his feelings.

Prom night unfolded the way it did because I was never supposed to go with Elijah. He stole that moment from Caleb. He was willing to carry that lie for the rest of his life. And still, some small part of me wants to know he recovered from the poison. My fingers twitch toward my phone, but instead, I walk to the bathroom. The shower beats down on me, hot and heavy, and I let it, feeling defeated.

How did I get here? How has everything turned upside down? I tell myself I should do something other than crawl straight into bed. What would I even say to him? What can I say?

By the time I lie down, I feel more tired than I did before the water touched me. How can someone be this exhausted after a four-day nap? Tears slide quietly into my hair, not having the strength to wipe them away. The last of my fight slips out of me, leaving me hollow.

My world is shattered. Everything I thought I understood has crumbled. I think of learning to dance, to ride a bike, to swim. Back then, I lived inside wide-eyed, innocent dreams. Now the world feels stained red with wrath, and I can't tell where the anger ends, and the grief of what I've lost begins.

Coldness seeps in where warmth once lived, and my body shivers from the ache of it as the weight of everything I've been trying to outrun settles on me. The truth presses in with a cruel finality.

My heart doesn't ache for what I've lost. It stings from the fantasy of what could have been, a fragile dream I kept trying to breathe life into. I turn on my side and let exhaustion drag me under, hoping sleep will hold back the darker thoughts creeping at the edges of my mind.

I wake feeling heavy, not only in spirit. There's weight on me, real and unmoving. I force my eyes open and find myself swallowed by darkness. I try to sit up, but can't. It's not something pressing on me. It's someone. A large presence lies behind me, an arm slung across my waist, pinning me in place.

Panic sparks through my chest. I twist to escape, but the grip tightens. Their hand clamps down over my mouth before I can release the scream clawing its way up my throat. Their other arm drags me back until my spine is pressed against solid muscle and heat, trapping me in the darkness with them.

"I know you didn't think you were sleeping by yourself tonight, Little Bird," a familiar voice caresses my ears as his familiar scent invades my nostrils. I continue to struggle against his grasp, only to find it tighten like one of those damn Chinese finger traps. "You're never sleeping by yourself again," he says, his voice a low rumble.

I huff out a breath and still myself, for now.

"I was going to knock and come through the front door, but I think your dad would've tried to put a bullet in me after my performance at the mating festival. I hope you don't mind me using the window," he continues, his breath hot against my neck. My chest tightens at the thought of the last person who used that window.

"It would be a shame if I had to kill your dad for thinking he could keep you away from me. Now I'm going to remove my hand, and you're going to be a good girl and not scream, right?" His tone is soothing but commanding. I nod slowly in agreement as he pulls me flush against him. The heat from his chest seeps into my bones as we breathe in sync. Then there's a shift in the air that feels charged. His body feels too close as his breath skates along the back of my head, making me shiver. I've been trying to avoid thinking about this, but my mind goes back to that night, two years ago, on prom night. I press my thighs together in a futile attempt to douse the heat that blooms in my lower stomach. On cue, as if he lives in my head, Caleb shifts his arm onto my lower belly.

"Cal—" He clamps his hand back over my mouth.

His fingers skate down my side until they reach the hem of my oversized T-shirt. The fabric bunches up as his cold hands explore underneath, gliding back up my side before falling to my waist, firmly resting above my belly button.

"North or south?" he asks, knowing I can't answer.

"North it is," he chuckles, finding my breast and caressing it feverishly while his thumbs play with my nipples, which harden under his cold touch. My body feels on fire, my chest rising and falling frantically.

"Maybe south," he says, his hand trailing lower, causing me to shiver in his grasp.

He passes my belly button and continues south as I begin to struggle in his hands once more. I honestly don't know why I'm resisting. I want this on a deep level. I've been anxious about everything happening and need the release.

His fingers toy with the hem of my panties, moving back and forth.

"Should I?" he teases, and I nod, breathless, feeling like I'm on the verge of combustion.

He slides his hand beneath the waistband of my panties while simultaneously placing his legs between my own to create easier access. His hands dip between my folds, rubbing circles around my apex, adding pressure as my back arches at the sensation. He continues to increase the pressure, and the room is pitch black, but I can see stars.

He moves his fingers further south until he reaches my opening. "Do you want me here?" he asks as he continues his delicious torture. He places gentle kisses along my jaw while guiding one finger inside, pumping lazily. "Look how wet you are for me, Little Bird." Then he adds another finger, quickening his pace.

"Only for me," he says, adding a third finger, which causes my entire body to tremble, my breathing becoming sporadic. My stomach tightens, and my legs clamp around him as I reach closer and closer. Just a little more, I think. A few more strokes.

He removes his hand, and I feel empty. He flips me onto my back, his hips hovering over where his hand was. He reaches in between us and begins circling my sensitive nub while removing his hand from my mouth. He holds my braids and pulls my head back taut, exposing my neck to him.

"Tell me to stop," he urges, kissing my neck tenderly while continuing the assault on my clit.

"Tell me to stop," he repeats, and now that his hand isn't over my mouth, I can't find the words. I don't want him to stop.

He places himself at my entrance while his hands continue. I don't know up from down or left from right. I just know I don't want this to end.

"Say it," he urges, pressing his forehead against mine as I keep my lips sealed tight.

He pushes in, stretching me, causing an intense burning sensation. I gasp in response, and he kisses me deeply. He doesn't move for a moment, giving me time to adjust. Then he begins.

"Tell. Me. To. Stop." He punctuates each word with a thrust. The burning sensation begins to dull as I start to grind upward to meet each of his punishing blows. This isn't lovemaking. It's claiming. Him claiming me and me claiming him. Us claiming each other.

"Don't stop," I whisper as my body begins to tremble again, my stomach tightening once more.

"What was that?" he teases.

"Please?" I beg, desperation lacing my voice.

"Please what?" He thrusts deep. I can barely think, barely breathe. I can only feel it. "Say it again," he urges.

"Don't?"

"Don't," he taunts.

"Don't st—stop," I finally manage to let out.

Then he loses it, pushing in and out with such force that the bed's feet scrape across the floor. So much for being subtle. He wraps his hand around my throat, squeezing a little on the sides while placing gentle kisses along my jawline. "Mine," he whispers repeatedly, like a ritual.

The kisses he places in between are so different from the brutal thrusts. My head feels light, and I don't know if it's from the impending orgasm or the lack of oxygen. My body begins to tingle as I clamp my legs around his waist, bringing him closer, grinding against him. I arch up into him and let out a blood-curdling scream, which he muffles by clamping his hand over my mouth. He continues for a minute before following along with his own release.

My body shakes with the aftershock as he has to manually disentangle me from him.

"Keep that in there for me," he says, placing one last kiss on my lips as he moves my panties back to cover me. I should be embarrassed by that, but I can't bring myself to care. I've never felt pleasure like that before. The guilt claws at me, but I can't find a single care to give.

Caleb slides back to the side of the bed he occupied before and pulls me flush against him as I drift off to sleep, feeling weightless and satiated.

"My dad's gonna kill you," I murmur right before I lose consciousness, and I swear I hear a distinct growl in response.

I wake the next morning, deliciously sore, the aftermath of our encounter lingering in my muscles. I turn to find the spot where Caleb had been empty. The window is locked from the inside, a clear indication that he left. I glance around for my phone and find it sitting on the nightstand. The screen lights up with messages.

Just as I'm about to text Caleb, a message comes in from him:

Meeting at the den. Fill you in later.

Like hell, later. I want to know what happened now. What's so important that he had to leave without even saying good-bye? I mean, I'm risking a goddamn UTI for him for God's sake.

I scramble out of bed, a sense of urgency propelling me forward. The remnants of last night fade into the background as dread fills my chest.

I quickly shower and dress, throwing on the first clothes I can find, and rush out of the house. The air is brisk, and I drive toward the den, my mind racing with the implications. What happened?

As I pull up to the den, a sense of foreboding washes over me. I step out of my car, the gravel crunching underfoot, and make my way toward the entrance. I can feel it in the air, thick and suffocating.

Inside, the familiar faces of Caleb's pack are etched with concern, their conversations hushed. I push through to the meeting room, where the air buzzes with uncertainty. Caleb is at the center of it all, his jaw set in a hard line, his expression unreadable.

"What happened?" I demand as I enter the room, my heart pounding.

Caleb's eyes flick to me, then back to his pack. "It's my dad. He's been taken to the hospital. He's hurt."

"What happened?" I press, my stomach twisting in knots. I walk over to where he sits, taking the only free seat to his right.

"He was attacked."

"Where?"

"He was looking for some information for me. He went to Khalid's bar." Everyone's faces around the room hold varying looks of worry.

"Khalid?" I ask, confusion lacing my voice.

"It's a rival pack's bar," Allie answers.

"Rival? Rival for what?" I ask, my mind racing.

"Resources," Lucas replies.

"And you think this rival pack attacked your dad?"

"God, your ignorance is annoying," Moyra, sitting two seats down from me, scoffs in my direction.

"Better to be ignorant than desperate," I shoot back, my patience wearing thin.

"Enough!" Caleb bellows from my right.

"It wasn't Khalid's people who attacked him. We have an agreement with that pack." Caleb's tone is firm.

"How could you possibly know that?" Moyra sneers. "You mating with her has sent rumors throughout the entirety of The Scath. This has put a huge target on our backs. All of our backs, bigger even than the one the bind created."

"I know because it was my cousins," Caleb replies. "Khalid was kind enough to send me a video of his back alley, where they attacked him. They did it there, hoping we would retaliate without thinking and start a war between the packs."

"War breeds chaos. They would have depleted our pack of the numbers we needed and our resources. We'd be open for attack from the Varros pack, and others," Lucas interjects. Caleb nods in agreement.

"Well, what are we going to do about it? They attacked one of our own," Moyra says, her voice rising. "If we don't retaliate, they're going to think we're weak."

"Who gives a fuck about that?" Lucas shoots back.

"We can't act on emotions," Caleb replies, his voice steady.

"You sat on Kali like a guard dog after you mated. We couldn't move her for hours, but you want to talk to me about emotions?" Moyra yells, the vein in her neck straining against her skin.

"We're not going to war over this. Things get lost in war and people get hurt." Caleb's tone is controlled, though red is seeping into the color of his eyes, which happen to flick over to me.

"I don't care," Moyra says, holding her chin high. "We aren't running from a fight."

"I do care," Caleb says, his eyes now completely red. The power rolling off him is palpable, dousing the room in anxiety. Everyone's eyes switch back and forth between Caleb and Moyra. He takes deep, controlled breaths, but I can tell that if someone doesn't de-escalate the situation, it will be a bloodbath.

I place my hand on Caleb's arm, feeling him calm down slightly and begin mindlessly twirling my fingers in random patterns, feeling the anger slow and the anxiousness around the room decline significantly.

"We have to address this issue with your grandfather's pack. It doesn't have to be violent. Today it was your dad and tomorrow it could be someone else." I speak directly to Caleb, forgetting everyone else in the room. "What's to stop a copycat from doing the same thing if we don't set boundaries on what we are or aren't willing to accept from others?"

"You'll look weak. They don't deserve grace," Moyra argues.

"And you keep throwing yourself at someone, at your Alpha, who is mated. Just because there's a reason to not give grace doesn't mean it shouldn't be given. We're better than that," I shoot back.

"I'm just trying to give my Alpha what he clearly doesn't get from his mate," she says smugly. I continue rubbing swirls on Caleb's arm, my anger rising.

"I suggest if you like the blood in your body being on the inside of your skin, you shut the fuck up," I threaten, still looking at Caleb's forearm.

"Did I strike a nerve?" Moyra taunts.

"Imagine being so obsessed with wanting MY mate when you couldn't even keep yours." My voice is steady.

"Fuck you, you cunt," she spits, standing up and storming out of the room.

"Did I strike a nerve?" I shout after her, feeling a surge of adrenaline.

I look across the table; some faces sport pleased expressions, others are shocked, and a few older wolves look confused.

"I'll make a decision and let you all know," Caleb says, dismissing the meeting. As everyone filters out through the large double doors, Caleb and I remain seated.

"You could've at least bought me a coffee," I say, trying to lighten the mood. "Or a Plan B." I raise an eyebrow at him. He widens his eyes in response. "Kidding, I've been on the shot since I was sixteen." My doctor thought it would help me start my menstruation. Joke's on him, it never came. But at least I won't get pregnant. Now that I think about it, I wonder how much me being a Siren has to do with that.

"We'll figure this out," I assure him.

"I was supposed to be there with him. I was supposed to go with him, but I couldn't stay away from you," he finally admits the guilt that's been lacing him as he hangs his head in shame. "I saw the text messages," he says, a grim tone edging into his voice. "The ones between you and my cousins. Why didn't you tell me they were already following Knox?"

"Why was I supposed to say anything, Caleb? I didn't even know if I could trust you. You seem all too happy about this bind situation, and they were threatening Knox. What would you have had me do?" I hang my head as tears threaten to spill.

"Have you talk to me?" Frustration laces his words.

"How can I trust you when you won't even acknowledge that this thing, whatever it is, isn't just affecting us? How can I trust your judgment when you show no emotion towards Paris or Elijah? Tell me: do you think that's a person who's trustworthy?"

He stands and begins pacing back and forth, his frustration evident.

"Do you think I didn't want to tell you? Do you think it felt good for me to date your best friend just to be in close to you? When I heard you moaning and screaming Elijah's name, I wanted to tear your fucking door down and pull him off of you. Do you think it's easy for me? That I'm just this person, a person that lacks ethics and morals. Do you think I wouldn't have rather it be me from the beginning? I did what I was told. I had to. Your dad set the rules, I just followed them. As much as it tore me up inside, as much as it fractured what little bit of heart I had left."

"You should've said something," is all I can manage to say.

"Say what?" he yells.

"Anything!" I yell in return. "I thought it was from Eli." I held the necklace up to him. "It's the only reason I started to date Elijah. At the time, I thought it was the sweetest thing someone could have ever done for me. My dad told me it was a special stone, and that someone must have gone through great lengths to get it and give it to me. I thought that was Eli, but it was you! Again, if you had been honest with me, no one would be getting hurt right now." I walk up to him, craning my neck to look into his face, his expression unreadable.

"If you want honesty, I have loved you since the first day I saw you in kindergarten. I didn't understand it then. For a long time, I thought it was just a crush. I kept telling myself that if I looked at other girls, kissed other girls, did anything with other girls, it would fade. But it never did. As we grew up, liking you turned into something else, and then into wanting you more than anything. Basically an obsession. All of it started that first day when Brian Penn pushed Lucas into the sand, and you walked up and kicked him in the dick."

I smile at the memory.

He lets out a breath, almost a laugh, but there's nothing light about it.

"All these years, I've been borderline obsessed, and you've just been living your life while I stayed on the outskirts of it."

I place my hands on either side of his waist, grounding us both. His breath stutters.

"I'm not staying on the outskirts anymore, Little Bird."

"We both made mistakes." My voice softens. "And I'm willing to move forward, but there can't be any more lies. Caleb, I need to be able to trust you explicitly." Tears swell in my eyes, beginning to spill over my lower lash line. "Two people I trust most in this world now hate me because of this, and I need to know that you'll be honest with me, and that I can trust you."

"Kali..." he starts.

"No. Either say you're going to be completely honest with

me, and that I can trust you, or I don't see how this is going to work."

"Of course, you can trust me," he says, hurt lacing his eyes, their blackness a stark contrast to his golden skin tone.

"I also want you to tell me that you're not going to abandon Elijah," I say.

"Kali…" he says again, his tone more annoyed this time.

"I'm not saying it's what he does or doesn't deserve. I'm just saying that as a leader of the pack, you can't put how you feel about Elijah because of me in front of doing what's right for the pack. Especially if you expect the pack to help protect me if your customs are to retaliate when provoked? When a member of your pack is attacked, that's what you need to do."

As he's about to answer me, my phone starts ringing, Paris's name flashing across the screen. The timing is strange enough that my stomach dips.

I answer. "Hey, Par, can I call you back?" I begin, but a voice cuts me off.

"Not the best time for her either."

A man. Smooth, confident, smiling through the words.

"Who is this?" My brows pull together as I turn the phone on speaker so Caleb can hear.

"Don't tell me you forgot me already, my sweet Siren," the voice purrs. "You don't remember killing my brother in the woods, you bitch?"

Ice sweeps through my chest.

He continues, almost playful. "Guess what. Your little best friend is about to be left in the same woods with nothing to protect her. If she dies, it depends on how fast you can find her. Now you know how it feels to watch someone you love die."

The line goes dead.

Silence floods the room.

My breath stops in my throat.

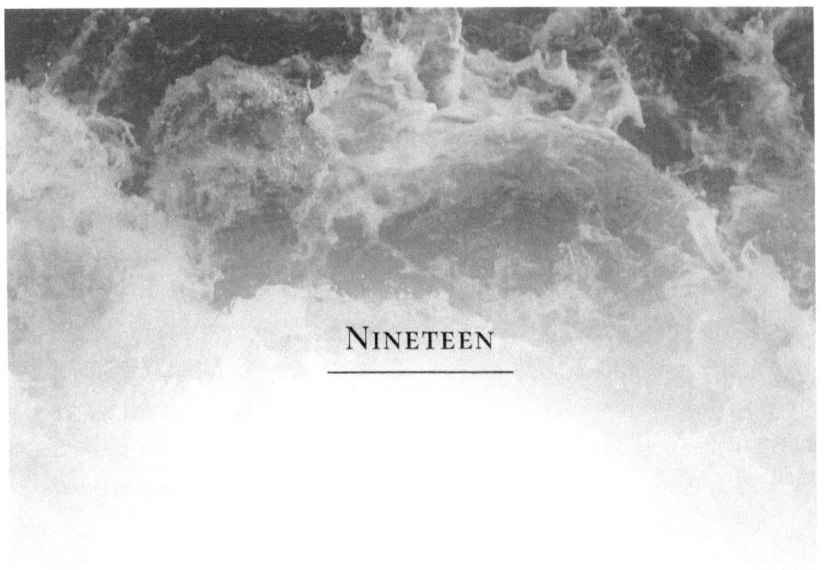

NINETEEN

I can't breathe, think, or speak clearly, but I force myself to stay steady. Sitting in the same meeting room as before, I'm surrounded by Caleb and his pack, waiting for the next move. My elbows rest on my knees, not in defeat but in focus, grounding myself so I don't waste energy on panic. I tried to get to my car the moment the call ended, ready to track Paris down myself, but Caleb stopped me and dragged me back so we could form a plan. As much as it irritates me, he's right. Charging out blind would not help her.

There's no soft way to look at this. Elijah was attacked, and now Paris, who has nothing to do with any of this, has been taken. I don't know what they're doing to her, and the thought burns a hole in my chest. My stomach twists, but I steady my breathing until the nausea loosens its grip. This isn't the moment to fall apart.

Things should never have spiraled this far. Paris is strong in her own way, but she's not built for fighting. We both stand tall at five-foot-ten, but our bodies are different by design. Mine is shaped by sport and discipline, built to hit back when life tries to knock me down. Paris is soft where I'm sharp, a scientist with a gentle heart, curious and peaceful. She should never have been dragged into a war that belongs to me.

I place my head in my hands while Caleb and the others argue, their voices rising and falling like a storm ready to break. My body trembles, not from fear but from the force of holding myself back. Every thought of what they might be doing to Paris pushes against my composure, demanding to be acknowledged.

When the plans are finally set and the search teams organized, I learn more about how the pack divides itself. Some wolves are trackers, some specialize in close combat, others in distance or support. A few can even camouflage. The younger and inexperienced wolves will remain behind while the trained and capable head out. Five will comb the hundred acres around my parents' property, some being state land.

"I'm not risking my life for a Maylard, a hunter, because she chose the wrong friend," Moyra says, her voice sharp enough to frost the air.

I lift my head at that. I'm not fragile enough to pretend she's completely wrong. Paris is in danger because of the mess surrounding me, but that doesn't make her any less deserving of help. She's a person, not collateral.

Caleb steps in before I can respond. "Her being a Maylard has nothing to do with this." His tone is steady and unyielding.

"It kind of does," Lucas shoots back. "What are they gonna do when they find out?"

A spark of hope flickers in me, but dread follows close behind.

"Well?" Caleb asks, his gaze sweeping the room with sharp authority. "I'm only doing this if everyone is on board."

I hold my breath. Will they stand with him, or will they turn away when they realize who they're risking themselves for? Will they help find Paris, or leave her with whoever took her?

Lucas glances at Allie, his expression serious. "I'm in," he says. Allie nods in agreement. One by one, the rest give their reluctant yes. Moyra is last, rolling her eyes and releasing an irritated, "Fine."

"I'll call my parents so they're not blindsided when I show up with a pack of wolves searching our property," I say, pushing to my feet. Energy returns to me now that we have a team and a direction. Caleb still has explaining to do, but this isn't the moment to unravel his habit of leaving out details. Paris needs me, and everything else can wait.

By the time Allie and I leave, the sky is sliding into evening, streaked with the last traces of fading light. I ride with her to my parents' place, much to Caleb's irritation. But now isn't the time to pick a fight. Finding Paris comes first.

Pulling up in record time, I notice the tires crunching over gravel are loud in the tense quiet between us. The air feels heavier out here, thick with unspoken fear and everything we still don't know. My heart beats to the point I can feel it in my throat, but I push the doubt back where it belongs. I need my head clear.

I decide to stay with Allie's group, not knowing enough about their search formations or why certain wolves are placed where they are. The last thing I need is to disrupt a working system. Being in Caleb's group would only pull our focus off the mission. We would end up watching each other instead of watching the woods.

We fall into a line formation and begin sweeping the woods, each group assigned a specific section of the property. My team takes the quadrant furthest from the house, following the trail that winds toward the old training facility. Caleb's group searches the next acre over, close enough that I could probably hear them if anything went wrong, but far enough to give me the space I asked for.

Once we reach our designated area, we spread out, keeping each other loosely in sight while covering as much ground as possible.

With every step into the trees, a chill creeps along my spine, the kind that whispers of eyes hidden between the shadows. The forest stretches tall above us, ancient and brooding, branches shifting in the evening wind like they're trying to warn us. We move in silence, ears tuned to every sound. A rustle that isn't ours. A breath that's not the wind. A voice swallowed by the dark.

The tension hangs heavily around us. Every crack of a twig snaps through my chest, sending my heart racing harder. We search and search, and every minute without a signal from another group confirms the same horrible truth: no one has found her yet.

This has to work. There's no version of this night where we fail her. I refuse to think about what I'll say to her parents or what I'd have to carry if something happens to Paris because of me.

I force my focus to the ground, scanning for any sign of a struggle. Broken branches. Drag marks. Footprints out of place. Anything that proves she came through here.

I lift my head to shift directions, and the realization hits me hard.

I'm alone.

I spin, searching the shadows as panic presses against my throat. The woods stretch silently in every direction.

Where is everyone?

To my left, I notice what looks like a staircase rising out of the forest floor, leading into nothing. No platform. No building. Just old stone steps swallowed by moss and shadow. I move toward them, trying to ignore the uneasy twist in my stomach. Lifting my foot to test the first step, I hear a voice cut through the silence behind me.

"I would not do that if I were you."

The voice is smooth, but danger coils beneath each syllable, sending a shock up my spine. Part of me is drawn toward it, pulled by something I can't name, while another part urges me to run.

I turn slowly.

A tall figure stands behind me, emerald eyes glowing with an unnatural depth. He towers over me, his features sharp and precise, almost sculpted. His clothes are an odd mix of elegance and practicality, a flowing top paired with leather pants and a utility belt that carries nothing yet seems anything but useless. Everything about him is striking. Beautiful. Dangerous. A lure wrapped in skin.

Recognition clicks into place.

It's the same man I met in the woods what feels like a lifetime ago. Aleron.

"Why are you here?" I manage to ask, heart racing.

"Why are you?" he replies, an enigmatic smile playing on his lips.

"If you're not going to give me a straightforward answer, then I'm leaving," I say, turning to walk away, the instinct to flee growing stronger.

"No," he commands, and my body freezes. I will my limbs to move, but it feels as if they're encased in ice.

"We aren't done with our conversation, love." He steps closer, his voice low and alluring.

"What the hell?" I whisper, trying to regain control over my body.

"Speaking will do you no use," he says. "The others can't help you. They can't protect you. Not from me. They can't even hear you." He speaks as if I'm in danger. Nothing in his lax stance, soft eyes, or gentle tone gives me that impression. But I guess most murderers don't give the impression of being a murderer. I beg my throat to open so I can call for Allie, Lucas, Caleb. Hwll, at this point I'll even call out for Moyra if that's what it takes. The woods feel suddenly alive, the shadows stretching and twisting, as if they have a will of their own. I can hear distant voices calling my name, but they seem to fade into the background, the sound muffled like I'm underwater.

"Stay away from the wolf," he continues, and I roll my eyes. "He's not who you think he is. He's going to hurt you in more ways than one. The Omegas will use him against you, as will others. And he'll absolutely turn on you." His words are a chilling whisper that hangs in the air like a storm cloud ready to burst. "If he hasn't already."

I feel a tremor of fear. The stranger takes a step back, and I find my voice again. "What do you mean? Who are you talking about? How can I stay away from him? We're mates?"

"Trust your instincts and let the wolf go." With that, he turns and walks away, not a sound echoing behind him.

I'm left standing alone, breathless, my heart pounding against my ribs. I look around, but he's vanished, as if he'd never been there. Leaves crunch close by, and I spin around to find Elijah standing before me, concern etched across his face.

"What are you doing here?" Is all I can say as the weight of the moment crashes over me.

"Liam told me about Paris," he replies.

"Well, she's not over here." I walk past him, back toward my group. I don't want to dive into what just happened with that stranger, needing to focus on the task at hand.

"Can we talk?" Elijah asks, his voice steady.

"I don't think now is the time," I answer, my heart racing again.

"Not now," he says sheepishly, "but I would like to talk at some point."

As I'm about to respond, the wind blows from behind me, and I smell him before I can see him: pine trees and sea water infiltrate my nostrils.

Without saying a word, Caleb walks up to us, grabbing my hand and pulling me behind him and away from Elijah.

"Let go," I demand, trying to shake off his grip.

"No." Caleb's voice is firm and protective.

I don't understand why he's treating me like a child. I'm no one's possession. But as Caleb drags me away, the words of the mysterious stranger echo in my mind: Trust your instincts. Don't trust the wolf.

I want to rip my hand from his grip. I'm not his child. He doesn't get to dictate who I can and can't talk to. This isn't going to be that kind of relationship. But even as he drags me along, the words of the beautiful stranger echo in my head again: Trust your instincts. Don't trust the wolf. Caleb's actions point to him, but my gut doesn't. Dammit, why didn't he just give me a name?

"I'm staying home," I say.

He's basically already dragged me back to his car and is opening the passenger side door. He stands there, one hand gripping the door while the other moves to his hip.

"You can get in, or I'll put you in."

Usually, I would argue, but there's something in his aura and on his face that tells me this isn't the time or place. Reluctantly, I throw myself in as he slams the door behind me and walks around the hood to the driver's side. He gets in the car, and we drive in silence. This isn't going to be a fun night.

When he finally slams on the brakes, he sits there in silence for a moment, gripping the steering wheel in a death grip. I look up to see if we're at the same cabin he brought me to after the mating ceremony.

"What the hell, Caleb?" I turn to him. His hands are still locked onto the wheel. He seems more upset than he should. This can't just be because he saw me in the woods with Elijah. He reaches into his pocket, pulling out a crumpled piece of paper. It looks wet, as if it's been rained on. The paper reads:

Dear Big Bad Wolf, dressing up in Grandma's clothes won't make you innocent or worthy. Sirens are for kings, not mutts. I let her go tonight in the woods because I enjoy the chase. But sometimes, I like to enjoy other things. To my rare Siren, I'll be seeing you again soon.

I drop the paper in my lap, Caleb snatching it immediately.

"What happened out there tonight?" His tone is edged with concern.

"We were searching for Paris." My gaze is fixed on the darkened windshield.

"Was there anyone else out there…besides Elijah?" His question is sharp, cutting through the tension in the car.

I want to tell him yes, to be honest with him, but the words are stuck in my throat. The haunting warning from that handsome stranger echoes in my mind: Don't trust the wolf. Vocalizing the lie will make me physically ill, so I simply shake my head, staring down at my hands as I twist them nervously.

Caleb exits the car, coming around to my side to open the door for me. I reluctantly follow him inside.

"I should've stayed home," I murmur, following him through the foyer into the open entertainment space.

"Yeah, well, I thought you might not be so accepting of your parents hearing us, again" he replies, a hint of sarcasm in his voice.

"I meant I should've stayed home by myself, me, alone, without you." My frustration bubbles beneath the surface.

"Well, that's just not happening anymore." He steps closer, cupping my face and leaning in to kiss me, his lips warm and inviting. After a few tender pecks, I pull away, breathless.

"I know what you're doing," I say, trying to regain my composure. "You can't keep me here forever, Caleb. I have a life to get back to. We have a life to get back to."

"You're being hunted." His voice is low and serious.

"I can protect myself." Defiance sparks brightly in my chest.

"You only have so much energy to do what you do, Kali. If anyone learns that using your powers drains you to exhaustion—"

"No one is going to find out that bit of information," I snap, cutting him off.

He exhales sharply, frustration flickering across his face. I see the moment he decides he's done arguing as he runs a hand through his hair, muttering something under his breath, and turns away from me, exasperation in every step as he heads toward the bathroom.

The door stays open, steam spilling into the hallway. A part of me wants to chase after him, to keep pushing until we settle this, but my focus fractures. The bind pulls at me from every direction, my emotions scattered and raw. I want to stay angry, but the mating bond makes it impossible to ignore how much I feel him.

Beneath it all, the stranger's warning echoes relentlessly.

Do not trust the wolf.

I drift after him anyway. Reaching the bedroom doorway, I stop, mesmerized by the sight. Warm water cascades over his skin, droplets tracing down the curves of muscle I'm trying not to stare at.

Trying and failing.

I bite my lip, heat curling low in my stomach. Logic is fading, replaced by the magnetic pull between us. All I can think about is the one thing I want, but he walked away to stand under a stream of hot water like he doesn't feel this bond tearing through both of us.

I position myself at the edge of the bathroom door, most of my body hidden from sight.

Am I hiding? Yes.

Do I care that I'm shamelessly watching him? Not even a little.

I watch as he runs a rag over his body, washing his broad chest and down his sculpted abs. My gaze trails lower, fixating on his pelvis and the rock-hard member standing at attention, making my mouth water. I can't tear my eyes away as he pumps himself a few times, completely transfixed. I follow the movement of his hand, up and down his shaft, twisting around the head again and again.

"Enjoying the show?" he asks, catching me off guard.

I jump, heart racing. "I…um…was just—"

"You were just staring," he teases, his smirk widening. "Admit it."

"Okay, fine! I was staring." I roll my eyes, trying to mask my embarrassment.

He steps out, wrapping the towel around himself, which hangs dangerously low on his hips. "You like what you see?"

The confidence radiating from him is intoxicating. "You think you're all that, don't you?"

"Pretty much." His tone is playful.

He walks over to me, fully opening the door behind me and leaning down to whisper in my ear, "Shower, eat, then get eaten."

I've never taken a shower so fast in my life. Emerging from the bathroom, I find a single T-shirt and nothing else on the bed. Guess these are my pajamas for the night. I hastily slip it on and pad through the house, looking for Caleb. Truth be told, I'm a little hungry for both food and something else.

Following the smell of noodles, I make my way to the living room. When the hell did he order Chinese? I arrive at the couch where he sits, doing my best to cover my nether regions with the slightly oversized shirt. He hands me a box with noodles just the way I like: vegetable lo mein with no bean sprouts. A wave of longing washes over me, threatening to bring tears to my eyes. Elijah always forgets to specify no bean sprouts. After all these years, Caleb remembers. I can count on one hand the number of times he's heard me order Chinese food. Why would that guy say not to trust him? What is Caleb still hiding from me?

"You officially broke up with Paris, right?" I ask. I can't keep the guilt out of my voice, even though I know there was nothing I could have done to stop it.

"Yeah. Officially," he says. "I got called an asshole more times than I can count, a few *dicks* for emphasis. But, no knives this time. I'm counting it as a win." He plays something on the science channel, and we eat in silence, listening to a documentary on whales.

As I slurp the last of the noodles, he takes the box from my hand, gathering the garbage and taking it to the kitchen. He returns to the couch, standing in front of me as I crane my neck to look into his eyes, my body buzzing with anticipation. He caresses the side of my face with his large hand, rubbing his thumb back and forth across my lips before sliding down my neck, gripping it gently—not applying pressure but holding me in place. He looks deep into my eyes, as if he's scouring my soul. Prickly heat travels up and down my spine, igniting every nerve ending.

Then he drops to his knees before me, his height still forcing me to look up at him. He bows, lowering his forehead until it touches mine, then pulls me into a kiss. It's wild, hungry, and everything I didn't know I needed. I pour everything into it, and so does he. Our tongues dance in a caressing rhythm, his fingers toying with my sensitive nub, and I gasp, trying to comprehend the sensations flooding my body. His kiss holds my lips hostage as he continues his exploration. He replaces his fingers with something hard, and I don't realize until I feel powerful vibrations against me that he's slipped his other hand down. He turns the vibrations to a higher setting, causing me to pant into his mouth, unable to breathe or think clearly. I try to say his name, to say anything, but the kiss keeps me silent. My body begins to shake in tandem with the vibrations. I'm so close to the edge when he suddenly turns it off.

Finally releasing my lips, he presses his fingers against the sides of my throat, effectively keeping me quiet while he pushes me into a lying position on the deep couch. The backrest is high enough to prevent my head from lying flat, forcing me to look at him as he lifts my leg over his shoulder, exposing myself to him. I should feel ashamed, but I couldn't care less. All I want is my release.

His head moves lower as he does exactly what he promised —he begins to eat.

My eyes roll to the back of my head. I think I black out as he pulls my sensitive nub into his mouth, sucking until white spots dance in my vision. As if that isn't enough, he licks broad strokes with his tongue through my folds, again and again, until my legs shake once more. He alternates his motions, pushing me to the brink as my legs go from trembling to clamping around his head, begging him to stop the onslaught. But he doesn't relent, adding more pressure to my throat, prolonging the blissful torture.

It isn't until the darkness around my vision starts to close in and my legs slacken against his shoulder that he finally lets go. Climbing up my body, he captures my lips in another kiss, forcing me to taste myself on his tongue. He doesn't say anything else, and I don't have the strength to speak as he lifts me into his arms, carrying me through the house to his bedroom. He places me on the bed and crawls in beside me where we both drift off to sleep to the soothing sound of rain pattering against the floor-to-ceiling windows. I'm glad to once again let my physical exhaustion drag me away from my mental exhaustion.

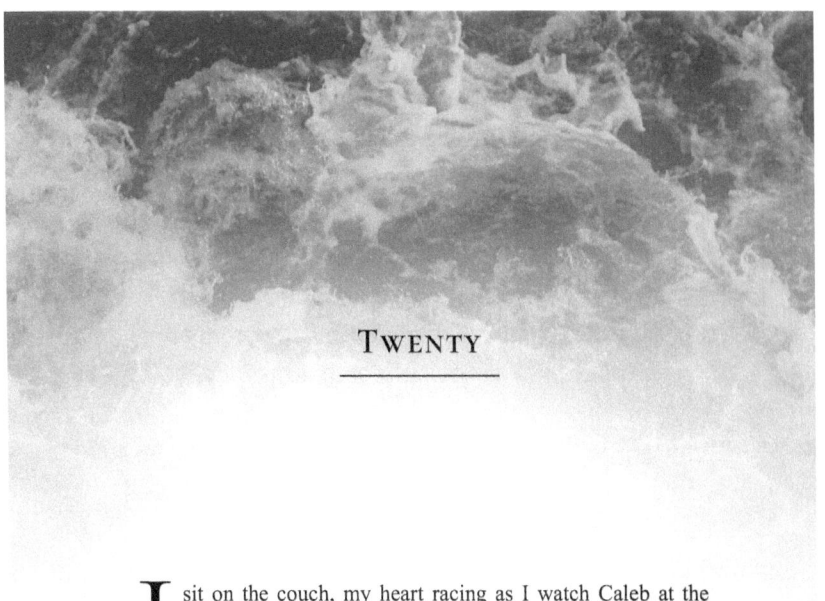

TWENTY

I sit on the couch, my heart racing as I watch Caleb at the
onyx-stone island in the open kitchen. The evening sun
sinks lower, casting an orange glow over his caramel skin,
illuminating the chiseled contours of his back. I find myself
analyzing him more than watching, entranced by the way his
wide shoulders taper down to a slim waist. Veins snake around
his forearms, his biceps bulging at the center. My eyes trail down
his back to his perfect chiseled ass. I get why he's so cocky. But
no matter what, my mind still goes back to Paris. We couldn't
find her last night, but the pack went back this morning to see
what they can find in the daylight. Nothing. I wonder if this is all
a wild goose chase. But, they have her phone. Lucas contacted
his dad to see what he can do, but we still have nothing to go on.
Usually, I know Paris's day in and out, but I don't even know if
she's still living in the apartment. And after that note from last
night, Caleb refuses to let me leave his sight. Although, I do
have a feeling he's keeping me here for other reasons.

"Like the view?" he asks, glancing back at me, a teasing
smile playing at the corners of his lips.

"I know what you're doing." I try to sound nonchalant but fail as heat creeps up my neck.

"And what is that?" He turns fully to face me, sipping from a mug emblazoned with "Alpha Daddy." The sight both amuses and irritates me.

"A gift?" I raise an eyebrow, taking in the absurdity of it.

"From Moyra." A smirk ghosts across his lips. I narrow my eyes at him, unsure whether to be amused or annoyed.

"I'm leaving." I stand, feeling a rush of determination.

He sighs, a bored expression crossing his face. "And where are you going?"

"Why are you keeping me here?" I shoot back, my pulse quickening. "We haven't really gotten an update on Paris."

"You seemed preoccupied. I didn't know you still wanted to know." His tone is casual as he takes another sip.

"You've been keeping me occupied. Why wouldn't I want to know what's happening with my best friend?"

"Ex-best friend," he corrects, his gaze sharp.

"Screw you." I cross my arms defiantly.

"You already did that." His smirk widens. "Several times over the past few hours, if my math is correct."

"Don't flatter yourself. I was just hot and bothered by—"

"By who?" He tilts his head as he prowls toward me. Dipping his head, he brings our eyes level. "Who got you all hot and bothered, Little Bird?"

"Why would that matter to you, Alpha Daddy?" I lean forward to maintain our intense eye contact. "You'd do well to remember I can vaporize four wolves and luckily for me, you're only one."

"You think you can take me?" His eyebrow arches, a challenge in his gaze.

"Haven't I for the past few hours?" I counter, raising my own brow. "You can give me the information I need, or I'll get it elsewhere."

"You think my pack will bend to you?" His tone darkens.

"Maybe not the wolves still in YOUR pack, pup." I shrug, letting the weight of my words settle between us.

"What did Elijah say to you in the woods?" His voice drops, the tension sharp enough to cut.

I sit down and lean back, crossing my legs and arms, a silent refusal to answer.

"What were you two discussing?"

"It was nothing," I insist. "Just…trying to figure things out."

Caleb invades my space. "Trying to figure things out with Elijah?"

"He's my friend," I snap back.

Caleb's expression darkens, his gaze intense. "He's not who you think he is, Kali. You need to be careful."

Before I can respond, the doorbell rings, breaking the tension thickening between us. "Who the hell is that?" I ask, bewildered.

"Pizza," he says, casually walking toward the door.

I watch him go, my heart racing with anticipation. As he opens the door, a chill crawls up my spine. The energy shifts, and I sense something is off.

He stands there for a moment, his body rigid, and when he steps back, I catch sight of two figures. Paris's parents. My heart drops as her father raises a gun, pointing it directly at Caleb's head.

"Where's my daughter?" Mr. Maylard demands, his voice sharp.

"I told you what I know," Caleb replies through a clenched jaw. When did he speak to her parents? Is this why we're hiding out here? What is in that gun that has Caleb backing up? I've seen him heal from worse.

"I know what you said, but that's not the truth, is it, Alpha?" her mother interjects. How does she know Caleb is the Alpha? The words "Don't trust the wolf," echo in my mind.

"What are they talking about?" I stand, suddenly aware that

I'm wearing nothing but one of Caleb's shirts, which barely leaves anything to the imagination.

"How cute, the wolf and his little fish whore," Mr. Maylard sneers.

I gasp at his harsh words. "Mr. Maylard..."

"Exactly how long have you been planning to stab my daughter in the back? You snake!" Mrs. Maylard spits.

"I didn't. I wasn't...it's not like that," I ramble, trying to defend myself.

"No? What's it like? Hopping from bed to bed? You were always ambitious, I'll give you that. Went ahead and bagged yourself an Alpha, huh?" She rips through me with her accusations. "Pity Paris was stupid enough to consider you a real friend."

"I was her friend!" I protest. "I am her friend."

She turns her nose up at me, pivoting back to Caleb. "Forty-eight hours. Or I won't be the only one losing a child," she states, coldly as they back out of the front door.

When the door finally closes behind them, I collapse onto the couch, suddenly feeling exhausted. I curl into a ball, resting my head on my knees, squeezing my eyes shut tight. My entire body begins to shake, whether from fear or exhaustion, I'm not sure.

"Little Bird?" Caleb's voice is filled with concern as he kneels beside me, trying to pry my hands away from my head.

"Please, just take me home," I beg. A beep comes from his phone. He sighs, standing up and walking to another room. A moment later, he returns, tossing a pair of sweats and a hoodie onto the couch next to me. I stand to get dressed, following him out of the house. He drives me home in silence, the weight of Mrs. Maylard's words threatening to pull me under.

We sit outside my house for a while. I don't want to leave, and I'm not sure why Caleb is even letting me go. I need to work through this stuff about Paris alone, and it doesn't help that I'm sleeping with the main problem.

"It's not your fault," he says, breaking the silence.

"No?" I ask, my eyebrows furrowing. "Whose fault is it?"

"Mine." He looks me in the eye, sorrow lacing his expression. "I should have come clean to you. I should have told you from the beginning. I tried, but your dad...it's my fault. I could have waited, should have waited. Paris didn't deserve this. Neither of you did."

"While I would love to blame you," I say, a small smirk playing on my lips, "it would be dishonest of me. This"—I gesture between us—"was set by fate. We couldn't have stopped it even if we wanted to." I offer him a small smile, truly believing it. The binding is one thing, but mating, interspecies mating at that, is another. I still don't know how this is possible. We can fool ourselves into thinking we could have stopped it, but there's no chance. He's the last standing piece of glacier ice, drifting and slowly melting until consumed by the sea of Kali. It seems most people in my life end up consumed by me, directly or indirectly.

"I'm gonna head inside."

"Do me a favor tonight," he says. I look over at him as red begins encroaching on the gray in his eyes. "Go somewhere. Don't tell me where. You're going to need to hide for the night."

"Why?" My eyebrows knit together.

"It's a full moon."

"Okay?" I don't understand.

"I've never had to deal with a full moon as a mated wolf. I've heard it can be difficult to focus."

"Focus on what? What difference does being mated make when we were bonded before?"

"You remember how I said being a wolf amplifies everything about you?"

"Yeah." I'm still confused.

"Well, it doesn't only amplify physical capabilities, it amplifies emotions as well. When I'm mad, I feel wrath, and when I'm horny…" He smirks, leaning closer. "I'll lock you away in my cabin for a week, if I'm not careful."

"I'm confused," I say, frowning.

"Between our visitors this morning and the last twenty-four hours we've had, I'm feeling a bit of both. That won't be good for either of us," he continues. "So you need to hide. Don't tell me where you're going to go. Don't tell anyone where you're headed. Just go and stay there until morning."

"You'll be back to normal in the morning?"

"I'll be back to myself. I don't know if that's what you'd consider normal," he clarifies. "Find your way to where you're going to hide before the sun sets tonight and the moon is at its apex."

"Um…okay." I'm slightly dazed as he gets out of the car, walking around the hood to open my door. He stands at the front door of my house, lingering, as if he wants to say something. He looks at me longingly, as if there are so many words he'd like to say, but not enough time to say them.

"Just say it," I encourage.

Cradling my cheek with sorrow in his eyes, he says, "Before the moon is at its apex." He drops his hand and walks back to his Jeep.

I walk through the house, checking to see if anyone's home. To my pleasant surprise, I'm all alone. Somehow, my feet bring me back to the hallway that leads to my dad's office. We're usually not allowed to go in there, but since he isn't here, I figure, what the hell?

I glance at the wall with the map of the Rysen. I've always loved how the enlarged map makes our tiny town seem not so tiny, though it's mostly surrounded by water.

As I scan the office shelves, my eyes land on a book slightly pushed out from the others. Of course, I can't let it be. I walk over, pushing the book in and take note of the weathered spine, reading the title: *Tales of The Scath*. How have I never seen any of these books on the shelf before? Or have I seen them, and my dad erased the memory? It's so frustrating not knowing, always having to question, not being able to trust my own memories. As I go to draw out the book, another with a similarly weathered binding catches my eye. The faded words along the spine read: *Facts About Lycanthropes*. I pull it out, intrigued more by the latter. There's no author, just the title repeated on the front. I decide to take it for some light reading later as I try to come up with a suitable place to hideout for the night.

I make my way to my room, feeling even more of an ache in my body than I had an hour ago, as I ponder over places that one could hide from an Alpha.

A few hours later, I hike across the beach at The Cove with my go bag slung over my shoulder. Caleb asked me to hide from him and put as much distance between us as possible until the full moon passes. He doesn't trust what the mating bond will do, and I refuse to test it. The pier is the furthest and safest place I can think of. The seawater will mask my scent and is far too deep and violent for him to swim through if instinct takes over. I tell no one where I'm going, so not even he can coax the truth out of them.

I set up my small tent and unroll my sleeping bag on the isolated pier, the old boards creaking under my weight. The sun sinks toward the horizon, painting the water in molten colors while I sip from a thermos of coffee. With everything happening, I have no desire to sleep. At least with Caleb nearby, I usually feel safe. Out here alone, exposed to the open sky and the rising tide, that safety is gone.

My cheeks warm as memories surface. The last time I was here with Caleb feels like a lifetime ago, like it belonged to another version of me. If that girl looked at who I am now, she wouldn't know me at all.

I settle into my camping chair and watch the sun vanish, the moon slowly taking its place in the sky. The wind sharpens, bringing the scent of salt and storm. The tide rises, waves crashing harder against the supports beneath me. I retreat into my tent before the gusts can whip sand into my eyes.

Inside, I switch on my lantern, its soft glow pushing back the shadows. I pull out the old book I borrowed from my dad's library, which I chose to learn more about my so-called mate. If I'm going to survive the night, I need every advantage I can get.

Inside, I flip through the book and find a table of contents on Lycanthropes and Werewolves. My eyes skim the chapter titles until one word jumps out at me.

Swimming.

I open to the page.

"Yes, wolves are strong swimmers and enjoy water. Their webbed toes and comfort in water allow them to swim long distances in search of food, territory, and mates. In the wild, wolves may swim across rivers and streams, and some coastal wolves live with two paws in the ocean."

I stare at the words.

Why did I not read that earlier? I mean, my scent should be masked. His cabin and the den are thirty minutes from my house and in the opposite direction of The Cove. That distance should be enough. Technically, he shouldn't be able to find me.

A long howl echoes across the water.

My heartbeat spikes instantly. I sit up straighter, listening harder. Something splashes against the base of the pier, loud and sudden, the kind of sound that shakes the boards under my feet. I pull my jacket tighter around me, grateful for the thin tent behind me but wishing it were thicker.

I unzip the flap and step outside, lifting my flashlight. The beam sweeps across the water's surface, catching nothing but shifting waves and foam. But my pulse doesn't settle. My mind keeps pushing images at me of Caleb cutting through the dark water like it's nothing.

I stand there for what feels like forever, the wind slicing at my face, and the flashlight trembling slightly in my grip. After ten long minutes, I force myself to breathe, to think. The ocean is loud. The wind is cruel. I'm alone, exhausted, and on edge. Maybe it's nothing.

I lower the flashlight and check my watch.

Just past one in the morning.

The moon is past its peak now.

Whatever that means for him…it's already happening.

I mean, technically, I don't even know who wrote this book or whether any of it's true. I take a deep breath and let out a quiet laugh at the idea of worrying about Caleb swimming thirty feet through rough water just to reach me. The more I picture it, the harder I laugh. The whole situation is ridiculous.

Until the smell hits me.

It sneaks in beneath the salt and sea spray, faint at first, then stronger. Pine. Sharp and warm and achingly familiar. My whole body starts to shake, not from the wind.

I turn.

Glowing violet eyes stare back at me.

I don't know what I expected to see. Maybe a wolf on all fours. Maybe something monstrous. Definitely not Caleb standing there, fully himself, in shape but clearly not in mind. Something else is in control. Or maybe the moon has simply stripped away everything he usually hides.

I step back until the railing presses against my spine. He tilts his head, a slow, curious movement that feels both human and not. Then he steps forward, placing his arms on either side of me, caging me against the rail without touching me.

One of his hands glides up my side, deliberate and possessive, settling at the back of my neck. His other arm traps me in place as he lowers his head, dragging his nose along my throat and inhaling deeply, drinking in my scent as if it's the only oxygen he knows.

He breathes one word against my skin.

"Mine."

"Caleb," I whisper, my voice trembling along with the rest of me. He lifts his head, eyes flicking over my face, studying every line and shadow like he needs to memorize them before the night steals me away. The moonlight is the only thing illuminating us now—at some point I must have dropped my flashlight. But his eyes glow brighter than the moon, violet fire drawing me in.

The longer he holds my gaze, the further I fall into him. My fear, my logic, every reason I came out here scatters like sand in the wind. I stop caring how he found me or why he's here.

I stare until it feels like the light isn't coming from the moon above but directly from him. His glow, his light illuminates me. It feels warm and slithers over me from the crown of my head to the soles of my feet. He moves in for a kiss—harsh and brutal. All of his gentlemanly ways have slipped away as he claims me. I match his energy, claiming him myself, nipping at his bottom lip until I taste a burst of metallic coating my tongue. But even then, we don't stop. Our touches lash out at each other as we both move our hands all over one another hastily. He grabs my face firmly, forcing me to look into his eyes as he declares, "Mine," once more.

I wake the next day to the sound of waves lapping against the shore and the sun beating down on the top of the tent. I stretch my hands over my head, feeling incredibly sore and unable to remember anything from last night after Caleb found me. I stumble out of the tent, scanning the area. Well, I'm really looking for Caleb. To my surprise and disappointment, I find myself alone, wearing a shirt and panties. Memories from last night swirl beyond reach, fragments shifting through fog. His glow. His voice. His hands. His eyes.

Everything else is a blur.

I walk over to the other side of the pier, tilting my face upward to soak in the vitamin D. "Morning, Little Bird," a voice says behind me. I spin around, holding my chest.

"Jesus, Caleb! Are you trying to give me a heart attack?"

"You do know wolves are great swimmers, right?" He ignores my question.

"Well, yes, I've learned that now." I try to maintain my composure.

"So, I say to hide…" He smirks.

"How did you find me?"

"You're my mate. I'll always find you."

"So what was the point of telling me to hide?" Annoyance creeps into my voice.

"Well, as you know," he starts, leaning against the rail next to me, "I've been going through a lot of changes in my life recently. I didn't know how it would play out when I shifted again, so I'd rather try to keep you safe than be sorry."

"What happened last night?"

"You don't remember?" He raises an eyebrow.

"If I remembered, I wouldn't be asking."

"Hmmm…we should get you home." He begins walking across the pier to the stairs leading to the beach. "Coming?" He looks back at me and my questioning eyebrow.

"Well, I don't want to give anyone else the wrong idea," he says, though he adds, "however, I might be inclined to kill someone else if they were to see you in your underwear."

"Someone else has already seen me in my underwear."

"I couldn't stop that before. You'll learn I don't make the same mistake twice." He walks down the steps, leaving me standing there with what is probably the dumbest look on my face.

I snap myself out of it, grab my bag from the tent, and hurry after him. Yanking my sweater from the pile of gear, I tie it around my waist like a makeshift skirt and follow him across the beach. We walk in silence, the boards of the pier creaking beneath us as we make our way back toward TKS's parking lot where I left my car the day before.

"I'll have someone grab your other things later," he says.

"Why won't you tell me what happened?" I ask as we head toward my car. "And what happened to my pants?"

He doesn't answer, stepping around to the passenger side, then moving to open my door as if that somehow excuses the avoidance.

"You're not going to dodge the question forever, Caleb," I say as he closes the door and walks off without acknowledging me.

The drive home is quiet, the kind of quiet that presses on my ribs. I keep replaying every fragmented image from last night, trying to force them into something coherent, but nothing settles.

When I finally pull into the driveway, the house feels strangely still. I push the door open and call out, "Mom? Dad?"

Silence.

No footsteps. No movement. No voices. The place is empty.

I drop my keys into the bowl by the door and head upstairs, still trying to untangle the foggy threads of memory from the night before. Caleb walks in behind me like he owns the place, cool and composed, while I feel like my brain is trying to rewrite itself.

"You're not going to avoid answering the question forever," I repeat over my shoulder as he passes me and heads straight up the stairs toward my room.

I follow him, frustration simmering beneath the confusion. I need answers. He's acting like last night was nothing more than a midnight stroll.

Meanwhile, I can't stop wondering what happened between the moment he whispered mine and the moment I woke up alone.

"What exactly do you think you're doing?" I ask, rushing behind him.

"I figured I'd lay down a little. It's not like I got my sleep last night." He winks, walking over to my bed and laying directly in the center. It's a queen-sized bed, but he makes it look like a twin.

"What the hell happened last night?"

"One hour, Little Bird." He closes his eyes, effectively indicating the end of this conversation.

"Thank God you want to be a vet because your communication skills suck." I spin on my heels toward the bathroom to take the shower I desperately need.

I stare at myself in the mirror, my eyes wild, my hair frizzy, my lips swollen and bruised. I look crazy, but more so, I look alive, more alive than I have in a while. I peel my sweater over my head, revealing bruises in the form of handprints on my breasts, the sides of my hips, and my upper back. What the hell happened last night?

When I emerge from the shower, Caleb is still laid back with his eyes closed. I walk over to the dresser for some leggings and move to the closet, searching for a hoodie.

"Not that one," he says, one eye opening to glare at me.

I look over to find him lounging on the bed, his expression firm. "This is one of my favorite hoodies."

"Your favorite hoodie smells like Elijah, and I really don't want to have to smell that."

I decide not to argue and quickly find another sweater at the same time his phone rings. Where's mine?

I've been so wrapped up in everything going on that I completely forgot about everything else: Paris, the missing kids, the Omegas. I've forgotten about everything.

"The new wolves?" Caleb inquires, putting the phone on speaker for me to hear.

"Doing better," a woman answers. "Although I think they'll be doing their best, since they won't have to worry about being attacked because the Alpha mated with a Siren," she continues.

Attacked? I shoot a questioning glance at Caleb, swinging my eyes to him accusingly. He shakes his head no at me, indicating that this conversation can be had later.

"Look, I say we can just let them have her." I'm guessing it's Moyra who says it.

"Do you ever shut up?" Allie mutters under her breath. I roll my eyes. Caleb says nothing again. I don't know what Moyra's problem is, but at some point, she's going to piss me off enough for me to find out. He hangs up without a goodbye, his head falling back on the bed as he shuts his eyes.

My mind is racing a thousand miles a minute. I wish I could go back to life when it was weightless, and I didn't have to care about all of this.

A memory rises to the surface.

"You're quiet," Allie says.

We stand in one of the knife-throwing rooms beneath the den, where young wolves train in hand-to-hand combat. Not every Lycan shifts, but even those who don't are trained in weapons. Everyone serves the pack somehow.

"Observant today, aren't we?" I mutter, remembering how she commented on the bags under my eyes earlier.

"Maybe I can help," she offers.

"Can you find a way to make me not your Alpha's mate?"

"Our Alpha," she corrects gently. "Which makes you an Alpha too."

"I am not like Caleb. He earned his place. I was just born into mine."

"You think the pack doesn't like you because you're not like him?"

"I'm observing." I throw a knife, and it thuds dead center into the carved wooden wolf's eyes. "They probably want an Alpha with similar traits."

"Hmmm...you might have more in common with him than you think." Allie walks over, examines the throw, plucks the knife free, and brings it back to me.

"Something tells me our morals and ethics don't exactly align," I say.

"All leaders look different. Yes, Caleb is ruthless, and the pack respects that. But he's more than that to a lot of people. If you zoom out, look at the whole picture, you might see something different than the version you built in your head." She offers me the knife.

I take it, then mutter, "How can someone like Moyra shift, but someone with an actual heart can't?"

"Who says I can' shift?" Allie laughs, arching a brow.

"You...I thought because with Lucas..."

"Kali, I don't shift unless necessary. Yes, in part because of Lucas and the frail male ego. Consideration is part of a relationship. Though," she adds with a giggle, "if you ever see Lucas truly angry, you'll understand why the world is safer with him not being a Lycan, as a werewolf, him turning into a three-hundred-pound beast of rage is more than enough." she laughs to herself.

I snort despite myself.

She grows a little more serious. "Nature dictates the mating bond, Kali. You and Caleb may be bound by forces you didn't choose, but mating itself is rare. It doesn't happen unless it's meant to, and it doesn't happen for many."

She hesitates, then adds, "And Moyra...there is more to her than meets the eye. She wants the title more than the man. She wants to be the Alpha. She admires ruthlessness, so she thinks that's what a leader must be."

Allie gives me a small wink. "You should try to remember that."

Caleb sleeps for exactly an hour before rising like someone pulled a string attached to his spine. No explanation, no lingering look. He just stands, dresses, and heads for the door. The bond tugs at me like a pulse under my skin, restless and distracting. Since I came home to an empty house earlier, following him feels easier than sitting alone with my thoughts.

I change into leggings and a fitted shirt, tie my hair back, and meet him outside.

The summer heat hits immediately. The sun is high and merciless, nearly afternoon, turning the driveway into a sheet of warm stone. Cicadas rattle from the woods, loud enough to vibrate the air. The scent of sun-warmed pine and baked asphalt clings to everything.

The drive to the den is quiet. Caleb keeps one hand on the wheel, his jaw locked tight, his expression unreadable. The AC struggles against the heat, pushing cool air against my skin while sunlight flickers through the trees overhead. The bond hums between us, dragging up flashes of last night that I try hard not to replay.

We pull into the den's gravel parking lot, dust kicking up behind the tires, glowing in the harsh sunlight.

Inside, the den feels alive—hot with summer bodies, voices echoing through the stone halls, wolves training in every corner. Metallic thuds from weapon practice, laughter, the smell of sweat and sunscreen, and warm stone.

Caleb doesn't pause, walking straight across the main room and taking his seat on the elevated platform that overlooks the space, the same spot the Alpha always occupies. His posture is relaxed, but there's a tightness in his shoulders that hasn't left since he woke. From that height, he can see everything. Everyone.

Including me.

Moyra notices.

She drifts forward from a cluster of pack members, stepping directly into my path with a smile that glints like broken glass. Sunlight catches in her hair, copper threads sparking.

"Rough morning?" She tilts her head, her tone sweet as poison. "You look like you barely slept."

It's a direct jab.

I keep my shoulders squared, refusing to give her a blink of insecurity. Her gaze flicks to the platform, to Caleb watching from above, then back to me, her smile widening in silent challenge.

She steps closer—not enough to touch, but enough that I have to shift my stance to avoid her. Purposeful. Predatory.

The air between us tightens, the summer heat pressing down on my skin, thick and suffocating. My senses sharpen, catching everything: her citrus perfume, Caleb's pine and smoke lingering from earlier, the distant clang of steel on steel.

Kali Marrinos is not the type to back down.

I meet her stare, steady, unflinching.

Across the room, Caleb finally drags his attention away from his phone. He lets out a sharp, irritated sigh directed squarely at Moyra.

"Moyra," he says, voice clipped and full of warning.

I walk toward the elevated platform, heading for the empty seat beside Caleb. The wood is warm from the summer sun pouring through the windows, the air thick with heat and too many watching eyes. I feel Moyra's stare burning into me, but I ignore her. I can't kill a member of the pack just because jealousy twists through my veins. They would never trust me if I gave in to that impulse. And she knows it.

She wants a reaction.

My pulse pounds in my temples, a mix of the bond, irritation, and something darker. Rage. No—deeper than rage. Bloodlust. It swirls with my thoughts until everything blends together, hot and suffocating.

I take my seat.

Moyra decides to make her move.

She glides up the steps as if she owns the place, pausing long enough to lock eyes with me before turning her back and lowering herself onto Caleb's lap. She settles there, facing forward like she belongs, shoulders straight, chin high.

Caleb stiffens beneath her, annoyance rolling off him in waves.

Every breath in my body goes still.

Allie's voice from our conversation flickers through my mind: Moyra respects ruthlessness. She pushes because she wants dominance answered with dominance. But that isn't who I am. Not naturally. Not by choice.

But she's pushing me anyway.

The bond thrums like a warning, a fuse sparking.

I stand.

The movement is quiet, but the room reacts instantly. Heads turn. Conversations stop. The training floor falls into a heavy, anticipatory silence. Even Caleb's attention snaps directly to me.

"Hmmm. Alpha, my ass," Moyra mutters loud enough for the entire room to hear, tilting her head slightly as if testing how far she can shove before someone breaks.

The rage that's been simmering under my skin clamps down in a single blinding surge. The entire world narrows to her.

Black edges my vision.

What I want is red.

I take the steps down from the platform.

I reach the floor.

I turn.

Then I leap back up the three steps in one smooth movement, landing squarely in front of her, so close she has to tilt her head back to look at me.

She's still perched on Caleb.

But she won't be for long.

Gasps ripple through the room behind me, feet scraping against the floor as wolves instinctively shift their weight. None of it matters. My focus narrows to the two wolves in front of me.

Before either of them can react, I drive my knee into Moyra's stomach. The air whooshes out of her, and she folds for me to press my new fourteen inch dagger—my father's gift—against her chest. The tip settles above her heart, pushing into the fabric of her shirt.

Good thing I grabbed it on my way out this morning.

Moyra's hands fly up, gripping my wrist in a desperate attempt to force the blade back. I can feel the moment power drains from her body. The second she realizes she isn't strong enough to push me off, her eyes widening in fear.

I lean forward, adding a slow, deliberate pressure to the dagger until the fabric dents under the point.

"You know, Moyra," I say lightly, almost conversational. "I would really like it on record that I tried with you. First, I tried being nice. When that didn't work, I tried being cordial. But you don't want either of those."

Her breath comes fast and shallow against the blade.

"No. You only respect blood. Don't you?"

Her eyes, sharp and defiant a moment ago, flicker with some-thing else—uncertainty. I raise an eyebrow.

"You know, I'm actually a little curious about what a silver knife embedded with Wolfsbane might do to a Werewolf."

"I am a Lycan, not a Werewolf," she snaps, breathless and furious.

"I don't fucking care." My voice is low and even. "Now that we've cleared that up, you're going to give me your word that you'll stop screwing with me. Right now. Or you and I are about to conduct a very interesting study on the long-term effects of this blade in the heart of a WEREWOLF."

I put my full weight into that last word, letting it echo through the room.

Silence.

Every wolf in the den finally understands I'm not the one to test.

"Seriously?" she asks, exasperated. I dig the tip of the dagger in slightly.

"You have my word that I won't fuck with you anymore," she says.

"And?"

"And I won't make any advances toward Caleb."

"Good. Now apologize." I press the blade further.

"I'm sorry," she squeals.

"Thanks, but I wasn't talking to you." I raise an eyebrow at Caleb.

"I'm sorry, Little Bird," Caleb drawls.

"For?"

"For treating you as anything less than my equal, than my mate."

With an eye roll, I spin and head down the stairs of the platform as the pack erupts with cheers and yelps. At some point, Lucas and another wolf lift me onto their shoulders and begin chanting "Alpha!" while others howl. Moyra, clearly upset at my acceptance into the pack, runs back into the meeting room. Caleb sends me a knowing glance and bows his head.

After the pack finishes their cheering, they finally let me down from their shoulders. I wander off to the side where Allie awaits me.

"Well, she finally made you snap," she says.

"I know. Once upon a time, someone told me she respects ruthlessness." I bump into her shoulder jokingly.

"I never want to be on your bad side," she says, eyeing the dagger in my hand.

Behind me, I can feel Caleb before I smell or see him. His presence is ominous yet dominating.

"Can I talk to you?" he asks, eyeing the dagger in my hand. He turns to head to the library, and I follow.

"What do you want?" My patience is waning. How can I want to be near someone all the time, but also want to punch them in the face?

"I'm sorry," he says warily, still eyeing the dagger.

"Should I care that you're sorry?"

"I'm not just talking about Moyra," he continues. "I'm talking about all of this." He sits down in a chair close to him. Even with him sitting, his height still puts him just below my eye level. "You're kind, smart, and beautiful. You don't deserve any of this. I wish I didn't have to bring you into it. But I'd be lying if I said I wasn't glad it's you."

"Caleb—"

"Just let me finish," he continues. "I thought your dad was never going to tell you about the bind. I thought you wouldn't accept me or the pack once you found out what I was. I thought...I thought I couldn't trust you." He hangs his head. "Mostly, I was afraid that you wouldn't want me."

I lift his chin. "I can accept and want anyone I trust," I explain. "The question is: can I truly trust you?" I raise an eyebrow. "Honesty is what I need, Caleb, not just want. There's a lot I can get past, but lying to me isn't one of them."

"I haven't—" he starts.

"—Omitting information is a form of lying, Caleb. You can't go through loopholes with me. This isn't a fleeting high school relationship, this is a lifelong bond. We're mated. I need to be able to trust you completely."

"You can." Determination fills his eyes.

"Then tell me the truth. What's going on with Paris, the

Omegas, and the new wolves? How do Paris's parents know about The Scath?"

"Can't we start with one truth?"

"I want all of it, Caleb, or I don't want any of you." I need to be able to lean on him, and if I'm being honest with myself, I'm already falling hard. Maybe I'd fallen years ago, the love gradually building over time. Like a water-soluble stone, love has embedded into me until I'm so filled that I have no choice but to be drawn toward his polarizing energy.

TWENTY-ONE

I sit in my room, attempting to steady my thoughts after this afternoon. Caleb comes clean about everything, I think. He explains how Paris's family belongs to an old hunting line called the Maylards, an organization that tracks Supernatural creatures in The Scath. Their history is darker than I expected. The Maylards once lobbied against the creation of The Scath altogether, and they still hate everything about it. But by naming themselves protectors of humanity, they were able to gain the freedom to hunt any Supernatural creature they chose, which lasted until the creatures began killing back. When the violence rose, a new worldwide authority called the Supernatural Intelligence Agency, or SIA, stepped in and took control of the checks and balances between humans and The Scath.

Even after that shift, the Maylards stayed powerful, brokering the old Scath Accords. They've had eyes on Alphas for generations. My mind is spinning that Paris is attached to this in some way.

They've also taken a special interest in me, apparently, although he can't explain why. I assume it's because they don't know enough about what I am, and caution makes sense. But

I've been best friends with their daughter since kindergarten. If I'm a threat, someone would have known years ago.

Caleb isn't proud to admit it, but part of him dating Paris was leverage against her parents, who inherited the family business.

There was also another attack on the new wolves, the younger ones who turned this month. He doesn't know if the strike came from the Maylards, the Omegas, or another pack entirely. My head spins from the conversation, but I feel better knowing the truth.

When I pull into my driveway, I receive a text that says,

Dinner at my place at eight—Caleb

I glance at the dashboard. Three hours. Enough time for a jog to clear my mind.

The house is empty again, which isn't strange. It's always been like this, everyone scattered, busy with their own tasks. Still, with everything happening, I send a quick text to my mom and dad. Not that it's needed. Every entry point has a camera so they know I'm home.

I check out the window, noting I have about two hours of daylight left, and change into jogging clothes. I know exactly where I want to go and run the familiar trail to the small waterfall on the property. Stepping onto the flat stone at the top, I feel the pressure is less today. I lie back with my legs hanging over the edge, braids trailing in the spillway. The water runs over me, soaking me from head to toe. The day's noise thins to water and breath, and I let the calm take me.

I realize Caleb gave me a lot of information about what happened, but he never told me what happened that night at the pier. The gap bothers me more now that I know it's there. I search for the memory and find nothing but fog.

A prickle moves over my skin. Sharp fear and heavy guilt. Neither feeling belongs to me. They pass through like a cold hand brushing the inside of my chest. It feels like another emotion brushes against mine for a breath. Not mine. Not entirely human. It passes so quickly I almost doubt it and push the sensation away. Trying to relax, I blame it on nerves.

Off in the distance, I hear leaves rustling. I sit up and listen hard, ears straining past the constant crash of water below. Something shifts. Footsteps?

I lie back on the stone and let the water run over me again. The calm lasts only a moment before I hear a clear branch snap. I shoot upright, my gaze sweeping the treeline from left to right, sharper now, every muscle tight.

Then I see him.

The wolf from Graybeard's pack stands to my left, the one I met on the first day at The Cove. Heath. The catalyst to all of this. That day feels like a lifetime ago. Gone is the playful light I remember in his eyes. Now there's only sorrow, heavy and raw. The tension in the air is so thick I can taste it.

"You know, suicide is one thing, but willingly walking into your death has to be the stupidest thing I can imagine." My voice cuts through the roar of the falls. The stone beneath me is slick and cold, but I stay seated, legs still draped over the edge. Rage coils inside me, steady and deliberate, but not frantic.

"I'm not here to fight." He stands at the treeline, palms lifted in a trembling plea. "I just didn't want to run into your pack. You're mated to their Alpha. Packs with Alphas kill first and ask questions later."

"No. You're here to collect your Siren, right?" My tone stays level. The falls vibrate through the stone and into my bones, a deep pulsing hum that centers me.

"This isn't what I signed up for," he mutters, his hand dragging along the back of his neck.

"What did you sign up for?" I don't move, not needing to. He can feel the weight of my attention from where I sit.

"I thought we were going to be a pack. A real one, just different. We were all Omegas and came from bad situations. I signed up for a family, not kidnapping and killing. This is out of control. Someone else is pulling the strings. He's not like this."

The fear and guilt I sensed earlier brush against me again. It was him.

"Not like what?" I ask. "Not like a kidnapper. Not like a murderer. Which part of him am I supposed to excuse?"

He flinches at the words. "I just want to make things right."

"Then start simple." My voice lowers, not softer, but heavier. "Where is my friend?"

The forest holds still. Even the leaves are quiet. Only the relentless crash of water fills the space between us. His eyes dart past me, unable to meet mine.

"I'll bring her to you." His shoulders slump under the weight of his promise.

"When? Where? Why not now?" The questions leave me calm and sharp.

"I'll bring her to you," he repeats.

I finally lift my chin, a small motion, but enough to pin him in place. The air tastes metallic on my tongue, the cold spray of the falls misting across my skin.

"Sunrise," I say. "Or I wear your family on my skin."

His jaw clenches at the threat, despair flickering in his eyes. Then he turns, steps crunching through the underbrush as he retreats into the trees.

I don't move until the forest swallows him whole, the last traces of guilt lingering long after he's gone.

My mind races with possibilities of who or what else might be moving through these woods. Aleron flickers across my thoughts like a dark shape at the edge of the trail, and instinct pushes me into motion. I leave the stone and sprint toward the house. Summer air clings to my skin, thick and heated, carrying the scent of sun-baked pine and wildflowers crushed under my steps.

I feel like something is watching from the trees, which only makes me run faster.

I reach my room and shut the door, the soft click echoing in the stillness. My pulse is a drumbeat in my ears, adrenaline humming through my limbs. I sink to my knees and wrap my arms around myself, not in fear but to gather all my scattered pieces back into place. The floor beneath me is warm from the day's heat, grounding me.

My breath evens. My heartbeat slows. I rise on steady legs and walk into the bathroom.

The girl in the mirror still drips river water, hair damp and curling in the humidity, but her eyes hold the same steel the forest felt. I wash off the grit, re-braid my hair, and choose a black dress that clings where it should and leaves me cool in the summer heat, showing the confidence in my shoulders, the strength in my legs.

I slip on simple jewelry, nothing that catches too much light, and swipe a little gloss across my lips. By the time I finish, the sun hangs low enough to cast long golden bars across my room.

A quiet settles in my chest. Not peace, not exactly, but something like readiness.

I grab my keys and step outside. The summer heat wraps around me, soft and dense. Cicadas hum in the trees. The sky bruises into deeper shades of pink and orange as I drive. Every mile between me and the encounter at the falls feels like peeling away another layer of tension.

Caleb's property appears at the end of the long, winding road, the lights already glowing like warm lanterns through the trees. I park and walk up the familiar stone path, the air smelling of salt and warm earth.

I expect noise, people, a spread of activity in the backyard like every other event I've attended here.

But the yard is quiet.

Only one figure sits on the back patio steps, elbows on his knees.

Caleb.

The moment I step onto the stones, his head lifts as if the air itself tells him I'm here. His eyes flash violet for a heartbeat before fading back to black. He stands and walks toward me, the night bending around him with that familiar pull.

The space between us hums.

"What kind of dinner is this if you're wearing what you always wear?" I tease, giving him a quick once-over.

He lifts a brow. "Do you know, my family doesn't normally eat out here," he says with dramatic sarcasm. "You do know we have a dining room."

"Ha ha. Hilarious." I roll my eyes as I take his hand. His palm is warm, steady, as he leads me up the patio steps and into the house.

We pass through the kitchen, soft lights glowing off polished stone. As we near the dining room corridor, I hear chatter ahead. Voices. Laughter. Too many for a quiet dinner. I glance at Caleb. He gives a helpless shrug that tells me he's just as confused as I am.

I round the corner and stop short.

Cloudy white eyes meet mine from across the long dining table, set in deep brown skin and a face I recognize immediately.

"Duke," I breathe, my brows drawing together.

He isn't alone. Qora. Zori. Noah. All dressed to the nines like they stepped out of some high-summer gala rather than a last-minute dinner invitation. The table is already set with flickering candles and dishes I don't recognize.

"What are you all doing here," I ask, half-laughing, half-stunned.

"Sorry I missed you at Wraithstone," Qora says as she leaps up and pulls me into a tight hug that smells like citrus and summer wind.

"Yeah," Duke adds from his seat, "Noah woke up, didn't see you, and started checking every corner of the damn place. We had to talk him down from a full search mission."

"Well, hey, hey," Noah says, flashing a grin as bright as his aura. "It's not every day you get saved by a Siren. I only wanted to show my thanks. Be grateful. You know. Normal stuff."

"Normal," Qora scoffs. "We just wanted to make sure you weren't planning some over-the-top grand gesture."

"However, she wants me to show it." Noah winks at me with zero shame.

A laugh slips from me as Caleb nearly combusts beside me.

"Same old Noah," I say as I move to one of the two empty seats.

"Not the same old Noah," he corrects, hand to his chest. "A Noah indebted to you." He bows his head with theatrical sincerity.

I wave him off. "There's no debt."

My gaze travels around the table. Their eyes follow me with warmth and something like pride. The weight of it settles strangely in my chest, soft but firm.

"So," I say, lifting a brow, "anyone want to tell me why you're all here?"

They glance around the table, eyes shifting from one person to another in playful guilt. Caleb takes the empty seat beside me and leans in, his breath warm against my ear.

"I thought it would be nice for you to spend some time with your friends," he whispers.

The word friends hits something in me I didn't notice was hurting until now. Paris used to sit in that space, used to fill that word.

"They seem to make you..." He hesitates, searching for something true. "Happier."

"Not happier," I say, tapping a kiss onto his cheek. "Just happy."

And I am. Sitting here with them, I feel the weight behind my ribs loosen. But the thought forms as quick as a sting: Who does this for him? Who thinks of his happiness while he tries to carry everyone else's?

I look at him and wonder if he's ever had a night arranged for his sake alone.

"So what's it like to be mated?" Zori asks suddenly, eyes sparkling with nosy excitement.

"That is so not a personal question," Qora snaps, elbowing her.

"I just want to know what—"

Zori's words cut short as Caleb's phone rings.

He checks the screen, and everything in him shifts. His shoulders go rigid. His brows pull together. Whatever voice is on the other end drains all light from his face.

The others sense it too. The table stills. Qora, Zori, Duke, and Noah all lean subtly forward, eyes narrowing with pack-trained alertness. I watch each face for clues, but all I see is tightening tension.

Caleb rises. "I need a moment."

We all nod. The scrape of his chair drags across the floor. He steps into the hall, and we hear his shoes scuffle, a stumble, a hissed breath.

Several things happen at once.

Duke and Noah push back their chairs and face the doorway.

Qora and Zori draw weapons from hidden places with alarming ease.

Instinct hits me like a spark.

A knife is suddenly in my hand. I don't remember reaching for it, as I feel the cool weight of the blade settling against my palm.

Caleb bursts back into the room and shoves me behind him. His stance drops low, muscles locked, every line of him prepared to tear through whatever waits beyond the wall.

The air thickens.

The room holds its breath.

The door begins to open.

I peek around Caleb's shoulder to see what has everyone so tense. My breath catches.

Paris stumbles into view, bruised and exhausted, with Heath at her side. Her skin is mottled with dark marks, her steps unsteady. I don' let my mind imagine how she got them. Not now.

"Before sunrise," Heath says, nodding once toward me, his eyes not leaving mine.

Caleb immediately shifts to block his line of sight, muscles tight, jaw clenched. He glances back at me, sharp and accusatory, as if asking without words why Heath is showing up with my friend like this.

"Leave," I tell Heath.

He starts to retreat, but Caleb's voice cracks through the room like a command. "Town." Authority rolls off him. Unshakable.

Heath lowers his gaze and backs out, disappearing into the night.

I look around the table. Confusion shadows every face. Qora's blade is still in hand. Noah's shoulders stay tense. Duke's cloudy eyes track the doorway like something might come back through it.

Caleb turns on me, eyes narrowed, questions simmering behind them.

"Can we talk about this later?" I ask, brushing past him toward Paris, who sinks into a chair, limp with exhaustion.

"What do you need?" I ask her gently.

"Sleep," she mumbles, her voice barely above a whisper.

I lift a brow at Caleb, giving him a silent, pointed look. This is his house. His territory. She needs somewhere safe, and he damn well knows it.

"She can sleep in the guest house," he says. His tone stays hard, his gaze locked on me like I'm another mystery he doesn't have the energy for but refuses to ignore.

"Okay," I say quietly.

He steps forward and scoops Paris into his arms. She folds against him with no resistance. He carries her out of the dining room, heading toward the path that leads to the guest house by the pond.

I follow closely, silent.

Watching him hold her twists something in me. The way he moves with her, careful, protective, familiar. A pulse of jealousy flares hot in my chest, sharp enough that I almost stop walking. The instinct to tear her out of his arms flashes through me before I can contain it.

I swallow it down.

I love her too much. She's my best friend. She needs him right now.

Despite everything I try to tell myself, the truth simmers low and honest in my chest.

He's my mate. If jealousy burns in me, who can blame me?

Seeing Paris in Caleb's arms as he carries her down the path ignites something deep and relentless inside me. A truth I can't shove down anymore. There's no turning back. No pretending I don't feel this. I'm so tired of justifying it. Tired of lying to myself.

I'll have to face the consequences of my choices and feelings, but not now. Right now, Paris comes first.

Caleb sets her on the bed in the guest house, his voice low and soft as she leans back against the pillows. The tenderness in his tone burns through me. My blood runs hot, jealousy flaring bright and instinctive once again. But she needs and deserves that comfort. She's always been a good friend to me, far better than I've been to her, no matter how many excuses I try to make.

When we step back outside, Caleb pauses. I can feel the

questions rising in him before he speaks. He wants to know about the wolf—how I got Heath to bring Paris back alive. He wants answers.

But I'm hollowed out, every part of me feeling threadbare.

We walk back toward the house in silence. His curiosity lingers between us, thick as summer humidity, but he doesn't push.

Back in the dining room, I tell everyone I have to leave. I thank them for coming and apologize for dinner being ruined. They protest immediately. Qora grabs my hand, Duke shakes his head, Noah insists nothing is ruined, and Zori even gives a soft smile.

I leave before the weight in my chest breaks me open.

I can't look at anyone at the table, least of all Caleb. Their eyes feel like questions I'm not ready to answer. I slip out the door with a quiet promise that I'll reach out later, even though I don't know when I'll actually be able to breathe again.

I park my car just before the gate and sit there for a moment, hands gripping the wheel. The pressure inside me finally cracks as tears claw up my throat and spill over, hot and relentless.

The sky answers.

A low rumble rolls across the clouds, distant at first. Then another. Then the first hard drop of rain hits the windshield, followed by a second. Within seconds, the sky breaks open. Lightning slices the horizon. Thunder shakes the air around me like the earth itself responds to the pain I've tried so long to swallow.

Guilt, hate, betrayal, all of it erupts inside me in sync with the storm. I've spent so long telling myself I'm good—that I do the right thing. But good is subjective, and if I hold myself to the same standard I hold everyone else, then no, I'm not a good person. Not right now.

A heavy stone rises and falls with my heartbeat. Under it sits a truth that has stalked me for weeks: I wanted it to be Elijah. I wanted him to be the one who gave me the necklace. I clung to that fantasy because it was easier than accepting the truth.

But deep down, I always knew.

It was Caleb.

That realization aches so sharply it almost feels physical. My denial has touched so many lives. Hurt people I care about. The storm outside roars as if echoing the chaos in me.

When my tears slow, the rain only grows heavier. The storm is full, wild, alive.

I step inside the house, clothes damp from the sprint to the door. My mom is in the living room, a soft old love song drifting from the record player. The warmth of the house contrasts painfully with the thunder still rattling the windows.

I'm too tired to pretend I'm okay and head straight to my room.

I crawl into bed, still shaking. My life feels like it's ripping apart at the seams, everything I tried to hold inside spilling free. I curl in on myself, arms wrapped tightly around my chest as the storm rages outside my window, the thunder almost matching the tremors coursing through me.

I don't remember when sleep finally drags me under.

Sunlight wakes me. Weak, pale, nothing like last night's fury. For a moment, I expect the smell of pine and sea salt, some sign that Caleb came.

But the room is still. Quiet.

Just me.

I reach for my phone. No messages. Not from Caleb. Not from anyone.

I hide here for the rest of the day.

The hours pass slowly. I pull out the books I took from my father's library, stacking them on my bed like a shield. Their pages smell of cedar and dust and old magic. I sink into them, reading about The Scath accords, Siren lore, and bloodlines that weave through centuries.

By the time I look up, it's almost six.

I close the books one by one, feeling a strange mix of exhaustion and clarity.

I take a long shower, letting the hot water beat against my skin until the tightness in my chest loosens. When I finish, I dress in my usual black skinny jeans that hug every curve with confidence and a white shirt with a small patch logo that reads The Kill Spot. Familiar clothes, familiar armor. I breathe deeply and steady myself.

The house is quiet as I head downstairs. Grabbing my keys, I move toward the door. It's been a while since I helped at the bar, and Killian could definitely use an extra pair of hands. Work sounds grounding and simple.

I reach for the handle.

"Kali."

My father's voice slices through the air behind me.

Damn it.

I close my eyes for a beat. I know he thinks everything he did was for my protection. For my future. Maybe it's true. But the fallout of his choices has cracked open every part of my life. I've lost so much because he chose secrecy over trust.

Even if I've gained things too, I can't ignore the truth.

If he'd been honest with me from the beginning, so many people wouldn't have been pulled into the wreckage with me.

I turn slowly to face him, following him to his office, resentment simmering like heat under my skin.

"Hey, Kalibunga," he says, trying to keep his voice calm, as if he's trying not to scare me away.

"Father," I respond, emotionless.

"Wow, Father?" He makes a face. "You only call me that when you're truly angry."

"I'm late to head to Killian's, Dad." My heart aches at the way his eyes lower slightly, and his smile wanes just a little at my harshness. I've always been a daddy's girl, wanting to impress him, to be the best version of myself, to make him proud. I look up to him more than anyone else, more than I look up to Mom or my siblings. It's always been him and me.

But I can't justify what he did, even if it was done with good intentions. Sometimes good intentions aren't enough. Sometimes we have to make tough decisions, and I can't help but feel like he didn't want to make a tough decision when it came to me.

"Right, I'll make this quick." He reaches behind his desk and pulls out a necklace box with a locket inside. The necklace and pendant are gold with two stones on either side of the oval locket. I take the necklace box from him, examining it before pulling out the locket and turning it over in my palm. On the back is engraved, "The sea gives life, but it also consumes."

Opening the locket, I find a picture of him and me on one side. On the other, an inscription glints in delicate script: *For you, I live. For you, I die.*

My eyebrows pull together as I look up at him. There's a weariness in his eyes I haven't noticed before. He looks older, more fragile. Shadows sit beneath his eyes, and even his smile feels tired.

"Is everything alright, Dad?"

"It will be," he says. "And so will you." He steps forward and pulls me into a tight embrace, holding me as if the world might break us apart if he loosens his grip.

"You just gave me a necklace. Remember?" I'm hoping he'll explain why he suddenly feels like he's saying goodbye.

"I spoke with Caleb." His tone shifts, and my heartbeat jumps. "He thinks you're afraid of your power. Among other things."

"I'm not afraid of it," I say, crossing my arms, heat rising in my face.

"No," he says gently, "but you are afraid of using it."

My gaze drops to the floor. "When I use it, I become weak. Weakened."

He lifts the necklace between us. The stones catch the light with a faint, shifting shimmer. "These stones are mined from deep-sea caverns. They draw energy from the world around you. The more you learn to channel and pull from your environment, the less it takes from your own body. It could help you."

I watch the locket glow softly against his fingers.

"Your abilities are like a muscle," he says. "You must train them for them to grow stronger. I thought what we did here would be enough. But it's time for you to have real training. Formal training."

"From where?"

"When the time comes." Something unreadable flickers in his expression. He fastens the necklace around my throat with careful hands. "Now go."

He gives me a gentle push toward the door, the locket settling warm against my collarbone as if responding to my pulse.

The necklace feels different the moment it settles against my skin. He's given me jewelry before, but it feels like this carries a weight I can't define. Not physical weight. Something deeper. As if the metal remembers hands other than his. As if the stones recognize me.

There's something different about the exchange too, something unsaid crouching between us. I tuck that feeling away for later. I don't have the time or the emotional energy to unravel it now.

I head to TKS. When I walk inside, everything is the same as always. The bar hums with summer chaos. Drunk college kids slur their words. Frat boys try to fight over nothing. Killian drags two of them out by their collars before they can throw punches. It's loud, messy, and predictable.

But no one from the pack is here, only a scattering of football guys I barely recognize.

There's one kid at the bar who keeps catching my attention. Something about him feels familiar, though I can't place why. He gives me easy smiles and tips well, but that's where the interest ends. Nothing strange. Nothing dangerous.

The night drags on. As the last stragglers finally stumble out, I stay behind to help Killian clean. I wipe down tables and bar stools, the scent of citrus cleaner mingling with spilled beer and pine from the doorframe.

Finished, I grab my bag and head toward the exit.

The bell above the door chimes.

I don't need to turn around. My whole body knows who it is before my mind catches up. His presence hits me like the shift in air before a summer storm. Warm. Electric. Impossible to ignore.

God. I swear I can smell him even in my dreams.

There he stands in a charcoal henley and tailored jeans, sneakers soft against the worn floorboards. His hands rest in his pockets as he walks toward me, shoulders tense, eyes locked on mine.

"Can we talk?" he asks.

"Nothing but time and opportunity," I say with a sigh.

The honesty of it stings. I'm happy to see him, and I hate myself for that flicker of relief. Anger coils under my ribs, sharp and familiar. My mind races through every scenario of what could happen when he's not there. Every danger. Every crack in the world he keeps trying to hold together.

How did I go from hating him two weeks ago to wanting him near me all the time. It has to be the mating bond. It has to be. I never wanted to be around Elijah this much. Not even close.

"Can we go for a walk?"

I glance toward the bar windows. The beach stretches out beyond them, moonlit and quiet. Waves roll in and out in steady breaths, brushing the sand with silver. The tide won't rise for another hour, which gives us time. Enough to walk. Enough to talk. Enough to say the things we can't risk anyone else hearing.

It's the only place we can go where no ears are listening.

I nod once, slow and deliberate. "Yeah. Let's go."

I lead the way outside, Caleb falling into step behind me. We move down the steps and onto the warm night sand. The ocean glitters under the moonlight, quiet except for the steady rush of waves folding over themselves.

"So—" I begin.

"I wasn't with Paris last night," he cuts in.

The words stop me. A breath I didn't realize I was holding drops out of my chest.

"Okay," I say softly, letting that truth settle.

"I was with the pack," he explains. "I've been trying to reach the Maylards to let them know we have Paris so they won't retaliate."

"Oh." It's all I can manage. The Maylards retaliating is a nightmare I don't want to imagine. "How is Paris doing?"

"Better." His tone shifts, heavy with worry. "But she says she doesn't remember what happened. She woke up in the guest house with no memory of anything after they took her. Not the transport. Not Heath. Not arriving at my place. Nothing."

A chill runs through me despite the warm summer air. "That's weird."

"Yeah. Tell me about it." He looks at me sideways, eyes sharp and searching.

He exhales. "I wanted to come by last night," he admits quietly. "I was wrapped up in pack issues, and it looked like you needed space."

"I did," I say with a short nod. "Thank you for giving it to me."

He opens his mouth as if to say more, but a low growl rumbles out of him instead. The sound is primal, deep enough to vibrate through the sand under my feet. His head snaps up, eyes scanning the dunes and tree line with sudden focus.

"Caleb," I whisper, but he's already moving.

He grips my wrist and pulls me toward the water, stepping

backward into the rising tide. Cool waves lick at our ankles as he positions himself between me and the shore.

His gaze sweeps the dark in tight arcs, muscles taut, senses locked on something I can't see.

The night, moments ago calm and bright, feels different now.

Something is out there.

And it's coming.

"Caleb," I whisper.

He doesn't answer. His growl still vibrates through him, low and warning, his body angled protectively in front of mine. I shift to peer around his shoulder.

Graybeard and his pack stand at the forest line. A solid wall of bodies between the trees. That can't be right. Caleb told me he killed him at the hospital. Yet there Arnold stands, tall and unmistakable, the same silver-streaked beard catching the moonlight.

And he isn't alone.

It's only Caleb and me out here, ankle deep in the rising tide, the ocean at our backs. But across the sand, just beyond the surf, there are far more figures than I remember. Graybeard used to have six wolves. Maybe seven.

I count quietly under my breath.

Ten.

Fifteen.

No. Twenty.

Twenty shapes. Twenty bodies. Twenty wolves standing shoulder to shoulder like a small army. Far enough that I can't see their faces, but close enough that I see the way they shift restlessly, like coiled wires waiting to snap.

They look young. Terrifyingly young.

My stomach drops as everything clicks at once. All those teenagers who have gone missing these past months. Eli's explanation that some were born wolves, but others could be created. Lycan made, not pack made. A painful process. A deadly one. Something most humans don't survive.

So why would they put children through that?

Is getting me that important? And important to whom? Graybeard isn't smart or powerful enough to orchestrate this alone. Someone else is using him. Someone with far bigger plans than collecting a rare Supernatural creature.

Allie's warning echoes in my mind. Young wolves are volatile. Their strength can rival any Beta. And here we are. Caleb, a single Alpha, against at least ten new wolves on the front line alone. Maybe more waiting behind them. My power is limited. Even with the necklace warm against my skin, I don't know how long I can fight before exhaustion takes me under.

We're cornered.

Just him and me.

The tide creeping higher behind us.

The riptide waiting to drag anyone careless into its pull.

I want to kick myself for not telling Killian we went for a walk. For not sending a text. For not doing anything that would give someone a trail to follow.

No one knows we're out here.

Caleb's expression shifts, his eyes hardening into something final. Resigned. Ready.

He's already decided what he's going to do.

"It seems you don't want to answer my texts," Arnold calls out. His voice rolls across the sand with a mocking lilt. "I left you notes. Texted you. You know it's not nice to ignore people."

"What is he talking about, Caleb?" My heartbeat climbs into my throat. "He was dead," I whisper.

"He didn't tell you," Arnold says, sounding delighted by the secret. "I've been contacting your mate for weeks. I told him we could do this the easy way or the hard way." He tilts his head, studying us. "Poor Paris. She really didn't deserve any of this. First her best friend steals her boyfriend, then everything she endured with us. A disgusting twist of fate."

Cold dread curls through me.

"Who would've thought she was a Maylard?" he continues. "Very interesting. I even managed to get the Maylards to blame your pack for her disappearance. That took real creativity on my part."

He smiles like the devil.

Then his gaze sharpens. "Oh, and my twin brother is dead." His eyes lock onto mine, murderous and bright. "Imagine my frustration when my niece called to tell me the bad news."

He gestures to the girl I first saw on that fatal day in the woods. She stares back at me with cold pride.

"Although he was an Omega, he left the pack. Ambitious and stubborn. But he was still blood." Arnold gives a small shrug, but his eyes never leave my face. He speaks to Caleb, but the hatred is aimed at me.

Caleb keeps his focus forward. He doesn't look at me once, but I can feel the calculations happening behind his eyes. He's trying to find a way to get us out alive. There's none that doesn't involve a fight.

I already know the truth. If we try to fight our way out, there's a real chance neither of us makes it. But Caleb will never hand me over. Not to Arnold. Not to anyone.

And if I'm honest with myself, I don't know what waits for me if I go with Graybeard's pack. The questions are endless. The outcomes all feel fatal in different ways.

But one thing becomes certain inside me, sharp and steady.

I'm not something to be traded or claimed or dragged into darkness because of what I am. Caleb stands in front of me like a wall, and I refuse to let him stand alone.

If we fight, I fight with him.

If we fall, we fall together.

I lift my chin, power gathering in my chest like a rising tide.

I'm done running.

Graybeard's pack descends the beach in a wide, deliberate line, their silhouettes growing sharper as they step out of the shadows. Caleb and I keep our backs against the rising tide, the cold water pulling at our ankles as we stand shoulder to shoulder. The wolves spread out across the sand, forming a semicircle that tries to pen us in. None stand on Caleb's side. All nine on my side move as one, their eyes locked on me, while Graybeard stands in the center of the formation with his attention fixed entirely on Caleb. Something in me knows he's underestimating me, and for a brief moment, I feel a spark of satisfaction at the mistake he's about to make.

The pack surges forward. Caleb launches himself into the first wave on his side, claws flashing with Alpha precision. The air fills with growls and scraping sand as I brace myself against the nine rushing toward me. They're young, barely more than children, their movements sharp with desperation rather than skill. They have no idea what they've been forced into, no understanding of the blood they're being asked to spill.

"You don't have to do this," I call out, hoping even one of them might listen.

The girl who attacked me in the woods steps forward, her voice dripping with venom. "Oh, but we do. You killed my brother. And that ex of yours, you have no idea what I wanted to do to him just to make you suffer. Then I realized you don't even care about him." Her smile widens, cruel and gleeful. "You must care about your best friend, though. That's why you're sleeping with her ex-boyfriend."

The words hit their mark. The thought of Eli in their hands cuts deep, but the taunt about Caleb hits deeper and pulls something hot and feral loose inside me. My power stirs under my skin, reacting to the surge of emotion.

"Me killing your brother wasn't enough for you?" I let my anger sharpen my tone. The tide pulls harder on my legs, the necklace warming against my chest. "If you want to see him again so badly, don't worry. I'll make sure you see him sooner than you think."

Her eyes widen with rage, her control snapping. Exactly what I need.

She lunges forward with a snarl, claws extending as her hand slices through the air inches from my face. I lean back enough to avoid being shredded, the rush of her strike cutting through the space where my skin had been moments before. Using her momentum, I bend low and sweep my leg across hers, knocking her feet out from under her and sending her crashing into the wet sand and rising water. The moment she hits the ground, the other eight close in on me. Their shadows blur together as I fight them off with everything I know. A strike to the nose with Tiger Balm coated fingers sends one stumbling. A blow to the gut folds another. A kick to the chest drives a third back. Every lesson I ever learned rings through my mind in my father's voice, telling me my legs are strong and to use them. So I do. I kick out again and again, a sharp knee to a rib, a heel to a jaw, my body moving on instinct and training.

Then a howl splits the night. Not a victory cry. A cry of pain so raw it tears through my chest. I spin toward the sound and see Caleb on the ground. Graybeard stands over him, his claws raised high, ready to strike. Fear slams into me, and I gather every shred of energy in my body, ready to erupt and blast through the wolves surrounding us.

Before I can release it, hands clamp around my neck from behind. A wolf drags me back, cutting off my air. I slam my elbow into their ribs again and again, striking blindly until their grip loosens. I twist, gasping, only to face the girl from earlier as she drives her claws straight into my side. Pain explodes through me, and hot blood pours down my hip, soaking into the sand as the world tilts.

I can't see Caleb anymore. I can't see anything at all. My head pounds, and my whole body trembles, unsure if it's pain or fear or the shock of how fast everything has gone wrong. The hands choking me dissolve into water that slips between my fingers. The girl in front of me flickers, her form rippling like a reflection on a disturbed pond, then she disintegrates entirely into a splash that vanishes into the tide.

The beach on my side is suddenly empty. Every wolf who stood against me is gone. My gaze locks on the one figure still standing. Graybeard.

I try to move toward him and the several werewolves standing above Caleb, but my legs fail beneath me. I collapse into the shallow surf, knees sinking into the cold water. The scene unfolding in front of me feels distant and unreal, like a horror film I'm forced to watch from inside my own body.

"Looks like you're out of energy, Little Bird." His voice drips with satisfaction. Hearing that nickname from his mouth twists something sick inside me.

Caleb is still on his knees. Barely. Graybeard steps close, claws raised. He swings, and Caleb falls into the water, swallowed by the rising tide.

A cold certainty cuts through me. If nothing changes, someone dies here. Maybe both of us.

I reach inside myself for strength, for power, for anything at all. My limbs are dead weight. My vision swims. I can't even count the ones already gone. I only know I'm too weak to move.

Then the water touches me.

It glows where it meets my skin, a faint blue shimmer that pulses with the rhythm of the tide. The ocean shifts around me, not pulling or pushing, but waiting. Listening. Recognizing.

The locket at my throat begins to heat. Then it burns.

I drag everything I have left into one place inside me. My

fear. My rage. My grief. The ocean answers, pulling toward me like a living thing. I feel it rushing from the depths, swirling through the tide, racing through my veins. The power is immense, almost unbearable.

The locket surges with cold blue light, spiderweb fractures racing across the stone. The water around me rises, swirling into a bright, spiraling vortex that lifts the remaining wolves off their feet. The air hums. The light intensifies.

Then it happens.

The necklace cracks and bursts.

A ring of blue fire explodes outward, fed by the ocean itself. It hits the wolves in a single sweeping wave. Their bodies dissolve on contact, vaporizing into mist that vanishes before it reaches the ground. Not blood. Not bodies. Nothing. Only steam that curls upward and disappears into the dark.

The energy drains out of me all at once. My body collapses forward into the tide. I hear a distant howl, sharp with shock and fury. The world tilts, water rising to meet my face as the last flicker of power fades from my broken locket.

Then, as if the sea itself exhales, the water stills.

The tide stops moving. Not a ripple. Not a pull.

The ocean rests after giving me everything it had.

Darkness closes over me.

TWENTY-TWO

The familiar scent of Caleb envelopes me, anchoring me to the moment. I wake up, disoriented and unsure of my surroundings. I turn my head slowly, careful not to disturb him. His face is relaxed, peaceful—like a serene painting. For a moment, I marvel at the youthfulness in his features, but then I notice the subtle lines etched into his skin, the toll of stress and responsibility that's aged him prematurely.

As I watch his chest rise and fall, the events of the last night crash back into my mind like a wave, causing my heart to race. Suddenly, I bolt upright, panic flooding my senses. Caleb shuffles in his sleep, turning to the other side, blissfully unaware of my turmoil.

I slip out of bed, my bladder demanding immediate attention. I close the bathroom door silently and hurry to the toilet, praying that the flush won't wake him. After washing my face, I make my way back to the bedroom, determined to piece together what happened.

To the left of the mirror, atop the armoire, I spot an old, faded photo. Stretching to retrieve it, I find a picture of Caleb and I from summer camp over a decade ago. Memories flood back, filled with laughter and innocence. I remember how his family hosted that camp for local kids by Lake Missouri, but I can't recall the moment this photo was captured. A tight knot forms in my chest as I realize how little I noticed him back then, how he was always there, quietly hoping I would see him.

The weight of nostalgia presses down on me, bringing tears to my eyes as I consider all the times Caleb has been in the background of my life, waiting for me to recognize him. He kept this photo all this time, and the thought of it is both beautiful and heartbreaking.

"You know I have strict rules about people rummaging through my sentimental stuff?" Caleb's groggy voice interrupts my thoughts. "There's a hefty price to pay for that," he says from over my shoulder. I didn't even hear him get out of bed.

"Does saving your life suffice?" I shoot back, a smirk creeping onto my lips.

He steps closer, pressing his body into mine, warmth radiating from him.

"Sleep well?" A hint of concern laces his voice.

"Depends on how long I was asleep?" I'm still processing everything.

"Six days," he says, the gravity of his words sinking in.

"Six days?" I'm astonished. Even with the necklace, the fight took a toll on both of us. "I thought I lost you." His voice is heavy with emotion.

"I thought the same thing."

I turn to face him, placing my hand under his chin, lifting his gaze to meet mine. "Unfortunately for you, I'm still kicking."

"I killed—"

"Don't blame yourself. You saved us both," he interrupts.

"Those kids—"

"Got dealt a bad hand, and it's not your fault."

"What happened?" I need to know what happened. The memories of the beach and the fight are still hazy.

"You happened, I guess," he says, his tone steady. "I don't even know what you did" He nods solemnly. "None of them made it."

A wave of nausea rolls through me. I know I shouldn't blame myself, but my existence seems to cast a dark shadow over so many lives. Caleb, my family, and now these young wolves. It feels like a burden I can't shake.

"You have a big heart, Kali. You're more compassionate than any of us. I know you think your existence is the reason for all this pain, but life is unpredictable. People live, people die, often for reasons beyond our control. You chose me just as I chose you, and that decision came with risks."

"How did you know what I was thinking?" I'm surprised as his words sink in, resonating deeply within me. I chose him despite everything, despite the weight of our pasts and the fears that loom over us. "But what about Elijah? What about Paris?" My voice trembles.

"You'll have to let that go." Caleb steps closer, his expression fierce yet tender. "We belong to each other now. There's no room for doubt."

He leans in, capturing my lips with his in a heated kiss. The world around us fades, and for a moment, it's just us, lost in each other, drawn together by forces beyond our understanding. I melt against him, my body instinctively responding to his, and I finally, once again, try to accept the truth: he is mine, and I am his.

As we break apart, his mood shifts from blissful to serious. "There's something else you need to know."

His hand sneaks around my waist, but the playful motion doesn't reach his eyes. The pools of black bloom with violet swirls as he struggles to speak, his eyebrows pulling together.

"Did the Maylard's make good on their promise? Do they

know that we got to Paris in time?" I ask, anxiety rumbling through me.

"Not the wolves," he clarifies, and I let out a breath I didn't realize I was holding. "Okay," I say. "So what happened?"

He hesitates, long enough that my heartbeat starts to ache in my chest. His mouth opens, then closes again, as if the words are too heavy to force out.

"Kali," he finally says, voice rough. "I-it's…it's your brother. And I need you to understand this before anything else. We don't know who killed him. There's nothing pointing to anyone yet."

The floor shifts under me. "What are you talking about? Knox?" The question barely makes it out.

He drags a hand over his face, eyes unfocused as he shakes his head. "His car was still in the bar's parking lot when we got to the pier. That was the first sign that something was wrong. I called the pack to come assist with you before I went inside."

He stops and swallows hard. "But when I went in, I found him."

My knees start to fold under me, and he catches me before I can drop. My breath turns sharp and fast, and my vision washes in red as thunder booms somewhere far away or maybe inside my skull.

Then everything goes black.

Three days later, I crawl into my bed, still wearing my black funeral attire. There's always so much to do before funerals. You're surrounded by so many people giving their condolences, but once they're gone, all you're left with is your thoughts consuming you until there's nothing left. I'm exhausted, surprised I'd even managed to make it to the funeral. It was small, just family and Caleb, of course. Not even friends. Krystal hugged me as silent tears slid down her face, while Kristina shot me an accusatory look. Knox sat on the bench by the gravesite with his head hung low. I stayed with him most of the time.

I've been in and out of consciousness, the pain of knowing he isn't here pulling me back into the abyss every time I wake up. I make an effort to not let the pain consume me, just for today. Just so I can see him one last time. I've taken up permanent residence in Caleb's cabin. He thought it best. He's probably right, there's nothing stopping me from going after Paris, her family, or anyone I think could have possibly had a hand in my brother's death.

Caleb has done his best to keep me occupied with physical activities, trying to get me out of my head, but it all comes back to one thought: revenge. I've never been a violent person, but I want everyone who has ever spoken ill of my family to pay. I want to wash myself in their defeat and death. I realize I'm not good to be around right now. I want revenge, and my mind keeps thinking up different ways I can get it.

Fortunately for him, from what I've recently learned, mates can't kill each other. The bloodlust they feel can be directed at someone else, but it's never directed at your mate. It makes sense that he's keeping me away from everyone. Who knows what will trigger me?

I lay on his black silk sheets, watching as a thunderstorm rages outside.

Caleb, who left for a meeting at the den, comes back as I'm waking. He scoops me out of bed, bringing me to the bathroom with him. It's been like this for the past three days: me in a silent daze and him taking care of me. He lifts the black dress I have on, making me stand as he peels my stockings and underwear down my legs. My lower half is bare before him. He unclasps my bra, letting it fall to the floor between us. His palms find my breasts, and he begins massaging them. My eyes meet his.

"What do you need?" he asks, cocking his head to the side.

"To forget," I reply.

He shakes his head no. "The time for forgetting is over." He looks at me with hard eyes. "What do you need?"

Admittedly, it's a loaded question, mainly because I don't know what I need. I know what I want: several people to die. I want to kill them myself. I want my brother back. But, what I need? I haven't thought about that.

"I need to feel something other than the pain."

He leads me to the large shower as he strips off the sweats and henley he put on after the funeral. He takes a hair tie and places my braids into a high bun as he walks into the shower with me, grabbing the loofah and slowly spreading soap over my body. He pays particular attention to the spot between my legs, and my head rolls back in tortured bliss.

Too fast for me to process, he wraps his arm around me, lifting me so my legs wrap around his waist as he impales me on him. One of his hands has a firm grip on my throat. I can't process what's happening fast enough. He slams into me repeatedly, my body clenching around him while I hold on to his shoulder for dear life. He uses the bun he created as leverage to drag my head back, pushing my breasts into his chest as he nibbles and kisses my neck and collarbone, until his head dips, and he takes a nipple into his mouth, sucking hard.

I push my body into him more, driving myself down onto him while simultaneously pushing my breasts into his mouth. He kisses his way back up my neck before biting down hard. Stars begin to pepper my vision as his fingers squeeze the sides of my throat. I can feel when his teeth break the skin as he laps the blood with his tongue.

"Who do you belong to?" he asks, continuing his punishing thrusts.

"You," I strain to get out through the pressure of his hand.

"Who?"

"I belong to you."

He releases my hair, my head falling into the crook of his neck as he reaches between our moving bodies to play with me, sending me over the edge. My entire body begins to shake with the overwhelming feeling of my orgasm. My thighs tighten around his waist, pulling him deeper into me as I ride wave after wave of pleasure, while he spears up into me. Finally catching his own release, he bellows out a moan, and I can feel him pulsing inside me. I feel sore and tired, but at least this is a pain I can manage.

He cleans me and washes himself, bringing me back to the room and dressing me in his shirt and boxers. He brings me tea to drink while I lay on him, his hand stroking my head in a caring manner. With the exhaustion from our earlier activities pulling me under, I whisper a thank you before closing my eyes. I dream of three babies with violet eyes.

I wake up the next day, deliciously sore as I stretch my hands above my head. Caleb is sitting by the window reading a book.

"Hey," I say.

"Sleep well?"

"Better than I have in a long time." I rub my eyes as he watches me.

"Have any interesting dreams?" he asks.

There's no way he knows, I think to myself. "Same old, same old," I answer as I sit up in bed. He looks at me inquisitively. "Why?"

"You were tossing around a lot," he explains, which I don't believe.

"Why are you up so early?"

"Got a call from Luna. The whole thing with the Omegas was bugging me. I was trying to find out who sent them. I was sure they were working with the Maylard's, but Luna had a meeting with them. It wasn't them, though. They actually scoffed at the idea of working with any Supernatural creatures from The Scath."

"Any other theories?" I ask as he shakes his head no. "And what about Killian?" My chest tightens at the sound of his name.

"They say it wasn't them. They sent their condolences," he says as I scoff. "There's something else you should know. They had your dad search Paris's memory, and he could see what happened while the Omegas had her."

"Okay. What did he find?"

"Nothing."

"Do you think it could have been another Kelpie who wiped it?"

"I thought of that. Interesting theory. There's something else," he continues.

"Can you just say everything at once?" I sigh.

"They also had him wipe her memory," he says, finally getting to what he really wants to say.

"Of?"

"All of it, anything that had to do with The Scath…including me and you." He eyes me warily. The knife in my chest turns slightly, knocking the breath out of me. "It was for the best." He walks over to the bed. "This way she doesn't suffer anymore."

"She's my best friend," I whisper, bringing my head down to my knees.

"I know." He rubs small, soothing circles on my back. If I'm being honest, this is for the best. Paris is human, and I'm not. At least I still have the memories of us. The problem is that this hurts just as bad as a breakup. Paris deserves better. It hurts me to know that her parents had to be the ones to make the decision.

Caleb goes to the bathroom as my phone beeps, signaling a new message.

KRYSTAL

We need to talk now.

I ask Caleb to drop me off at home so I can figure out what's going on. He reluctantly agrees, only after I promise he can come back later. The second the door closes behind me, I can already tell something's wrong.

As I walk deeper into the house, heading toward my room, voices drift from the living room. Krystal, Kristina, and Liam are all sitting on the couch. My sisters look tense, and Liam, Kristina's boyfriend, sits between them like he's bracing himself. He's also Elijah's brother, and the sight of him alone is enough to set my nerves on edge.

A meeting like this is never good. My mind instantly jumps to Killian. Maybe they found out something. Maybe the pack finally uncovered a lead. The thought sends a cold twist through my chest.

"What's going on?" I ask, stepping into the room. The silence feels heavy, like the seconds are stretching too long.

Krystal looks at Kristina before speaking. "It's Elijah. He's been attacked again. Liam called this meeting because he just got the news, but we don't know where he is or what happened yet."

My heart drops. Another attack. Elijah left Caleb's pack months ago, so why are they still hunting him? He is not even my mate. None of this should be following him anymore. None of it should be following me.

Liam sits to Kristina's left with his head lowered. His whole body is tight with anger, the kind that shakes beneath the skin. I can feel the turmoil rolling off him, the pressure of trying to stay loyal to the pack while fearing for his brother's life.

"You don't know where he is?" I ask, keeping my voice firm.

"We don't know," Liam says. He finally lifts his head, and his glare hits me full force. His anger is hot, but I refuse to take a single step back from it. He's terrified of losing his brother. I understand that. But that doesn't mean I'll shrink.

"We'll find him," I say. Calm. Certain.

"I think you've done enough," Kris snaps, her voice sharp.

Krystal cuts in before anything escalates. "This isn't helping.

We need to figure out who has him." She pauses, thinking. "And I don't think it's the Maylards."

"Then who could it be?" Liam asks, frustration rising.

My phone rings. A blocked number. The timing alone makes my irritation spike.

I answer immediately. "Who is this?"

"There's my Little Bird."

His voice is smooth, like he thinks he has the upper hand. He doesn't.

My brows lower, unimpressed. Before I can respond, Kristina steps closer, trying to get my attention, and Krystal leans forward, mouthing, *Who is it?* Liam edges even nearer, eyes narrowed. They want answers, and fast.

I hold a hand up to quiet them, then switch the call to speaker. "Say that again," I tell him, my tone cool.

"Now, now, Little Bird, I've been looking everywhere for you. Where have you been hiding?"

"Who are you?" I ask, my voice unwavering.

"You don't remember? The other night at the bar?" he taunts.

"Should I? You sound like someone who thinks being annoying counts as a personality."

"You're hurting my feelings," he says with a fake pout in his voice.

Krystal shoots me a questioning look. I shake my head once. I don't know him, and he's not worth my time.

"You have a problem answering questions directly," I say. "Are you slow or just stalling?"

"Oh, that mouth. Sounds like you need it filled," he purrs.

I smile, cold and sharp. "Here's how this is going to work. You tell me exactly what you want, right now. If you don't, I'm ending this call."

I keep my thumb hovering over the end button, making sure he hears the threat in the quiet that follows.

"What about poor Elijah?" he replies.

Chains clink in the background, followed by a muffled, pained growl. My eyes snap to Liam. He's already on his feet, fists clenched so tight his knuckles whiten.

"I'll bite, though," the caller continues, his voice dropping to something that tries to sound dangerous. "I was at the bar the other night. Gave you all those tips. You remember? You kissed me to make that sack of shit jealous."

A cold wave rolls through my stomach, but I refuse to let it show. I keep my voice steady. "What do you want?"

"I thought you were beautiful. And who wouldn't kiss a beautiful girl, right? But then this…obsession hit me. I couldn't stop thinking about you. And then I saw what you did at The Cove. Holding the entire sea back to protect the Alpha. You must really like him."

He pauses long enough to revel in his own words.

"I wondered how I could get your attention. Then I took a little walk through your room and saw all those photos of you and Elijah. So I thought she might be messing around with the Alpha, but this little wolf right here means a whole lot more to her."

Liam sucks in a sharp breath. Krystal's hand flies to her mouth. Kristina steps closer to me like she's ready to restrain me or support me depending on my next move.

"But you?" the caller goes on. "You're worth even more to me. I can't get you out of my head, no matter how hard I try. And trust me, sweetheart, that's bad for business."

My jaw tightens, but I keep my breathing steady.

"So here's what's going to happen," he says. "You're going to come down here and reverse whatever it is you did to me. Or he dies."

I don't flinch. I don't gasp. I don't break.

I stare at the phone, then at Liam, whose entire body is coiled like a wolf moments before a kill.

"Good," I say. "Now we're getting somewhere." "And where is 'here'?"

"I know you're constantly surrounded by all those wolves," he says. "But you should let them know that if any wolf comes with you, it dies."

"Just send me the address," I spit, refusing to give him the satisfaction of hesitation.

"You're a big girl. I'm sure you can figure it out," he replies, and then the line cuts.

Silence drops into the room like a weight. I feel every pair of eyes on me. The house vibrates with tension long after the call ends. Outside, the sky has darkened completely, the kind of heavy night that presses close to the windows. I check the time, surprised at how quickly the hours slipped away. The moon is high, casting pale light across the living room floor.

"You're not coming," I tell Liam immediately.

"This is my brother's life at stake, Kali," Liam says. His voice is tight, desperate, but his eyes burn with determination.

"I'm bringing him home alive and safe," I say, staring straight into him. "We're doing this my way."

The tension thickens until the room feels too small. Liam's jaw locks, his shoulders rigid, torn between his instincts and the reality that he can't fight me on this. I'm terrified, but I bury it so deeply no one can tell.

I text Qora to meet me at my house. If I go to the den, Caleb will insist on coming, and I can't risk that. Duke and Zori decide to come as well. More hands, more experience, more options. I ask them to bring weapons from Wraithstone.

A roar slices through the quiet, sounding like a motorcycle engine about a half an hour later, then another. The low rumble rolls across the house, and every head snaps toward the front door. Krystal goes to open it.

Zori is the first to step inside when the door swings open. Her braid hangs over one shoulder, her boots muddy, her eyes sharp with purpose. The second she sees me, she walks straight over and pulls me into a fierce hug. "I know you didn't think you would do this without us," Zori says.

Behind her, Duke follows, tall and silent, his expression unreadable but focused. Even the air around him seems to shift, like the shadows stretch a little farther to reach him.

Kristina stares at him with thinly veiled suspicion, but Duke doesn't bother acknowledging her.

Qora looks at each person in the room, her gaze lingering on Liam, then Kristina, then Duke. She folds her arms and turns back to me. "Tell me everything." I do.

"And how exactly do you expect to find this guy?" Kristina asks me. Her tone is flat, almost bored, like she's daring the situation to impress her.

"Me," Duke says simply.

"And you are?" Kristina asks, not bothering to hide the rudeness in her voice.

I push aside the fact that I've not fully thought through how we'll track Elijah. My focus has been on assembling a team capable of extracting him once we get there. I don't know how many enemies are involved, and my power is still something I don't fully understand. At The Cove, I pulled from the ocean. Does it have to be natural water? Open water? What if that was a fluke? What if I can't rely on it in combat?

At least the Wraithstone team has lived their whole lives preparing for this kind of situation. Technically, I have too, but I've not had the chance to prove myself in a real fight. And this isn't exactly a low-risk trial run.

"Incubus are very good trackers," Duke continues.

Kris scoffs. "Of course she would stumble into The Scath and manage to find the bottom of the barrel to hang around with."

My patience snaps like a pulled thread.

"Look, I don't need your snarky, bitchy comments right

now," I say, pinning her with a hard stare. "You can either shut the hell up and help, or you can leave. Your choice."

The room stills after my words, and for the first time since the call ended, I feel like the ground beneath me is solid again.

"Liam doesn't want to leave his brother's life in the hands of the girl who ruined it," Kris snaps.

"With a sister like you, who needs enemies?" Qora replies, her tone cold and effortless.

Kris whirls toward her. "What the fuck did you just say to me?"

"I sai—" Qora begins.

"We don't have time for this," I cut in, stepping between them before the room explodes. I turn to Duke. "What do you need to find Elijah?"

"A picture of him will suffice," Duke answers.

"That's it?" Kris asks, disbelief dripping from every word.

"God, does she ever shut the fuck up?" Qora mutters.

"Only when she's asleep," I say under my breath as I take the stairs two at a time.

The upstairs hallway is dim, lit only by moonlight leaking through the windows. My heart beats fast, not with fear, but urgency. I reach my room, go straight to the dresser, and pick up the last photo Eli and I took together. It was after his team won the football championship last year. It had poured that day. Eli's clothes are soaked and covered in mud, and he's smiling like the world belongs to him.

It feels like a lifetime ago.

I turn the photo over in my hand, focusing on his face, letting the memory settle for a moment.

A presence shifts behind me.

I spin around.

Duke stands in the doorway, silent, his eyes unreadable. The shadows in the room seem to lean toward him, drawn like metal to a magnet. He steps forward, gaze lowering to the photo in my hand.

"That will do," he says quietly, before turning to go back downstairs. He looks back at me, saying, "Sometimes there are things we wish we could change, and there are many things that we can change, but destiny and fate aren't one of those. Sometimes we have to be happy with the time we've had with someone. Be grateful for it. But when the time is up, you have to move on." He turns, leaving the room.

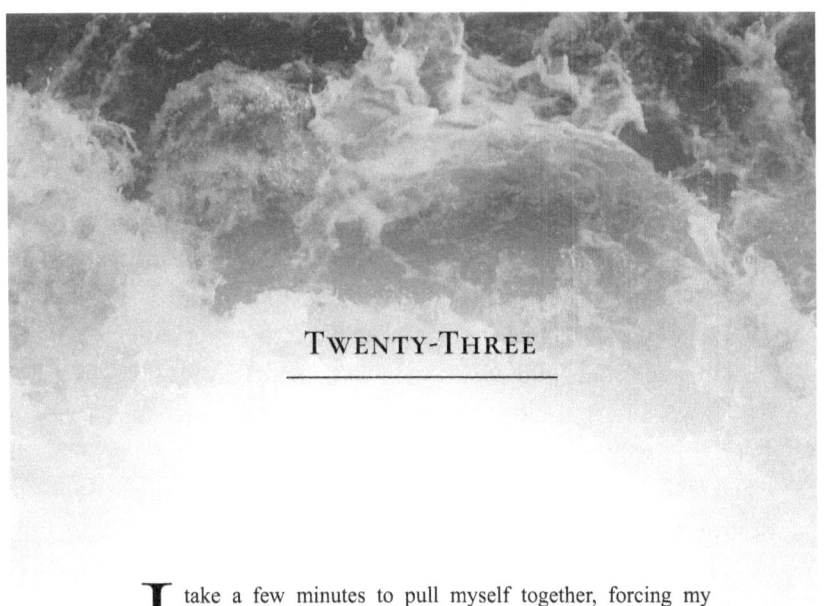

TWENTY-THREE

I take a few minutes to pull myself together, forcing my thoughts into order instead of letting them spiral. I change into a full black outfit: a long-sleeve, skin-tight bodysuit and cargo pants. Practical, silent, and loaded with pockets for every blade and tool I might need. I don't know exactly what we're walking into tonight, but I refuse to show up unprepared.

I send a quick, sharp prayer into the universe that Duke finds Elijah, that we get him out, and that everyone who steps into this returns. My mind churns through every possibility of who could have taken him. I keep circling back to the guy from the bar, but he was too ordinary and too human-looking. But that's the problem, isn't it?

Who the hell is this man, really? This all seems highly calculated and less of an advantageous coincidence.

By the time I head downstairs, the house is humming with movement. Everyone is gearing up. Qora has already divided the group into teams, laying out markers and a plan with military precision. Duke needed less than a minute to lock onto Elijah's trail. The scent leads toward The Cove, an abandoned warehouse past The Kill Spot. Convenient. Too convenient.

A cold knot settles in my stomach, but I clamp down on it.

We pile into the cars, engines rumbling to life in the warm summer night. The interior smells like leather, steel, and the sweat of all of us bracing for what comes next.

The headlights cut through the night, flashing across trees and abandoned fences. Every bump in the road shakes the weapons strapped to my legs. The whole ride feels too quiet, too tense, like the world itself is holding its breath.

I look down at my hands and think of Liam. Leaving him behind made something inside me twist. I hate that I had to make that call. Even if we lose Elijah tonight, I can't let Kristina lose Liam. He's the only person who keeps her from slipping into what I could only call Moyra's darkness. Losing him would destroy her in a way none of us could repair.

The thought sits heavily on my chest for the rest of the drive.

We pull up to the warehouse, and the place looks completely abandoned. Zori and Qora sweep the perimeter for any sign of movement, finding nothing at all. No cars, no voices, not even the usual echo of distant machinery. It feels empty in a way that makes my skin crawl.

"Are you sure this is the place?" Qora asks Duke.

"Are you questioning my talents?" Duke lifts a brow.

"I am," Kris says, shouldering past him and bumping him hard. "Well, we're not going to find him standing out here arguing all night." She heads for the large front door.

"Maybe we should wait," I say, catching her hand. "I have a bad feeling."

"Let go of me. Look, I get that you're too scared to go, but I'm not dealing with a shredded boyfriend because you're too chicken shit to do anything," she snaps. "Elijah deserves better than you." She slides open the door, which makes almost no noise at all.

Krystal goes in after her. The rest of us exchange looks. Zori lifts a shoulder in a small shrug and steps inside.

The knot in my stomach tightens, but I follow them into the warehouse. Qora comes after me, Duke taking up the rear.

Inside, it's dark except for the slivers of moonlight filtering through the holes in the torn roof. The warehouse is carved into sections by steel makeshift walls. Sheets of plastic hang from the ceiling, rustling softly whenever a breeze slips in through the cracks. Each step echoes faintly, swallowed by shadows.

We move in a line, careful and quiet. I strain my ears, listening for anything beyond the steady drip of water somewhere deeper in the building. Kris, as usual, walks ahead without hesitation. She moves from room to room as if nothing here could possibly touch her. The rest of us, who still value staying alive, stick together. Kristina pushes onward with Krystal close behind.

The moment we enter the next room, something shifts. The air feels wrong. Heavy. I can't place it, but it crawls across my skin. More plastic sheets hang around us, creating narrow corridors that twist the faint moonlight into distorted shapes. We search carefully, checking corners and scanning the floor for any sign of Elijah.

The others gather near the far wall, finding nothing at all. I step toward the exit, ready to move on, when an arm snakes around my waist and yanks me back. A hand clamps over my mouth before I can make a sound.

A breath brushes against my ear.

"Shhh, Little Bird. We wouldn't want to scare your friends, would we?"

My heart slams against my ribs. His voice is unmistakable. He told me no wolves should be involved. If Caleb is here, Elijah's chances are already disappearing. The only question that slices through my mind is how he found us so easily.

There's only one place my thoughts go.

Kris.

I look up in time to see Duke standing in front of me. His

eyes sweep over the scene with cold irritation. "I knew you were idiots, but I didn't think you were suicidal," he says.

Caleb answers with a growl that rolls from deep in his chest, low and dangerous enough to vibrate the air.

"What's going on?" Qora calls out as she steps back into the room, weapons drawn and eyes sharp.

"What did you do?" I whisper to Caleb, my pulse hammering as I stare at him. My voice shakes from anger, not fear.

He presses one finger to his lips, silently telling me to stay quiet, then points toward a hallway to our right. We move quickly and silently in the direction he indicates, weaving through the narrow path of steel walls and plastic curtains.

The corridor opens into a large central chamber. We're on a second-level balcony, the metal grating cold beneath our boots. Below us, in the middle of the open space, Elijah hangs from chains, his arms stretched above his head. An IV line runs into his arm, filled with a yellow liquid that glows faintly in the moonlight.

"Wolfsbane," Zori murmurs. "I can smell it from here."

Our group gathers tightly along the railing. My gaze snaps to Kris, and beside her, confirming my worst fear, stands Liam. He looks terrified but determined. At least the entire pack didn't come. That's the only mercy in this mess, and it's a small one.

We scan for a way down and spot a narrow metal staircase twisting to the lower level. The structure looks unstable, rattling even from this distance.

Caleb steps forward, intent on descending.

I grab his arm and pull him back. "Stop. Think for once."
"Something doesn't feel right. This is too easy."

"Maybe he got scared and ran off. Everything isn't always something," Kris snaps as she brushes past Caleb and heads down the stairs, Liam following without hesitation.

Caleb turns to me, his hand warm against my cheek as he searches my eyes. "What is it?"

"I don't know. It's just a feeling."

"We go together," he says.

I give a small nod, and the rest of us descend the staircase to meet Kris and Liam below.

Krystal works quickly to remove the Wolfsbane drip from Elijah's arm. His skin looks pale, almost gray. I can't shake the feeling of eyes on us. My gaze sweeps the balcony that wraps around the room. Sheets of plastic hang from several sections, and anything could be hiding behind them. I check the lower walls and corners, but there are no doors or exits. Only the staircase we came down.

We're trapped. Sitting ducks.

Everything happens at once. Bright lights blast on overhead, blinding us. Liam tries to haul Elijah's arm over his shoulder. I throw up a hand to shield my eyes, but the glare is too strong to see who stands behind it.

"You know, I really thought you would listen, Little Bird. I said no Werewolves. Especially not your Alpha!" the voice from the phone roars. I still can't see his face, only the silhouette behind the light.

"Screw you!" I shout.

Caleb steps in front of me, growling as he blocks the man's view of me.

"Will you?" the voice replies.

A gunshot cracks through the room. Liam collapses beside me. At the same moment, Qora draws a knife and hurls it toward our right, hitting her target with violent precision. A body crashes from the balcony above.

"Jace," a new voice screams from the opposite side of the balcony. More gunfire erupts. So there's three of them.

We sprint toward the shelter under the balcony. Something small and cylindrical hits the ground in front of us. It pops open, and smoke floods the room in thick gray waves.

Caleb starts coughing hard, each breath harsher than the last.

I yank my hoodie up to cover my nose and mouth as the smoke grows denser, swallowing the room and blinding my sight completely.

Caleb collapses to the ground, and a surge of blind rage tears through me as I watch him fall. The sound of his body hitting the floor is enough to snap something inside my chest. I reach out through the space the way my father taught me, searching for the pulse of the one who threw the smoke bomb. I lock onto a source close by, focus hard, and pull with everything I have until I hear a sharp, wet pop, like a balloon bursting.

"There's some kind of Wolfsbane mixed into the smoke," Zori shouts through the haze.

I try to find the man behind the blinding light, but he's either already retreating toward the exit, or that locating by blood thing was a one time deal. Qora, Zori, and Duke race up the staircase after him while I drop to my knees beside Caleb. My fingers press against his neck. His pulse is weak, but it's there. Relief cuts through me, but it lasts only a second.

A scream tears across the room behind me.

My stomach twists, nausea rising like a wave. I turn and see Kris kneeling over Liam. He's not moving. His chest is still. His body is riddled with bullet holes, and the blood leaking out is dark as ink. Wolfsbane. Too much of it.

Kris clutches him, shaking, her sobs breaking the air. "No. No. No, not him." Her voice fractures with each word.

I sit frozen, unable to move, unable to think. Krystal gathers Kris into her arms, but Kris refuses to let go of Liam. Elijah lies beside them, barely conscious but untouched. Liam shielded him. Liam died shielding him.

Time loses meaning. I stay beside Caleb as he sits up, gathering himself as best he can, until a shadow falls over me. Duke stands there, breathing hard, face tight with worry.

"We have to go," he says.

I try to move, but my body doesn't cooperate. My limbs feel

heavy, locked in place. I don't ask whether they caught the man or if he escaped. I don't ask anything at all, only stare at the faces around me, each one carrying fear, grief, and the dawning horror of what this night has become.

"This is your fault!" Kris screams at me. "All of this is your fucking fault." Her grief tears from her throat like something feral, and for a moment, she looks right through me, as if I'm the only thing in her world worth hating.

Duke moves past us, stronger and steadier than I expected. He carries Elijah first, then Liam, lifting both of them as if the weight of their bodies means nothing compared to the weight of what's happened. Krystal drags Kris toward the cars, whispering to her, trying to keep her together. Kris keeps fighting her, sobbing so violently her whole body shakes.

Caleb and I head for his Jeep, hidden in the trees behind the warehouse. He leans on me, each step slower than the last. The Wolfsbane still claws through his veins. His breathing is unsteady, and his skin is too cold for summer air, but he refuses to let me take all his weight.

Ahead of us, Qora and Zori are already pulling away, racing Elijah to my parents' house. My mother can help save him if anyone can.

I help Caleb into the passenger seat. He sinks back with a low groan, he tries to hide. I take the wheel, and the silence between us feels heavy, buzzing with everything we can't bring ourselves to say yet.

The night outside presses close as we drive. The forest is dark and still, but the echoes of gunshots seem to follow us anyway. The smell of smoke clings to my clothes. My hands shake on the wheel. Every mile puts more distance between us and the warehouse, but none of it feels like enough.

Caleb stares out the window, jaw clenched, fighting the Wolfsbane, I assume. I keep my eyes on the road, trying to swallow the truth burning in my throat.

Kris blames me.

And part of me wonders if she's right.

Two funerals in one week has to be some kind of record, though not one anyone should ever have to set. Krystal was the only one willing to give me the details. Kris still hasn't answered a single message. I know she's shattered, drowning in a grief that no one should face alone, but it still hurts that she won't let me be there for her. She shuts me out like I'm part of what she lost.

We gather around the gravesite dressed in black. The summer heat settles over the field in a suffocating blanket, thick and unmoving, as if even the air is mourning. The scent of freshly turned earth mixes with the sharp bite of cut grass. A low breeze moves through the trees but offers no relief.

Most of the pack has come. Their presence fills the space with quiet strength and shared sorrow. Their father stands at the front, rigid and unreadable, his hands clasped so tightly they tremble. Elijah sits beside him, looking fragile, still bruised and recovering, but he's here. He's alive. There's a small spark in his eyes, a thin thread of hope that didn't exist when we found him chained and fading.

Kris sits next to him, her posture stiff, her face blank. A wall has dropped between her and the rest of the world. Krystal stands behind her chair, one hand lightly touching her shoulder, as if she's the only thing keeping Kris from falling apart in front of all of us.

A few seats down, a man I don't recognize watches the service with too much interest. He looks out of place among us. His clothes are crisp, deliberately chosen. He sits unnervingly still, and his eyes keep drifting toward our group. When his gaze lands on me, something sharp skitters up my spine. It isn't grief in his expression. Not sympathy. Something else. Something colder.

The hair on the back of my neck rises.

Whoever he is, he's not just here to mourn.

As the service draws to a close, Kristina finally lifts her head. Her eyes cut through the drifting haze above the graves like blades. The anger radiating off her is almost tangible. I steady myself, knowing this moment would come. Grief has reshaped her into something fierce and volatile, and if she needs a target to survive this, then I'll take it.

She steps around the grave, slow and deliberate, until she stands directly in front of me.

"I'm so sorry, Kris," I say quietly. My voice wavers, not from fear, but from the weight of everything we lost.

She doesn't answer.

Her hand flashes upward. The slap cracks through the silence, sharp enough to turn a few heads. Pain blooms across my cheek, but I stay still, absorbing it.

Caleb reacts instantly. He's at my side in a heartbeat, one arm around me as he pushes her back. His growl rumbles low, more warning than sound.

"I never want to see you again," she spits. The venom in her words burns more than the slap. She turns away before I can respond, storming toward the path. Elijah rises with visible effort, following her, his expression torn between worry and exhaustion. His hand presses to her back, guiding her as they leave together.

Caleb's glare follows her until she disappears past the tree line. Only then does he look at me, his eyes softening, concern etched deep into every line of his face.

We walk back to the Jeep in a silence so heavy it almost presses the breath from my lungs. The world around us feels muted, drained of color. When I slide into the passenger seat, he closes the door with more force than necessary and circles around to the driver's side. The Jeep roars to life, and he speeds away from the cemetery, gravel spitting under the tires.

The drive feels endless.

My mind spirals through every choice, every moment, every

damn decision that led us to this. I know Liam's death isn't my fault. Kris is the one who told him where we were. But guilt slithers its way in anyway, cold and familiar.

If I had never dated Elijah.

If I had never gone to that bar.

If I had never kissed that man.

Liam would still be alive.

Kris would still have her boyfriend.

Elijah would still have his brother.

And none of us would be burying the consequences of my existence.

TWENTY-FOUR

Once we arrive at the cabin, I head straight to the bedroom without turning on a single light. I climb into the bed and pull the black silk sheets around me like they can keep the world out. They're cool at first, soft and slick against my skin, but my body is still shaking too badly for the comfort to settle in.

Caleb joins me a moment later. He slides in behind me and wraps his arm around my waist, his chest pressed firmly against my back. Our legs tangle together on instinct, as if our bodies know how to calm each other even when our minds are falling apart.

His strength is returning. I felt it on the drive here, that slow shift in his breathing and the faint heat creeping back under his skin as the Wolfsbane finally began to fade. Meanwhile, I can't stop the tremors running through me. Anxiety, anger, panic, and something else I don't want to look at yet.

Caleb doesn't ask anything. He just holds me.

I didn't realize how much I needed that. To be held. To feel someone warm and alive against me after so much blood and smoke and terror.

But sleep isn't gentle. Every time my eyes close, I see the warehouse again. The bright white lights that blinded us. The choking smoke. The moment Caleb collapsed.

And the moment after.

The one I've refused to examine.

The one where I reached out with my power and felt someone's blood in the air. Where I pulled so hard that his body made a sharp, wet sound. I didn't see his face. Didn't know his name. He was alive one second and gone the next because he hurt Caleb.

The thought circles in my mind like a slowly tightening coil. My stomach knots and unknots until breathing becomes work. I try to bury the memory beneath the silk sheets and Caleb's touch, but it rises again. Heavy and unavoidable.

What did I do?

What does that make me?

Would I do it again?

A quiet, ugly truth sits in the back of my mind. If it meant saving him, yes. I would.

The realization scares me more than any enemy ever could.

Eventually, exhaustion drags me under. Caleb's arms stay locked around me, steady and sure. His scent, pine and sea salt and something wild, anchors me to the bed until sleep finally pulls me away.

I wake to the sharp blare of Caleb's phone. The sound cuts through the quiet room like it has claws. The soft purple glow of dusk washes through the floor-to-ceiling windows, painting the forest in a strange, dreamlike light. Shadows stretch across the wooden floor. Everything feels still, almost peaceful.

Caleb groans beside me. He keeps his eyes closed as he pats

around for his phone. His voice comes out rough and sleepy when he answers. "What?"

The voice on the other end is frantic. I can't make out the words, but the tone makes the back of my neck tighten.

Caleb shoots upright.

"Mom? Mom, what's wrong?"

The fear in his voice chills me more than any nightmare.

"Caleb," I call out, but my voice barely reaches the empty doorway.

Before I can push myself up, he's already out of bed. I hear the cabin door slam. A second later, the Jeep engine roars to life. He drives away so fast that gravel sprays against the cabin walls.

He doesn't look back.

Panic surges through me, sharp and immediate. The same panic from the warehouse claws its way up my throat, the same cold sensation that something is about to rip open again.

I scramble for my phone with trembling hands and call Caleb, Allie, and Lucas. Once. Twice. Again and again.

No answer.

The silence on the other end feels worse than any scream.

Alone in the cabin, heart hammering against my ribs, I feel it settling over me.

Something is wrong. Terribly and unmistakably wrong.

And I have no idea what I'm about to face next.

As I move through the living room, my steps are measured and steady, but inside my chest, something tightens every time I glance at the door. The cabin is quiet, too quiet, and the weight of it presses against my ribs. I know better than to panic. Panic clouds judgment. Panic makes mistakes. So I keep myself moving, pacing slowly, keeping my senses sharp.

Still, the quiet gnaws at me.

Outside the window, the trees shift in the wind. Normally, the movement centers me, but tonight the unease beneath my skin refuses to settle. Caleb is somewhere out there, unreachable, and every hour he stays gone makes something cold spread through my chest.

My mind keeps circling back to the warehouse. The smoke. The gunfire. Caleb collapsing. And then the moment I reached for the man who threw the smoke bomb and ended him before I even saw his face.

I'm not falling apart over it. I know what I'm capable of. I know what I was trained for. He was a threat, and I removed him. But there's a part of me that can't ignore how easily the kill came. How natural it felt. How quickly I chose violence the second Caleb went down.

I'm supposed to be in control of my power. Instead, it felt like it controlled me.

By the time morning light filters through the windows, I'm still awake and waiting. When the door swings open, Caleb stumbles inside. He looks wrecked, his clothes rumpled, eyes bloodshot, shoulders sagging under some invisible weight. He looks like someone who's been fighting shadows all night.

I should be furious that he ignored every message. I should demand answers. Instead, I watch him collapse onto the couch, and the only thing I feel is a painful squeeze in my chest. Whatever happened, he's hurting.

I approach him carefully and sit beside him, close enough that our shoulders almost touch. I place a hand on his arm, steady, offering comfort without smothering him.

"What do you need?" I ask, trying to keep my voice soft but not fragile. I want him to know I'm here, not clinging, not demanding, just present.

"Space," he says.

The word hits me like a blade sliding between my ribs, sharp and precise. I pull my hand back and keep my face neutral, but something inside me shifts. He wanted me close every moment since the mating ceremony. Now he won't even look at me.

I know the bond ties us together. I know it cost him things he never said out loud. But hearing him ask for distance feels like confirmation of something I've tried not to think about. The fear that he's realizing the price of being bound to me might be higher than he's willing to pay.

I stand slowly, keeping my posture steady so he won't see how deeply the word cut. I leave the cabin without another sound. I won't beg him to explain. I won't let the bond make me cling where I'm not wanted.

The air outside is cold and clean. I breathe it in until my lungs stop aching and follow the trail behind the cabin, trying to make sense of the hollow feeling slowly filling my chest.

My phone rings, Allie's name appearing on the screen.

"Hey," I answer. My voice is steady, but I know she'll hear the strain beneath it.

"Hey. I'm sorry I didn't get back to you yesterday. A lot has happened."

"Like what?" My curiosity sharpens, but beneath it another fear stirs. If everything is falling apart this quickly, I need to know how far the damage spreads.

"Didn't Caleb tell you?" Allie asks. Her voice tightens, shifting from casual to cautious. "His mom was attacked yesterday. We spent all of night trying to figure out who did it."

The words hit with brutal precision. My knees give out before I can brace myself, and the forest floor rises to meet me. I'm not collapsing from weakness. It's the shock. It lands clean and hard, like a strike I never saw coming. The air seems to thin around me as the pieces rearrange themselves in my mind.

Caleb's mom. Attacked. And he said nothing.

"No. He didn't tell me." The whisper feels scraped raw. I force myself to steady my breathing, but the betrayal threads through every inhale. Why would he hide something this important from me? Why would he choose silence over trust?

"Kali, I'm sorry," Allie says quietly. "He asked us not to tell anyone."

"I'm not just anyone," I snap. The anger rises fast, sharp enough to cut through the shock. "I'm his mate."

The admission leaves a bitter taste. Mated, bonded, tied together in ways that should have meant honesty. Instead, he shut me out again. A long silence stretches on Allie's end.

"Just talk to Caleb when you can," she says finally, then the call ends.

I stare at the screen, the weight of it pressing down on my ribs. The truth settles in with chilling clarity. Caleb wanted space because some part of him blames me. Kris does too. Their grief and fear spill outward, and I'm the common point where it all collides.

Every tragedy keeps circling me as if I'm the center of its gravity.

I get to my feet slowly, bracing myself against a tree. I don't break. I don't crumble. I simply absorb the pain, let it settle, and decide what to do next. I need someone who will not twist the knife deeper, someone who sees me as more than the damage orbiting my life.

I call my dad.

He answers at once, and within twenty minutes, his car appears at the edge of the trail. The sight of him grounds me. His presence has always been steady, a reminder that I'm not as alone as the world keeps trying to make me feel.

I lift a hand, letting him know I'll be only a minute. I owe Caleb that much. Even hurt, even doubting everything, I won't disappear without telling him.

I take a breath, straighten my spine, and turn back toward the cabin with purpose burning beneath my ribs.

Inside, Caleb is still on the couch. He hasn't moved since I left, staring at the ceiling like he's watching something I can't see, something far away and unreachable. He doesn't look at me when I walk in, doesn't even flinch.

"I'm going home," I say.

The words drift into the room and disappear. Nothing changes. He doesn't turn his head, doesn't so much as blink. He gives me nothing, not even the courtesy of acknowledgement.

The indifference stings harder than I expect. I've now faced enemies who wanted me dead, creatures who saw me as prey, people who blamed me for things completely outside my control. None of that hurt like this. This is a cut delivered without effort, quiet and precise.

It's almost impressive how easily he can make me feel invisible.

I stand there for a moment, waiting for something, anything, from him. A nod. A glance. A word. But there's only the hollow emptiness of the room and the sound of my own breathing.

Fine.

I turn away and walk out of the cabin. The door closes behind me with a soft thud that feels too final. The air outside is heavy, thick with the scent of coming rain. Dark clouds churn overhead, slow and ominous, mirroring the storm rolling through my chest.

I climb into my dad's car and let myself sink into the seat. His presence has always been steady, a silent reminder that I'm not alone even when the world feels sharpened against me. He doesn't push for answers, only drives, letting the silence settle.

Rain begins to fall, sliding across the windshield in long streaks, and the wipers sweep them away in slow, steady arcs. The pattern is hypnotic, the only thing holding me together.

I feel my dad's eyes flick toward me, full of pity he tries to hide. I look away, not wanting pity. I want clarity. I want answers. I want to understand why the one person who should never shut me out is choosing to bury himself in silence instead of letting me in.

By the time we reach the driveway, the clouds have thickened into a dark, roiling mass. I'm out of the car before it fully stops. The first rumble of thunder rolls across the sky as I push through the front door.

Inside the house, the quiet wraps around me. I run to my room, sliding down to the floor, my back pressed to the door, my knees pulled close. The storm breaks outside, rain hammering against the windows. The sound fills the room like a cocoon, loud and relentless.

I let myself feel everything I've tried to hold back. The hurt. The confusion. The fear that Caleb is pulling away from me. The fear that he regrets our bond. The fear that I'm losing pieces of my life faster than I can gather them.

At some point, I force myself to shower. The hot water burns against my skin, grounding me enough to keep moving. Eventually, I crawl into bed, exhausted in a way sleep never seems able to fix.

I drift off for what feels like minutes before a knock breaks through the haze. My mom stands in the doorway. I turn to my alarm clock, the dial showing it's a little after 10 am. It's odd that she's home. It must be her day off.

Seeing my mom step into my room is a surprise. I turn on my back, staring at the ceiling, letting my thoughts twist into shapes that make less sense the longer I sit with them. I only shift my eyes when she moves closer and sets something on the night-stand. By the faint scent of chamomile and honey, I know it's tea before I look at it.

"You need to eat something," she says quietly. "And you can't shut yourself in here forever."

"Why not?" My voice is flat. "It's safer for everyone if I stay put. When I'm around people, they get hurt. They die. At least if I'm here, the only ones who might die are the ones who created me."

The bitterness slips out before I can leash it, hanging in the air between us like smoke.

She lets out a slow breath. "Well, Knox, who did not create

you, also lives here. So that's not entirely accurate." She tries for a weak smile, a thin attempt at humor.

"Right. Accuracy and efficiency. The only things you respect," I snap back. The words are sharp, and I know they cut deeper than she deserves. I feel it immediately, a sting of regret under the anger twisting in my chest.

She studies me for a long moment. Her expression softens in a way that almost hurts to look at. "Hurt people hurt people, LiLi."

The nickname hits harder than anything else she could have said. My throat tightens as I feel the emotion rush up fast, raw and unexpected. She hasn't called me LiLi in years. I remember the exact night she stopped. The argument, the way she asked me to slow down with Elijah, how furious I became at the idea of being controlled.

I remember spitting venom at her, telling her to mind her own business. I remember the look on her face when I told her I hated her.

Since then, she's only used my full name. Formal. Distant. Safe.

Hearing it again cracks something open in my chest, letting in memories I would rather avoid. Memories of how I've treated the people who have loved me without question. People who have protected me even when the cost was heavy. Kris. My parents. Everyone who stepped into danger because of me.

The guilt rises like a tide, cold and suffocating. It claws at me, whispering that I don't deserve any of them. That the darkness in me is easier to believe than their love.

My mom kneels beside the bed, close enough that I can feel her presence, but far enough that she gives me space to choose whether I let her in. I stare at her hand resting on the comforter. I don't take it, but I don't push her away either.

"I know you feel like everything falls apart around you," she says softly. "But your existence isn't the reason people get hurt.

Choices, circumstances, enemies, fate, all of those things play a part. You're not the root of every tragedy."

I want to believe her. I truly do. But the ache in my chest pulses with everything I've witnessed in the last week. Everything I've caused, directly or indirectly. Everything falling apart around me.

The darkness pulls at me again, tempting, familiar, convincing. It tells me I'm the problem, and that distance is safer than connection. I feel myself slipping toward it, that cold place that swallows everything warm before I can reach for it.

I close my eyes for a moment, trying to breathe through the heaviness. My mom stays there, steady and patient, letting me find my footing without pushing or pleading.

Then my mom does something I don't expect. She climbs into the bed beside me and gently runs her fingers along my braids. The gesture is soft and familiar, something she used to do when I was young and overwhelmed by emotions I didn't yet know how to control. For the first time, I feel myself breathe a little deeper.

"I know I haven't always been around." Her voice has that quiet weight it only carries when she speaks from truth rather than duty. "I want you to know that there's not a single second of my day when I don't think about you. My children are always on my mind."

She hesitates, choosing her next words with care.

"I don't say this enough. I probably should, especially with you. Sirens feel everything more intensely, and that can turn the smallest wound into something heavy." She brushes a braid behind my ear. "But I am proud of you. Truly proud. I didn't agree with your father keeping this part of you hidden, but I am proud of how you've faced all of it. You carry yourself with more strength and grace than you give yourself credit for."

The compliment lands like a weight on my chest, heavy and unexpected. I feel my throat tighten.

She leans down and presses a soft kiss to my forehead, a tenderness I haven't felt from her in years. Then she rises and walks toward the door.

Once she's gone, everything inside me surges. Sadness, pain, anger, guilt, love. It feels like a storm pressing against my ribs, desperate to break free. I bury my hands in the sheets and force myself to breathe through it.

My mom may be wrong about many things. She's made mistakes, and so have I. But she's right about this one truth. I can't change the past. I can't undo the damage. I can't reverse death or turn back time. But I can protect the people who are still here. I can fight for them with everything I am.

That resolve settles into me like stone.

I push myself out of bed. My legs are stiff, but I move with purpose and pull on a black outfit, practical and familiar, a second skin that reminds me of who I am when I stop drowning in emotion.

By the time I reach the Carwell residence, my mind feels sharper. Focused. The air is cool as I walk up the steps and ring the doorbell. I want to check on Caleb's family. I want to make sure they're safe, even if he refuses to let me into his world right now.

The door opens, and I'm surprised to see Caleb's younger sister standing there.

"Hey, Kali," she says. Her voice is thin, shaky. Her eyes are red and puffy, the unmistakable look of someone who's cried more than slept. She tries to smile, and though it's small, it's brave.

My chest tightens. I can't imagine the weight she's been carrying. Grief settles differently on everyone, but on her young shoulders, it looks far too heavy.

"Is your mom home?" I ask.

"Um, no. She went with Caleb to a doctor's appointment."

"Oh." The word feels awkward and small on my tongue, and

I turn slightly, preparing to leave. I don't want to intrude. This house is already full of enough hurt.

"You can come in and wait if you want," she adds quickly. Her voice wavers with something that sounds like loneliness.

"Are you here by yourself?"

She nods.

A quiet tug pulls at me, something protective and familiar. She's always looked at me with a kind of trust I don't feel I deserve, especially now. Still, I can't bring myself to walk away from her when she's clearly struggling.

"I guess I can stay for a little while," I say. She steps aside, and I enter the house.

The living room feels dim and strangely still, like the grief has seeped into the walls. We end up on the couch watching a terrible Christmas movie, the kind with bad jokes and overly dramatic snowflakes. Eventually, she leans into me, her breathing slowing as exhaustion takes over.

By the time she falls asleep with her head in my lap, I find myself gently rubbing her back. The small rise and fall of her shoulders is a quiet rhythm in a life that's felt too chaotic lately. Something inside me softens.

When the movie ends, I carefully ease myself away so I don't wake her. The house is silent, the kind of silence that feels both peaceful and lonely. I wander without thinking, my feet carrying me down the hall, which eventually leads to me going upstairs.

Of course, I stop in front of Caleb's room, his scent bellowing out from it's depths.

I step inside, drawn by a mixture of curiosity and something deeper. His trophies line the shelves. Football. Martial arts.

I run my fingertips across the edge of a plaque, his name engraved in bold lettering. The memories come easily here. He was my dance partner for Paris's sweet sixteen. We'd moved so easily together, like our bodies had always known how to match each other's rhythm.

How could I have known him for so long and known so little about who he really was?

I inhale slowly. The room smells like something distinctly him. Familiar, comforting, and suddenly foreign. I had no idea he was a Lycan. Or that his entire world was built on a truth I was never allowed to see.

My dad took my memories. My mind has been stitched together with holes in all the wrong places. Maybe I sensed it anyway, that something about Caleb was different. Maybe my instincts had whispered it all along. I just never understood what I was feeling.

Standing here now, I realize how much has been kept from me, how much I still don't know. It sends a quiet ache through my chest, a reminder that the gap between us is wider than I thought.

But I'm here.

By his dresser, I pause at a small shelf crowded with stones. Some are familiar crystals, smoothed and polished. Others are pitch black, inky and lightless, as if they're carved from shadow itself. One in particular draws my attention, gleaming strangely, almost alive beneath the soft bedroom light.

"You know it's not polite to snoop," a low voice drawls from behind me.

I don't jump, though the sudden sound sends a ripple along my spine. Instead, I keep my gaze fixed on the stones.

"Well, it's not polite to ignore your mate." My tone is calm, cold, controlled. "I guess we both forgot our manners."

I feel him before I see him. His presence moves in close, a warm pressure at my back. He lowers his forehead to the back of my head, the gesture intimate in a way that makes my breath catch for reasons I'm not ready to admit.

"I just needed space," he murmurs.

"Well, you got it." I step out of his reach, forcing distance between us. The air cools instantly where he stood.

"Little—" he starts.

"How's your mom?" I cut in, my eyes narrowing. He's not going to slide past this conversation with pet names and soft apologies.

He rubs the back of his neck, jaw tight. "Better now."

He glances toward the hallway as if checking for footsteps that aren't there. "I'm sorry," he adds quietly.

"Yeah, I've heard that before." The words come out sharper than I intend, but I don't take them back.

He opens his mouth to respond, but my phone rings before he can speak. The name on the screen makes my heart pulse once, quick and unexpected.

Qora.

I swipe to answer. "Miss me already?" I tease, because with Qora it's safer to use humor than emotion.

She snorts. "You're hilarious. Truly. Do I miss being almost murdered in a filthy warehouse? No. But that isn't why I'm calling. Fenrir wanted me to tell you he got some information you requested."

"He couldn't call me himself?" I ask, incredulous.

Qora laughs under her breath. "You know he has the emotional communication skills of a brick. The dude acts like he's from the fifteenth century. Dad had to threaten to fire him just to get him to adopt an electronic filing system for the library."

I remain silent. "The answer is no, he wouldn't call you. See you soon, little Siren," she says before hanging up.

Caleb stays behind me while I talk to Qora. He doesn't move or speak, only presses himself against my back, solid and warm, his hand sliding around my waist as if the closeness can fix what he broke.

When the call ends, his grip tightens, and I feel his breath at my shoulder.

"Just let me go, Caleb." The words scrape out of me, rough with strain. I push his hand away and step forward, spinning to face him.

He looks at me like the ground shifted beneath him. "I wish I could." His voice is low and heavy, frustration woven through every syllable.

The answer sends a sharp pulse of anger through me. "So what does that mean? That I'm supposed to be here when you feel like reaching for me? That I'm supposed to take whatever you give and pretend the rest of it doesn't hurt?"

He flinches slightly, but I keep going.

"I'm expected to hold everything together when everything's been falling apart. My brother died. Your mother was attacked. I hate that any of it happened. None of this feels fair. But you don't get to push me away and then pull me back in whenever it suits you."

His jaw tightens, and he takes a step toward me.

"I may not be fully human, but I feel things too," I continue. My voice is steady now. Strong. "You don't get to decide when I matter. You don't get to choose the moments when you want me as a mate and ignore me the rest of the time. That isn't how this bond works, and I won't let you treat me like that."

Caleb opens his mouth, ready to argue, but the words don't matter anymore. I walk past him, brushing his arm with my shoulder, and head toward the door with sharp, controlled strides.

"Don't walk away from me," he calls after. The command in his voice cracks with something desperate.

I don't slow. "I need SPACE."

I take the stairs two at a time, the anger pushing me forward, the ache in my chest shifting into something sharper and cleaner. For once, I let myself choose distance instead of chasing after answers he refuses to give.

At Wraithstone, the sun casts everything in a warm afternoon glow, bright and golden. It should be beautiful, but all I can think about is how sharply it contrasts the storms that have battered us for days. The calm sky feels almost taunting, as if the world is choosing to shine while my life splinters apart beneath it.

I walk through the courtyard and into the quiet halls of the university, my steps purposeful. Today isn't about emotion. Today is about answers. Whatever Fenrir uncovered, I need it more than I need peace with Caleb.

The library is cool and still, its tall windows flooding the room with late sunlight. Fenrir stands near the circulation desk and nods once, his expression controlled but not cold as he holds out a thick file folder.

"I believe this is the information you were seeking.". His tone is clipped in that professional way he favors, but there's warmth beneath it. "There are also a few additional insights that may prove useful."

I take the folder. The weight of it is substantial, almost heavy enough to drag my shoulders down. I thank him and slip past the tables until I reach a secluded desk in the far corner. It's quiet here, tucked between two towering bookshelves. Perfect for thinking.

I sit and open the folder.

The first thing that hits me is how full it is. Papers, photo-copies, old yellowed news articles, handwritten notes, diagrams, even some outdated hunter sigils. Fenrir went out of his way, which means the information is either extremely important or extremely dangerous.

Maybe both.

I begin sorting through the documents. My heart clenches when I find a section devoted entirely to Paris's family. Names, dates, associations, records of contracts and alliances. Detailed enough to be useful, vague enough to be concerning. I scan each page slowly, taking in far more than I want to.

But then another name appears. Bold. Underlined in red ink.

Kludde.

I stop.

I've never heard that name before. Not from Caleb. Not from the pack. Not from any Scath text that's ever been shoved down my throat.

Why?

I flip through the pages more quickly now, scanning for patterns. Kludde appears repeatedly across decades, each time in connection with violent disappearances, Supernatural conflicts, and covert operations that make the Maylards look almost predictable.

Who are they?

Are they part of the Maylards? A faction within it? Or something entirely separate that moves through their shadows?

A cold weight settles in my chest. The implications are obvious. If the Maylards already stretch farther than I expected, then Kludde expanding into the picture raises more questions than I can stomach.

The sunlight across my desk shifts, and for a moment, I feel suspended between two worlds: the quiet library and the storm waiting outside the calm of this building.

Whatever Kludde is, it's not small.

Fenrir included a detailed map that stretches across the entire United States, the paper worn at the edges from how often it's been handled. Thick black ink marks out territories controlled by the Maylards. Dark red symbols, jagged and unsettling, indicate Kludde influence. The pattern isn't random. It looks strategic, intentional, as if two unseen armies have been moving pieces across a global board for decades.

I study it, tracing the lines with my fingertip.

It feels like a chess game with stakes I don't fully understand. Every territory marked in red suggests power, resources, and reach that rivals anything the Maylards hold. And yet I've never heard that name spoken aloud. Not once. Not even in whispered conversations or buried warnings.

The next packet in the folder draws my attention. It's labeled in Fenrir's neat handwriting: *Mating Contracts and Genetic Pairings within The Scath.*

My pulse quickens.

I open the pages carefully. The first sections cover ancient family lines, their loyalties, and the contracts that sometimes guided mate bonding. Most of it reads like old political maneuvering, but the last page stops me cold.

Contrary to everything I've been told, I learn that I never could've mated with anyone except Caleb.

My breath catches.

Suddenly, the fear in Caleb's uncle's threats and the disappointment in his grandfather's eyes lose their power. Even if they successfully manipulated the bind, none of it mattered.

Because the truth is simple.

I would have mated with Caleb anyway.

The idea sends a strange ache through me. Not painful. Powerful. A realization I can feel deep beneath my skin.

The text explains that true mating isn't political. It's biological. Emotional. Genetic. Two people whose chemistry, instincts, and DNA are uniquely compatible. There are no duplicates. No alternatives. No backups. Caleb's genetic code is singular in the world. So is mine.

We were made to find each other. Even if the bind didn't choose us.

We would have been mates regardless.

The thought is overwhelming, not because it traps me, but because it frees me. It means I'm not tied to Caleb because someone forced it. Our bond formed because it always would have.

Fate didn't care about their contracts or their opinions.

I close my eyes for a moment, breathing in the truth as it settles in my chest like a steady heat.

As I sort deeper into the folder, another document catches my attention, listing substances harmful to Werewolves, their effects, dosages, and variations. Then the section for Sirens appears, far thinner and less certain. No Sirens existed for testing, only legends, guesses, old scars of knowledge lost.

Some of the listed toxins make my stomach tighten. Some are familiar. Too familiar. I fold that page carefully and tuck it back inside. Information is power, but some of it carries weight I can't even begin to unpack.

The sky outside the library has shifted to dusk by the time I gather my things and leave the quiet halls, the folder pressed to my chest. The sunlight is gone, replaced by the soft violet glow of early evening.

My steps carry me toward the parking lot, and I'm surprised to find a small group waiting for me near my car.

Noah leans casually against the hood, chewing gum with that permanent half-grin. Duke stands with his arms crossed, eyes scanning the shadows out of habit. Qora offers a short wave that's more of a chin tilt but warm in its own way. Zori steps forward, her presence grounding and steady.

They're not my pack.

They're not my family.

But they've shown up anyway. They've shown up for me.

And something inside my chest loosens. Just a little.

"Heading out?" Noah asks.

"Yeah," I say, feeling the weight of everything I just learned settle across my shoulders. "A lot to think about."

Qora snorts. "You do enough thinking for all of us. Try to keep your head intact."

Duke nods toward the file. "Careful with that."

I raise a brow.

Zori smiles. "Safe travels, Kali."

Their simple presence feels strangely comforting. For the first time today, I don't feel entirely alone with the truth I uncovered.

"You always have a place here, you know," Noah says as he pulls me into a tight embrace. His arms are solid and familiar, grounding in a way I hadn't realized I needed. For a moment, I let myself lean into the comfort, allowing the warmth of it to cut through the tension coiled in my chest.

"Only if I get my own room. Zori snores far too loudly," I tease, letting a small smile break through the heaviness sitting behind my ribs.

Zori rolls her eyes. "I don't snore."

Duke snorts. "You definitely snore."

Qora smirks. "Loud enough to scare off low-level demons."

Zori narrows her eyes at all of them. "I hate every single one of you."

My smile grows, thin but genuine. "I might just take you up on that offer." I step back and give Noah one last appreciative nod. "All of you."

They watch as I slip into the driver's seat, heading toward the gates, the golden dusk stretching my shadow across the stone path. There's a bittersweet ache in my chest, a mixture of gratitude, exhaustion, and something that feels like hope trying to surface through the mess of the last few days.

No matter how fractured everything else feels, I'm not alone.

Not by a long shot.

TWENTY-FIVE

My heart sinks as I step into my bedroom, letting my bag fall to the floor with a dull thud. The room is nearly pitch black, the blackout curtains swallowing what little light remains from the fading day. As I walk farther inside, a familiar scent meets me, subtle at first, then unmistakable. Pine and sea salt. It wraps around me like a phantom embrace I'm not ready for.

"You do know you have your own house, right?" I say, yanking the curtains open. Twilight spills into the room in a soft wash of purple and gold, illuminating the shadows that had swallowed everything whole.

The light falls over Caleb, seated against my headboard with his legs crossed and his hands clasped loosely in his lap. He looks exhausted, hollow in the eyes, tension drawn tight across his shoulders. There's something raw in the way he watches me.

"This is starting to feel borderline obsessive." I try to force some humor into the air so it won't suffocate us both.

"You didn't pick up your phone." His voice is rough, threaded with fatigue. A faint shadow darkens his jaw, and the warm-toned freckles dusting his nose stand out more in the low light. He looks human in a way he rarely allows himself to appear.

"I needed space," I answer, giving him the same words he threw at me. The same wound. I want him to feel the edge of it.

In a single heartbeat, he's in front of me. Too close. Fast enough to steal the breath from my lungs. He presses me back until my spine meets the cool glass of the window.

"This isn't a game." His voice is low, intense, vibrating with something dangerous and desperate all at once.

The air between us crackles. Not magic, not fate, not the bond. Emotion. Raw and unfiltered.

"Great, because I'm not playing," I fire back. "You don't get to shut down and disappear while I'm left to piece everything together alone. You don't get to tell the pack to keep things from me. You looked me in the eye and told me we were equals. You told me I could trust you. Tell me, Caleb, would you trust you right now?"

The words land sharply. He steps back as if I struck him. Maybe I did. Maybe he needed to feel the sting for once instead of pretending everything could be smoothed over with apologies and silence.

I'm not here to be his afterthought. If we are mates, then he needs to act like it. I won't be convenient only when he feels ready.

"I'm sorry." His voice softens into something quiet, almost fragile.

"Yeah, you say that a lot." I cross my arms, holding my ground. The memory of him ignoring me, leaving me in the dark, still burns hot in my chest.

"I am trying, Little Bird," he says. "What do you want me to do?"

"How about trying harder?" The words come out like a blade I've been sharpening for days. "How about you stop freezing me out the second things get complicated? How about you tell me the truth instead of deciding what I can handle? How about you stop instructing the pack to keep me uninformed?"

He flinches slightly but doesn't look away.

"Look, Kali, it's been a rough couple of days." He runs a hand through his hair. The frustration is there, but so is the exhaustion. "I'm trying to do the right thing, but every time I turn around, I end up hurting you. You have to know that this is never what I want. Things with the pack are chaotic right now. I just need you to trust me. I never want to intentionally hurt you. I'm responsible for a lot of people, not just you. So many depend on me. I just... I was overwhelmed. I'm truly sorry."

He steps closer slowly, giving me time to move away. I don't. His hands slide around my waist, pulling me into him with a gentleness that contrasts with the rough edges of the conversation.

His forehead comes to rest against mine, his breath warm against my lips.

But the question remains.

I'm not sure an apology alone can fix the pieces he's cracked.

"Caleb, I'm here as your partner." I keep my voice steady, even though a frustrated heat coils in my chest. "You can talk to me about this stuff. I accepted you and the pack. You don't get to fight for us," I gesture between us, between the bond tightening the air—"and then have them shut me out the moment things get hard. It isn't fair. I want the truth. What's been going on?"

He drags a hand down his face. The exhaustion carved into his features makes him look older, harder, worn thin.

"Ten new younglings have gone missing," he says quietly.

The weight of it sinks into the room.

"Younglings?" My brows draw together. I think I've heard him use the term before, but not in a context like this. The ache between us shifts as I force my hurt aside long enough to listen.

"Newly changed Werewolves," he clarifies. "Most shift around sixteen, but some shift earlier. Twelve. Thirteen. Younger if their genetics are strong." He exhales sharply. "They're volatile at that age. Their emotions are too big for their bodies. That's why we keep them in the den. The older wolves help them control the shift and keep them stable."

"And now they're out there alone?" I ask quietly.

He nods. "When the full moon comes, they'll shift, whether they're ready or not. It can destroy them emotionally. Sometimes physically. A forced first shift without the pack can break a wolf."

A chill crawls up my spine. "How early did you shift?"

He hesitates. "I'm different."

"That isn't an answer." I raise a brow, refusing to let him retreat behind that familiar wall.

He meets my gaze for a long moment before speaking. "I shifted at nine."

My eyes widen. Nine. Children that young are still figuring out handwriting, not their animal form. The thought of him enduring something that intense so young twists something sharp inside my chest.

"Like I said, I'm different," he murmurs as he leans in, nuzzling into the crook of my neck. His breath brushes my skin, and despite everything else, a shiver trails down my spine.

He inhales once more, then stiffens. His voice sharpens. "Why do you smell like another wolf?"

I blink. "What?"

"I sa—"

"I heard you." Thinking through my day, I know I'm constantly surrounded by wolves. Then it hits me, "I was at Wraithstone today. Noah hugged me before I left. They all did," I clarify.

A low growl rolls through his chest, deep enough to vibrate against my skin. His grip tightens at my waist. The air thickens, charged with a tension that's equal parts protective and possessive.

"Simmer down, pup," I tease, though my pulse skips as his eyes darken.

"He was bold enough to leave his scent on you for me to find," Caleb mutters. The black in his irises swirls and bleeds into red.

"Calm down. He had no idea I was going to see you today."

"We're mates," he shoots back instantly. "Of course I would be seeing you today. I see you every day."

I step back slightly, irritation flickering. "Not on the days you need space, so apparently not."

His jaw flexes. The retort on his tongue dies, replaced by urgency. Then his eyes glaze over, occupied by something that's not present.

"I have to go to the den," he says abruptly, shifting the topic again, slipping out of the conversation like water through clenched fingers.

"Can this not wait until after we finish this conversation?" I ask. His abrupt shifts are giving me whiplash, and I feel the frustration twisting tight in my chest. Caleb doesn't even respond. He's already moving, gathering tension like a storm preparing to break.

But something about this moment is wrong.

His phone never rang.

So how does he suddenly know he needs to be at the den?

A quiet unease forms beneath my ribs.

"I'm coming," I say firmly. I'm not leaving him to handle this alone, and I refuse to be shut out again.

When we step into the hallway, the front door swings open.

Krystal enters with a bag of groceries, her hair pulled up in a loose bun, her eyes tired but alert. She takes one look at us and pauses. Krystal and Kris are twins, two halves of the same storm, but shaped by different winds. And in this moment, Krystal's face carries all the worry Kris would never allow herself to show.

I tell her I'm heading out, but before I can move past her, she touches my forearm.

"Kris left town," she says quietly.

The words land heavily, my chest tightening.

Of all people, Kris is the one who would rather burn her own heart than let anyone see her hurt. And she's my older sister. Impossible. Stubborn. Sharp. I know she pushes people away, but she's always been mine to protect in some strange, backward way. Kris and Krystal came into the world together. I came later, but somehow, I still carry this complicated pull toward both of them.

Part of me wants to stay, to comfort Krystal. To chase after Kris even though she would shove me away on instinct.

But Caleb stands behind me, tense and restless in a way that sets my instincts on edge. Something's happening at the den. Something urgent.

I swallow hard, feeling torn cleanly down the middle.

"I'm glad she's taking time," I say, pulling Krystal into a hug and pressing a kiss to her cheek. "She needs space. You both do. Tell her I love her, even if she doesn't want to hear it."

Krystal nods, her eyes softening. She squeezes my hand once, understanding too much without needing words.

"I have to go," I murmur, guilt and duty warring inside me.

Krystal steps aside, and Caleb follows me out.

Outside, I stop short.

His Jeep isn't here.

I turn to him slowly. "How did you get here?"

He avoids my eyes.

"Fine," I say. I lift my keys from my pocket. "We'll take my car."

Caleb hesitates, but I'm already unlocking the doors. If he won't tell me what pulled him toward the den, then I will drive him there and find out for myself.

When we arrive, the atmosphere hits me immediately. Heavy.

Thick. Wrong. We've been here for over an hour, but the rest of the pack is still assembling for a meeting Caleb apparently called, which only makes his sudden urgency even more confusing.

Moyra is pacing like a restless viper, snapping at anyone who speaks too loudly. Liam's absence sits like a crater in the center of the room. Every conversation feels weighed down by it.

The grief presses on us all, and for a moment, I drop my head, letting it wash through me.

A sharp shout slices through the tense air, dragging my attention toward the door.

Someone is yelling. Something is happening.

The room shifts. The pack tenses. Caleb stiffens at my side.

Whatever peace existed here moments ago fractures instantly.

We surge out of the meeting room together, the tension in the air snapping into panic the moment the shout echoes through the corridor. The pack pours toward the front of the den in a chaotic wave, claws scraping against concrete, bodies brushing past in a frenzy of movement.

The moment I reach the entrance, everything inside me stops.

A wooden spike has been driven into the ground.

And on it rests Liam's severed head.

Caleb steps in front of me in an instant, arms spread as if he can shield me from the sight. But it's too late. I've already seen it.

My heart plummets. The world narrows. I feel the ground sway beneath my feet as the image sears into my mind. Liam's eyes are open, lifeless. His hair is matted with blood that's dried too dark to be real. The sight is grotesque, cruel, and deliberate.

A horrified gasp ripples through the pack. Then chaos explodes.

Wolves shift on instinct, bolting into the woods in a blur of fur and claws, howling as they search for a scent, any scent, any sign of the monster who did this. Others sprint back inside to pull up security feeds and check the perimeter, voices raised in frantic shouts.

Someone reaches for the spike, intent on removing the head. The moment his hands make contact, he screams and drops it immediately, stumbling back as his palms sizzle and blister in front of our eyes.

The smell of burnt flesh hits me like a slap.

Lucas, eyes wide, steps closer. "It's Lunashard," he says grimly.

The word sends a chill up my spine. Lunashard metal. Poison to wolves. Toxic even when diluted. A material most hunters won't handle without thick gloves.

"What does that even mean?" I ask, struggling to keep my voice steady.

"I don't know," Caleb replies. His shoulders are tense, his jaw clenched so hard the muscles twitch. The threat in his stance is unmistakable. "But I'm going to find out."

"We have to put it back," I say.

My voice surprises even me. Firm. Certain. Heavy with a duty I didn't expect to feel.

Allie steps closer and nods in agreement. "She's right. It's disrespectful to leave him here."

Caleb turns to me, concern creasing his brow. "Are you sure? You don't have to do this."

"If I don't, who will?" I answer quietly. "I owe him at least this much."

And not only Liam.

Kris.

All the pain she carries. All the guilt.

I step forward, pushing through the pack until I stand directly before the spike. My heart hammers hard, but I don't let myself shake. Swallowing the revulsion burning in my throat, I peel off my jacket.

Carefully, gently, I wrap it around Liam's head.

The weight of it is terrible, too heavy for something that used to laugh. Something that used to breathe. Something that shielded Elijah with his last breath.

I hold on anyway.

Caleb moves with a controlled fury as he leads the way back to his Jeep. Allie and Lucas fall in behind us. No one speaks. The silence is thick and suffocating, broken only by the sound of crickets and the distant growl of wolves tearing through the forest.

We climb into the Jeep together, the tension hanging over us like a storm. My jacket sits in my lap, wrapped around what remains of someone we all failed to save.

As Caleb starts the engine and pulls away from the den, the gravity of the moment settles over all of us.

Liam deserves peace. And whoever did this deserves fear.

As we travel, voices swirl around me in fragments. Everyone is arguing, guessing, insisting they know who might have done this. But none of it lines up. The pack swore they killed every Omega from that night they attacked Caleb and me on the beach. Luna insisted the Maylards weren't involved. And nothing about this feels like the kid from the warehouse, even though part of me can't stop thinking about him.

Why desecrate Liam's grave?

Why sever his head?

Why leave it at the den?

My gaze drops to my lap, to where Liam's head rests, heavy and terrible.

My hands are steady. My skin is fine. I feel no burning. No stinging.

I'm holding something coated in Lunashard without a single blister.

A quiet pulse of confusion moves through me.

Lunashard is toxic to wolves. Wolfsbane can be worse, as it

has lasting effects, I've been told. The combination is lethal. The wolf who tried to lift the spike screamed as his skin blistered instantly.

Yet here I am. Unaffected.

Just like in the warehouse. The smoke hurt Caleb and Zori badly, but it barely touched me. Everyone said it was Wolfsbane.

At the hospital, they blamed my symptoms on Wolfsbane residue from when the Omegas attacked me.

But if it was real Wolfsbane at the warehouse and real Lunashard now, and I feel nothing...

Then whatever affected me before was not Wolfsbane.

My pulse dips, then quickens. I keep the realization tucked tight inside my chest. I don't look at Caleb or breathe a word. I simply watch the road as the pieces click together with slow, unsettling certainty.

Something else poisoned me that night.

Something I have no name for yet.

Something I probably wasn't supposed to survive.

Caleb parks in front of the graveyard. The atmosphere feels wrong the moment we step out, thick and charged, almost electric. The air tastes metallic on my tongue. Instinct pushes me forward before logic can catch up.

"Wait," Caleb calls.

Too late. My feet are already carrying me toward Liam's grave.

When I reach it, I realize no one is beside me. The rest of the pack stand several feet back, rigid and pale.

"What's wrong?" I ask, confused by the sudden distance.

Their eyes drop to the ground around me. I follow their gaze.

They stand frozen, faces drained of color.

Caleb's voice hits me first, loud and harsh with panic.

"Kali, stop. That's Wolfsbane root and Lunashard."

I look down slowly. "The grave's surrounded by it," he continues.

"Kali!" another voice shouts.

I turn as Krystal races toward me, her braid flying behind her, the hilt of a sword bouncing against her shoulder. Since when does Krystal have a sword?

She skids to a stop outside the toxic ring. Her eyes widen as she takes in the sight.

"What are you doing?" she demands, her voice breaking with terror.

She's staring at me like she's seeing something she can't explain.

"I was just…" The words trail off as something clicks in my mind. I turn toward the headstone again and freeze.

Liam's grave is untouched.

No disturbed soil.

No claw marks.

No signs of digging.

Nothing.

Just grass beginning to sprout across the fresh earth, undisturbed and peaceful.

Confusion slams into me. "What the hell," I whisper, stepping closer, my heart thundering.

A voice slices through the air behind me. "I wouldn't do that if I were you."

The tone drips with malice, cold and deliberate. My stomach drops.

I whirl around.

Paris stands several feet away, gun drawn, her smile stretched too wide, too sharp. A manic gleam lights her eyes, like she's been waiting for this moment and savoring every second of it.

"Paris," I breathe out, fighting to keep my voice steady, even as dread pulses through my veins. "What is this? What are you doing?"

"Giving you exactly what you deserve," she says sweetly. Too sweetly. The kind of sweetness that hides poison. "I know you didn't think your dad's little memory wipe would be enough."

The world tilts slightly under my feet.

Then my gaze shifts past her, and my heart sinks.

Behind Paris stands a cluster of familiar faces.

The missing younglings, Elijah, and Kris.

My blood runs cold.

"What the hell, Kris?" I shout, disbelief crashing into me so violently it nearly knocks me back. "What is this?"

Kris meets my eyes with a smirk that twists her face into something unrecognizable. "Doesn't feel too good, does it? Dedicating your energy to someone and losing them to someone else?"

She turns to Elijah before I can speak. And kisses him.

Deeply. Deliberately. Like she wants me to choke on the sight.

The betrayal hits me like a punch to the gut.

"I didn't kill Liam!" I scream, the words ripping out of me. "You told him where to find us. You killed him!"

My voice breaks, but not from weakness. From fury. "And now you're making out with my ex?" I spit, shaking with rage. "For what, exactly? What is this supposed to prove?"

Kris pulls away from Elijah slowly, her smug smile only widening.

Something inside me snaps.

"Making out?" Paris scoffs with a laugh that feels jagged and wrong. "Oh, please. They've been fucking all over our apartment."

Her voice drips with triumph, her eyes shining like she enjoys every second of tearing my world apart. The words land like blows, each one aimed with precision.

I feel myself slipping, my mind racing. Anger. Hurt. Disbelief. Betrayal. All of it collides inside me so violently I can barely separate one feeling from another. My gaze snaps between

Kris and Paris, the two people I trusted in such different ways, now standing united in their cruelty.

Behind me, Caleb's voice cuts through the tension. "Paris, what are you doing?" He sounds furious and shaken, like he can't decide whether to fight or protect.

Paris doesn't even spare him a glance. "You're not the one I want," she says lightly.

Then her gaze flicks to me, and something inside me tightens. That manic glint in her eyes sharpens into focus.

"Who I want is right here," she says, lifting her chin toward me. "Pity your parents never told you what you really are. What you really hold. I didn't understand it myself until the Omegas took me. But you...you were always under my skin."

She smiles in a way that makes my stomach drop.

"Every forehead kiss, every hug, every quiet moment," she whispers. "They drove me deeper into obsession. And then you threw me away for him. When I threw him away for you."

Her words rattle around in my head like broken glass.

"Paris," I say slowly, carefully, trying to steady my voice. "You told me you didn't want to be friends anymore. You ended things."

She tilts her head, her smile widening. "I don't want to be friends anymore. Are you not listening?" Her voice rises slightly as she takes a small step closer. "I'm in love with you. And if I can't have you, he certainly won't."

She raises the gun, her movements exaggerated, deliberate.

My heart skids sideways, the world narrowing to the barrel pointed at my chest.

"Paris, please," I breathe, hands lifting slightly, palms open. "Don't do this."

She scoffs and gestures toward Elijah and Kris. "Elijah has moved on, thanks to your Alpha."

A low, vicious growl rips from behind me. Caleb.

"Or should I say your MATE," she continues.

"What do you mean?" I ask, my voice sharp, distrust slicing through the fear.

Paris smiles like she's been waiting for that question.

Her finger taps the trigger lightly, playful, like she's savoring the tension of the moment.

Everything around us feels like it's seconds from shattering.

"Well," Paris begins, drawing out the word like she's savoring the moment. "Let us just say your sister and Liam were bound in their own way. But since he died, both she and Elijah went to Caleb for the blessing to keep it in the family. If you catch my drift?"

My breath catches. "What?"

Paris's grin widens, sharp as a blade. "He gave them his blessing to be together. You know only the Alpha can do that. This entire situation wouldn't even exist if Caleb hadn't said yes. Makes you wonder why he did it, does it not?"

Her words hit me like a punch.

The betrayal slams into me. It feels physical. My vision tunnels, my heart beating in my ears like a drum. Heat surges through me. I shift my stance, daggers drawn before I even register the movement.

I'm ready to strike.

But a voice interrupts.

"But since I don't agree with any of this," Paris says lightly, as if she's discussing the weather, "I'm giving you free reign to kill them both."

My grip tightens around my blades.

Paris tilts her head. "Although..." Her smile bends into something darker. "You may notice you feel a little strange."

Before I can react, she gestures to powder on the ground. The particles shimmer as they catch the moonlight like crushed glass.

A strange, metallic scent fills my lungs.

"This dust is known to inhibit the powers of Aquatic Super-naturals," Paris explains with a sing-song rhythm, delighted by my growing discomfort. "Which means you'll have to kill them fair and square."

A cold, crawling sensation begins to spread under my skin. My pulse stutters, then lurches forward in a quick, unsteady rhythm.

Paris shrugs casually. "It also tends to increase bloodlust. So, Darling…" Her eyes gleam with unhinged satisfaction. "How are you feeling?"

The world around me shifts.

My heartbeat pounds louder.

My vision sharpens, colors brightening unnaturally.

Something deep inside me stirs.

Something hungry.

Something ancient.

Paris watches me unravel, smiling like she'as already won.

I spit to clear the metallic taste rising in my mouth, but it does nothing. I can't think past the pounding in my ears. My pulse roars like a storm inside my skull. My entire body burns, every nerve lit with fire, and the only thing that feels like it could extinguish it is blood.

Kris's blood. Elijah's blood. The thought hits me like it belongs to someone else, but it coils hot in my gut, impossible to ignore.

I've never been violent. Never. But there's nothing holding me together now. None of the necklaces my father made. None of the jewelry that dampened the Siren in me. My energy builds from the top of my head to the soles of my feet, rushing in a relentless wave that demands release.

Kris steps forward, daggers gleaming in her hands like she was born with them. Her eyes are cold, merciless.

The world tilts.

And then it snaps.

The fight explodes around us.

I lunge at her, tackling her to the ground. We slam into the dirt, our blades clattering against each other as we wrestle for dominance.

"Get off me!" she shrieks, thrashing wildly.

But I'm beyond hearing her properly. Everything is a blur of adrenaline and rage. My hands grip harder. My limbs move faster. I can't tell if it's instinct or something else entirely.

"Why would you do this?" I shout, grappling with her, my voice raw.

"Because you're weak!" she spits back, shoving me hard enough that my teeth rattle.

A gunshot cracks through the night.

Then another.

Paris fires over us, bullets slicing through the air so close I feel their heat whip past my cheek. My body reacts before my mind does, twisting to avoid the deadly arc of Kris's dagger.

Chaos erupts in every direction.

Wolves roar. I see the younglings charge out of my peripheral vision. The ground shakes beneath the surge of bodies.

Somewhere in the distance, I hear the growl of Caleb's Jeep engine and see the car tearing over roots and vines, pushing toward us despite the Wolfsbane barrier.

I try to center myself, but the bloodlust drags its claws deeper into me. Kris slashes again, and I duck under her blade, catch her wrist, and use her momentum to twist her arm hard.

She screams.

I rip the dagger from her hand and spin her to the ground, pinning her with every ounce of strength I have. The dirt is cold against my knees, her breath ragged beneath me.

Power floods through me in a brutal wave, hot, heavy, and consuming.

For one horrifying heartbeat, I realize how easy it would be to end this.

Krystal's hands clamp down hard on my arms, trying to hold me back, trying to pull me out of the frenzy I'm sinking into. Her nails dig into my skin, her voice frantic in my ear, but none of it reaches me the way it should.

Kris tears herself free, rolling to her feet with a predator's grace. The air between us crackles like something electric. We both move at the same time, blades cutting through the space in sharp arcs. Every instinct in me sharpens, all the training I've ever had spiraling up from memory and melding with the rage boiling through my veins.

I pivot low, sweep her legs out from under her, and knock one of her daggers spinning across the ground.

But she recovers too fast. Too practiced and angry.

She lunges again. Her remaining knife flashes in the dim light, and the blade slices across my thigh. Pain explodes upward, hot and blinding, but instead of slowing me, it fuels the fire roaring through my body.

We both regain our footing. The world narrows into movement and breath and the metallic smell of blood. Krystal's voice shouts something behind us, begging, pleading, screaming for us to stop, but the sound dissolves beneath the rush of adrenaline pounding in my ears.

There's no reasoning left in me.

Krystal steps protectively in front of Kris, her arms spread wide. Her eyes glisten with fear, but she doesn't move.

"You can either move out of my way or die with her." The words leave my mouth without hesitation, dripping with the venom of the bloodlust coursing through me.

Her voice trembles. "Kali, think about what you're doing."

"Death it is," I reply.

I move before either of them can react, knocking both sisters to the ground. Krystal's longsword clatters loose. I snatch it up in one smooth motion, the weight of the blade familiar and perfect in my grip. Rage surges, wild and consuming, as I lift the sword high above my head, ready to bring it down on Kristina.

Somewhere behind me, Caleb's grunts rip through the chaos

as he fights off the younglings trying to restrain him. There's the sound of bodies colliding, claws scraping, panicked shouting. But none of it matters.

The only thing I focus on is Kris beneath me.

The girl who betrayed me. The girl who blamed me. The girl who chose them over her own sister.

My pulse roars as I tighten my grip.

Then someone steps into my path.

A figure moves between me and Kris, solid as stone. The sword I'm swinging collides against another blade with a loud, metallic ring.

My father stands there.

His sword drawn. His stance unyielding. His face carved with determination and fear and heartbreak.

"Kali, stop!" he shouts.

But I'm too far gone. Too consumed. Too lost to the fire.

The world tilts, red haze pulsing around the edges of my vision, and my father stares at me like he's watching his daughter slip into something monstrous.

He swings the butt of his sword toward my ribs. I twist, barely dodging the full force, but the blow clips my side and sends me stumbling backward. Pain flares hot, sharp enough to steal my breath for a second. The rain pours down around us in a relentless sheet, pounding the earth and sliding cold against my skin, mixing with the sweat and blood already dripping from my face.

I spit to the side, tasting iron from the cut Kris gave me earlier, and lift my gaze back to my father.

I'm far from finished.

Thunder rolls across the sky like the world is shaking with me. My father's expression is tight with fear and sorrow.

"You're not thinking straight, Kali," he pleads, rain streaking down his face like tears.

"She dies here." The conviction in my voice is terrifying, even to me.

I surge forward again.

The world narrows to motion and instinct. I move with ruthless precision, every hour of training snapping to attention as I drive myself into the fight. I knock Krystal back with a sharp strike to her wrist and kick Kris hard enough that her dagger skids into the mud.

But Kris refuses to relent. She comes at me again, eyes blazing with fury, blade raised high. She thrusts toward my heart. I pivot, catch her wrist, and shove the dagger away before plunging my own blade into her left thigh. Her scream cuts through the storm.

My father is on me again, grabbing my arms, trying to restrain me. His touch feels like chains I can't bear while Krystal fights to hold her own twin back.

"Let go!" I roar, twisting violently out of his grasp.

I fling another dagger at Kris without hesitation. It sinks into her shoulder with a dull, sickening sound. Satisfaction surges through me, dark and primal.

Before I can strike again, my father grabs me from behind, arms around my torso. His grip is strong, but I can feel the hesitation in it. The heartbreak. The fear of hurting me. The fear of losing me.

"Kali, please," he whispers, voice breaking.

I whirl around, consumed by something that's no longer reason.

No longer restraint.

A final dagger is already in my hand.

My body moves faster than my mind can catch up.

I drive it forward.

The blade sinks into his chest.

Time stops.

My father's eyes widen, stunned, the pain flickering through them eclipsed almost instantly by something worse.

Grief.

Regret.

Love.

"No," I breathe, the word barely a sound.

His hand rises, trembling, and he places it gently on the back of my head. He leans forward and presses a soft kiss to my forehead, the same gesture he gave me when I was small, when I cried after training, and when he needed me to know I was his heart.

Then his body collapses.

The world tilts. Rain pounds against him. Against me. Against the blood soaking into the ground.

Memories slam into me with brutal force.

His laughter.

His guidance.

His pride in me.

His warnings.

His love.

His faith in the daughter he thought he was saving.

And I killed him.

The truth crashes into me with unbearable weight. My vision blurs. My knees buckle. Pain tears through my chest until it feels like something inside me rips open.

I fall.

The storm rages around me, drowning out every thought. My body shakes violently, my breath breaking apart in gasps as the world goes dark around the edges.

I reach for him. For anything. For an anchor. For the father I just lost.

But the darkness swallows me whole.

I collapse completely, sinking into unconsciousness as thunder roars above like the sky itself is mourning.

Voices echo around me, muffled and distant, like I'm underwater. Hands lift me. Someone shouts my name. Someone else cries.

My eyelids feel heavy, weighted with regret and blood and rain.

And then, everything goes black.

"The MRI doesn't show any brain damage. We just have to see what happens when she wakes up. She was severely dehydrated. Honestly, I'm surprised she didn't pass out earlier," a voice says nearby, clinical but edged with concern.

"Thank you," my mom replies. Her voice trembles in that way she hates—the way she only lets slip when she thinks I can't hear her.

I try to speak, try to reach her.

But my tongue is heavy, my throat dry, my body a sinking weight.

Darkness pulls me under again.

"Fly back to me, Little Bird," Caleb whispers.

His voice drifts through the dark like a warm current, sweet and haunting. I try to answer him, to reassure him that I'm still here, that I haven't flown far at all. But the darkness grips tighter, and I fall back into it.

"You need to go home and get some rest, honey. I'm here. I've got her," a woman says.

Liz. His mother. A steady presence even through the fog.

"You didn't see how she looked at me when she found out what I did," Caleb says, breaking, unraveling. "How did I let Kris and Eli bind? I didn't know they were being used. They said they would leave. I didn't even know what Paris used to get control of them. Kali told me all she wanted was to trust me

447

fully, and not even twenty-four hours later, I broke that trust. She doesn't deserve this. I don't deserve her."

His voice cracks.

Something warm brushes my cheek. A kiss, maybe, then another.

Thunder grumbles outside, echoing the storm inside my chest. I drift again.

"Come back to us, Kals. Please," Knox's voice urges, soft and earnest. Rain begins to tap gently against the window, steady and rhythmic. I cling to the sound...then slip away.

"Hey, LiLi. I'm here with your sisters," my mom's voice says softly. I can hear her smile, hear her fear. "I know it's safe in there, but you have to come back to us. We all want you to come back. Me, Knox, Krystal."

Another rumble of thunder. Another pull downward into the dark.

But this time, I don't fall into nothing.

I fall into memory.

My dad stands before me, vivid and whole. We're walking the trail from the training facility, the late afternoon sun filtering through the trees. I sip water, breath coming fast from the drills he pushed me through.

"I won't be here all the time, you know, Kalabunga," he says, his voice warm and teasing.

"Planning a trip, old man?" I reply, grinning as he messes up my twists.

"You're one of my greatest achievements." His voice softens in that rare way that always makes something swell in my chest. "I'll always be here for you. Even if it's not physical. I'll be in your memories. You'll always be able to find me. Just not for now."

He hugs me and kisses my forehead as our house rises into view.

The memory dissolves like mist.

A new one takes its place.

Wraithstone, a few weeks ago.

We sit beneath the gazebo, the night air cool around us. Lanterns sway above with the breeze. My father sits beside me, posture relaxed, the hint of pride in his smile.

"You know you'll always have a place here," he says. "This place was kinda built for you. I can only teach you so much. But here...here you can find yourself. Here, you can have another home."

"I already have a home," I answer, voice quiet.

He shrugs. "Maybe you'll find more. Maybe you'll find where you belong. Maybe you'll find your own pack."

Another hug.

Another kiss to my forehead.

Another piece of him tucked into my heart where nothing can reach it.

The memory fades slowly, gently, like it's giving me time to breathe before it leaves.

And then everything crashes back.

The graveyard.

The rain.

The blade.

My father falling.

The scream trapped in my throat.

My world tearing apart.

And the truth I couldn't see through the bloodlust.

I gasp and open my eyes.

The room blurs into focus.

The storm outside roars.

My heart thrums like lightning under my ribs.

In that moment, clarity strikes through me with brutal force.

I know exactly what I need to do.

Exactly who I need to become.
Exactly what my father meant.
I know my path now.

ACKNOWLEDGMENTS

I must first acknowledge the writers who paved the way before me. To those whose imaginations shaped universes with fewer tools than we have today, your creativity and determination have inspired generations of novelists, me included. I am profoundly grateful for the foundation you've laid and the stories you've gifted to the world.

To my brilliant editor, Kate Black, thank you for your unwavering guidance and patience in shaping my novels. Your wisdom and dedication gave me the confidence to persevere, and your belief in my work has meant more than I can express. You went above and beyond, and for that, I am eternally grateful.

To my family—my siblings Jeremy, Channon, and Mikiya, and their spouses—You have been my unshakable foundation through every twist and turn of this journey. Your love and support have anchored me through the storm, and I am reminded daily that my success is only meaningful because it is ours.

To my coworkers, friends, and my cherished book club girlies: Thank you for your constant encouragement, for cheering me on when I doubted myself, and for reminding me why I started this journey in the first place.

Finally, to you—the reader—thank you for taking a chance on a newly minted author. By stepping into my mind and exploring the world of Coved, you've given my imagination a home in your heart. Thank you for letting this story be your escape from reality. Your trust means everything, and I hope these pages bring you as much joy reading them as they brought me in writing them.